THE IRANIAN DECEPTION

Captain Edward M. Brittingham Sr. USN, Ret.

ASW Press
Richmond, Virginia

*THE **IRANIAN** DECEPTION*
Copyright © 2008 by Captain Edward M. Brittingham Sr.
Published by ASW Press

For more information please contact:
captemb@peoplepc.com
or
info@arborbooks.com

Book design by:

Arbor Books
244 Madison Avenue, #254
New York, NY 10016
www.arborbooks.com

Printed in the United States of America

*THE **IRANIAN** DECEPTION*
Copyright © 2008 by Captain Edward M. Brittingham Sr.

LCCN: 2005932050
ISBN: 0-9727859-3-0

THE IRANIAN DECEPTION

DEDICATION

With honor and belief in what the United States Navy protects our own harms way, the founders of Surveillance Towed Array Sensor System are overwhelmingly proud of this display of integrity.

Admiral Ray C. Witter has carried on this ongoing successful adventure by continuing the Small Water Area Twin Hull which has been the answer for littoral or coastal regions.

Chief Warrant Officer (CWO4) Edward Haney has been my coordinator as a Commander Oceanographic System Atlantic and as many of the staff that support these systems.

And I must be remiss if I did not mention Captain David Williams, who is my guiding light in the undersea world!

TABLE OF CONTENTS

"How many roads must a man
walk down,
Before you call him a man?
How many seas must a white
dove sail,
Before she sleeps in the sand?
Yes, how many times must the
cannon balls fly,
Before they're forever banned?"

"Blowin' In The Wind"
A Bob Dylan Lyric

THE IRANIAN DECEPTION

PREFACE

A series of short, unrelated spurts of data sometimes reveals a chance at being exact. These spasmodic occurrences happen when in the ocean mass. We are told that this amazing event occurred during World War II, in which pilots were detected when crashing into the sea near Midway Island. This historical phenomenon was capitalized on early in the 1950s when the Oceanographic Systems began placing a ring of listening devices, with which, for all intents and purposes, the entire east coast was planted. Then came the outskirts of Bermuda, and finally Iceland was included in the net. This was the Cold War that was labeled in the early 1960s. Many objects were noticed on the initial outer shores of the Atlantic/Pacific Ocean. An appreciable amount was fathered in the Gulf of Mexico. The subjects are watercraft; boats ranging from shrimp boats, transfer boats to/from the oil rigs, tugs that reposition the bigger ships, and plain old fishing boats.

Suddenly, a tugboat with a long afterboard began powering through the seas. It was a sturdy boat, powerful enough that it could be used for towing and pushing. Several varieties were noticed, and then one day a nautical engineer had a brilliant idea. His counterpart worked in Gulfport and was head facilitator of the new frigates being built. A dream was the tug/vertical–stabilized bow and aft, so the ship could tow us away. The idea caught on in the civilian shipping world and that of the United States Navy. Soon the ship, Surveillance Towed Array Sensor System, as it was called, was in Operational Evaluation (OPEVAL), and it flunked miserably! Commander Naval Electronics System Command was on the bottom of the list as the sole ability was not doing its job when the array was deployed. Several other factors ballooned as the fixers wore at each other's throats! A study revealed that the bow thruster let one position a boat in difficult situations. Also a stern thruster, in combination with the bow facilitator, would allow greater maneuverability in high seas, which the ship needed. The second trial commenced in late spring of 1980. The ship certified its sole capability; its satellite worked amazingly, and was verified as a "go."

In September 1980, the Operational Navy/COMNAVEX-EL commenced the briefing trial. Finally, the Secretary of the Navy was happy and then the Department of Defense was next. Around the end of September 1980, SURTASS was approved and 12 ships were bought.

Inevitably, this ship, called SURTASS, played an exciting and predominant role until the Soviet Union bowed out. Soon the cutbacks were phenomenal. For example, every counterpart took a fifty percent reduction across the board. Many ships, submarines, battalions, Air Force bombers, were chopped, giving us a meager fighting force level of half the structure we had during the Cold War era.

This prompted the rise of the terrorists, who had been lurking for some time. President Reagan commented in the early 1980s that this action was uncalled for, and yet the average male during that time could not fancy the thought of living in the United States. That blunder and numerous subsequent slip–ups brought this destiny to a reality on September 11, 2001.

United with the terrorist bands of some forty clans, each has its own individual traits, but all form under the diocese of Mumand. There is no Al Qaeda network that can be held responsible for all actions against the United States of America. Each hand is sliding money from every faction to another for training, weapons and whatever is needed to get the job brought to an end.

With help from the Union of Soviet Socialist Republics, Iran has suddenly become a front runner in the Middle East. This creates a group of desperate terrorists who seem to have their mind set on the weapons the United States is about to expose to the nuclear submarines. A new torpedo is a dream of the Iran processors of three conventional submarines, which represents a corpus delicti, is the final verdict.

CHAPTER 1

JULY 1981

Doctor Bandar Abbis was hard at work at his vibrant desk looking for an improvement to the MK–48 ADCAP torpedo. An advanced lightweight projectile is to be used for the fast, deeper and more specific submarines. Naval Undersea Warfare Center has instituted an OTTO fuel, which is used in the external combustion cycle of an MK–48 torpedo engine. This fuel is allowed to enter the fuel tank, pressurizing the liquid and pushing it into the combustion chamber. After this process is finished the doctor finds favor with the system. Results of the OTTO fuel process simplifies the seawater mixture for naval submarines. Thus, the improved reclamation process has the capacity to mandate OTTO fuel and seawater ingredients from submarines in San Diego and Pearl Harbor, which are shipped to Key West in tanks. This volume, which is 350,000 pounds, adds up to $1 million dollars being subdued each year. Principally, factoring the costs and avoidance of waste disposal costs results in a net saving of $960 million per annum.

Created on October 1, 1998, "Naval Station Newport's mission is to maintain and operate facilities, provide services and material to support operations per tenant activities, support activities and visit fleet units, and to perform such other functions and tasks as may be directed by higher authority."

To understand the development in the Narragansett Bay area, one must first examine the history of Newport, Rhode Island. Nichols Easton and son set up a four–gun battery to protect the future of Newport. Following the trades of the Triangular Trades countries brought this as a high during the Colonial Period.

The Revolutionary War brought to bear the American Navy, which was founded in 1775. This force was instrumental in the throwing out of the British Navy and bringing the French Navy to quell the surrender of the Brits at Yorktown in Virginia.

The actual history of Navy development began in 1869 with the establishment of an experimental Torpedo Shop on Goat Island. This fostered development of the Naval Undersea Warfare Center, which was tasked to develop torpedoes, equipment, explosives and ancillary electrical equipment. The physical size of the Torpedo Station grew and, during WWI, approximately 3,500 workers were engaged in producing 80% of the torpedoes made by the United States.

The Second World War was an expansion device in itself. Finally, an air station, Naval Air Station, Quonset Point, was commissioned in 1941. Newport underwent a tremendous surge during this period. Warships, as well as convoys and fighting ships, were amassed at Newport. As many as 100 ships of the Navy were home ported in Newport.

The Naval Underwater Systems Center of NUSC is the present name of the underwater arm of the U.S. fleet. By the mid 1980s the Naval Underwater Systems Center had become the largest command because of manpower and bucks. During the 1990s it was added to the Naval Undersea Warfare Center. This addition of new labs gave paramount labs, which provide full spectrum research, development and testing for all submarine and underwater systems.

At the home of the Naval War College in Newport, Rhode Island, is the Undersea Warfare Center Division. The McLaughlin Research provides NUWC with precise proposing and implementing of complex technical problems throughout the past three decades for cost–conscious customers. The MRP currently provides NUWC issues the area directorates and includes launchers, combat systems, periscopes, targets and engineering management support for which NUWC is always in need of appraising. Interestingly, we have the torpedo as well as its strategic strength to deaden the insurgent.

Primarily among all of the academic verbiage of this list of tasks is the Torpedo and Underwater Vehicles. Dr. Bandar Abbis' chief function is the NAVSEA list of functions, to provide the life cycle, including all torpedo types, services and the mobile targets currently in use. Lest we forget, the entire interactive course wear involving operational trainer vis–à–vis as an in–post and lightweight launch of the MK–48 ADCP and the light versions of this torpedo.

Anticipation of the U.S. authorities gave birth to a new technological advantage of the Soviets, noted during 1960 through the 1970s. Pursuant to this event, studies of the MK–48 led to an Operational Requirement by the Chief of Naval Operations and advanced threat led to the MK–48 ADCAP technology, which keeps track of the Soviet submarine improvement program.

In 1979 the appearance of the Alfa Russian nuclear submarine charts showed that the ADCAP heeded post haste. Also necessary were improvements made to increase the depth, and the necessity to increase the speed was, without a doubt, a critical benefactor. Finally, the ADCAP provided sustained long acquisition range, minimized environment and countermeasure efforts, and enhanced target engagement capabilities.

Bandar was born in Iran in 1954. The country was known as Persia but became an Islamic republic in 1979. Commemorate with this the Shah was forced into exile. A theocratic system of government, the ultimate control authority vested with a learned religious academia, ruled as if divinely guided. The U.S. Embassy in Tehran was seized on November 4, 1979, and held until January 20, 1981. From 1980 to 1988 a bloody war with Iraq caused an indecisive row over uncontrolled lands. Lastly, popular discontent with the government has been prompting poor economic conditions, plus a nation that has been reaching for political reform.

His parents, Rosi and Inez, were living in the capital city of Tehran. His father and mother were college graduates living among the affluent mask of society. His Dad majored in political science, which landed him a substantial job in the judicial branch of government. He worked mostly at night, where he got a law degree. He soon became a judge, which gave him more status vis–à–vis the political party of Islamic Republicans.

Bandar was a spectacular student from the outset. He joined the soccer program and was adept at chess and another game with which he could test his finesse. He had two other children, one boy and girl, who filled up his time. They were bright, but did not possess the true intellect of Bandar's ability. He breezed through elementary school and took all excelling classes, which inspired him to reach out for membership in the Islamic Republic in 1979.

Through many windows passed an appointment to Harvard University for a master's degree in 1981. He went to the United States with his Dad, who is the most prominent judge in the legal arena, by his side at the airport. He was met after customs in New York by Rafson Bahti. Rafson was to meet, greet and take him to become registered at Harvard. The primary objective achieved, Rafson took him home to meet the family. He was introduced and was rediscovered by a host of Iran followers.

Bandar entered Harvard with a wealth of knowledge, particularly in the use of English. He took courses in physics, chemistry and some technical courses in the engineering field. He returned to Rafson's house for dinner once a month, and then he noticed a young girl later eyeing him. As you know, they spoke Iranian when they met in Bahti's home. Bandar spoke of this encounter with this girl.

"Is it cool if I date her?" he asked.

"But of course," he said in their native language.

Mary, the name she used outside the house, was a pleasant girl and she wore a veil, which is the length of cloth covering the head and shoulders, principally the face. Mary and I often met in the coffee shop near the school. We talked of many things, then about us. Finally, I took her to my apartment. It was there we talked of what has happened during the last ten years. We centered our opinions on the recent Iran–Iraq breakout, which had started outbreaks of war in certain areas in 1980. This ferocious beginning was the murderous waste of men and elements of war.

Nine months before achieving a master's degree from Harvard, Rafson met him outside the physics department. His college told him of a job he had planned for him and it would involve working in a torpedo development and theory task force working for the United States Government. This job was a government service 14, equivalent to big money. Bandar thought this was acceptable but he had to pass the test and become qualified as a U.S. citizen. The couple went to Bandar's apartment and filled out the application. The following Saturday they went and filled out the paperwork for U.S. citizenship.

On June 4, 1981, Bandar Abbis graduated cum laude with a Master Degree in Physics with separate side majors in Chemistry and Engineering. To his surprise, his mother and father were in attendance. He was pleased as he hugged both of them and they celebrated at a nearby restaurant. Bandar's parents met Mary and they looked curiously at Bandar. Eventually, he told his parents with Mary at his side that they were going to marry sometime that year. They were thrilled and kissed the loving couple.

Two hours later the party was alive with dancing, eating and enjoying the drinks of Iran. Bandar had just finished dancing with Mary. Rafson came to his table and whispered something in his ear. He got up and he followed Rafson out of the room. They stopped outside the restaurant and proceeded to a car.

Once outside Rafson spoke to him of his job. He was to report to the security department of the McLaughlin Research Company in July 1981. All of his paperwork will be inspected, U.S. citizenship, social security number, driver's license, and so on.

"Yes, you have a job with the Undersea Warfare Center Division, which is at the Naval Station in Newport, Rhode Island," said Rafson.

The submarine and torpedoes are subjects that go hand in hand, and a history of one must necessarily include the study of the other. The undersea boat and the undersea explosive charge had experimented their development and the same cradle of the deep, deep sea. Fathered in New England by David Bushnaur, it proved that the submarine has an express purpose for carrying an underwater demolition, and thusly the modern torpedo evolved as an engine designed to deliver the charge to the target.

Obviously the torpedo's performance has a direct influence on all submarine operations. It is up to the submarine to detect to adjust the range and to properly unleash it at the proper time. Let it fumble, falter or otherwise fail, and the whole play goes askew. Such failures may cost the submarine its life as a naval weapon. It goes without saying, as well as submarines that might be lost through torpedo failure; an entire campaign could be threatened where submarines are forced to fight with faulty weapons. As in the beginning, as it is in WW II, the US sub force entered the war with such a weapon, or the torpedo. It was not until late 1943 that the serious situation was adequately tested and demonstrated to perform as advertised. Now let us discuss and go through the trials that Kelling, on behalf of the Navy's torpedo, the men who made good with it and the men who made it good.

The multiple torpedo carrying 18 pounds of gun cotton enabled to sustain a 6 knots speed was a wonderful integrate device, but in comparison to today's modern submarine, it was a contrivance as simple as a naphtha launch.

Weighing 101.25 tons, with a maximum effective range of over 9,000 yards, the modern self–guiding submarine torpedo is, in effect, a robot submarine. Those employed by the US Navy at the beginning of WW II were ejected from the torpedo tube by compressed air. Once ejected it would level off at a predetermined course and then go streaking down the straight line to the target. Imagine if the projectile, when fired from the gun, could so spur to the right or left for a target around the corner. This projectile also predicted the ability to dive and to rise to the level of a suitable trajectory.

Steam generated by forcing a spray of water through a torch of burning substance, such as alcohol, supplied with motive power, it becomes a handy way to get something going. A delicate hydrostatic device regarding to water pressures governs depth control. And, finally, the explosives carried in the projectile's warhead contain about a quarter of a ton of TNT. The blast was detonated by an exploder mechanism, which worked by contact or by magnetic influence when the torpedo passed through the steel ship's magnetic field. Certainly the weapon or torpedo in a door with a remarkable status "one of the most devastating engines of destruction ever produced." All in all, by and large, in fact, it didn't work.

In action it proved to be a curiously temperamental provider, much like the prima donna who starts brilliantly on one occasion, but falls on her face on the next occasion. One day the torpedo may run hot and normal. On another, it may explode to the target, it may fail to explode on Thursday, and on Friday the only reliable feature of the torpedo was its unreliability.

Defective torpedoes are not easily brought to book — especially those which display all sorts of defects. The band in question made circular runs, purposed, ran cold, but sometimes just flat–ass refused to run. Quite baffling were the effects and design of the torpedo and the exploder mechanism. As described, some torpedoes ran certain depths. They exploded prematurely, they sometimes never even hit, but more than likely were called duds. Most baffling of all was the fact that they did work according to Hoyle and ran through their paces with a perfection that left nothing to be desired. They sank enemy shipping, tons of it, and proclaimed much of the difficulty in locating their flaws. Nonetheless, there were many officers in the submarine course that the torpedo could and should have been corrected, long before it was. Many people pointed to Admiral Lockwood's position and authority in grinding out the minute faults of this super weapon. Though for two years the U.S. submarine effort was seriously retorted by defective torpedoes, and it was not until autumn of 1942, and only then after the forces had stepped in to solve the problem, that the submarines were finally equipped with a weapon worthy of their skill.

Until the Mark 18 torpedo went to sea in Sept 1943, most torpedoes that were used by the submarine force were the Mark 10, or like "S–Class submarines" and the "Mark 14 for fleet types." The Mark 10 torpedo was a veteran with well over a decade of service. It was 21 inches long in diameter, it weighed 2,215 pounds, and when it was ready for a war shot, the warhead carried 497 pounds of TNT. The Mark 3 exploder was fitted with a simple contact device, designed to detonate the head upon impact of a wall or a stone or, ideally, a target.

The Mark 14 torpedo, 21 inches in diameter, was longer, heavier, faster and had a greater range than the Mark 10. When the war broke out, it was the most recent model in quantity and in production. It had two speed adjustments that could be fired with either speed, 46 knots to a range of 4,500 yards or a speed of 31 knots to a distance of 9,000 yards.

The original Mark 14 warhead contained 507 pounds of TNT. Improvements during the war boosted the explosive charge to 668 pounds of high explosives. This was filled with an exploder and it was designed to explode by magnetic induction when passing through the magnetic field in or around any vessel made of iron or steel.

The Mark 6 exploder has been a long time in development and its production has been a top secret. In fact, it emerged behind such thin scales that at the time of Pearl Harbor, it was a little more than a rumor to many submariners. It was not issued until the summer of 1941, and even then the commanding officers and torpedo officers didn't even know a gosh darned thing about the device. It was soon apparent that they were required to acquire some experience in handling the device, but it was this Mark 6 exploder rather than the Mark 14 torpedo itself that played the arch villain in the melodrama of malfunction.

The torpedo is an expensive machine. For example, the Mark 14 costs about $10,000 apiece. When they were fired in target practice, neither the warhead nor the exploder was used. Instead, an exercise head was employed. This exercise head was filled with water and so designed that at the end of the torpedo run, the water was expelled. This reduced the weight of the unit in order to prevent damage to the torpedo. Regulations called for a depth setting, which insured the torpedo would pass under rather than hit the target.

Such target practice procedures provided a check on the submarine commander's ability to make an approach and an accurate attack. It also tested the abilities of the torpedo men, but it provided no check on the exploder mechanism, nor did it provide a check on deep running torpedoes, which have exposed themselves by striking the target. The submariners had to accept these matters on faith, and the U.S. Navy, an entire generation of submarine personnel who had never seen nor heard the detonation of a projectile, was faced with this Mark 14 phantom from hell. Torpedo defects began to crop out as soon as submarines went into action. Difficulties with the deep performance, that is 500–700 feet, were not taken into strict advantage, and by August 1942 misses caused by erratic depth performance, were finally ironed out. Finally, the depth performance requirements of the Mark 10 were most exacting. For this torpedo to hit the target, it must really be right on target center. Thus, a miss with the Mark 10 was literally as good as a mile. The Mark 14, detonated by magnetic influence, would explode if it passed under a target. As these wrinkles had their source in the magnetic exploder, an explanation of the action of this mechanism, is in order.

Magnetic exploders — TNT — is an explosive which is not easily detonated. Under normal conditions neither fire nor shock will cause it to explode. In the torpedo warhead this wave is produced by the firing pin striking the primer cap which, in turn, sets off the detonator positioned within a cavity at the base of the booster charge. The explosive of the detonator sets off the booster. The booster produces the detonation wave that causes the TNT to explode. So, not one explosion, but a series of three, which will occur with the rapidity of chain lightning, finally creates the final explosion or blast.

The function of the exploder is to inaugurate this series at the proper moment. The Mark 6 exploder, weight 92 pounds, was designed to reblaze its firing pin upon contact with the target or passing through the target's magnetic field. This dual capacity — to work for impact or from magnetic influence — was a much prized feature of the world famous mechanism.

Equipped by an exploder that can be activated by magnetic influence, the torpedo will have a direct hit.

The exploder mechanism maintained another important feature — a device that disarmed the torpedo for safe and easy handling. In the unarmed position, the detonator was drawn from the booster, and this feature presented any additional shock, concussion or jolt getting off the booster and the main charge. When the torpedo was fired, its rush through the water activated a spinner that operated a chain of gears that moved the detonator into the booster cavity. Yes, the torpedo was then armed.

The 450 arming run was a feature that served to protect a submarine from the explosion of its own torpedo close aboard. But the full 450 yards was not required for this protection. It extended another arm for another purpose. During the first lap of the run, a torpedo is subject to the drastic changes of speed and direction. It hunts depth settings and seeks its preset course.

Having accomplished this, the armed torpedo was all set to explode. But now another contrivance stepped in as a control. This was an "anti counter–mining" device, which is designed to prevent the torpedo from being blown up by a nearby explosion. It would not do to have one torpedo blast detonate other torpedoes coming in for a hit.

So the armed torpedo would explode only when it passed through the magnetic field of a steel or iron vessel or struck the hull of a vessel, that is if the exploder were working properly. The contact feature of the Mark 6 was a relatively simple affair if the torpedo struck an object with sufficient force. This released the firing pin, which set off the works. This magnetic influence employs a more complicated device. When the torpedo passed through a ship's magnetic field, the electromagnetic force, EMF, generated in the exploder induction quarls under way of change. Amplified by vacuum tubes, this change of EMF caused release of the firing pin.

What was the extent of the ship's magnetic field? How close did it bring the exploder under the influence? At the war's beginning, submariners were instructed to run their torpedoes 10 feet under a battleship or five feet under a lighter vessel. This presumably allowed a good margin considerably below the depths that they were concerned with, operating with both contact and magnetic features, one torpedo exploding anywhere from the target's waterline down to 10 or 20 feet below the gale.

Sponsors of the magnetic exploder asserted that the device not only expanded the target, but gave the submariners a wider mark to shoot at. Literature, correspondence and instructions on this subject repeatedly stated that an explosion a few feet below the bottom of the vessel was three times as effective as one against the side.

That there can be no gain saying that a workable magnetic exploder widened the target for torpedo marksmanship, the hedge came in the qualifying objective: "workable". The magnetic exploder was new to naval warfare. The contact exploder dating back to the spar torpedoes of the Civil War was an old and tried pure verdict of newness and of proven merit. Nevertheless, the Mark 14 torpedo with the magnetic exploder, the Mark 6 was the primary submarine weapon at the beginning of the war.

So confidence and the reliability of the Mark 6 exploder waned rapidly during the first six months of 1943. Imperfections in the exploder mechanism necessitated an exchange of considerable correspondence between the submarine forces and the Bureau of Ordinance. As intricacies, the previous secret mechanism became none to many, but there were theories and suggestions for improvement. Minor design changes were made by the Newport Torpedo Station and torpedo shops that submitted exploder mechanisms through rigid tests before issue to individual submarines.

On April 27, 1943, the Bureau of Ordinance stated that the Mark 6 was susceptible to pre–maturing when set for

12–foot depths or less. The Bureau of Ordinance and foreign Admiral King stated that the effectiveness of the Mark 6 would be increased by 10 to 30%, increasing the arming distance from 450 to 700 yards. Between these two latitudes, torpedoes would be set at gale depth, or less, and the influence exploder would be kept operable. On July 24th, Admiral Limitz, Commander in Chief Pacific Fleet, ordered subcompact and the destroyers to activate magnetic exploders on all torpedoes. But because of probable enemy counter measures, because of ineffectiveness of the exploder under certain conditions and because of impracticability of selecting the proper condition under which to fire, that settled the magnetic exploder for Admiral Lockwood's submarines.

A Bureau of Ordinance letter on the Mark 6 dated August 31, 1943, outlined the magnetic features used. This letter went on to discuss the conditions under which the exploder would be expected to work and those under which it would not. Magnetic latitude targets, magnetic course conditions of degaussing, beam of target, graph of target in depth of torpedo, were factors to be taken into account.

When Admiral Lockwood in June 1943 ordered the inactivation of the magnetic exploder device, his force believed that the torpedo worries were all but over. Submarine commanders were ready to forego advantages for the magnetic exploder in order to obtain torpedo heads against the sides of enemy submarines. There was at that time no reason to doubt the contact mechanism of the exploder was anything less than reliable.

Quality, or lack of it, was not the only torpedo problem that bedeviled the submariners in the early months of war. Quantity was another matter. Quick work and removal under fire saved the remainder of the torpedoes that were destroyed in the Cavite Navy Yard on December 10, 1942. As has been related, some of the pioneer submarines went on patrol only partially loaded with torpedoes.

The crisis was relatively brief, considering that this was the first major torpedo war in the U.S. Navy's experience. By January 1943 the production crisis was over, but, believe it or not, transportation difficulties slowed the delivery and shortages continued to exist in the southwest Pacific until mid 1943.

After the United States entered the war, several private concerns were induced to engage in torpedo manufacture. Most of the submarine's steam torpedoes were manufactured at Newport, Rhode Island. Many parts were being subcontracted to a diverse list of manufacturers. Westinghouse produced the Mark 18 electric torpedo, introduced in the late summer of 1943. With Newport and Alexandria producing the steam torpedo, the Mark 18 electric torpedo kept pace with eventual expenditures, which soon reached $5,000 per month.

Early endorsements on patrol reports recently applauded extreme economy even for parsimony in the use of weapons. This encouraged commanding officers to wait for setups. Fortunately, the need for parsimony did not prevail. Thanks to the manufacturing resources of American industry, the torpedo supply problem was quickly and rapidly solved.

The war would have been foreshortened and many American lives saved had a reliable torpedo been available from the very beginning. This was the consensus of the Veteran U.S. Submarine Force.

CHAPTER 2

A FRENCHMAN COMING TO THE USA

In 1910, George A. Chartier and his lovely bride set sail from France to the United States. Her parents were native Frenchmen but were given the same treatment — a lowly peasant palace in Paris. They met quickly by accident two years ago. George was a salesman in the street and practically ran over Joan. She was carrying a basket full of clothes she had washed, pressed and ironed, and was taking this laundry back to its owners. Poor George hit her blind side as he was looking the other way. Joan fell down and tipped over the clothes in the basket. George was embarrassed immensely and stooped to pick her up. He was so sorry and he offered her money to solve the laundry problem. Her hair was a pretty bronze color and she sported a cute figure. They introduced each other and

George asked her for a date that weekend. This is how they met and fell in love.

A search or a chivalrous enterprise in gaining resource or involving an adventurous journey played an important part of their lives. Joan's father was a printer who demanded many hours at work. She wanted George to be at home more and not tied to his jobs. George's dad was a part–time alcoholic who kept the family vying to keep the family across the board.

In the past two years before their marriage they saved plenty of money. George's sales well exceeded forty percent. They both refreshed themselves with the American language. His wife was coming along but he had to take the upper hand in this affair.

The reason why George and Joan Chartier went to the United States was George's brother, who lived in Gulfport, Mississippi. Clinton was a budding printer who started a newspaper about ten years ago. He had built up this neighborhood and had encouraged numerous businesses to setup in this town. He asked George to come over and to assist him in his overflowing job.

The trip to Mississippi brought many hours of trains and buses. The trains were slow but chugged along at a reasonable speed — 25 miles per hour. It took forever to transit to the south. They finally made it by bus to the Promised Land — Gulfport, Mississippi.

The story of Mississippi begins with the portion of land that it occupies: one–quarter of 198th of the universe. The state consists of 47,000 square miles and it is the thirty–first in size among the great fifty strategy states. To compound this state, the outlander and native reveal that this is emphatically a white/black society, deeply bound together to the land.

The state is bound by one of forests, agricultural fields and small towns. The metropolitan areas take second place, with Jackson, Gulfport, Biloxi and Pascagoula as the picture cities. The empty space is encumbered by six national forests, the layout holding areas of Mississippi. Among the total capacity of reservoirs and recreational areas, this state is ranked first in environmental air quality.

The road system is immense in this territory, linking it to all other adjacent stations. The magnificent locale Nathez Trace is a little known road that runs from the south all the way to the northeast, where it eventually goes into Nashville, Tennessee. You are in a sleepy countryside with long distances and, of course, that's what the song says: "What I like about the south."

Water, water, everywhere — ruins, oxbows, bayous, lakes, swamps and catfish Ponds. This is where life itself began. The waters of the sloughs and in geological time the Gulf of Mexico covered one–fifth of the state of Mississippi. Dated from the Pleistocene Period, this state is blessed with rivers running north to south, with mossy swamps and emerald woodlands.

The Almighty has given to this state a climate full of growing opportunity, with an average temperature of 62 degrees. Yes, there are torrid summers and bodacious humidity.

The highest recorded temperature is 115 degrees and the lowest is below, or bordered close to, zero. There is languor to our Novembers when the fuliginous is profound with the landscape is suffused with a golden warmth. Occasionally, during their snowstorms, you find the wild frolic of young children playing in it, but overshadowed by dogs trying to bite the descending flakes!

This is a land of ghosts — the land of the vanished Indians. Hernando De Soto traveled the almost jungle in 1540, which would later be called North Mississippi. This region was already populated by Chickasaw, Natchez, plus many other smaller tribes.

These tribes were driven off by each white nation and many live in the state today. In country lingo, many names of the cities, rivers and countries reveal the native Indian Yazoo (River of the Dead), Tallahatchie (Rock River), Bongue Chitto (Big River).

It was my river because it meant so many things to all people. Twenty–eight miles to the west of Yazoo City was a living presence coincident to the people. Its mighty traverse, its bluffs, oxbows standing out in the sun, its tales and lore, and countless treacheries. Mark Twain once noted that the Mississippi gives and takes on fifty–four rivers that are navigable by steamboat. There is more commercial activity on the river today than ever before. Many tugboats travel the river, pulling about anything that will drag or haul its appointed load. The U.S. Corps of Engineers has pretty much claimed the river with concrete embankments here and continuing deviation to prevent a rushing tumultuous outpouring to the river below. History and the land are immutably combined, or the time has been with us that will unfold our valiant individuality. Mississippians are a singular people!

The Gulf Coast is one of the six sectors that we will concentrate a common center or focus on. Look at the map of the great state and we find that thirty miles upstate, north of the Gulf, is known as "the smell of salt in the air." The land is different in that it is flat and open, marshy with huge oaks laden with Spanish moss appearing here and there. And, but of course, people of different ages are fishing the land. Coastal Meadow includes the remote backwood marshes and all of the ponds, streams dotted with an occasional bayou.

The coastline is still available for construction. Many of the old contours remain — the sheltered homes with great porches, and outdoor staircases facing the sea. Pelicans and gulls are etched against the high banks of clouds and meandering bayous. Still, there are plenty of old houses for rent on the warming Gulf surrounded by emerald green live oaks or pungent blooming magnolias. This is where the twilight over the water during the outbreak of a storm made the words of a popular song cry out: "The sun went out just like a dying ember, that September...in the rain."

In 1699 the French established the first permanent settlement in the Ocean Springs land. This has been the most heterogeneous state in the region by far. "The people were Catholics," Falker wrote. The Spanish and French flood still showed in the names and faces. But it was not a deep one, if you do not count the sea and the boats on it: a curve of beach, their broken line of estates and apartments, hotels owned and inhabited by Chicago millionaires, standing back–to–back with another thin line, this time the tenements inhabited by negroes and whites who ran the boats and worked in the fish processing plants.

Rich vacationers had come to enjoy the Promised Land in the nineteenth century from New Orleans, and many northerners' summer styles suited all decorative cut out work made the style. Since 1880 the Gulf coast has been a prominent fish supplier for the nation. The sandy soil was a plus, but this remains a paradise for onshore and offshore fishing. Offshore fish like flounder, white and specked trout, and offshore catch — redfish, king mackerel, lemon fish and shrimp — are abundant. The commercial industry specializes in shrimp, crabs and oysters. On a clear day you can see the barrier islands, where most of the offshore fishing takes place.

Thought to be one of the oldest structures in the entire Mississippi Valley is Pascagoula. The Biloxi Indians excited themselves when they drowned themselves rather than be enslaved by a hostile tribe. West from Pascagoula we came to Ocean Springs, located on the waterfront and surrounded by pecan orchards. West of Gulfport the beach road goes through such a vivid display of gardens — roses, crepe myrtle, fences overgrown with wisteria and honeysuckle.

Such is life with the skies yielding to the exquisite, profound shores of beauty. Le Havre, two hours away from Paris, was the disembarkment center for the Chartiers. Once the ticket was bought they began packing. Joan's mother was apprehensive about the ocean travel. She helped pack the necessities, such as panties, warm underclothes, with an occasional sweater. It was March, yet the coldest of air was still upon them.

George was basically the avid of all weather systems. He packed freely with close attention to the cold.

Finally, all the bustle and speedy adventure was at last a reality. They said goodbye to loved ones and climbed aboard a train for Le Havre. The rain paid them a welcome call as they sped to the waiting ship. La Champagne was the ship that would take them to the United States of America.

The disembarkment at Le Havre was slightly easier, being directly from the steamer's main decks into the "Omar des Transatlantiques." This was the French Lines equivalent of the Landing Stage, although it was not afloat. Between ship and masonry pier, intermediate floating camels permitted passengers and mail alike to offload on parallel gangway–ladders. Hence, at low tide a steep climb up/down the ship was steep!

There were few open–sided sheds that made a March arrival/departure very frigid with humidity very damp. The main facility was a modern brick train shed surmounted by an equally modest clock–cupola.

Once aboard the ship they took 30 to 40 minutes to reach the sea through a torturous, twisting channel. After maneuvering carefully into the deeper water, they passed through home port to the Channel, where numerous sightseers and fishermen waved "bon voyage."

Once debased, inoculated and sprung from the port encampments, they went downstairs to be assigned their beds. This was an unpleasant task, as one person was allocated 100 square feet. Each berth was six feet long, two feet wide, with 30 inches between bunks. The bunks were a laughing matter. The bunks were padded shelves with mattresses made of straw and sufficient sheets and one blanket for cover. There were no stools or chairs available for dressing. There was no place to store bags, so the belongings were left in the beds. Incidentally, there were no wastebaskets or trash bins. Privacy was left to the imagination!

The transverse across the Atlantic Ocean was a precarious adventure. The food was enjoyable but each person was given a fork, spoon and an individual lunch pail. George and Joan were sometimes freezing during the night and sometimes the oceans wing–tipped high velocity waves brought in water to their sleeping quarters. Privacy for women was impossible as ship employees roamed sometimes during women's dressing times. Last, but not least, the bathrooms were hideous. Joan was mortified at the showers and bathroom facilities, but survived this procedure.

Finally, the view of Ellis Island and the outline of Upper New York Bay came into view. The trip across the Atlantic Ocean was to end at this island, which served as an immigrant station. After the La Champagne was docked, the disembarked passengers were moved to the passenger line at Ellis Island. Here they were checked in, bags checked and then the shot drill begins. They were kept there for two weeks before they entered the United States.

As George and Joan stepped off the bus they smiled and hugged each other. He took the two bags that they had been carrying and went inside the local store. He found the pay phone and called his brother. Clinton and his wife Jane came about fifteen minutes later. Clinton was tearful as he hugged his younger brother. The word that came out was foreign according to all passersby. Jane had not met Joan but the friendship was immediate. They talked of being alone and dirty most of the last three months. Jane was an American girl raised in God's country by the Gulf Stream. She had two children whom she had left at home with a nanny. With the bags loaded, they started the Ford and headed for Clinton's abode.

The breeze from the Gulf filled the air as the beginning of honeysuckle burst the scent of the afternoon. The houses were ultimately beautiful two–story palatial palaces with four or five

bedrooms on the second floor. Finally, they turned into a bodacious house right on the Gulf Coast surrounded by green oak
trees with blooming magnolias. Once the car stopped, the door
opened on the porch and two children came out running to
meet them. John and Cathy were their names: five and three
were their ages. They unloaded the car and George and Joan
met the nursemaid, who was black, with a great smile. Miss
Betty shook hands with them and escorted them to the upstairs
bedroom. It was lavishly purple with curtains and covered with
white cloth with bows hanging over the king–sized bed. Miss
Betty pointed out the bathroom and told them to clean up and
be downstairs for a cocktail in thirty minutes. She excused herself and shut the door. George was amazed and the two were
above looking out the window at the water. Joan turned and
looked into George's face and they hugged and eventually
kissed as their dream became true.

The next morning George and Clinton left for work. The
newspaper, the Gulfport Times, was a weekly edition of the
local events in town. The door was unlocked at 8:30 in the
morning. Clinton told his brother that he would be the salesman of the paper printed matter that went out each week via
special at a special rate, become a "printer's devil," and finally
become a printer to spell Clinton. He sat down and he began
the printing elements of the shop. At 9 o'clock the secretary,
Diane, was introduced. Clinton explained that he had just
come from France. He had a lot of English learning to do! The
next item was to review the sales contracts so Clinton could
catch up with the newspaper happenings. George had a few
questions but they were answered by the boss as he lead him to
a local restaurant for lunch.

In two weeks' time George was beginning to take root. He
rented a small cottage for a year and bought a secondhand car
for peanuts. His wife got a job in a clothing store and was
doing quite well in language/selling. They invited the Clinton
household to a Sunday outing. They had everything you could

imagine, shrimp, crawfish, potatoes and all the trimmings. It was hot and all the kids enjoyed splashing in the water beside the Gulf. At 7 p.m. the breeze started to cool the pent–up heat that they had subsided. Clinton said what a good job he had accrued at the newspaper. The sales had jumped another 10% and now he will concentrate on the elements of printing next month.

The next four years yielded a host of activities that George and Joan accomplished. First and foremost, let's break down and acknowledge them both for buying a new oceanfront house, advancements in both newspaper and in sales, and for Joan, she was with child! George and Joan had wanted a baby but never had time for her to conceive. It was the glass of wine before intercourse that did it! The world was upset, in that a World War was forthcoming. In 1914 this turn was properly applied because of the great powers of Europe, Russia, Japan and, eventually, the United States would get connected in between the hiatus of power. During this time, the economy of Europe was transformed by the Industrial Revolution. So, therefore, the use of iron and steel was preferred with electricity to power/operate the vehicles of war. When the inevitable crises came to the forefront, mobilization was ordered instantly. From a technical viewpoint, the war was of an internal combustion engine. From another perspective, the wireless telegraphy was to transport orders, which crystallized point to point communication. Basically, the cause of World War I was the blameless murder of Archduke Francis Ferdinand, heir to the throne of Austria–Hungary.

The Gulfport Times, with Clinton and George as co–owners, decided to print three times a week and hired an accountant and two other employees. They installed another printing device that would augment the main functioning apparatus and a ticker tape machine that printed telegraphic information on the news of the day. The big news was the war and how the countries described their battles. George was amazed with his handling of the war. Essentially, the war was fought through vast trenches. In this center of two lines of battle was a land wired with barbed wire. The first trench was a firing trench, from where the men fired at the enemy. The second trench was a cover trench, usually empty but it may contain an additional supply of troops. The other ditches are for reserve troops to final in the main force. This was a mystery until the plan was proved at battle.

In July 1915 the baby arrived, a girl named Mary Elizabeth, with blue eyes and weighing seven and one–half pounds. The couple worked on the extra bedroom buying a baby crib, curtains and a fresh coat of paint. Quickly they hired a nanny, whom Clinton and Jane approved. After three days in the local hospital, Joan brought the baby home. Nanny loved her the moment she saw her. Joan told her that she needed to nurse her and without a schedule for feeding her.

By and large the war carried on until the United States entered the conflict on April 6, 1917. The culprit was Germany and the American troops landed in France on June 24, 1917. The battle was tough, being overrun in the trenches numerous times. Finally, the troops rallied and began the final offensive on the Western front. On September 26, 1918, the Germans signed an armistice, or truce.

1920 was a surprise, as little John came from his mother's womb. Joan was pregnant, but by accident. She kept having morning sickness, but suddenly she missed her period. A doctor's visit and she was with child. She carried the baby but always had feelings of morning sickness and did not want any signs of sexual play. This was a dismal time for the two of them that went on an extended period of deployment!

Mary Elizabeth, they called her Beth, was all around John. She helped her mother change his diapers, wash him, with questions of "What's that?" "How come I don't have a pee–pee?" As the baby was six months old her Mom let her hold the baby. Mom and Dad enjoyed Beth, as she volunteered to give him the last bottle for the long sleep over the right house.

The deep depression locked the United States, including Mississippi. Gulfport was in need of a sedative to tranquilize the nervousness of many people without jobs. Clinton and George suffered through this period of stockholders going broke and, often enough, attempted suicide!

As the severity of money passed over the country, the necessity of being prepared bothered the United States. The Germans were gearing up their military and pushing the Hitler regime with killing of all Jews within their country. At age 18, John was finishing high school. He had worked diligently in all his efforts in sports, work and in being a thoughtful individual. His Mom and Dad were both exultant of his character, his aggressiveness in sports, and barely missed the honor roll of his senior class. Even his Dad thought highly of the work he did at the newspaper, which had again expanded to a newly constructed building. The night before graduating, John entered the living room and talked to his Dad.

"I have decided to join the Navy, Dad," he said. That upset his Dad but he listened as he went on with his decision. He recounted the events over the past three years and stated that it was inevitable that there was a war brewing. He had planned to visit the draft board the day after graduation.

His Dad was in turmoil; he wanted him to attend college, but no, he didn't want to. Finally, he hugged John and he wanted him to promise him that someday he would enroll and finish college. John agreed and then both went to find his mother and sister to tell them the news.

Great Lakes, Illinois, was the location of the Navy Training Command, and they were eager to see recruits. They processed them and away they went to receive their doctors' physicals and tests. Then they were divided up by forty souls who were positioned in a barracks. A Marine Gunnery Sergeant met them and had them fall into ranks. This took a lot of time, since neither sailor had ever heard of such a simple manner of routine.

By routine the steps were followed by the squad. The Gunnery marched them to the regimental haircut, to the uniform/clothes shop, and back to the barracks. Here each candidate got his sheets and watched closely how the Marine tucked in the sheets. Then the sailors launch into the bed–making, which was destroyed by the Sergeant, which was half–assed done. Things to be said about this is there will be an inspection each morning at 0800 hours. This includes all beds; drawers open revealing proper folding of undershirts, briefs and the individual manner of dress, and his shoes, spit and polish! This took quite a bit of training in one week to get a seaman a 4.0 grade at morning inspection.

Next, they were challenged with the physical requirements of a seaman. Pushups, rope climbing, running and numerous activities like the obstacle course. This, coupled with brain teasers which the students participated in, got sleepy in class. Next, marching with rifles, swords, knot string and assorted tasks; then came the true skill of what the seaman wanted to do. John liked all sorts of jobs, but his focus was on mechanical endeavors and, after almost six months of robotic training, he was assigned to Naval Training, Memphis, Tennessee, with two weeks Christmas leave.

John surprised his parents by writing letters every week. He told them of his orders but he did not want them to be surprised. The bus stopped at Gulfport. He came off the bus with his long duffel bag that contained all of his personal belongings. He caught a taxi that let him off at the newspaper building. John stopped at the receptionist's desk who, when she saw John, came around the desk and hugged a fully dressed, bell–bottom trouser wearing, white capped sailor. The commotion was making all heads turn, and finally George came in the entrance of the showroom and shouted, "John. You have come home!"

CHAPTER 3

PICKING OUT A CAREER

George and Joan Chartier had the marvel of having a Christmas full of happiness and wonderment — John is with us! John and his sister Beth were reunited and he wanted to know all about Ole' Miss. The Chartiers had sent her to the University of Mississippi, where she studied to be a teacher. Her graduation was the following May. Their primary concern was how the four of them were going to celebrate Christmas. Mother got out the handheld chalkboard and they made plans for the coming of the Christ child. It was December 17, 1938, a Friday night, and the plans were made. The Christmas tree, the decorations, both inside and outside the house, food, including a turkey, and, of course, presents. John elected to help Dad and Uncle Clinton at the newspaper. Monday was a worthwhile day, as John was fixing a printing device that prepared data. The gear ran perfectly after it was properly oiled and after all the gunk was cleaned off the printer head. On the way home John met a friend who had gone to high school with him. Joy greeted him with a hug and they sat down in a drugstore and talked about old times over a Coke. She went to college, Mississippi Tech, and she was somewhat disappointed. John dated her on and off, but he became interested in her again as she had her hair done differently. He relayed all the factors about Navy life and, after two weeks at home, he was to report to Naval Training Center, Memphis. He took her phone number and promised her she would hear from him the next day.

By Friday night he had dated her twice, both times to the movies. She was coming over for dinner to meet his parents. At six o'clock sharp she rang the doorbell. Beth met her at the door and was pleased to see her. They came into the living room and John stood up and introduced Joy to his Mom and Dad. She looked like Venus, knowing that she was right for him. She enjoyed a red wine while John stuck with his Budweiser. They socialized for about thirty minutes and then she went with Mom and Beth to serve dinner.

Dinner was exceedingly well done. The pot roast was enchanting, the vegetables and the rolls brought out the effervescence that showed the cook's exhilaration. Beth had a date, so Joy and John washed, cleared and put away the dishes. Yes, it was Christmas Eve, and they joined the family in the living room, where the Christmas tree had been put up and was beginning to be decorated. Both heads turned and Joy hugged John.

"Merry Christmas," she said. John acknowledged and said he loved her. Joy knew he had been thinking about what to say to her. George broke the moment by inviting them to help with the tree. After an hour the old pine tree of seven feet tall looked like a thing of beauty. Many rows of popcorn, gold intertwined the tree, beautiful Christmas balls scattered over its green needles, and tons of icicles covering pine cones with green branches. All was complete with apple cider that had a bite as they saluted the symbol and the Virgin Mary on top of a woody perennial plant.

They said goodbye as the clock struck ten. In the car they exchanged different heartfelt feelings about the friendship that Joy had felt. John, too, lauded her presence that enables one to establish a distant relationship with his parents. They drove in the driveway and walked up to the front door. She asked him to come in and look at the tree. John entered and walked into the living room. The tree was magnificent and Joy went to pick up a present. John was surprised as she said, "Merry Christmas." He stood back when she gave him this gift. John reached in his right pocket and held the ring box in his right hand. He kneeled down on his right knee and said, "Joy, I love you with all my heart. You have renewed our love, so I give you this as a token of love — that same day when I am ready you will marry me!"

Joy was crying tears that she meant to sacrifice herself to the load of eventful bliss. She opened the small box and there was a ring made of quartz and navy blue. John said that the navy jewel represented him and the quartz white was as pure, colorless and transparent as her soul. Joy tried on the ring and it fit. She pulled up John and kissed him, opening his mouth, giving and taking his tongue. She broke apart quickly saying, "John, I will wait for you," breathing deeply. He complied and started kissing her again. Joy started unbuttoning his shirt and said not to worry because her parents were at the Christmas Eve service. John removed her sweater, which revealed a bra that was filled with overflowing breasts trying to be released from her undergarment support. Both had their shirts/pants removed, and now they lay down side by side with John opening the gates of treasure and kissing her protruding nipples. Ten minutes later Joy wailed in ecstasy, as she came with John right after her. They hugged, kissed and, fifteen minutes later, they repeated the lover's march to the pledge of being married.

Christmas Day was a happy occasion. John went to Joy's at noon and then he met her at the door. "I love you, my sweet," she said. He kissed her and they went inside. Her parents were just the same as he had met them previously. Her grandparents were there and wanted to know why he was going, when and where the war was going to occur. They had dinner with wine and then they talked about any and everything.

Monday the 27th of December, John called the Greyhound bus terminal from work. He found out that the best time to leave Gulfport was at 12 noon on the 30th to make the necessary connections to Memphis on New Year's Eve. He told his Dad that he planned on telling Joy that evening. She cried slightly but she wanted him as much as he wanted her. She told him she was going back to school to make a go of it. It would be doubly difficult to study as now she worried and thought about John. The next three nights they planned several dinners and ate and made love at various spots.

Mom, Dad and Joy bid John goodbye as the Greyhound roared off toward the north. John had to admit he had tears in his eyes, but Joy, God bless her, said she would wait for him.

The waiting and gathering of people at the public transportation center was atrocious. Maybe it was the holiday, the coming of a major, or maybe it was that John worried about his life and the partner that he would spend it with.

The Greyhound stopped at Jackson, Mississippi, to change buses. The bus he was supposed to get on never arrived at Jackson. The bus was late and then broke down at Meridan. He stayed the night at a hotel and left at 8 o'clock the next morning. The Greyhound system was cleaner when they counterbalanced the number of passengers. For example, they have standby buses that could eliminate a big burden at that junction. At the Naval Training Center in Memphis, John arrived at 12:30 in the afternoon. They took him to the security department at the Naval Training Center. The Chief signed his travel orders and then the driver took him to the barracks.

The next morning was New Year's Eve, but John walked down to the Naval Exchange. He bought some toiletries and went by the barbershop for a haircut. He was assigned to the Aviation Mechanic's School and it met on the 2nd of January. That night he went to the Seaman's Club and had dinner. There was a band with plenty of champagne and horns.

Sunday was for telephone calls. Joy was called and she was elated that John had arrived safely. He gave her my address and she said, "I will miss you!" Mom and Dad were home and they wanted to know how he liked Memphis. Dad said he would take care of Joy for him.

At 8 o'clock in the morning John and his fellow students met in a classroom near the mechanical shop. The Senior Chief called out their names and most of the men were airmen, while some had already climbed to Petty Officer Second Class. Senior Chief Davis passed out some literature that asked or answered many questions all of the 20 people had. The room was a classroom, one of those that they would experience when they had completed the course. Looking at the academic schedule, the first week dealt with mathematics, diagrams and engineering problems. The second week started out with aircraft engines, which later on dealt with labs that concentrated on repairs to the aircraft engines. Throughout the weekly schedule they had target practice, calisthenics and whatever. At 9:30 they went to the clothing store to be issued a blue short–sleeved shirt and matching pants. This was the issue for school.

At the end of the first week John had met new friends. He learned their names and recognized their homes from which they came. John also took the top grade on Friday and bought the first round of beer at happy hour at the club. The weekend was Joy's time and he knew she was at college. He wrote her religiously until he called the college and awaited her voice. She answered and he said he missed her. She told him that the girls admired her ring and wanted to meet him.

"When will the semester end?" John asked.

"The end of May, but I don't know the date. The school ends on the last of the fourth week in May."

"Maybe I'll get leave and come see you," he said.

The training became real interesting as the labs turned out to be aircraft engines. They identified what the problem was, checked out the instruments in which to restore it or deliberately deal it as worn out, unfixable power plant. One engine trainer to four big propeller planes, a one–day check or a full maintenance check they could accomplish with no problem. His class was phenomenal in that they were the hardest, meanest and most rewarding young mechanics in the Navy. Grade–wise, he was the top contender. Chief Davis talked with every man in this class. John wanted what the Senior Chief wanted, a good reliable man to meet the beginning of World War II. Corpus Christi, Texas, was cranking out pilots at a given rate. There were more barracks being built for the sailors that would come if such a war took place.

On the last Friday of May, 1939, they had a graduation, which enabled those 20 seamen to lie aside, marked with truth and integrity; they were proud–headed as they received their certificate for completing A School. The second ceremony was the sewing on of the patch ADR, and John sewed on ADR3 as his highest grade won him his advancement in rate. His orders were NAS Corpus Christi, where a PBY squadron was located. He had to report in a week's time, at one o'clock in the afternoon. ADR3 Chartier, with his new grade, called the Naval Air Station to see if there were any rides to the south.

"Where do you want to go? Wait a minute. We have a plane going to Gulfport, Mississippi," the Petty Officer said. The Petty Officer said that he should come on over and then he would know if the Lieutenant could take him. "Where are you from?" asked the man. The Lieutenant was from Gulfport, Mississippi. Lt. Bang was going to fly to Gulfport and stay until Monday, he said. "Would like to go and return with him?"

"No," said John. "I would like a ride to Gulfport."

At 1500 local time the DC–3 aircraft took off from Memphis. John made the flight, had all his clothes, and nobody knew he was coming home. He and three officers were riding along and introduced themselves. About an hour into the flight another officer on his flight said let another aviator do some flying. Lt. Bang was a nice guy and introduced himself. He stated that his best friend was going to get married on Saturday near Gulfport. John told about himself being from Gulfport all his life and having joined the Navy last year. Lt. Bang thought that "good hard work" meaning the war with Germany was just about to start.

The DC–3 landed at 5 o'clock local time and it taxied over to the Navy Department and shut down. John thanked Lt. Bang for the ride. John went in the detachment and found a phone. His Mother was surprised when she heard his voice. He said where he was, and told her to look for the Navy hangar, as he would be there. He also asked her to call Joy!

They met in front of the hangar where he hugged and kissed his parents. They got all the clothes, the elementary stuff and went home seeing who wants the best gabbler! They marveled at John's crows and asked him all about Memphis. Just as the Plymouth turned into the driveway, he asked about Joy.

"Yes, she is home," said his Mother, "but I told her you were at the airport."

The front door opened and there was Beth running down the steps. She hugged John and immediately John said, "Congratulations, teacher!" Beth said she was nominated to teach at the West Gulfport elementary school. She accepted and would be teaching second grade. Dad had his duffel bag and Mom had the rest, so they went in the front door.

After getting out of his whites, a shower and a tooth brush, they went out to dinner. They had fried chicken with assorted vegetables and apple pie a–la–mode. Joy was on the line so John took the receiver from Mom.

"Hello, dear heart!" John exclaimed. Joy was excited and explained that she had gotten home the day before, after supper. She had finished up her freshman year but she was undecided whether she would return in the fall. "Come on over," John said.

"I'll be there in fifteen minutes." Joy said.

Joy was a wonder that he had been dreaming of. Her hair, her vivacious smell and a quick hug told him she was the one. George and Joan joined them in a joy of celebration. Wine and John's favorite beer hit Joy's wine glass. They talked about an hour and a half then they left for bed. John could not stay away from Joy as he kissed her all over. John turned off the lights and he joined her on the couch. The shirt did not stay on her amorous breasts. Their climax was quick as they heard a car door slam. It was Beth, as they scrambled for their clothes.

"Hello," said John. Beth went out to her girlfriends and they chatted. Soon Beth said she was headed for bed. Again Joy was all over him and they enjoyed themselves more than ever before. They got dressed and walked outside to her father's car. John said he had to leave for NAS Corpus Christi in five days, so they should make the most of them.

Saturday was going to be hot and humid. He went over to Joy's and saw her family. After an hour he took a trip down to the Gulf of Mexico. They went to a beach near Long Beach. They sat and talked about everything they had done during the previous five months, however, it was not complete being alone. He was burning on his back, but Joy put some tanning lotion on it. His back would be all right the next day — brown. Suddenly, Joy had to go to the bathroom. Under certain circumstances she had to go home because she had started her period.

The sum of four days was a whirlwind of many events. John helped his Dad at the newspaper and with many conversations; and his Dad found him a nice used Ford sedan. John, who had been saving his money, bought the car outright. It was a good deal, which included a state inspection. Additionally, Joy and John talked about their living together and being married. They were young, 19 or 20, but the times were beginning to press one's mind. It was argued between the two that after the tour in Corpus Christi they would set the date.

CHAPTER 4

JOHN BECOMING
A PBY FLIGHT ENGINEER

After leaving at eight o'clock on Thursday morning, it was a long trip driving the Model T. Joy was with him in mind and soul. The plans that they had worked out were formative and constructive. They would be married, he hoped, in a year. Mom and Dad were super, as they had some goodies for him on his trip to Texas.

At 1600 hours (4 o'clock local) he pulled into the Naval Air Station, Corpus Christi, Texas, on Saturday. The security officer checked him in and gave him a third–class sticker. He followed the directions given and pulled up at the barracks. Within thirty minutes he was in his room, bunk made, and all his stuff was put away in the locker.

The PBY training squadron at the NAS was for candidates who had gone through the pipeline and were ready to qualify for pilot/navigator training. On an isolated airfield in 1936, a small group of naval officers witnessed the first of three flights the brazen, awkward looking long wing aircraft flew. The era of modern maritime aviation was, without a doubt, being witnessed. The advent of the PBY (XP3–Y) was to be the odd and magnificent beast where this beauty would certify its splendor in wartime. Principally, it is called the long–range maritime patrol bomber flying boat. The missions — we'll name them when the war begins.

John was assigned to the Training Squadron 15, which was to train the pilots. He checked into the maintenance division, where he reported to the division chief (ADR). Chief Sims was his name, and he was delighted to meet ADR3 Chartier. He spent ten minutes meeting and greeting the whole bunch. Chief Sims showed him a display board of the 10 PBYs and when each scheduled maintenance function was performed. The PBY–1s, which were the first aircraft received at NAS, had the VW118D8–A and some airplanes had the modified B engines. John was checked out with a standard Naval Air Training and Operations Procedures Standardization manual. This book was all of the engine "nomenclature" and the mechanical "mumbo jumbo"

"A good guide to becoming a flight mechanic," said the Chief.

With that being said, Chief Sims told a third stash to show him his locker. Then he was to report to ADR1 Roberts. At the locker, John changed into a washed set of flight gear and marched out of the hangar deck to find Roberts. There were three PBYs undergoing various checks. Roberts was reviewing the work on the engines of aircraft number 3. He recognized a new hand and jumped down from the yellow check stand.

"Welcome aboard," he said. He spent about 30 minutes explaining all the gear that was needed to perform a 30–hour check. He spent several minutes going over the check, emphasizing the master checklist that each man must follow. When all was said and done, the completed work got its final "go" or "no go" from the check crew.

After a month in the maintenance division, John worked his way upward in that he understood all phases of the Pratt & Whitney engine, including all the dials that indicated its progress.

ADR1 Roberts was watching this guy and then he popped a question. "How would you like to be a mechanic"?

John was excited, but he had found that he had learned enough and said, "So when's the training that would permit me to fly this PBY–3?"

The course started in September, and meant passing a physical — eyes, and so forth. He studied hydraulics, boosters, engine nacelles, spark plugs, cylinders and all the numerous systems that should execute together. After studying in the classroom, the labs were open where the students analyzed a broken or malformed part and made it work.

Soon it became December and the final exams were at the end of the second week. The instructor said that the fifteen December flights that would have been stopped because of Christmas had been extended to the first of January 1940. John made the highest grade on the test. His evaluators were most excellent of him being vigorous and spirited throughout his pathway of success.

He left Corpus Christi Naval Air Station at 0800 on December 15. During his stay, he had purchased many items for his Dad, Mom and Joy. Also he bought several items for all of the family. At 1230 he stopped for gas, crackers and a Coke. Snow appeared but the chill was cold as he had been traveling due north. Finally, he arrived at home at 1700 (5 p.m.). His family was looking out for him as he approached the door. His Mother had him first and then Dad. They sat down and talked about his budding mechanic status, and went on to discuss Joy as his wife.

"I knew you were planning to marry her. When is the date?" his Dad asked.

"I don't know as of yet, but I plan to ask her parents if we can become engaged." With that being said, now he asked his parents about the best place to buy a ring. They thought a minute but both came out with the name Parks Jewelry. They discussed many other things, including when Mom could go shopping with him.

It was six o'clock by now as he and his Dad had a bourbon and water. He called Joy's parents and they were overjoyed that he had arrived home safely. Joy still had not gotten home as of yet.

"It's a busy Friday night as she was working at Sears and Roebuck," said her Mother.

She hung up after John told her he was coming over. A knock was heard at the door, so John went and opened the door — Joy. Into his arms she went.

"Surprise!" his parents cried.

PBY-5 Catalina flying boat in World War II.

"I do miss you," she said. They kissed softly while John told her that same endearment.

After exchanging hugs she took John out to her house for dinner. Joy stated that she was starting work as a sales clerk for Sears. She had calculated that she had made two raises in slightly six months. They talked about difficult things happening at Gulfport, especially with the Christmas season exploding with balls, ornaments and mistletoe. Her parents were at the front door when Joy arrived with the '37 Plymouth. Her Dad was happy to see John; so happy that he made a glass of eggnog for everyone. A toast was called for and John raised his glass and said, "Salute."

The meal was shrimp gumbo augmented with shrimp, mussels, okra pods and many other vegetables, plus hush puppies. The wine was white, as it soothed the zing of the soup. Conversation flowed throughout the meal, with Joy's mother getting more replacement bowls of soup. Joy was staring at John and he acknowledged her. Suddenly he felt a hand on his knee. Joy was killing the wine in her glass. She smiled at John as her hand moved even closer to his semi–hard condition.

The night went on with coffee, but John and Joy were quite ready to burst. They carried the dishes into the kitchen, but her Mom said to stack the dishes and she would do them the next day. They looked at the photos that had been taken since they were last together. Finally Joy's folks said goodnight and went upstairs. Joy went to John and kissed him as if he, too, meant the same release of passion, wanting, full of love, yet it was her body he had been dreaming of touching. John became aroused as she kissed him and she unzipped his fly. Joy motioned to him to go into the den. He complied and carefully closed the door.

Joy closed the blinds and said to John, "I love you, John." To which he replied, "The same."

Soon they both were free of clothes and they fell on the couch. John suddenly felt Joy kissing his penile area. He shifted her around until he could touch her female genitals. With his tongue he began kissing and agitating her private parts. Joy rose up and with her tongue licked the head of his penis, which moved him deeply. He found her orgasm spot and within thirty seconds she groaned as she just had vaginal contractions. Quickly she got up and kissed John, her nipples were ready to burst. She climbed on and resumed the dual climax, which she had reserved for her soul mate. If only God gave man the sole purpose of love through Joy, the sealing of ecstasy would be fulfilled for reality.

They lay together talking about getting pregnant, but John said, "Let it happen." She kissed him on each cheek and he nibbled each of her glowing breasts. That triggered an erection that turned into a phenomenon of love reaching all shades of fantasy and sexual embrace.

The next four days ahead, John helped his Mom get ready for the holidays. He bought a Christmas tree, many presents for the parents, and many things to decorate the house. Joy was exceptionally busy at the Sears store. He took her lunch the next day, which really did her heart good.

"I love you again and again," he whispered into her mighty fine ear. Joy took a fifteen–minute break and ate a BLT and a Coke. The store was packed as there were things going left and right. Joy, even though they were in a lunchroom, told John that she started her period that morning. When John heard, he was put at ease!

Next came his Dad, who needed some help down at the paper. The printer required ink, newsprint was low, and so on. That night, at seven o'clock, the newspaper had a Christmas party. The food was catered, the Coca Cola sales-men dropped off the final cases of drinks, and other goodies would be at the party. John helped set the dining–like table with a bar, well, sort of, and a stage with appropriate chairs. With 30 employees they expected around 80 people, including children.

Mom, Dad, Joy and John drove to the Christmas party. First of all they had cocktails and met all of the editor's writers, promotional leaders, secretaries, and finally the check man who waited, sorted mail and infinitesimal tasks. Then John's Dad went up to the podium and said grace, after which the caterers marched out with the food. Everyone formed in a buffet line and sat down at the tables provided. About 30 minutes later, all of a sudden Santa Claus appeared. The children gathered around old Saint Nicholas and he gave out presents. Then he helped Dad give out the yearly bonus checks. The party lasted for three hours, with the drunks the last to say Merry Christmas as a gesture when parting.

After dropping off his parents, John drove to Joy's abode. It was 10:15 p.m. when they arrived. Joy went upstairs to tell her parents they were home. She came down the steps with her nightgown on. They went into the den and sat down on the couch. She told John that she enjoyed the evening. John took a blanket and covered her shoulders. Her eyes were a little tired and he knew she had to be at work by 9 in the morning. John pulled her close to him and she looked at him — then he knew he had to kiss her. With his tongue in her mouth, moaning, and then she reached for his fly, unzipping it.

John said, "You are still on your period?" She nodded and then she took out his penis and stroked it until it was hard. After three minutes he had ejaculated kissing her breasts, as he had been relieved!

Two days before Christmas his Mom went with John to the Parks Jewelry Store. A lady introduced herself and Mom told her what they were looking for. Initially they had set a limit of two hundred dollars cash, for which John had the money. His Mom had in mind what size ring to get and suddenly the representative pulled out a display of engagement rings. Without a doubt, they were the cream of the crop. John and his Mother looked at all shapes and sizes. The one that was the consensus above all displayed was an exquisite diamond ¾ carats, which was placed in a platinum setting. The sales lady said the ring was two hundred and ten dollars. John said, "It's a deal." The store wrapped the stone in a ring box with a big bow on the top.

For Christmas Eve both families went to church, sitting side–by–side. The assembly was full and the joyous music made them realize that war was of the making. One by one they took communion, promising forgiveness as they left for home. Joy and John kissed goodnight, as she worked almost ten hours at work.

It was a quiet Christmas morning with snow showers skirting the coast.

"Merry Christmas," said John, as he was coming downstairs. Dad said the same as he hugged him. Mom was excited as she brought John a cup of coffee. They froze as Dad cut on the lights of the Christmas tree. They all had breakfast and then opened their presents. Everyone was shocked as John had got his Mom a beautiful sweater with earrings, and Dad got a Sears chamois leather long–sleeved shirt and a pair of pajamas. John got a light winter coat to wear around the house and got quantum socks, underwear and a new wallet.

Joy's parents were going to have them for Christmas dinner. They were to bring several dishes, and John was to bring the wine to go with the turkey. At one o'clock they bundled up with all the food, including presents, and drove over to Joy's parents' house. After going through the mistletoe line, Joy grabbed John and gave him a long kiss. Then the drinking began, with eggnog flowing, and then the present brigade started. Finally, all had gifts except Joy and John.

On his knees he said, "Joy, I am deeply in love with you. So, in front of your parents, will you be my cherished, to bind by a pledge to marry me?"

Joy began to cry and said, "I do, John." They embraced and then he gave her the box with a big bow on top. She opened it and everyone in the room thought the engagement ring was spectacular.

John returned to NAS Corpus Christi, Texas, with his mind on other things. He had Joy and the PBY–3 on his mind. He recalled the teaching from the last three months involving the specs and calculations of horsepower with related engine hydraulics, oil, gasoline and engine how–goes–it. Now that had been reviewed, he had to remember the dimensions of the aircraft. Oh, well. It was time to get ready for aviating.

Initially, the first set of students were given a week of review of all systems in the PBY–3. They went through a mockup of the flight engineer's seat. They were required, and if missed, they pointed out their mistakes and queried them again. On the third week of January, John was scheduled for his FAM, or his first flight. He met with his flight instructor, ADR 1 Michaels. He introduced himself and briefly went over the flight. The first portion would be a walk around the airplane looking for discrepancies. Before he went out to the airplane, he asked several questions, which John answered without any errors. Finally, ADR 1 Michaels asked, "What do the P, B and Y stand for?"

"Well," John replied, "P stands for patrol, B is for bomber, and I cannot figure out what the Y means."

John flew an excellent flight, and it was written up in his UBAA crew syllabus. There were four levels of performance which you could mark the individual: Unsatisfactory, Below Average, Average, and Above Average. Then that's it! Y, what is that which emaciates the brain! The moment he got back to his room he looked up and found what it meant.

John kept up with the chores of all the duties of plane captain. He was fueling the engines, putting oil in the engines, and showing top drawer performance in–flight. The engine analysis is a fine apparatus which is monitored every hour or when the engine malfunctions or coughs. This particular event happened on several flights. Both turned out to be engine failures after the engine was feathered. After landing, the sump pump found slivers of metal which exceeded the maintenance manual specifics — an engine change.

The final flight was scheduled for the end of April, 1940. John was confident and he excelled. The second week in May, he received a certificate and a set of wings, which he cherished.

When he pulled in the road to the house, his mother came to the door. She knew he was coming home today. She hugged and kissed him as he showed his mother a new set of wings. He told his Mom that he would be home for a month on leave. How was Dad? Could he help him? This was shortened by his Mom bringing in all his dirty clothes.

Dad was busy in the newspaper office, which was growing every step of the year. John hugged his father and was very proud to show him his wings that he had earned. His son said he would be home about thirty days on leave. He stated that he was ordered to Naval Air Station Jacksonville, Florida, for tactics and replacement training. Of course, his father had many things for him to attend to.

Joy came over after work and ate dinner with the family. After supper was finished, John talked to everyone about getting married to Joy. In one month from now he was to report to Jacksonville. That would take four months to complete. So, if he left the end of June, he would finish training and be ordered to an active duty squadron.

"So, you lady, would you take my hand in November?" said John. Joy hugged him and said yes. He told Mom and Dad that he would see what was in store when he checked in at Jacksonville. This situation was shaky, but clearly, they could only speculate.

The remaining ten days brought a smile between the two lovers. They figured out what church, dress of the groom and attendees. Joy went to the print shop downtown and looked at invitations. Flowers were included in the scenic view of the wedding. John calculated a rough cost for the wedding, which included the reception. Lastly, a list of who to invite was started to this grand occasion.

Time to leave for Jacksonville and Joy was crying. John knew he wanted to break down with her, but stiff upper lip, he promised he would call her when he had the date.

Jacksonville was a spacious place with many custom cars and young Navy sailors. The base was expanding every day, with housing units and Navy squadrons getting their share of the runway. He stopped at the duty office and checked in all his records. The duty yeoman gave him information on where he was to report the next morning. He thanked the sailor and proceeded to the Enlisted Barracks. Once he was in his room, he went to the Acey–Ducey Club to get some food. It was extremely hot, since it was obviously in the middle of summer.

The next morning he found out that a delay in his training would occur. This training would start about the first of August, 1940. There had been a backlog of pilots and so few planes. So, essentially, he had five weeks to kill. They made him the Assistant Squadron Duty Officer! John felt in charge after two days standing in. After four weeks taking this task, the Commanding Officer stopped by and shook his hand for a job well done.

At eight o'clock he called Joy and set the date, as this was the first day of training in the PBY Replacement Squadron. He recommended the second week of November. The training would constitute four weeks of ground and simulator practice with the remaining ten flights.

Already Joy had started laying the plans for the marriage. John said to look for a letter as he would send her a check for expenditures. They hung up and John was worried but he could not help it. That night, before he retired, he wrote a check along with a letter, which included a $500 check that was written on a savings account from a bank in Gulfport, Mississippi.

He started flying the day after Labor Day. Quickly reviewing some past work, he aced out his instructors. By the third week, in September, he found out about the first class exam.

After signing up, he took the test. Only the shadow would know who passed this test.

Tactics flights began in the fall days of October, which specified eye training search. The random square search was the first method taught. John picked this evolution up in a snap. They dropped bombs, water sand fills and even a few old depth bombs. The technique was the secret in blowing the shit out of a submarine. As November approached, John got his orders to VP–11, located at Kaneohe Marine Corps Air Station in Hawaii. On November 4, 1940, he checked out of the replacement squadron with orders to arrive at Naval Air Station San Diego, California, on December 1, 1940.

The day before the wedding they had a rehearsal, for which everyone was there. All of John's classmates and old girlfriends were alive! Afterward, they had a party, the likes of which had never before been seen in Gulfport. At nine o'clock the next morning, with his sunglasses on, John and his chap Dennis went to pick up the tuxedoes. Next, they visited the florist to pick up boutonnières. Now the story was, John shouldn't get to see Joy until she came down the aisle. Dad walked over and said he wanted to chat with him. He put his hand in his pocket and pulled out a key.

"Son, you have driven that Ford Model T into damnation and back. From Mom and I, here is your new car," said Dad. After walking out of the house, a 1939 Ford with a big bow ribbon was waiting for him. He gaped and hugged his Dad.

The wedding event went as planned and Joy looked sensational. After Joy had changed her things and John's clothes too, she threw the bouquet to the lucky girl. They walked out to the Ford, in which all of their belongings were. They kissed each Mother and Dad and were off to the West Coast!

CHAPTER 5

WORLD WAR II

In January 1941, the view of Hawaii was mobilizing, receiving supplies, and wondering what the Pacific Commanders should do. Meanwhile, over in Washington, D.C., the military was fighting Germany, assisting England, and had Japanese diplomats visiting the State Department. Three patrol squadrons that were based in Kaneohe Marine Corps Air Station in Hawaii were VP–11, VP–12 and VP–14. These units were assigned the earlier version of the PBY where a year earlier in San Diego, the latest version was being tested and given to VP–6. PBY–5 "Catalina" had the sharpest crew wring out this giant wing aircraft, similar to that of the B–17 Flying Forties. The Pratt & Whitney R–1830–92s made a substantial increase in horsepower in relation to the first engine. VP–6 was renamed VP–11 and therefore one aircraft (PBY–5) had arrived at Kaneohe Bay.

John and Joy arrived at the Hawaii airport the 15th of January 1941. He got government quarters and checked in with the VP–11 Squadron Duty Officer, which had only two–thirds of the squadron in place. The Squadron Assistant Duty Officer signed him in and he recognized the brand new second–class crow on his sleeve. The administrative arm had not checked aboard so he noted that his records were contained in the designated safe.

The hangars where VP–11 was situated were right next to the water. There were two airplanes in the hangar (PBY–3s) that were undergoing checks. John finally saw an office with "Plane Engineer" posted on the outside.

He met the senior mechanic, who was glad to meet him. In fact, there were three missing which caused throbbing headaches between the other mechanics. Senior Chief Fisher was the NATOPs evaluator and he wanted to know his progress in order to finish his flight syllabus. John said he had all flights with numerous deficiencies and received an outstanding rating. "We'll see," said the laughing senior chief. Fisher completed the bulletin board depicting ADR2 Chartier's presence and he was potentially the second mechanic of crew two. The next step on his checkout list was for the NATOPs manual, and all the flight gear he was supposed to have. Last, but not least, a locker to put his flight gear away. Then he led the way to the hospital where he got a checkup and was credited with an up.

Joy was busy back in the apartment surveying the kitchen. She made a list of needed pots and pans, including needed spices and all that lot. John came home about two o'clock in the afternoon and embraced his wife. She had on a short outfit, which would mark her as a lively young thing. John asked her if she was ready to go to the navy exchange and the commissary. She showed him what she had planned for the living and dining rooms. She hung curtains in the bedroom but she was excited about them. John accepted a glass of iced tea and then he climbed out of his uniform into a pair of shorts with the shirt. By this time Joy was ready so they climbed into his Ford, which made it to the Promised Land.

They found everything in the exchange, however, they had nowhere to go. They bought the necessary pots and pans with assorted cups for coffee and an occasional wine glass. Off to the commissary for food. They had a list of things to get but they had to have a useable refrigerator. Joy solved this problem by getting a block of ice (10 lb.) to put on top of the unit to chill meat, etc., to last for three days. They had lettuce, cucumbers and all sorts of snacks. John bought Cokes, beer, and Joy liked wine.

After 2½ hours of shopping they arrived at their apartment. They took in the groceries and put them in the cold refrigerator. No matter what time it was there was a breeze blowing through the apartment. Nevertheless, John was sweating and Joy was, let's say, perspiring. John had a beer and Joy had a Coke and then they tackled the draperies. John went out to the car to get a hammer, screws and a tape measure. He opened the screen door and found Joy comfortably nude and immediately kissed him, opening his shorts.

Later that evening they had steaks, hung all the curtains and took a walk throughout the neighborhood. Life in Hawaii was stupendous!

After receiving seven flights as an assistant second mechanic engineer, the NATOPs checker had him for a NATOPs flight. He rushed to the airbase and donned his flight suit and boots. He reported to Senior Chief Fisher, who began the brief. John understood all the ins and outs of the manual. Fisher asked him about flight rules regarding the conduct of the preflight in which he was to conduct. Finally, he presented him with five types of nuts, screws, or whatever that belonged to the aircraft that he was going to preflight. Amazingly, he found the places that had eye–opening faults and John finished in about forty minutes. He topped off the 115/145 gasoline tanks and verified that the oil was at the top of the full list. The brief at planeside was conducted by the plans commander. He spent two minutes talking over the safety procedures and asked if there was anything else. Chief Fisher commented on the NATOPs being conducted on ADR2 Chartier and he would be riding the seat.

Since this flight was a local flight lasting five hours, the PBY started up and with exact checks, the PPC sitting in the copilot seat announced the appropriate take–off condition. John got his lifejacket ready, sent belt locked, and they began their take–off. Once out of the water the drills began. After two hours of flying, Chief Fisher swapped seats and John was sweating like a big dog! The final two hours consisted of touch and goes ended a new second mechanic. Chief Fisher congratulated him and said he flew an outstanding flight.

In May, the members of the crew were formed. The PPC was LCDR Adams, who was in charge of the Operations Branch. John was part of VP–11's crew; three copilots (LTJG), four gunners or observers, a radio operator, a navigator (an LTJG) and John. They started from scratch on the readiness chart. They practiced bomb runs, mining exercises, and anti-submarine warfare tactics. Within two weeks they were classified as a category BRAVO aircrew.

In July of 1941, John had written his parents and told them that the ship level was at maximum with at least three carriers and many battleships. He and Joy wanted to see them, but travel across the Pacific was not a good escape. Joy had written her parents, too, with thoughts of seeing them far into the future. The flying had increased as the seven–crew squadron was tasked as much as the other two squadrons. Crew three practiced with a conventional sub and got 2 more qualifications. After a long, hot day John came home bushed. Joy had dinner ready and, after the dishes were put away, she took her husband for a walk. She was happy for no reason, and laughed as if there was a hidden thought that was about to burst within her. They stopped at the ocean, the waves pounding against the beach.

She looked at him and said, "Honey, I'm pregnant!" John looked at her dumbfounded, and then he broke into tears and picked her up and tried to hold Joy against his body. He was crying not because she was with child, but because they had been trying for several months.

"When will the angel come from within your body?" he asked.

Joy, kissing the tears from his face, smiled and said, "Based on the doctor's visit today, he will arrive in April next year."

It was near Christmas, the day before the infamous day of December 6, 1941. Kaneohe Bay is a sheltered cove on the western side of Oahu. It has a variety of beaches that color the first rays of sunshine reaching westward across the Pacific Ocean. As not previously mentioned, it was home to Kaneohe Bay Marine Corps Air Station, which was supporting VP–11, VP–12, and VP–14. For more than a month the Pentagon had been negotiating with Japan which, when looked with a shady eye, it spelled danger to those in Washington, D.C., who wanted a carrier to help fight the Germans on the east coast of the U.S.

VP–11 was fully manned in complement but short of PBY–5s, as originally planned. For more than a month they were placed on limited alert and the security guards were checking identification cards at the gate. There were many Japanese on the island and occasionally they worked odd jobs on the base. On December 7th, VP–14 launched two PBY–4s for routine daily submarine patrols. There were three anchored in the bay with the remaining parked in and around the hangar in neat rows with the VP–11 and VP–12 patrol aircraft. Half of the duty section was playing baseball and some were smoking cigarettes and making small talk while waiting for their comrades to return from breakfast at 0800. Kaneohe Bay was an air station that had to be protected. An advanced radar station was secretly installed on top of a volcanic mountain surpass. The range, they said, was about two hundred miles plus. They had the device manned twenty–four hours a day with a radio, which reported birds, aircraft and so on. Prior to 7 a.m. they reported a large mass of aircraft about 150 miles away. They contacted the Kaneohe Duty Officer, who was sleeping soundly. He woke up with the assistant duty officer's insistence and was told of the site's contact. He got up and said it was the B–25 flight that was expected that day.

The sound of approaching engines drew little attention moving south toward Pearl Harbor. The second wave came over their heads with the scream of low flying Japanese Zeros diving on the airfield. The morning stillness was interrupted by an explosion. Not only one, but also multiple explosions lit the blue sky with bright orange balls of fire. The time was 0800 on a Sunday morning, December 7, 1941. It was the beginning of the slaughter of sailors, the sinking of the Pacific Fleet of warships, and the beginning of the war with Japan.

John woke up at 7:45 a.m. and went to the bathroom to take a piss. He felt relieved, and since it was Sunday he brushed his teeth and returned to the bedroom, put on shorts and a T–shirt. He looked at Joy, who was asleep and now five months pregnant, and he slipped on his tennis pumps and went to fix some coffee. The coffee was ready, so he had a cup and went out the back door to the patio. A sound unrecognized by him was approaching and he knew by their markings they were attacking the air base. Back inside the house he woke Joy and told her he was headed for the base because of an attack. He kissed her, and as he was driving his Ford in a flash to the airfield at 8:00, he heard a series of loud explosions. He got as far as the gate and ran the rest of the way to the VP–11 hangar.

John could see for the first time that hell was breaking out all around them. Yes, they were Japanese Zeroes with machine guns, spitting fire as they raked the PBYs neatly lined beside the VP–11 hangar. Quickly he joined the men in putting out the fire of the aircraft that were burning, each catching fire from the rubbish from the next. He and three men went with flight machine gunners to get the mounted guns, two 50–caliber and two 30–caliber guns from this one aircraft. They got the 50–caliber free just as another wave of Jap planes few over striking other aircraft, not to mention hitting two of their working party. They left with the 50–caliber gun being set up and the next item was to break into the armory to get the BAR — Browning Automatic Rifle — to eventually fire back at these heathens of the Rising Sun.

Senior Chief Fisher joined them as they broke out ammo and machine guns inside the dump. Finally, they broke the glass and the BAR with ammo and went out of the armory to shoot down the enemy. As they came out of the ordnance shop they saw puffs of bullets hitting the ground and also heard the drumbeat of bullets against Hangar #3. The blast of Hangar #3 blew John to the ground. Dazed for a moment, Chief Fisher was dead — lying there with two bleeding wounds from his chest. John almost became teary eyed, but he knew he had to help his shipmates.

Hangar three was burning out of control and all of the PBYs were bullet scarred, some in flames, but the men had started spraying them with hoses to no avail. All around were bullets being expedited from the air and John's shipmates that he had known in almost a year were drastically wounded or living dead because of their horrific invasion. He ran missing a line of puffs to the 50–caliber machine gun that was vacant; the bodies were a mess. He grabbed the gun and started shooting the instant the planes made their strafing run. He stopped briefly when he noticed the smoke that began trailing one of the Jap planes and watched it plummet into the sea. He wasn't sure whether he shot that plane, but his shooting didn't matter. That son of a bitch was down; that was the important thing.

The Commanding Officer of VP–11 hugged him and asked if he was all right. John realized that he had been hit by fragments with a three–inch gash on his back, right behind his right lung. He was bleeding, but the Commanding Officer took him to the medical ward. As the enemy planes began to withdraw, there was a possibility that they might return at any minute. Hanger one had burned and hangar three was destroyed by a bomb. Every last PBY had been destroyed beyond use.

Now began the monumental task of cleaning up the debris, recreating the airfield, and organizing a quick defense to preclude this tragedy from happening again.

By 10:30 the back of John's head spit out fragments ranging from one inch to a three–inch gash right behind the right lung. He was banged up and got two shots; tetanus and penicillin. He left the makeshift hospital and then he thought of Joy. He finally reached his car and went home. He got out of his car and suddenly he knew he was hurt. Inside the house he called her name. She was nowhere to be seen. A knock on the door, and it was Julia, the wife next door. "John, Joy had a miscarriage, and I took her to the hospital. She is all right, but you ought to go to her."

The hospital was jammed with people helping each other that were in desperate need of medical attention. After 10 minutes of waiting he saw the nurse and described his wife, pregnant, and told her she had a miscarriage. She smiled when she found the admission list and directed him to the second floor. At the nurse's station he was informed she was placed in Room 7, which was right down the corridor. John entered the room and saw Joy. Her eyes were closed, under some sedation, but alive. John took a chair, moved it next to her, and, with a kiss on her forehead, he sat down beside her. His eyes started to water, and he wondered if this was the way to deliberate an unborn child to suffer a death caused by him, the surprise of the attack or whatever God had decreed. He prayed to God to forgive him and Joy and what may have caused this horrid state. As he was looking across her bed, Lt. Briggs was at his side. He stood up and the lieutenant embraced him and told him that Joy was all right but out like a light. He related that she was bleeding from her vulva and she had pains of giving birth. The baby was aborted and initially she was under the lieutenant's care. John thanked him but told him briefly about the Kaneohe Station, which essentially there were no aircraft remaining, with all hangars destroyed. He was told she should be out until that afternoon. John thanked him and he went to cover the rest of his patients.

John went down to the first floor to get something to eat. Yes, it had been sometime since he had breakfast. The Coke, hamburger, French fries, and a piece of apple pie made him happy. As he walked through the main alley of the hospital a particular section wanted blood, all kinds and shapes. He went over and an older Red Cross lady asked him if he could give blood with his back being bandaged. He told her that the wound was fragments and he was ready to give blood. "O positive," he said, and lay down and gave a pint of blood. After the donation he drank some juice and got a sign that said, "I gave blood."

It was 2 in the afternoon when he finally went to see his wife again. He had a vase of flowers, which were on sale on the main deck. He set them on the table next to the bed and sat down next to his loved one. He must have been napping but he woke alert and found Joy crying, with her hand holding his. He got up and caressed her, wiping her tears and then wiping his own.

"I am so sorry, but it just happened fifteen minutes after you left for the base," she said. John interrupted her and told her to be calm. He told her that he had talked with Dr. Briggs, who had said she was resting comfortably. The nurse stepped in and asked if he would step out.

The nurse came out of her room ten minutes later and wondered if he could feed her some soup and Jell–O. "But of course," he said. Joy was really hungry as she ate her lunch. Water came next with the nurse bringing her two more pills.

The period lasted 15 minutes and Joy was back to sleep. He kissed her and then he stopped by the nursing station and told her he would be back later.

The men were fighting the blazing hangars, with fire hoses drawing up the water from the bay. Big skinny caterpillars were pulling PBYs from the holocaust plus sailors who were burned alive, aside from the mass slaughter of men and weapons. John's men were sorting out machine guns, saving the ones that were operable. By 1800 the fire subsided as the VP–11 men uncovered the valiant horse Pegasus, brilliance and honor, it showed no sign of the sneak attack. The CO of VP–11 gathered his men around him and told them to go home and get some rest. As the squadron broke up and headed home, the two aircraft landed after a beneficial ASW exercise looking at the once beautiful landing area, which was black with aircraft burns and the smell of burnt human bodies.

A week later, Joy was released from the Navy Hospital. John had everything clean, bright eyed, and bushy–tailed. He had fresh cut flowers in the dining room and in the bedroom. Joy wanted to be alone with him — all alone. She went through the attempts of telling her husband what her doctor had told her. At present, do not attempt to try for a baby until a year from now. Use condoms at all times when having intercourse. John said he got the same forecast from the medic, but that they would cross that bridge when the time came.

April 1942, the airplanes were disseminated in Kaneohe Air Base, Hawaii, and were replaced from the mainland, which supplied them with PBY–5 aircraft. Soon both John and each crew practiced this object that detects and locates air/surface contacts. On April 30 two crews were sent to Johnson Island to conduct sector searches. On May 29, the detachment size was increased to six aircraft. John could see his crew's run next up. He went home and told Joy that he may be leaving soon. Calmly and before their lives became separate for an undetermined amount of time, Joy broke out two different plates, two brand new place settings, and served T–bone steak with wine as an aside. A toast was said under a candle shedding the glance of human flesh and love glowing in their hearts.

On the 22nd of May the three crews left, but they knew it was a secret. This led to numerous land–hopping detachments. The VP–11 planes were inundated with tender support, engine maintenance on planes hidden with camouflage, or whatever. The most gratifying of their flight were centered on the Landings at Guadalcanal. This was important to the Marines as well, as they bombed numerous dumps or barges pretty well scorched our tail feathers.

As the patrol antics were turning the tables on the Japanese nocturnal enemy, VP–11 among the night hunters became innovative at adapting their aircraft to ensure survivability during these nighttime forays. Using materials from the tender Curtiss, in August 1942, John and his mechanic friends concocted a mixture that covered the PBY–5 from the tail to the nose. At night, the sinister black bird made it also invisible to the surface ship. Case in point, the enemy can't see the Cat which flies under him. If, for some unforeseen event, the pilot called force only to have his depth perception distorted, whereby it's another factor yielding to the PBY.

Flying from Westpac in World War II, a squadron of black painted PBY Catalina flying boats, mainly at night, wrote a proud chapter in the history of naval aviation. They were known as "Black Cats," which war records led to those that were equally successful.

They were Black Cats because they ran a certain breed of Navy Patrol planes: seaplanes, flying planes, printed flat–black, which was in the favor of night operations against the Imperial Force. In the daytime they discussed detailed aircrews as well as pilots from bomber fighter aircraft.

The PBY flew with 9 to 12 crewmen, which were complemented like an airborne submarine. It had several bunks and all the amenities of being at home. The guns aboard ranged from 30–50 caliber machine guns with 1,450 gallons of aviation gas. It had 3,000 lbs. hanging under the wing plus assorted anti–personnel bombs inside. With a wing span of 104 feet and two Pratt & Whitney engines driving her, she and the crew rarely gave up.

The Black Cats were officially designated on December 14, 1942 by Commander C.E. Coe. The slow speed and light armament caused great concern when used by the Allied leaders. The squadron got equipped with the ASE radar, which spotted ships out to twenty miles on the ocean surface. Thus, the VP–11 Pegasus painted black under the wings, hull and flew "targets of opportunity" beginning in October 1942. In essence, these black night flights were raids and reconnaissance of the Japs. Normally the Cats carried four 500–pound bombs or one torpedo under their wings. To complete the envelope there were high–powered illuminating flares plus many fragmentation bombs. One final weapon that caused a certain degree of havoc and which brought fear as they sought cover during these air raids was the whistling, blood–chilling screech caused by dropping empty beer and Coke bottles that gave the Japs insomnia.

The act of night–bombing merchants, barges and tankers was developed by the incredible dynamics of the PBY in conjunction with the specialty skills of the Navy aviators. Yes, the average age was 24 years old — the more they flew it, the more they trusted it.

One night, Lt. Jim Cobb took off for Guadalcanal, where he gave the Jap troops going ashore "a taste of their own medicine." Wing racks loaded with ordnance and anti–personnel bombs stashed inside in every inconceivable hiding place. They would pass over the troops dropping 3 or 4 weapons. After each pass the plane would wait a short period of time and then attack again. This technique would be tried again, to be called "Louie the Louse" flights. This really got General Geiger fired up. So he sent a short cryptic note:"THE BLACK CAT FLIES TONIGHT!"

Another story of a classic nature was when the operation officer flews with his crew. The Operations boss was often busy with move reports and/or course changes. The Pegasus was split up on two difficult missions, but basically they were realistically the same. John was filling out a log of engine performance when he looked outside the starboard window. He saw the Jap sub and the co–pilot reported it. The submarine crash–dived and was below the surface of the water when two 650–pound depth charges followed. The charges went off and about 2 minutes later a large quantity of oil remained on the surface. A kill of I–172 was later announced as a crew commanded by Takeshi Ota was lost with all 91 aboard.

Joy had been heard from by mail five times. She was working in the Navy Exchange, saving money because she did not know what to expect. His letters were like godsends

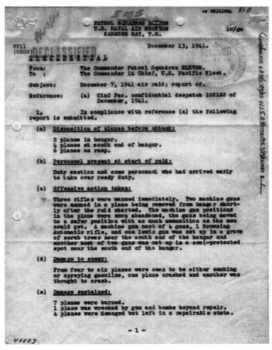

VP-11 letter concerning the attack of December 7, 1941.

from paradise. She cried when he told her of his moments of sadness and despair. Joy told him of the joy of the Midway Island airplane attack, with many of the Jap carriers going down at sea.

LCDR C.C. Marcy, the CO of VP–11, wrote a letter to his bride stating that they were returning from combat and for refit home leave in February 1943. He asked her to put the word out that they were returning to Naval Air Station San Diego, California. The captain's wife put out the word at officers' wives coffees, chiefs and enlisted parties. The first news that the squadron was back was when Joy got a telegram. A DC–3 was able to ferry some wives back to the states. Joy met John on the run at the local airport. She was crying, kissing and visualize your mate is not muted image. John had been there for three days and he found quarters for four weeks. He rented a car and loaded Joy's baggage and went to the quarters. Champagne was iced, roses were flowing in the bedroom — welcome home! They toasted each other and talked, kissed, and finally both took off their clothes going into the shower.

Later they talked in bed about what they wanted to do. The facts were John was to go on leave today for 3 weeks. This time could be spent with her parents or even his mother and dad. The plan was this: they decided to visit each parent for about seven or eight days — money no object. John then made known that he was a mechanic first class, to which Joy was exuberant. Joy had close to $5,000 in the bank from working at the Navy Exchange. Together, they felt the urge that makes married couples violent in ecstasy. John kissed her and both of her rapidly developing to mature nipples. Yes, she had lost her flabby weight since the miscarriage.

John and Joy met their parents after flying from San Diego to Corpus Christi, Texas, and then a short flight from there to the Gulfport Army Air facility. They split up the first night and his parents were as proud as they could be. They listened with great intensity as he described the events of the malice of Pearl

Harbor. As a spin–off, he told with great agitation the troubled event of Joy's miscarriage. Mother broke up, and with John beside her she was calm, knowing that her words were comforting yet despairing for a marriage that would never end over such a catastrophe.

The next day John went with his Dad to the newspaper office. The building had grown again, however his uncle's sudden death from a heart attack somehow molded the institution into a circulation frenzy which everyone in the building is striving with the world war centered on two elements of belligerent behavior. John was gladdened by the aggressiveness and the vitality of the workforce, each fighting for the freedom which the USA offers for its citizens. He knew that they were happy to see him. "How is the war going in the Pacific?" a young reporter asked.

John met Joy late in the afternoon at their lovely house. Their house was full of relatives, each smiling, offering congratulations, asking what it was like flying the airplanes — it's great to know who you are living, dying, and each God–fearing soul is immovable, steadfast. After six days of enjoying their families, John called space available at Gulfport Army Air Base. They had a flight which took off at 1300 and did not get to San Diego until 11:30 p.m. Pacific Time. Their names were placed on the roster and they were to report at 1100.

John looked superior in his whites with two rows of ribbons. "When are you going to make chief?" his Dad asked.

"One of these days," laughed John.

John took their bags over to the checkout counter. He walked by and gave Joy her tickets, or stubs, when she went aboard the plane. The parents had a sandwich plus a piece of cake. Joy hugged her parents, and John kissed his Mom, who was crying. Dad was a tad upset, but John was ready and this war would end soon. Fifteen minutes later the plane began boarding. Joy held John as they took off westward.

As John returned to work, he cut his leave bank short of 2 weeks. Most of the personnel were still on leave as the aircraft were being updated and engines replaced. The rest of the morning was left to a technical representative to explain the changes which evolved an R–1830–92 engine, which produces 1,200 horsepower. Additionally, the gross weight, which mechanics figured out, grew from 26,200 pounds to 35,000 pounds when the war gear was added. In several weeks the squadron would fly back to Kaneohe and wait for the ground personnel to join them.

Joy accepted the news with overwhelming cheer and she joined her husband when she got an available spot on a steam liner to drop her in Hawaii. She left Sunday to be back on Wednesday. By the 10th of April 1943 the squadron was reformed and each plane was breaking in all of its pilots. On the morning of the 20th of April 1943, they cleared everything out of all lockers, including flight gear, and flew west for Kaneohe Marine Air Station. About nine or ten hours later they saw the island and landed. The airfield had changed since that infamous day. The hangars had been built again yet they had many protection devices in place and something new was added, all of the wives and girlfriends were there to meet us them.

They began in earnest by conducting patrol flights over the ocean in the Hawaiian area. By the third week in May they were ready to deploy to Perth, Australia. All of their combat training had been finalized with their airplane showing the perfection of its maintenance department. The night before he left, John and Joy spent some time talking about everything. They both decided that they would throw away all of the condoms, update their wills, and finally all was in order.

Perth was exciting in that they had to assemble the ground force. They were under Fleet Air Wing 10, flying patrols in the southwest Pacific. In September 1943 the squadron headed for Brisbane, and then to New Guinea and Palm Island. They were officially the Black Cat outfit upon relieving VP–101.

On November 1943 Lieutenant Jack Cruse and his crew were especially busy as they attacked Japanese facilities in the Bismarck Archipelago and the Solomon Sea. Severe weather conditions contributed to disabled enemy merchant vessels, barges and several shore installations/wharves. They uncovered a Jap task force, and Cruse made a low–level bombing run that destroyed this large transport. This pilot was awarded the Navy Cross for his gallantry.

On the 30th of December 1943 the squadron returned to Palm Island and was taken off combat operations. Routine flights, such as administrative and passenger flights, were conducted for the other islands. VP–11 continued to conduct operations for the next six months. All of these sites were not as nice as a grand hotel suite, vis–à–vis sleeping in a cove covered with vines doing an oil change on one of the PBY engines.

One of the many exploits that VP–11 did would have shown their explicit determination by changing this defensive search into a bodacious powerful surge. This squadron utilized the bold potential of this plane, striking day or night in masthead glide–bombing to ensure vital hits on the target. Denying the enemy the sea route and preventing him from reinforcing important bases, this is a tribute to the courageous fighting spirit of the men. On inspection at quarters, Fleet Air Wing 17 gave the Presidential Unit Citation to the squadron.

There were plenty other avenues of success, but the Japs were running out of gas. The ships were fallen below the sea, aircraft were flown by untrained young aviators, and the veteran rate was low, giving the kamikaze pilot his social crash on a carrier the final move of the Japanese.

From October 1944 VP–11 was designated VPB–11, whereby the missions of air–sea rescue and routine ASW patrols were conducted daily. On 14 November the group was moved to Wendi, where the squadron was told to break off from combat and departed for return to NAS San Diego on 19 December 1944. This was to be a Christmas of all, Joy!

CHAPTER 6

A NEW BEGINNING

With the war over, it was easy to fantasize over the past five years the memories of the places they had experienced. Hawaiian landscapes with outright vivid, bloody times fighting in the remote islands protecting their life's blood and their predecessors. Joy and John were thankful to be home with their parents and to start anew with their college education before them. John had filled out the necessary paperwork for entrance into the University of Mississippi. He processed out of the U.S. Navy when the squadron was decommissioned.

The GI Bill was known as the Montgomery GI Bill — Active Duty (MGIB), which stated:

- Help the members of the Armed Forces to adjust to civil service.
- To give those who cannot afford the money to get a higher education the chance to get one.
- To restore the education and the readjustment to service members who lost opportunities because of their active duty.
- To promote and assist the All–Volunteer force program of the military.
- Keep people in the Armed Forces.
- Develop a more highly educated and productive work force.

This group of highly skilled manpower could and would encourage membership in the Selected Reserve and the dedicated National Guard. Finally, this bill offered educational opportunities to children whose experiences in life were interrupted by liability or death due to a parent. And lastly, it helped prepare the surviving veterans' spouses who had succumbed to death or disability to support themselves and their families.

Thus, on June 22, 1944, President Franklin D. Roosevelt signed the GI Bill of Rights. After much intense debate and maneuvering, this legislation has been observed as one of the most important acts of Congress. An uncertain beginning, most or many felt that the bill was overbearing. The program got off to a rapid, yet appropriate start.

The University of Mississippi built row houses that would hold married World War II G.I. Bill candidates. John and Joy moved in August with their goods. He helped her organize the house with staples, such as living room, kitchen facilities and a bedroom suite for the bedroom. After the second day he went for a battery of tests. He, like several others, headed in and took many testing parameters. Finally, the criteria were completed. Each individual was accessed as to what skills could be further improved while taking certain courses, and after four years, he would graduate. He was notified that his aptitude test indicated his major would be engineering. He agreed and Joy was proud of him. Joy had found a job working in the college book store. She had met friends there and was very amicable. The first week of class was earth–shaking! The books her husband brought home were never–ending. As a matter of fact, she didn't see her husband much of the first week. He got home about five o'clock and was back at the library at six–thirty until the library closed at ten o'clock at night. At the end of the first semester her husband got straight As. She was so proud she took him out to dinner. He plowed on with a new determination that grasped all and spat it out like a new–fangled hand–held computer. When the first year was finished, they proceeded home to Gulfport. His Mom and Dad were waiting for them to arrive. They talked and went to church together. John helped his Dad at work. The business that he and his staff developed was growing leaps and bounds. Since the last time he had walked into the place, it had grown immensely. The reason why he helped his Dad was to get money to assist the shortfall of the G.I. Bill.

The beginning of his final year Joy desired to have a child. She went to a doctor and was examined. She told the physician the story of her first child, which she aborted. Also she recanted that she would not get pregnant until the doctors gave the golden word. The doctor examined her and gave her an excellent exam. The doctor said to go ahead and see if she could conceive a child. Joy ran home, excited as can be. She went to the grocery store and bought a steak, flowers and a bottle of wine. She knew she should not have done it, but what the hell, she wanted John to plant a seed in her that would become a beautiful precious being that they could love and cherish.

John walked in the door at precisely 5:30 p.m. Joy had the steak almost done with salad on the table, plates and silverware, wine poured, and, with the oven opened, out popped two roasted potatoes.

He noticed the table and said, "What's the occasion my dear?"

"Sit down and tap the wine," she said. With that statement he sat down and tried the wine. Not bad. She then placed a steak, medium rare, on his plate and one on hers. He questioned in his mind, what was the occasion for this festive happening? They ate because the meal was delicious, despite the heat in the kitchen. After two servings of wine and a piece of key lime pie, there was coffee. Then Joy told him of her visit with the doctor. He examined her and told her that she was ready to have a child. He held her close to him as they both cried. They both worked out her ovulation period of each month. They were both excited. If Joy became pregnant, they had to plan when the baby would be born, in what month.

They tried the first month, but to no avail. Her husband was totally upset when she started menstruating. They held each other with the belief that next time would ease the pain. He continued on with his work, labs and structural analysis, reports, and, finally, exams. In November they went out to dinner on Saturday night. Their friends met them at the restaurant. They were from Alabama and served on a naval battleship. His wife was with child, their third one. She talked about the other children, in that the first was extremely difficult to deliver after fourteen hours. The second child was born in three hours! They had a great time as the boys debated the hazards of engineering lingo and other founding principles.

That night Joy told John that she was late for her period.

"Not to worry," he said. "Haven't you a doctor's appointment next week?" She agreed and they both recklessly fell asleep. Her husband came home a week later to find his wife smiling. "I am with child," she said. They hugged each other then led to a quick climax on the living room floor. That might not matter how tough, hard, his courses were this semester, because he was going to take and nurture her mission to deliver a safe and wholesome child.

That weekend, no matter what the cost, he would bring home flowers every five days. After five or six weeks she noticed how nice the flowers were. She also saw how her husband emptied the wilting bouquet and replaced it with a bunch of new distinctive and characteristic fragrances. Christmas time was indeed a classic event. Both her parents and John's joined together for Christmas dinner. The parents for Joy were centered on the baby. Blanket, diapers, and clothes made the day. Joy's parents gave her the baby bed that she was born in and even an old baby carriage.

When April came it was exciting to visit the gym where all the representatives from each major tried to hire the graduating class. He looked and visited the engineering jobs that were there. The important thing was to sign up for all jobs, especially the ones you were interested in. From an engineering aspect, there were several jobs that he was interested in. Pascagoula Shipyard passed out a pamphlet with a need for highly skilled engineers. John had not been completely up to date with the news media, but the cracks were beginning to crunch over Korea.

At the end of May, the seventh month, Joy went to see the doctor. John went with her and the examination went great. The doctor told them that the baby was quite active as Joy nodded approval. The doctor said she was fine and her weight was right on schedule. Next month would be when the baby gains its most weight. Then he showed husband and wife how to treat pains or how to determine when the water has broken, or in other words, beat feet to the doctor! Finally, he suggested that if they had sex, take it easy on the baby!

The first week in June began the final exams. It was extremely hot with all windows open. Joy had an electric fan running and at least 2 gallons of iced tea to keep her husband studying. He did well and the letters from several engineering firms had corresponded with him. Pascagoula Shipyard was really interested in him. He sent a school form with grades and the shipyard wanted the results of the year. All in all, he averaged 3.75 overall in his class work endeavors. July 12, 1950, he walked down the graduation walk with an eight month's pregnant Joy smiling in the crowd for her husband.

With a bachelor's degree in engineering from the University of Mississippi, he headed home to Gulfport. The things that they had collected were equal to twice the amount from years ago. John's mother took over Joy and sat her down with a cold Coke. Dad and John unloaded the car, whereby the majority of big items went into the garage. After half an hour, the car and the two–wheel wagon was unloaded. John and his Dad and sat down in the shade with a cool gin and tonic with a slice of lime.

They had records and the reports of the doctor at school so they saw a family doctor in Gulfport. He greeted them and they went right into his office. He reviewed the paperwork and asked Joy if she would undress. The nurse escorted him to the front where he sat down. The doctor started by weighing her, listening to her heart, and finally she assumed the position and spread her legs.

"From all signs the baby is about to be born. The hospital is a block from here," the doctor said. Joy acknowledged. The doctors were very articulate when she started having pains so many minutes apart.

They left the doctor's office and it was lunchtime. They stopped at a drugstore and had lunch. Joy wanted some ice cream so they each had a vanilla cone. After dropping her off at his Dad's house, he went back to work at the newspaper.

That weekend John received a letter from the shipbuilding company. They offered him a sizable amount of money for him to work for them. The offer was good for a week. On Monday the 29th July, 1950, he called and accepted the job. Joy was pleased that he took the job, which started August 5, 1950. After a meal that featured shrimp, they all rested outside on the porch. Yes, it was time for Joy and the baby. At eight o'clock she had a stomach ache that led to the bathroom. That was the trigger for what was to transpire.

"Honey," she said as she walked out of the bathroom. He went and found her sitting on the bed holding her belly. "It's time, honey. It's about eight minutes between pains," she announced. He looked in the closet and got the bag they had prepared two months previously. John told Mom and Dad and started to go out the door with Joy, but Mom said she was coming to help her. So the three got in the car and went to the hospital.

At the emergency ward of the hospital, it was not too long as they took her in. The nurse took her name and the doctor's name. She went into a room where they undressed her and she got on the table. The nurse inspected her and revealed the opening of the birth canal was 2 centimeters. Accordingly, the pains had stopped. This was at 10 o'clock at night. The doctor arrived and looked at Joy. He decided to put her in a room and make the necessary preparation for delivery. The room was arranged nicely with two beds, a closet, a bathing sink and a room for a toilet. Mom went to work and helped her when the nurse got her hooked up to an intravenous injection. Then the assistant black nurse came in and shaved her lower parts. Now the plot thickens! With water in her system Joy was comfortable. Mom on the sofa about to fall asleep, and John asked if he could get something for Joy. He bent over and kissed her and told her not to worry. He went out of the room to call his Dad. "Nothing to report," he said. He went on to say that they are keeping Joy overnight.

At three o'clock in the morning Joy woke with a pain. John rushed to her side and helped her breathe so that the pain would subside. Every six minutes the pain would start and it would last for two minutes. After an hour the nurse measured the birth canal as up to 4 centimeters. She asked Joy if she wanted some Demerol and, quite frankly, she did. At six o'clock her doctor came in and pulled the curtain. John was standing by her side, the sweat pouring from her head, wiping her hair with a towel. Mom was holding her hand. Next, a gurney took her to the operating room.

Mom and her son had spent an hour in the waiting room. It was eight o'clock in the morning and in walked Joy's parents with John's Dad. He briefed everyone but could not be in the delivery room. Suddenly, a nurse who had been in Joy's care came to talk privately to John. She said she had given birth to a son but they could not stop the bleeding. She had a paper which, when he signed, gave the surgeon permission to remove all reproductive organs which had hampered the birth and the future of the life of Joy. He briefed his folks and hers and signed the paper. The nurse ran back inside the operating room. An hour later the doctor came out, removed the mask, and she was resting comfortably. He said her baby boy was A–OK and the dilatation and curettage (D&C) went well. He also added that she could still have sex; he meant that for her husband!

At one p.m. in the afternoon, John awoke as his wife stirred. He stood up and went to her. His kiss on her cheek made her eyes open and the smell of ether coming from her breathing. She wanted some water, which he got for her.

"Where is my baby?" she asked.

He told her that he was in the baby room asleep. "So, what will be his name?" he asked. The nurse interrupted and took her pulse, blood pressure, and asked her if she was hungry. Yes, she got that right. Next thing was the baby.

"Do you want to breast feed the baby?" the nurse asked.

"Yes," Joy replied.

The baby finally came to Joy's room. Joy looked miraculously better now, but she was tired. The doctor briefed her and she was feeling tired but well. The baby boy was given to her. John Clinton Chartier II, 6 lbs, 9 ounces, 21 inches long, and a shade of brown hair. The parents were there, expressing joy with oohs and aahs when they saw the baby. Finally, the nurse chased them out as Joy unbuttoned her gown and tried to feed John Jr. Finally, he nosed up to the nipple and enjoyed what little milk he tasted. The next morning he really chowed down as the milk was really flowing and Joy was full of love and elation that she had brought the child to living life.

CHAPTER 7

WAR, THE 1950s

On August 5, 1950, the Pascagoula Shipping Plant appeared to be a large group of real estate. All sorts of ships were being built, from trawlers, commercial fishing boats to merchant ships. The other part of the magnificent site was the World War II naval shipyard. Funny, not too much was happening there, so John parked the car outside the administration building. He took in the papers plus numerous items that he deemed necessary for proper checking in. The secretary received him and took the papers concerning the shipyard. Ten minutes later they took him into a room where he filled out numerous papers. Yes, he dug into his briefcase to get his social security card, birth certificate, service discharge, and, of all things, his driver's license.

By eight thirty he was finished with nearly a ream of paperwork. He finished up his second cup of coffee when the secretary popped in. "Are you ready to see Mr. Roy Parker?" she questioned.

"Yes, ma'am. May I go to the men's room first?" I asked. I made it first in time to the urinal.

Mr. Roy Parker was a tall man, dressed in a tie that looked like the ideal business man. With coffee provided, he talked of John Cartier, a World War II Navy flight mechanic, and now a holder of an engineering degree from the University of Mississippi. He reviewed his forms and he was pleased that his wife had a baby son last week.

"Thank you for monitoring that," John said. Furthermore, he asked Mr. Parker what the homes were like in the city. He opened the drawer and presented brochures containing real estate names, houses for sale and rent.

With this communication set aside, he embarked on the status of current events. Throughout the summer of 1950, the U.S. and the other involved United Nations states scrambled to contain North Korea's fast–moving army, assemble the forces necessary to defeat it and simultaneously begin to respond to what was seen as a global military challenge from the Communist world. Though America's Armed Forces had suffered from several years of punishing fiscal constraints, the end of World War II, just five years earlier, had left a vast potential for recovery. U.S. material reserves held large quantities of relatively modern ships, aircraft, military equipment and production capacity that could be reactivated in a fraction of the time necessary to build them anew. More importantly, the organized reserved forces included tens of thousands of trained people whose World War II experiences remained reasonably fresh and relevant.

It was a shaky recovery indeed. Beyond the organization havoc caused by a five–year long demobilization that stripped its fleet by 90 percent, the navy had lost a particularly acrimonious "roles and missions" battle with the air force only months earlier. In the fall of 1949 this bitter debate over the relative merits of and funding priorities for naval aviation versus land–based strategic air power erupted into full public view in what the news media soon dubbed the "Revolt of the Admirals."

Mr. Parker then grabbed his glasses and read, *"The advent of the Korean War found the Navy in the midst of a shaky recovery from the tumultuous months of debates on its roles and missions, the "Revolt of the Admirals," and the extensive downsizing of naval forces after World War II,"* by Dr. Richard P. Hallion.

"So, this is where we are today. We are entering into the Korean conflict which we (this shipyard) have not built a damn vessel," said Parker. "At 1300 today you will join a select few that will eventually propose what we can do for the Navy fleet as it proceeds into this appalling destiny of commission."

Prior to 1300 John had been examined by a doctor, had his picture taken and a badge was given to him to be worn at all times when at work. The plan was to meet on the second floor of the planning division. There was a café on the first floor that had sandwiches, nabs and cold drinks. They sold papers, and John paid five cents to see what his Dad had to say. At ten of one he started emptying his bag and wandered up the stairs to the conference room. His badge was displayed and the secretary, who had not seen his face before, asked for his driver's license. He walked in and met several attendees. The table at which they were seated had a placard with each person's name. The Plan's Officer, Mr. George Sett, was leading the group. He began by announcing that this brief was secret, and behind him a projector screen showed the message: "Brainstorm: What Can We Do to Support Our Country?" In total, twelve sat around the robust, sturdy clan of men. The speaker asked the new members of the clan to stand and introduce themselves. John stood up and acquainted himself. Another person was new and, when he had finished, the speaker took over.

The cause for concern was the Department of Defense sending message traffic requesting what to do with fewer ships and the lack of manpower in the Armed Forces. Specifically, the major ship builders were definitely behind the power curve. In South Korea, the infant navy had received its first significant ship, a former U.S. Navy 173–foot submarine chaser; the only Pacific Fleet Submarine was delegated to special operations; transports would definitely be needed; and the Navy assigned surface units to Hawaii, which would be chopped (moved) to Japan. The folders that were being passed out to them contained background information.

After driving 45 miles back home he was exhausted. Joy had come home in his absence. His and her mother brought them home. The baby was a cutie and was growing like a bandit. He opened the door and everyone looked, including the young son. He picked up the baby and kissed his wife. They talked for ten minutes and it was getting time to feed this child. They started him on pabulum and he liked the substance of rice. Then they tried some pears, which were not the highlight of the evening meal.

They finished up and went upstairs to get him ready for bed. Finally, Joy untied her blouse and the breast was ready for serving. John just sat there while she caressed his head, sang him a song, and last for only burping, then to sleep. Joy turned and her husband kissed her and her breast, which was out in the open. "I love you with all my heart," she said.

At eight o'clock the next morning he checked in to his office, which was relatively big in size. He had all of the draftsman particulars, including a book that he used to make a sketch or a rough draft. The group was supposed to meet at 1300. He sat down with a cup of coffee in hand and went through the classified section of his notes. First, he thought of the total ship force that could get underway. Next, he thought of the size of the ship with the type of men, firepower, fuel, munitions, and what it would take to keep Korea well supplied. The only combatant was the "Bak Dusan," which received the 3"/50 main guns before she was turned over to the Republic of Korea. That was a poor example of a fleet destroyer.

Taking into account the force that had been accumulated, there was a need for transports that were higher in speed. According to the information in each member's folder, several boats were on their way to Yokasuka Naval Base, Japan. There needed to be a design of this APD to determine if it could be altered one way or another to improve the rotation of troops/material/light vehicles/weapons for these ships.

That afternoon each candidate said they liked the scheme of things, but they cannot build up ships and could take at least 2 years. Finally, it was John's turn. He stood up and the projector operator cut on the light. He turned on the projector and introduced himself and reviewed all the pages in his secret folder. The screen now showed the APD. The Navy called them "high–speed transports," and they were being dispatched to Japan. Taking the few known ships today, his plan was making the ships a high–speed transport. Getting plans of the APD and modifying them for the comfort of troops, maintenance/supply/light vehicles and additional stores must be done as soon as possible. A third slide showed that the need of the shipyard could make necessary changes and fly those parts for installation to Japan.

The room was quiet for a moment, but then the questions came forth. They were answered completely and finally the moderator said, "Let's fill in the blanks and you can present this proposal to the vice president." An hour later the moderator showed him a secret message which was in draft stage. He needed several things which John was eager to fill in. Out the door the leader went, perhaps to get the message typed.

The house was beautiful and Joy liked it so much. Joy borrowed Mother's car and she came to meet John in Pascagoula at 4 o'clock. John called the real estate number and set up an appointment at 4:15. The real estate agent showed them two homes, but the last dwelling was their favorite. It had three bedrooms, a living room, including a front porch, and a two–car garage.

"When could we move in?" John asked her.

"The house is ready, and I assume you want a VA loan," she said.

The baby, who was asleep in the car, woke up. The real estate agent gave them a bundle of paper to be filled out. The "For Sale" sign on the lawn added another board, "Under Contract."

By mid–morning the plans included the strategy, which consisted of a hull of a warship, a likeness of a destroyer escort, and the superstructure of a carry/launch amphibious landing forces. The door opened and closed, not noticed by John.

"Good morning, John."

He looked up from his drawing board and there was the President of Pascagoula Shipyard. "Mr. Davis, how nice of you to stop by," he said.

"Well, I wanted you to know how proud you made me feel about aiding the high–speed transport. I have read over your résumé and with great intellect, coverage and ability, you have World War II, a GI education and an engineering degree from the University of Mississippi. Now John, this is creating a major interest in the Navy, and in fact you and I are leaving tomorrow morning early to fly to National Airport in Washington, D.C., to brief the Bureau of Ships at the Pentagon."

The plane took off at 0600, which was early for all concerned. This was the president's private plane. It had six comfortable seats and was cruising at two hundred miles an hour, estimating Washington in six hours. The flight was smooth and they landed at National Airport at 11:55 a.m. The Navy car took them to the Pentagon, where they ate lunch. The meeting was held in the Admiral's office on the fourth floor.

Commander Bly introduced himself and said he was an aide to Admiral Jenkins. He led them into the conference room and he got the slides/viewgraphs in order. At two thirty the Admiral had not shown up. At two forty–five, the Admiral came in the door. He introduced himself to President Davis, who, in turn, introduced him to John Chartier Jr., "the newest member of my firm, who advocates a high–speed transport."

Immediately, the Admiral was most interested in the ideals and the numerous facets by changing the inside of the hull. John stated that four APDs were headed to Japan. He pointed out that the troop transport could be designed to carry and launch amphibious forces. The Admiral interjected, "Can port and starboard boat sections or stations be capable of launching and recovering 4 landing boats?" Another slide showed the answer to the question by removing the centerline torpedo station in the destroyer escort. Other questions were brought forth by the team assembled watching the brief. Another slide showed additional armaments may be installed to make the ship battle–ready.

With the lights on, the Admiral took the floor. "John, your brief was concise and to the point. I am a firm believer that we had fallen into the depths as far as ship building, and I apologize to the men that for five years our defense has slipped. Let me make a phone call and I'll be back in fifteen minutes."

In summary, the Navy bought the four — lock, stock and barrel. The money for the four ships would be allocated to Pascagoula Shipyard. The project had to be done fast. John and Mr. Davis left for the National Airport. Before they took off the president called the shipyard: get busy, it was a go! He also passed a note to Mr. Parker's boss that the plans would be notified tomorrow which way to go.

The airplane landed about midnight. The vice president was there waiting for the owner. Both were pleased with the project and John gave an excellent brief. "Will call you tomorrow as soon as we get word from the Navy," Davis said.

It was a long trip home. John crept in the driveway only to see a light shining in the kitchen. He walked up the steps and the back door opened with Joy holding the baby. "I know you are worn out," she said.

He put his arm around Joy and the baby saying, "We got the contract!" Joy was so happy for him and his extra effort promoted his zoom to on top. As Joy held the baby, John told her of the events of the trip. Admiral Jenkins was the man he verified and he most certainly was able to state more clearly the precise modifications needed for the destroyer escort. Fifteen minutes later the baby was asleep. With the kitchen lights off, they went upstairs, put the baby to bed and joined each other in bed for another six hours.

This sudden escalation of work notified the apparent hiring of additional people. As the Korean War continued more work flooded the Navy site. John and his work force made a deadline and flew out to Japan as a verification of all the work that had been done to the APD class. The commanding officer of the ships had him over to address the officers. As soon as he walked in the mess, all the officers stood at attention. He felt proud as if he fought back the zealous self–esteem after a mission in a PBY–5.

The Yalta conference is often cited as the beginning of the Cold War. The definition of this phase is a conflict over ideological differences carried on without sustained overt military action. In other verbiage, the beliefs of conflict between the United States and the Union of Soviet Socialist Republics were not compatible. This meeting took place in I Czar Nicholas on the Black Sea on February 4–11, 1945.

Despite much pretense, national security had not been a major concern of US planners and elected officials. The historical record reveals this clearly. Few serious analysts took issue with George Kennan's position that "it is not Russian military power which is threatening us, it is Russian political power" (October 1947); or with President Eisenhower's consistent view that the Russians intended no military conquest of Western Europe and that the major role of NATO was to "convey a feeling of confidence to exposed populations, a confidence which will make them sturdier, politically, in their opposition to Communist inroads."

Similarly, the US dismissed possibilities for peaceful resolution of the Cold War conflict, which would have left the "political threat" intact. In his history of nuclear weapons, McGeorge Bundy writes that he is "aware of no serious contemporary proposal…that ballistic missiles should somehow be banned by agreement before they were ever deployed," even though these were the only potential military threat to the U.S. It was always the "political" threat of so–called "Communism" that was the primary concern. (Recall that "Communism" is a broad term, and includes all those with the "ability to get control of mass movements…something we have no capacity to duplicate," as Secretary of State John Foster Dulles privately complained to his brother Allen, CIA director. "The poor people are the ones they appeal to," he added, "and they have always wanted to plunder the rich." So they must be overcome, to protect our doctrine that the rich should plunder the poor).

Of course, both the US and USSR would have preferred that the other simply disappear. But since this would obviously have involved mutual annihilation, a system of global management called the Cold War was established.

According to the conventional view, the Cold War was a conflict between two superpowers, caused by Soviet aggression, in which we tried to contain the Soviet Union and protect the world from it. If this view is a doctrine of theology, there's no need to discuss it. If it is intended to shed some light on history, we can easily put it to the test, bearing in mind a very simple point: if you want to understand the Cold War, you should look at the *events* of the Cold War. If you do so, a very different picture emerges.

On the domestic front, the Cold War helped the Soviet Union entrench its military–bureaucratic ruling class in power, and it gave the US a way to compel its population to subsidize high–tech industry. It isn't easy to sell all that to the domestic populations. The technique used was the old standby — fear of a great enemy.

The Cold War provided that too. No matter how outlandish the idea that the Soviet Union and its tentacles were strangling the West, the "Evil Empire" *was* in fact evil, *was* an empire and *was* brutal. Each superpower controlled its primary enemy — its own population — by terrifying it with the (quite real) crimes of the other.

In crucial respects, then, the Cold War was a kind of tacit arrangement between the Soviet Union and the United States under which the US conducted its wars against the Third World and controlled its allies in Europe, while the Soviet rulers kept an iron grip on their own internal empire and their satellites in Eastern Europe — each side using the other to justify repression and violence in its own domains.

The Navy called them "high–speed transports," or APDs. Operating together or singly, these highly skilled ships led the way for the multinational raiding force that conquered the railway system of North Korea. These transports contained the hull of a warship, a destroyer escort, and the superstructure of a troop transport that could carry and launch landing forces. Being in a dual role, the APD carried 160 troops, while a crane handled light vehicles and equipment was placed further aft aboard each ship. Additionally, the centerline torpedo station was removed, allowing more room for port and starboard boat stations that were capable of launching and recovering four landing boats. In essence, the armament was accurately placed optically or through the ship's fire control system. The Navy, at the outset, had never found a more robust in firepower and outstanding in high–speed operations.

As the Korean War neutralized and peace was the established, orders for ships, submarines and airplanes moved upward. Pascagoula began the rising Navy ship producer in the late fifties. More Air Force commands were introduced with B–47 squadrons, Army and Marine divisions were left in place, and the Navy began moving patrol squadrons to make way for the VS squadrons' onboard carriers. Along with the increasing numbers of submarines, Oceanographic Stations became the act of assembling materials into a structure along the east and west coast relating to the fixed stations at sea that were monitoring the enemy submarines.

At home the boy was 5 years old and full of get–up–and–go. Joy had a part–time job, during which she used a daycare center for the boy. He already knew his ABCs and was starting to read. Every night before bedtime he took a bath, brushed his teeth and read, or tried to read, a story with Mom's or Dad's help.

P-3 Orion was anti-submarine's best aircraft during the Cold War.

The Moana Wave was the modified ship that passed operational testing and evaluation for the surveillance towed away sensor system.

CHAPTER 8

SURVEILLANCE TOWED ARRAY SENSOR SYSTEM

The first recorded commercial towing was done in 1815 by the steamer Enterprise from the Gulf of Mexico up the Mississippi River to New Orleans. Commercial towing started in New York when the steamer ferry Nautilus towed the sailing ship Corsair. The first propeller–driven tug was the Robert Stockton, built in 1839.

Tugboat or a towboat seems to complicate the matter. A tugboat is a small powerful craft that tows large oceangoing vessels (in harbors). A towboat is a type of pushing boat commonly used on inland waterways.

In British and French ports the tug pulls rather than pushes like the U.S. tugs. The harbor tugs push more at any point on the bow, sides, or stern of a large vessel being docked (undocked).

Towboats also push in a separate way. On Ohio waterways they have special bow pushers that look like kneelers. Pushers are firmly fixed on the squared–off bow of the tugboat and are made to fit into the notches or the stern of the barge being pushed (locking the craft together). The Navy and the Coast Guard employ many ships that are experimental, research and survey ships that support warship developments and operations. Experimental ships test hull designs, weapons and other devices.

The fleet tug or trawler was looked at by numerous companies. A trawler was a rock and roll type of guy when this platform was being considered for towing an array. It was looked at but the wave of reaction sought the T–ATF Powhatan fleet ocean tug. The Fleet Ocean Tugs were operated by the Military Sealift command and provided the Navy with towing and recovery of downed ships and aircraft. They also provided necessary salvage and driving, for which they could be used. Yes, towing in respect to coordinated targets for gunnery exercises could also be programmed.

Built at Marinetta Marine Corp., Wisconsin, it was patterned after the offshore oil or supply ship design. This ship was about the right length, and was big enough to add needed equipment. This particular vessel was selected by a boat company to test the advantages of towing an array. Often the ability to withstand the pulling of such array depended on the insight of stability of the system, the vertical depth that the array would be towed as in feet, and the overall capability the waves would have tracking crosswind.

The Moana Wave was a ship assigned to the University of Hawaii back in 1975. The R/V Moana Wave was constructed by Halter Marine Corporation. This was to be the University's open ocean in New Orleans as an AGOR class vessel for the USN, a vessel which suddenly had other plans. In January 1977 she was chartered by the Naval Electronics Systems

Command, which had undergone a structural change, and the Moana Wave was picked to test the concept of a towed array. First, the ship was sent to the mainland for extensive rework. The majority of the work was classified and required several months to complete. A large room was placed on the deck on the aft section of the ship. Inside were many computers and several gram readers. The satellite, the AN/WSC–6 CV1, was placed on the top deck of the ship. On the last one–third of the ship was the array on a spool that was guided by a rig above the spool. The array was approximately 5,000 feet long and was basically neutral being towed at three knots.

With most of the sensor equipment developed, the Moana Wave positioned itself at the Amphibious Base in Norfolk, Virginia. The first test that the ship had to pass was the VX–1 Operational Test and Evaluation (OPTEVFOR). Surtass flunked miserably the first evolution, as the satellite dish was not properly mounted and there was a problem concerning the ballast of the ship.

The year of 1968 was not looking very deep–seated, as John Jr. thought. He had graduated from high school and he had done quite well. He was ambitious in schoolwork and he had played basketball and had participated in spring track. His Mom and Dad were behind him and, as a favor, he achieved a 1,200 point score in the grade achievement test. Begrudgingly, he did not apply for college, but deep down inside he was worried about Vietnam and the ever–present Cold War. He knew that the draft would surely cut him off at the quick. A day after the ceremony was over, he asked his parents to listen to what he had to say.

"Dad, I wanted to go ahead and join the Navy when you were faced with the agony of the late 1930s," he confessed. Mom and Dad looked at each other and smiled.

"You did the appropriate thing, son, but don't make it a career," his father said. He and Mom/Dad embraced. The very next day he went down to the Navy Recruiter.

Seaman Recruit Chartier was busy making his bunk when mail call began. Two minutes later he heard his name and raced to get the mail. The letter was from his folks. All was well in Gulfport with an unusual hot spell. The shrimp fishing was exceedingly growing by the ton. Mom was making doilies for the church and she made a decorative mat that was exquisite. Dad was serious when he said take the twenty dollars and blow it!

"I am going into this shrimp business and really earn some moola!" said John to Joy. The shrimp task is big business. After several years as an engineering wizard he retired from the Pascagoula Shipbuilding firm. The next year he made $75,000 before expenses. The fishing got so tiring that he had to hire more people. One significant hand he hired used to be a quarterback from the university. He fit in with another lad who was in charge of dredging and spillway duties. The other chaps were hired working on boats and keeping the docks squared away. He grabbed the top ad of the local newspaper and the headline said, "Certifiable Idiot Finds Future in Naval Marine Experiment."

After two weeks of successful fishing, he made great jobs of many so he sent for Mrs. Tribble, an accountant, who would help him distribute all his money. Diversion! That's what the gentlemen suggested. He predicted that next year they would exceed the profits of this year with an excess of $190,000! With profits like that, you must reinvest them, and, therefore, the IRS cannot tax you into oblivion.

Out of the blue he formed a couple of corporations. Chartier's Shellfish Company, as well as Sue's Stuffed Crabs, were new places that had cropped up during the past year.

The quarter of a million became a half million, and the next year a million of them went on to a whopping five million a year in this business. From one shrimper to a fleet of many dedicated fishermen, the unit produced and was well known. Things had grown to real times as a quantum fleet of refrigerator trucks coupled with multiple shrimp, oyster and fishing boats. This got the town to acknowledge this as an important step in his image. His praise soon got him his own packing plant as well as an office building. This purportedly roused his investor to deal heavily in the real estate world by buying condominiums, shopping centers and leases of petroleum.

Before long he was paired with political warriors and was declared ready to run for political office.

John was told that Bubba was to open up a shrimp business. He showed him how to grow shrimps. He asked them the next day for breakfast. Home made sausage, fresh eggs and biscuits with molasses was the offering for openers. Then they climbed in a little boat headed toward the Bayou. The water was calm but there was a bit of mist on the water.

"Now," said Bubba, "here is where the salt tide comes in," and then he pointed to a slew that ran up the marsh. He mentioned that there were a lot of big ponds, so he would take us in that direction.

He piloted them into the slew and it became evident that a roof of a little shack where there is high ground. It used to be owned by a Mr. Tom LeFaiye, but he had been dead for four or five years. He looked and there were a couple of rowboats pulled up on the bank. You could walk them up, and probably they would float. By pole in further the old man had some duckboards running through the marsh down to the ponds.

The setup looked ideal. The shrimp seed was picked up in slews and bayous. It would not take much to start a business with this at hand. Another thing that bit their tongue was shrimp will eat cottonseed meal, which is cheap.

The main thing in establishing a means to block ponds with mesh nets and set about repairing that old house. After laying in supplies they worked their behinds off. In about a month they were seeing improvement in making the house hospitable and fixing up rowboats and duckboards on the marsh. With the duckboard apparatus they laid mesh nets around one of the ponds. Finally, the day came when they went looking for shrimp. John took a shrimp net and dragged it behind the boat. By nightfall they had fifty pounds, which they plunked into the pond. Next morning they got 500 pounds of cottonseed meal and threw 100 pounds into the pond. The pond #2 was prepared until all four ponds were designated shrimp bearers.

It was a fine day in June when they figured it was time for their first shrimp harvest. They went to the first pond and dragged it until it would not move. The problem with the net was there was no space for crustaceans! That evening they pulled in 300 pounds of shrimp in various sizes. The next day they went to Bayou Le Batre with a load of shrimp that nearly overturned the craft.

Soon the drilling, exercises and classes became commonplace. The drill sergeant was a blast, but you never let them know. Halfway through teaming the drill leader let Seaman Recruit Chartier lead the platoon, this time with rifles. Left shoulder arms, and when at attention he ordered salute with rifles. The lieutenant was off to the side and noticed this epitome of execution with moments with a weapon.

Three months and the final march was to begin. John's whites were shining and his orders were to Naval Air Station Millington, Tennessee, for additional training. He proudly served a Seaman apprentice on his left shoulder. After the parade he was proud that his company members displayed the esprit de corps. The bar served 3.2 beers, which all hands gathered and felt relieved. Each parted, going to different avenues of preparatory training.

John drove home to see Gulfport and his loved ones. They were proud to see him with his seaman apprentice stripes. He spent two hours at dinner telling of the stories he had been through. He was excited about his next training site; he had tested "suited for flight." Additionally, he had a girlfriend, sort of, that he told his parents about. They had corresponded twice with letters. The phone rang and his Mom, Joy, answered. After 20 seconds his Mom passed the receiver to her son. "Janet wants to talk to you," she said. "God bless her heart. She wanted to welcome you home."

She talked of many things, and finally she said, "When can I come see you?"

Janet met him at her house the next day at 6 p.m. She was five–feet–four, pretty blond hair, and a stunning one hundred and fifteen pounds. Her beautiful smile, outright conversion made his hug and a polite kiss on the side of her face absolutely erotic. He greeted her parents and then left to eat, talk and reveal what had been happening to them in the past four or so months. John arbitrated as he determined what restaurant to try. The Salt of The Sea was the place, and they were escorted to a table where they were overlooking the Gulf of Mexico. Margaritas, appetizers and seafood platters featuring shrimp/crab were star attractions of the evening. After dinner, they decided to walk on the beach. The moon was coming off the eastern horizon. Janet and John walked hand in hand, talking about when to return to Millington to complete his training. She stopped talking and wanted his lips. After kissing her sweet, richly luxurious lips, she told him she really liked him. John told her, "Me, too."

After spending three days at home and with Janet every night, John had one more night before having to leave. Tonight he went over to her house for dinner. He helped her father barbecue the ribs while having a beer. They finished up by having a freshly made, succulent, key lime pie. Wow, he was full! He helped Janet's parents clean up the mess and they sat down and watched television. Soon the parents retired and Janet slipped over next to John. At that precise moment they kissed, opening the mouths of babes. In his speediness, he opened her shirt and unhooked her bra. He realized she had ample motherly glands; in size, scope and in capacity — 38C! He began to kiss her nipples, which were hard, that he did not realize that Janet had opened his fly and her hand was feeling his manly shaft.

The next day, with all of his gear in the 1956 Chevrolet, his parents said goodbye. He stopped by Janet's and told her that he would never forget the previous night. Her eyes were tearing, but John promised he would write.

As he backed out the driveway he said, "I love you."

At "A" school in Millington he was in a classroom of twenty–five individuals. The Captain arrived with all hands at attention. "Be seated," he said. Captain Oliver welcomed the class and set forth the objections of this school. "The first four weeks will be dedicated to splitting or segregating numerous positions such as ship, submarine or aircraft. The remaining time will be devoted to learning your trade. The rules were laid down when you entered the Navy. There's no room for slackers, those who shirk professionalism or obligation," he said.

"Attention on deck," the instructor bellowed.

Each class all candidates were then given the rudiments of a surface ship, submarine and an aircraft. Classroom was convened on a mockup of a destroyer that created drills that point out the pitfalls of the Navy ship. Likewise, the submarine was similar, but more devastating when the submarine was underwater and traveling at 10 knots. Finally, there was the aircraft. Basically, the students went through a trainer who identified each officer and enlisted man in the back of a P–3 aircraft. The instructor took out a parachute, which he begins telling the student what the purpose of this item means. The CO_2 bottle of the "Mae West," the smoke container, plus the remainder of the gear were included. Then the examination, which judges each student's knowledge over the instructor's evaluation of the student. John did well; he chose an airplane and he got that position.

The anti–submarine warfare rating was beginning to start with the airborne enlisted rate. The Pentagon had just announced this rating, which would commence shortly. John started out with noise — sound of noise in the ocean — as he was granted a secret clearance. Being further amplified, the sound of noise related to propellers, shaft blades and all driven by revolutions per minute. Then passenger ships, merchants, tugs, fishing boats were the primary instigators of mass noise in the great body of water. Next charge a discussion of Jezebel. From a three–hour session on LOFAR grams the first unit that was introduced was the AQA–3. Principally, the writing appeared on the grams which were constantly being calibrated and synchronized. Grams led to ten point dividers who can correlate the second, fourth and fifth blade rate of a merchant contact. Heaven help us, they spring upon us the United States conventional and nuclear signatures on us! And, you guessed it — the Soviet submarines by class. So that being said, the process starts with the AQA–3, which leads to the AQA–4 system, which graduates to an AQA–5 system that gives a whole new meaning to detection. This section was about to commence, but it was time for a two–week lapse due to the holidays.

By and large, Christmas was just a passing fantasy — not this one. As John entered Mississippi, he made up his mind that Janet was the girl of his dreams. His mother would help him pick out an engagement ring. On the other hand, Janet had entered a small community college, where she was taking two courses and working part time. She was bright and enter-taining and had a good head on her shoulders. Additionally, John had saved most of the money from the enlisted pay that he got from the Navy.

It was the afternoon of December 16th when he pulled in to Dad's abode. The house was decorated with red bows and lights. Inside the house was a Christmas tree; it was ready for John to decorate it! They talked for an hour about life, the Navy, and how they were feeling.

Janet was overwhelmed when he met her coming out of class at Gulfport Junior College on December 12, 1968. She cried, kissed and hugged me until I was gasping for breath. "When did you get home? How long? And John, I love you," she said. These above all, were the questions she demanded of him. He drove her home and they met her mother, Eleanor. The table was set for three people, and then she caught on. John had called her mother shortly after breakfast. They sat down and Janet said she was due at a part–time job at Penny's at one o'clock. They ate hurriedly and waited while she changed her clothes, at which time he asked her mother if he could give her a promise ring, meaning he would be engaged to her until he was through the necessary schooling.

"John, I am proud of you and your parents. Yes, if you want to; I am acceptable of you joining my family." With those words of confidence, I embraced her.

At nine o'clock at night, I met her coming out of the store. Janet was full of wine, vinegar and love as she opened the car door, slid across the front seat and kissed me. We went to a local restaurant and then parked overlooking the Gulf. Her hair, her eyes and the color of her well–rounded being brought me to an immediate orgasm.

On Christmas morning I woke up, dressed and moseyed downstairs. "Merry Christmas, son," said Mom and Dad. John Jr. hugged them both. The tree was a symbol of glorious light signified by the effervescence of pine branches giving it the upheaval of the earth's crust.

Edward and Eleanor (her parents) and Janet arrived at one o'clock to have the holiday celebration and Christmas dinner with us. We gave presents, cheer, until it became time for me to give Janet a present.

I stood up and said, "Janet, with this present I wish to say that I love you, and with this gift I want you to marry me." She knew what I was trying to say. With the wrapping paper removed, she opened the box. She sighed. It was a brilliant one caret diamond shaded by a light blue color. Staring at the ring,

John moved next to her on bended knee. He placed the ring on her left ring finger. "Merry Christmas," he said.

John made the long trip back to the Naval Air Station Millington. John left off his studies with the newest Jezebel piece of gear. He learned the position quite well, which places paramount attention on the fixing and use of CODAR, which are Correlation, Detection and Recording. The meaning of this important fixing technique is dropping two sonobuoys (buoys) at 350 feet on a true course of 090. Then place 2 buoys on a true course of 180 at the same distance. When the sonobuoys are operational they detect sound being the submarine with a relation between a mathematical or statistical means, which causes a live pointing at the contact. Then another series of CODAR plants is dropped, yielding a fix.

The final portion of the A school academic training course was the active sonobuoy, which was called the SSQ–15. AQA–1 was the appropriate gear to display such a type of buoy. The SSQ–15 had a range of 2,000 yards. There were several tactical maneuvers which had to be completed before dropping this sonobuoy. Practice made perfect at this station.

The final week of this course the student found out which squadron and aircraft he had been slated. VP–10 Brunswick, Maine, and the P–3B aircraft was the choice for John. He was to check in at Patrol Squadron Thirty, Naval Air Station Patuxent River, Maryland, for an additional training in the aircraft. Two weeks leave was granted. On Friday he received a certification of "A" school, which also authorized Anti–Submarine Warfare. John Chartier was to wear the AWAN badge.

He arrived at home on the 15th of May 1969. He had 21 days to report to VP–30. Janet had a ball with Junior, as she called him. They both watched her ring as John figured out the date for their wedding. After four months at NAS Patuxent River it would be November before the promised day. After supper they shared their future with their folks. They made a list of bridesmaids and the bridegroom attendants. The date was set — November 6, 1969.

Lexington Park, Maryland, was a small town just outside the military establishment. The guards at the gate cleared him through the gate and gave him directions to where his quarters were located. Rising early he drove his car to the security office, where he got the appropriate sticker. VP–30 was the inherent of a massive hangar at the bottom of the hill. There were several planes coming up the hill headed for the taxiway, which was about three–quarters of a mile. After walking from the parking space to the administration office on the second deck of the hangar, it was eight o'clock straight up. After having checked in, the Chief told him to report to Bldg. 330 on top of the hill. My class was supposed to commence at 0900.

At 0900 Master Chief Biggs welcomed us as Class 7–69. He handed out our schedule for the next four weeks. Additionally, we were tested each Friday and that afternoon we had room inspection. The first thing that raised a hand was "What type of uniform should we wear?" Next, keep the syllabus, which listed the buildings, rooms, etc. Throughout the syllabus various groups broke off. For example, there were Aviation Ordnance, Aviation Warfare, Aviation Electronic, and Radioman in this room amounting to sixty people.

At the end of the month in August, the acoustic AWs went to the Fleet Airborne Electronics Training Unit in Norfolk, Virginia. This course was a refresher for me. Still, I learned more about submarines, especially the nuclear boats. On Wednesday I called Janet and wondered how the planning was coming. Everything was set and the bridegroom event was only 3. She missed me and, quite by circumstance, I asked to come to Norfolk for the weekend.

The acoustic test consisted of 20 grams which had to be identified, and 20 questions regarding the AQA–5/CODAR/AQA–1. I got a 3.90 on my test, which was the highest grade of the course. I thanked the Chief who was in charge of the course. He wished me good luck in VP–10. Out the door and on my way to the airport to get my lover.

Champagne filled both glasses as we drank a toast to two sweating souls. The Navy Lodge is where I was staying for the week as I added a couple of extra days. It was Labor Day week-end, and when Janet came out of the airplane she was pleasant-ly warm. We drank in the air–conditioned room and sudden-ly we were naked as jay birds. It was breathtaking — in and out, on top, sixty–nine, or whatever. "I love you, darling!" At eleven o'clock at night we went to McDonald's and pigged out.

Saturday morning, after I declared time–out, we took a shower together. The dream that I had of her can't describe the plentifulness of her chest. She dropped the soap so I bent over and her vagina was staring me right in the face. Immediately I began kissing her and touching the golden spot. She grabbed my shoulder and in a minute she reached an orgasm of the small erectile organ.

We spent time onboard the Norfolk Navy Base and saw everything, including a nuclear submarine. We talked of the wedding and got it all sorted out. We had dinner at a seafood place; I ordered shrimp, fish and a heaping order of fried oys-ters! We went back to our room with a six–pack of Miller Lite Beer. I opened one for Janet but she was ready for action. I stripped off all my clothes when I asked, "Is it time in your cycle to make a baby?"

"No baby. I just got off the pad Thursday," she said.

Driving back to Patuxent River I could not imagine having a wife like my beloved. Unpacking my gear and getting ready for classes tomorrow, I came upon a present. "For you, my Love," was the inscription on the face of the box. In it was a gorgeous Boliva watch. It was nine o'clock at night but I called her, questioned her about her flight and thanked her for the lovely timepiece.

This week was hell in that we studied the AQA–5 tactics such as logical comparative LOFAR, convergence zones, and basic tactical knowledge that we should have as AW operators. The last thing we did was to report to the maintenance shop and check out our flight suits, hard hat and so forth. On Monday we met our crew. LCDR Bob Fitch, LTJG Skip Fry and LTJG Bob Good were the training officers going to VP–10. The other three were an ordnance man, a non–acoustic AW, and a radioman. The training instructors were Lt. Armstrong and Lt. Smith. The reason for the meetings was to meet, discuss and to plan the navigation flight, which would occur on Wednesday and return on Friday. What this means to an acoustic trainee is to become familiar with the aircraft, NATOPS (Naval Air Training and Operating Procedure Standardization) manual, and learn the ditching, bailout and other procedures.

The tactics flights were labeled 1 through 10 but not all were flown. We have 3 or 4 Weapon System Trainees (WSTs), which improved our technique immensely. My instructor was fantastic, He let me go, that is, to conduct a preflight. He was loading a tape, annotating the tape, and briefed me on the present status of the acoustic system. AW First Class Fox was a professional. He noticed "my take care of the station," that he took me to take the AW3 test. He reported to the first class that the test was a piece of cake.

I was learning this and that as a result of the tactics flights. Mining was done in North Carolina, searchlight drill was to be conducted on Tangier Island, and the flights gave me time to do many prestigious jobs in–flight. Finally, it was all over. The officers threw a happy hour at the Enlisted Men's Club. We saluted VP–30, but really we were looking for the shaft of VP–10.

On November the seventh, I married Joyce with six bridesmaids and bridegrooms. The Catholic Church was packed as well as our families. We had our reception at a restaurant where alcohol was no limit. The bridge looked stunning with perfect cleavage and a close–cut gown. After lunch we changed clothes and threw the bouquet to a suspectant for the next grande occasion.

We went to New Orleans for our honeymoon, which lasted four days. Two days at home and we left for Brunswick, Maine. We got to Maine in three and a half days. Yes, the frost left the pumpkin but had settled in the Northeast. We went to base housing and found we were number 25 on the list. Well, bump that. So we looked in the Brunswick Times and rented a one–bedroom apartment in the city. We called the base moving and our shipment was there. Alas! The end of the week our apartment was all right for now with what little we had. On Saturday we went on the base, where I checked in to Hangar Four, home of VP–10. A second class flight engineer checked me in and I would report to the Duty Office at 0730 on Monday the 24th of November, 1969.

I chatted with the flight engineer on what was happening when and where. We said goodbye and I drove to the Navy Exchange, where I dropped off my sweetheart to see if she could get a Christmas job. Actually, I was in the market for a new uniform. I looked at the winter uniform, since I had already made it. I bought stripes (one stripe actually), and some shirts, hats, new shoes and some neckties. All of a sudden his wife came up beside him. "Guess what, honey?" she asked. "I got the job and I start Monday."

He met the Chief Petty Officer who introduced him to the AW Training Officer. Then he was handed a check–in sheet which took him the rest of the day to complete. Sure enough, it did take the whole six hours. I reported to the AW shop the next day where I was placed on Combat Air Crew 2, the Executive Officers crew. The disadvantage of this move meant that doomsday was rapidly coming. The reason why the ASW Evaluation was was December 1, 1969. According to scuttlebutt, the target was a U.S. nuclear submarine which was transiting the area. "Attention on deck," the Executive Officer, Commander Beach walked in and said. "At ease." The Chief introduced Seaman Chartier as his new acoustic man. The Executive Officer asked if he would talk to him in his office.

John sat down in the Executive Officer's office. "Would you like a cup of java?" he asked.

"Yes, sir," he responded. He talked about his enlistment, his background at A school, and his record at VP–30. He warned him about the ASW evaluation which tested all east coast for the "E" was forthcoming. John told him of his experiences with the Jezebel gear and his success in VP–30. He mentioned his wife and that they were number 25 on the housing list.

"On Friday at morning muster, I want you to be in dress blues to receive your AW3 designation," said the Executive Officer. John smiled and the executive officer was proud of him as he shook his hand.

It was Tuesday at five o'clock when the alarm went off. He quickly shut it off and went in the bathroom. He showered and came into the bedroom to find his wife fixing breakfast. They went to the briefing from where she took the car home in light snow. The main body of the crew was in attendance. The general brief was over but the acoustic operator and the Tactical Coordinator (TC) got the acoustic brief. The submarine had a sound device that put out as much as 5 miles radius of noise. Closer in to the target the normal noise appeared. Lt. J.G. Tan was the TC, and they had met before.

At 0830 the P3B vaulted into the sky headed south of the airfield. "Set Condition three," came over the loudspeaker. The gear was sweet so he reported same. An observer said that the previous five flights had no contact. The Antisubmarine Classification and Analysis Center brief said to put in a barrier at the designated area, road 090, a ten nautical mile spacing. After two hours of flying, Lt. J.G. Tan said, "Standby," and they started dropping sonobuoys. After dropping eight buoys, they turned north for 20 miles and then 270, where they dropped 8 more buoys. John was right on target. He reported every buoy up and no contact. He had a system where every 15 minutes he monitored all the sonobuoys. After thirty minutes he noticed something on buoy 18 that made him happy. He selected 18 and he heard cavitations. "TACCO from Jezebel. I have contact U.S. nuclear on channel 18," he said. Lt. J.G. slid down the rail next to John. John explained to him that it was a convergence zone contact. The tactical coordinator was no bimbo and directed the pilot to channel 18 to 000 degrees to 31 miles ASAP (as soon as possible)!

Sonobuoys went out with flying colors and so did two and three about one mile apart. "They came up with one having the strongest with a closest point of approach," said John. The TACCO had both CODAR plants figured out. Fifteen minutes later the fixing was achieved. John gave bearings until the observer said attack. They got a mad man, 2,000 yard up Doppler of a pinger, and delivered an attack with three practice depth charges the submarine acknowledged with a submarine track. This feat, by the way, was the only attack made on the nuclear boat. An ASCAC review of the grams conducted by the wing authorities selected VP–10 AWs, including six flights out of 11 had contact on their grams.

VP–10's Commanding Officer and the Executive Officer were furious at the results of the debacle, which left the Red Lancers in an arrogant disposition. Deployment was three months away and the acoustic AWs needed a kick in the ass. On the firing line were all AWs to be thrown into the fire. After several hours of bickering and pulling of hair they went before the Commanding Officer with the following plan:

- Administer a test to assess how the operators are doing, including grams of all targets, LOFAR system and LOFAR codar capabilities.
- Analyze their tests and set up the percentage of right vs. wrong based on the test.

- Make recommendations on how to solve these parameters.

After much heated discussion, the AW section was to follow the game plan and report to the CO in two weeks.

In the allotted time the acoustic Senior Chief reviewed the charts that showed the test scores of the AWs; test scores of missing nuclear subs or missing conventional subs; and new techniques, such as convergence zones, comparative LOFAR, etc. The charts told it all. AW3 John Chartier was the winner in all respects. "Well, Senior Chief, do we know what to do to put us back in ASW?" the CO asked.

In March of 1970 Janet kissed me as I was about to climb up to LD–2, destined for deployment. We had discussed the money issue as she was still working for the exchange. I would allot half of my payment to my wife so she could make the house payment. Just as I went up the ladder, she told me was pregnant.

Naval Air Station Lajes, Azores, and Naval Station Rota, Spain, was our split deployment. Seven aircrews, five planes were at Rota, and five crews with four airplanes at Lajes. Before I forget, I was the outsider or incandescent spark that made the AWs learn the fundamentals of acoustic analysis. It was me who taught all the systems that they forgot or never cared about. We were successful in every endeavor in Lajes or in Rota, Spain. We won the hook 'em award and the covenant Battle "E" Award for the East Coast in 1970.

Janet gave birth to a son on December 5, 1970. He was chipper and a slender child and loved his mother's milk. I was happy for the next two and a half years. I was elevated to Crew One as the PPC became skipper of VP–10. We rolled in acoustics as I made second class. There was something bothering me, the P3–C. It took about two years to get the bugs out, but it performed much better than the P–3A or B aircraft. In 1973 he received orders to Fleet Replacement Squadron, VP–30. Here he would gladly fly in the P–3C and to maintain the challenge to track or slay the Soviet submarine.

The training of young whippersnappers was a dare with a particular interest that drives young men to excel. He did that over the years as he made Petty Officer First Class. He made many friends in Patuxent River, Maryland, and when he was at the CPO Club. He was introduced to Mr. Bill Wise, who was retired from the Navy. After two glasses of beer he talked to John about a new program that the Navy was considering. "Wait a minute. Don't speak another word. How would you like to come down at VP–30 and tell me about your ship?" he asked. Well, holy shit. He drank the remainder of the beer, and they retired to the hangar.

After two hours of telling and emphasizing the need for a qualified young man who knew what a ship that pulled an array could mean to the Cold War. Thus, his response was to be blessed by his wife, he shook hands with Mr. Wise. After 11 years in the Navy he honored the many feats he had undertaken. With a yes from his spouse, he submitted to the paper an application to be discharged from the Navy on January 1, 1977.

Winter was already sweeping the East Coast of the United States. By December 1976 she had three snow storms in the Delmarva Peninsula. December 15th I took a week's leave to visit my new employees in Arlington, Virginia. My wife was with child number two and her parents were to arrive at National Airport at five o'clock that evening. In the meantime, I left Lexington Park at six thirty in the morning. The weather was frigid, with snow showers decorating the cars.

I arrived at the Naval Electronics System Command and was led by security to a conference room. I had on a suit and tie and was offered coffee. Another door bolted open as a Captain Ron Morse, an aide, and two other civilians entered the room. Mr. Bill Wise conducted the introductions and then all sat down around the conference table. Captain Morse was pleased to have met a riser in the Navy who had captured first class in a matter of ten years. He went on to say that his advisors had recommended his extraordinary analysis work to be a superior candidate for SURTASS work.

"Your presence today will get you the opportunity of planning, recommending and being a part of the Surtass refined team. You and Mr. Bill Wise will certainly have your work laid out. Are there any questions, John?" asked the Captain.

John asked several questions which pertained to his housing, pay and exactly how to dress. Mr. Wise said he could handle those questions. With that comprised the Captain stood up, as well as the others, and said he must go and meet the Admiral.

The remainder of the morning Bill provided his employment package, which was initially over 25% of his first class reimbursement. He suggested an apartment for the first couple of years. He suggested Saratoga in Springfield, VA, which had many new places opening up. John took the tour, meeting staff people who were wrapped up in marvelous secret projects. Then the stomach warned him it was time for lunch.

Bill spent the rest of the afternoon talking about the problems of a ship towing an array. The T–ATF 166, Powhatan Fleet Ocean Tugs, was the pattern of the proposed ocean surveillance vessel. He showed John a sketch of the ship, which was about ± two feet in length. The production ship had almost the same beam with a speed of eleven knots. The acoustical run was not detailed, but an off–the–shelf computer had been identified. The ship that was chosen to do the Operational Evaluation was the R/V Moana Wave. Halter Marine Corporation built the vessel in New Orleans as an AGOR class for the United States Navy. It, however, was sent to the University of Hawaii; charted by NAVELEXSYSCOM, she was to spend the next few years being modified. The work was being done in Gulfport, Mississippi!

By 3:30 p.m., the work hour was coming to a close. There was an office party at one of the nearby hotels. After he had parted with his sidekick he went over to the airport to meet Edward and Eleanor. They were coming off the plane when I recognized them. My in–laws looked good. They talked of their state and compared it to Washington, D.C. To me there was no similarity. Driving down Route 5, this was where they began to enter the countryside. Suddenly, it started snowing again; my wife's parents couldn't believe it.

Christmas 1976 was a prime model which ignited the tree when they came in to the house. Janet hugged each of them as they quickly kissed their grandson. Each had warm coats and had a warm sweater to boot. We played, went sightseeing and celebrated the Joy of Christmas. On the 26th of December all of us packed into the car to take them back to National Airport.

With Christmas gone and now we were blessed by the New Year, she and I were going house hunting. We looked at several places, but Saratoga Shopping Center was where we settled down. I had a week before I started work so we closed on this house and moved out of base housing. The new home would be ready in two weeks, so we rented a motel until the final day.

On Monday, as forecast, John was at work at 7:30. His secretary provided him with a cup of coffee and then led him to his office. It was a nice office with a desk, telephone, and a beautiful window filtering in the cold, rising sun. After the top coat and the sport coat along with it were hung up behind the door, John saw the work piled up in his IN basket. Most of it was inter–office memos, notes or an occasional letter that would need action or an action due date. He had uncovered several action items, but read various memos that he notarized. Finally, he concentrated on these items.

In Gulfport, Mississippi, the Moana Wave was being dressed out in SURTASS fashion. He was to join the gang there to see the plans of the acoustic phobia scheduled the next week. Additionally, the diagrams and related schemes of the satellite would also be discussed during this meeting house. Enter Mr. Bill Wise, as John looked up. The subject was the AN/WSC–6, which would supply the ship to communicate its contacts in the SHF capability to the Oceanographic Facilities Network. Bill and John attended this brief, which was well equipped. Navy questions came to rise. The satellite stations that were to convey the systems were planned and would be in orbit after 1980. The WSC–6 terminal supported a status rate at 9.6 kps (kilograms per second) for shore–to–ship circuits with 144 kps for ship–to–shore delivery. The installation was performed in three steps, in other words, the OPEVAL would be installed with one of the first global connectivity in 1979.

The cutting of steel sent fragments flying as he saw the future test and evaluation ship. John plus two other players were in Gulfport seeing this bulky action. The latter one–half of the vessel was stripped down to deck level with new components yet to be added. We were shown the particulars back in the conference room on the second floor. The satellite dish was the first thing that was new. It was mounted below the maximum height of the Moana Wave. Why was this super high frequency not at the top of the vessel? The next addition was the operational vase that controlled the contact breakdown and evaluation of the contact to send back to the shore station. The computer was talked about on the sly, but what did the sonic part (gram, etc.) resemble? The object here is what takes a man who is proficient in towing an array creates excellent at nabbing Soviet nuclear submarines? And homing into oblivion, what was the array wired best for looking for them? The last thing that would embrace the aft of the ship was the array wrapped above a big spool.

I called back to NAVELEX and corresponded to Bill Wise. I used a normal line but avoided mentioning too much. I told him that I was leaving that night to go to Dallas, Texas. He knew I was proceeding on course. Ace Hose Construction was the place I was after. There was no security guard and a haphazard secretary who called for my contact. Mr. George Able met me and I was escorted into his office. He was surprised after I showed him my secret uniform badge about not having an armed guard outside. "Well, you have to play a game with the Mexicans who are on the assembly end of the array, and so you say nothing," he said. On my list in my head of blunders, I have repeatedly cited; this is an unbelievable excuse!

I met the head of this establishment and Mr. Able took me for a walk through the plant. The array was about three inches in diameter and had wiring running through the cable. I asked very little as the array that was running off the assembly line was made for an oil company which they were dragging pursuant to detecting new oil fields.

In Arlington, I sent a memo, which I had finished while riding in the airplane, through Bill Wise to the head of NAVELEX. He was surprised when he saw the memo but he had seen the light at Dallas. He went to the Captain and discussed the complaint. This suddenly went to a higher ground for resolution. Apparently, the "Host Company" had a major shakeup, which classified the problems, a new security system was set up, and the Mexicans were still employed. In other words, the foreign employees worked on oil or other exploration gear, not SURTASS!

Lockheed arrived and assembled in a conference room where representatives came over from the Pentagon. They unveiled the CP–902, which was a derivative of the P–3C airplane. It was programmed similarly but had bytes up the electrical scale. ASN–86 Internal Computer handled the navigation, with inputs from the Global Positioning System, which was scheduled in 1989. The rest of the system was in logic unit two. Herein, like the acoustic display system with recall, comparison and final interpretation. The acoustic display was blank on the movie screen but there was more to come. And finally, according to all present, was the ANWSC–6 setup, including four or five units. This of course did not include the antenna and the ship mounting platform, which was mounted on top of the ship.

As the speaker was finished many questions transpired. John could not believe it, but a certain ton of people referred to is as a spy ship! Eight or nine questions were not answered because their producer was not there. For example, what are the arrays listening for what target?

Janet lay snuggled up against me asleep; her naked form had regained its shape after her 8 pound girl was brought into the world. What could I have done to let this creature pass me by? Suddenly she woke up yawning and, with her eyes open, she kissed me on the cheek. "I only love and adore you! I am sorry I have been running all over the United States. Please forgive me," he blurted out.

"Honey, I know you are doing the task set before you in true professional fashion. Knowing that I missed you, you always gave your best for me and the children." With that she hugged him and nibbled his chest. It was dawn just before the sun rose and she went to the toilet. She finished and John was right behind her. They both brushed their teeth and resumed their act of love.

July 1979 the ship was ready for the next step. Moana Wave made some preliminary tests before striking out to Fort Lauderdale, Florida. The actual hands–on gear was complete. Now the installation of sensitive gear was imminent.

With my concern for the project and the outstanding work that was performed, the Captain gave me a sizable increase in salary plus put me in charge of the analysis section on the ship. From my perspective, the job made me feel impossible in all respects.

The acoustic display was delivered when I arrived. Contractors followed the analyzer where it fit nicely. The fascination of the computer–run black gear was the data it stored in logic unit number 2 of the CP–902. Logic unit number two had every submarine cataloged and was computerized. Quite a system. WSC–6 also had a bed in which to sleep in the Surtass Operations

Center (SOC). The communicator/operator of this device will sit in the SOC. Routinely five or even seven men will share the responsibilities of the operation center, but time will tell.

The back–end of the Moana Wave was perhaps the most clever item on the list; the spool. Piled on this cylindrical device, which had a run or ridge on each side, was a linear array of 8,575 feet that was deployed on 6,000–foot tour cable. SURTASS array was neutrally buoyant. Another new item had been placed in the array, Vibration Isolation Modules (VIM). These items reduced the effects of ships noise coupled with cable strum. The cable to be used was the Pre–Production Baseline Array.

By the end of 1977 a plan was worked out with Operational Test and Evaluation facility to verify that this system was functioning as planned. The test would begin in June 1978. By then several projects were under study with training of operators, deployment sites, and the proverbial ocean waters it could operate in. So, in other words, half of the planned crew would be OPEVAL technicians.

War on SURTASS had just begun. The test required three months of testing, however, the test was aborted and the Moana Wave docked at Little Creek, Virginia, in sixty days. Apparently it was a major holocaust for towed arrays. Read 'em and weep:

- Array had problems, sharks attacking, not enough cable ends on board, etc.
- Satellite communications (WSC–6) were unsatisfactory. Only achieved 20% satellite coverage; antenna not installed properly.
- Computer locked up and was invisible 50% of the test.
- Acoustic sensor works except when the array malfunctions.
- The ship needs a configuration of ballast to improve the stability and control the craft while pulling a towed array in heavy seas.

CHAPTER 9

A STRATEGIC ELEMENT IN OUR MIDST

The unreal, unmentionable first was the outcome of what had been a prodigy, was full of incapacities that even the giant sharks would have applied. After all of the breakthroughs were analyzed, a plan of action of each act that was not in accordance with OPEVAL was marked and included. John said, although he warned the hierarchy that this mechanical system would fail, "Mr. John Chartier, you are project engineer, and by God you will make it work!"

The next attempt to shake off the elements was the period from January to June of 1980. Numerous tests were run and completed at home base in Florida. The satellite dish was placed with uppermost caution on most of Moana Wave. Also the antenna was larger than during the aborted test. This correlated with a study of how satellite communications could be as effective when responding to Mediterranean Sea, messages to Ocean System Atlantic or Pacific fleet, as necessary.

John's big take of this test is success of the failures. When the supreme justification of a pact detects a fault, we must acknowledge it and try to modify, week apart, or in essence, fix the damn problem.

May 1980 was a thing of beauty. The Operational Evaluation of SURTASS was a bona fide success. Everything worked in the system: satellite, communications, array settings, and above all, we had an occasional submarine. Commander, Operation Evaluation, was pleased except for a few minor discrepancies. The report was released by the end of June 1980. Then became the long trial of booting up the ladder for approval/production of twelve new ships. Many preparatory slides and words were run over, changed, and then tried again. Once Chief of Naval Operations was comfortable, the next step was the Department of Navy. Several minor changes were added and the system sailed right through his staff.

USNS The Stawart, the first operational SURTASS ship.

The initial brief was given to the Department of Defense czar of ASW. His background was twenty or so years relating to the breakdown of something, to be resurrected again with a dozen more bullets. On September 26th, 1980, SURTASS, a towed array ship, was signed for twelve ships. This brought all hands to toast all their warm feelings.

T–AGOS ships it was decided that they are operated by the Military Sealift Command and are under the administrative command of Commander, Undersea Surveillance. Then the fleet has their way by deploying under the operational control of Theatre ASW Commanders, CTF84 and CTF12. Civilian technicians who operated/maintained mission equipment manned the SURTASS Operations Center (SOC). Military detachments were required when embarked for onboard analysis with direct reporting to fleet units. In summary, the SURTASS mission lasted for 60 days while towing an array that detected acoustic data.

October 1980 was a preparatory trip to test out numerous "fixes." Several of the deficiencies were due to Moana Wave's characteristics, meaning noise and quieting noise from the ship. Slow speed while deployed operations was underway, was multiple in nature. This destructive power of force of the tension on the arrays above normal speed, reduction of excessive self noise of the boat, the quieting at lower speeds, and primarily the predominant reason for SURTASS (Gap Fillers).

Acting as the SOC (SURTASS Operations Center) we correlated way of the rock and roll discrepancies. The at–sea period was into the final days of the test. On December 26, 1980, we gained contact on a Soviet Yankee nuclear submarine. This was of significant posture to satellite this information to Oceanographic Systems Atlantic. The message arrived, but was not noticed until four hours later. This went through channels and wound up at the Pentagon Command Center.

OP951F, the SURTASS Officer, was called requesting he report to the Pentagon Operations Center on the morning of the 27th of December 1980. Moana Wave has contact and what should we do? The only thing that the project officer could do was to launch the ready duty from Bermuda and confirm this was a true by–God contact. The order went out to the Tactical Support Center and the P–3 was launched forty minutes later from Bermuda. The only thing they had to go on was a true bearing from the ship estimating 500 miles. After three hours of drinking coffee, the P–3 reported Yankee contacts, which made Pentagon Command Center very happy.

John and his troops soon were happy with the results. The next day John could not believe what was happening. A second Yankee had been detected. This true intercept was about 800–900 miles away, but it could not be a multiple of the first contact, which was still printing.

An Admiral was waiting in the command Center when the SURTASS officer arrived. He was amazed upon reading a secret noforn message. "Let's contact Bermuda and launch the ready," said Commander. He then went to the chart when they had the Moana Wave plotted. From Bermuda, the ship was plotted 135 true/250 miles. The first contact was plotted northeast at 500 miles and the second target was about 800 miles to the southwest. Confirmation from Norfolk said there was no relation, but similar in contact. Three hours later we had our answer.

When 1984 was off and moving the plans were rapidly being developed for the crew training. The specific site was the Fleet Anti Submarine Warfare School, Atlantic in Norfolk, VA. These men were trained in the SURTASS Operations Center (SOC) of 5–7 Lockheed Martin men. Each technical track was six months long, which included CMS qualification, considerable lab work, and back deck courses. In total the crew looked like 5–7 SOC personnel, 9–21 "Blue Suiters" was a CPO or Junior Officer as the SURTASS Mission Coordinator.

John was involved in the positioning of the satellites that would handle mission communications. Transmitting from satellite to downloading at a land base site was acceptable, but there had to be alternatives. In the Mediterranean Sea this became an obtainable. The only way was to choose a Naval Communication Site, transmit the message to them to pass via satellite to the action addee. The final episode was teletype it, which meant various senders.

SURTASS was envisioned to run sixty days and spend some time for replenishment at Naval Station Rota, Spain. A 10–15 day period was necessary in port for maintenance, with overhauls ranging 30 months. Arrays, substantial parts were positioned at this site. Rocky space was obtained, ready to receive the ship. Eventually, other sites — Glasgow, Scotland; Yakohana, Japan; Pearl Harbor, Hawaii; and Port Hunerve, California — were selected as ports of opportunity.

The Stalwart, Ocean Surveillance Ship arrived in the harbor at Little Creek, Virginia. It was October 1985, almost a year after it was projected to arrive. Basically, the builder, Tacoma Shipbuilder, Washington, had just submitted bankruptcy papers. This, plus the numerous negative factors of undersea phenomena falling by the wayside, spelt tension throughout the Navy's building hierarchy. Again, John was assigned to the system SOC evaluator. The Production Based Array was installed on the boat, which on the towed array was a linear array of 575 feet. The acoustic array monitored the lower frequencies, which were deployed on a 6,000 foot cable, plus it was mutually buoyant. Alongside this system were segments, when broken, and inept were replaced by the new tubes. Finally, the ship was ready to embark.

Underway, the ship followed orders and proceeded to the east beyond Bermuda. They dropped the array and began towing at three knots. Four hours after initial deployment a small part of the array was lost. After bringing in the array, a large fish, probably a shark, bit off a small segment. John and several others re–hooked the sequence up and tried again. This time the action continued and we had a Yankee submarine. We held the contact for about fifteen hours. Apparently the radar picked up a contact 15 miles away. It was just nightfall. The Captain of the vessel stated that if we suspected that this vessel was Soviet we might pull in our array. Three hours later they sighted a trawler, presumably Russian. The trawler followed the Stalwart with the array onboard. The ships began sending Morse code. "What are you doing? Are you catching fish?" the Russian asked. The ship replied, "We are sleeping for the time being," the Captain reported. All gear was in standby as initial response was sent regarding this stranger. Finally, after this was satisfactory, the Russian left. After 69 days of surveillance the ship cranked up to 11 knots and headed towards Rota, Spain.

In 1988, John was moved back to Arlington, Virginia. Despite a raise to GS18, he assumed coordinator of the newer version of towed arrays: Small Water Plane Twin Hull (SWATH). This, some years past, was a clandestine project labeled a SURTASS inventive ship that could perform well above the Arctic Circle. The Victorious Class craft were built on a small water plane tower hull, which gave it greater stability at slow speeds in high sea status in high latitudes. These ships were manned with slightly more men but had all the amenities of a civilian towed ship. The Victorious Class was built in McDewott Marine in Morgan City, Louisiana. With a greater length, similar capacity, its speed was only 10 knots, with towing at three knots. Of note is the AI80R Array, which was a commercialized version of reduced diameter array. This granted increased array gain in both mid and upper frequency regions.

CHAPTER 10

OSAMA BIN LADEN CONTROLS TERROR

The text of Worlds Islamic Fronts statement urging Jihad against the Jews and Crusades were faxed to Quad al–Arabic, signed by Shaykn Usamh Bin–Muhammad Bin Laden, the most prominent Saudi counterpart and others who were behind this man.

Praise be to God, who revealed the Book, controls the clouds, defeats factionalism, and says in His Book, "But when the forbidden months are past, then fight and slay the pagans wherever ye find them, seize them, beleaguer them, and lie in wait for them in every stratagem of war."

No one argues today about three facts that are known to everyone, we will list them, in order to remind everyone. First, for over seven years the United States had been occupying the lands of Islam in the holiest of places, the Arabian Peninsula, pilfering its riches, dictating to its rulers, humiliating its people, terrorizing its neighbors, and turning its bases in the Peninsula into a spearhead through which to fight the neighboring Muslim peoples. The best proof of this is the Americans' continuing aggression against the Iraqi people using the Peninsula as a staging post.

Second, despite the great devastation inflicted on the Iraqi people by the crusader–Zionist alliance, and despite the huge number of those killed, which exceeded 1 million, the Americans were once again trying to repeat the horrific massacres, as though they are not content with the protracted blockade imposed after the ferocious war or fragmentation and devastation.

Third, if the Americans' aims behind these wars are religious and economic, the aim is also to serve the Jews' petty state and divert attention from its occupation of Jerusalem and murder of Muslims there.

The best proof of this is their eagerness to destroy Iraq, the strongest neighboring Arab state, and the crimes and sins committed by the Americans are a clear declaration of war on God, his messenger, and Muslins.

Basically, and in faithful compliance with God's order, this is the fatwa to all Muslims:

The ruling to kill Americans and their allies — civilians and military — is an individual duty for every Muslin who can do it in any country in which it is possible to do it, in order to liberate the al–Aqua Mosque and the holy mosque (Mecca) from their grip, and in order for their armies to move out of all the lands of Islam, defeated and unable to threaten any Muslim. This is in accordance with the words of Almighty God, "and fights the pagans all together as they fight you all together," and "fight them until there is no more tumult or oppression and there prevails justice and faith in God."

This is in addition to the words of Almighty God: "And why should ye not fight in the cause of God and of those who, being weak, are ill–treated women and children, whose cry is 'Our Lord, rescue us from this town, whose people are oppressors; and raise for us from thee one who will help!'"

We — with God's help — call on every Muslim who believes in God and wishes to be rewarded to comply with God's order to kill Americans and plunder their money wherever and whenever they find it. Leaders, youth, and soldiers will launch the raid on Satan's U.S. troops and the devil's supporters allying with them, and to displace those who are behind them so that they may learn a lesson.

Almighty God said, "O ye who believe, give your response to God and His Apostle, when He called you to that which will give you life. And know that God cometh between a man and his heart, and that it is He to whom ye shall all be gathered."

Almighty God also says, "O ye who believe, what is the matter with you, that when ye are asked to go forth in the cause of God, ye cling so heavily to the earth? Do ye prefer the life of this world to the hereafter? But little is the comfort of the life, as compared with the hereafter. Unless ye go forth, He will punish you with a grievous penalty, and put others in your place; but Him ye would not harm in the least. For God hath power over all things."

Almighty God also says, "So lose no heart, nor fall into despair. For ye must gain mastery if ye are true in faith."

The word "fatwa" means judgment. Mr. Bin Laden uses many fatwas in the declaration of past judgments. This allegedly justifies his "holy war" or "jihad" against foreign enemies. "Usul al–fiqh" (Principals of Jurisprudence) are when the four factors are initiated: 1) It is right when relevant proofs, verified from Koran verses and habits; 2) It is received by one having completeness of heart; 3) Free from individual opportunity, and not depending on political servitude; 4) It meets the needs of the world.

As early as June 1998, a terrorist financier wanted by Saudi Arabian and U.S. authorities for at least two bombings appeared on U.S. Television on Wednesday and challenged the U.S. military to try him. Appearing on ABC News' "World News Tonight" and later on Nightline, Osama bin Laden spoke from what it was said was a heavily–armed camp somewhere inside Afghanistan, which had given refuge to the stateless Saudi Arabian and a group of his followers.

Bin Laden has vowed to wage a jihad, or holy war, against U.S. forces in Saudi Arabia because of U.S. support for Israel. He broadened his threat to include all Americans, civilian and military, in the Middle East. He also said, "We do not differentiate between those dressed in military uniforms and civilians. They are all targets in this fatwa…we must use such punishment to keep your evil away from Moslems, Moslem women and children."

The U. S. State Department has identified bin Laden as a major world sponsor of Islamic extremism. He is believed to have been a major financier of the two terrorist bombings in Saudi Arabia. The reported terrorist said, "We predict a black day for the United States of America."

On 12 June 1998, the State Department issued an announcement with respect to the Middle East and South Asia: The terrorist Osama Bin Laden reiterated his warning to the U.S. He said he did not distinguish between uniform and civilian. In a May 26 press review, he implied that some sort of terrorist action would likely be mounted in two or three weeks. We often take these actions as serious and we look at many government facilities as potential threats. Most assuredly, the State Department believes it is mandatory to alert Americans in the region to keep a high level of security in all working spaces. Thereby, Americans will maintain a low visibility when traveling, vary times and routes, and treat suspicious mail with great concern.

The pattern of Global Terrorism is stated by a quick review of all the organizations that formed a rebellion against the

United States. This criterion has force and intrigue that can destabilize a country as great as ours — September 11, 2001! This list of actives amounts to 50–odd foreign terrorist organizations. These factions are all intertwined, mutually involved activities and all are partially behind Bin Laden to justify his holy war against America. The al Qaeda has massive strengths, which include many artworks or umbrella organizations that include Sunni Islamic extremist groups, Egyptian Islamic Jihad, and numerous factions such as Harked ul–Mujahidin.

Here are a few of the sadistic scourge who are apt to coordinate with Bin Laden in respect to the training camps, money and supplying weapons:

A. Abu Nidal Organization (ANO). This group has carried out international terrorist organizations led by Sabi al–Banna. In 1974 he split from the PLO and they are made up of political, military, and financial doers. There activities have been attacks in 20 different countries. The major attacks have been in Rome and Vienna in the airports in December 1985 though January 1991. Their location of operations has been centered on Iraq since 1998. Al–Banna also has a presence in Lebanon and several Palestinian refugee camps along the coastal areas. Apparently, he has been offered and accepted a great deal of money (funds from Iraq, Libya and Syria) that augmented his support for future action.

B. Al–Gam'at al–Islamiyya (Islamic Group, IG) Egypt's 1970 militant group, which has been active since 1970, is an organized party. It issued a cease–fire in March 1999 but has not conducted an attack in Egypt since 1998. The group signed fatwa but it still supports Bin Laden. Al–Gam'at has launched several attacks against Egypt tourists in

1992, but became famous when they killed 58 foreign visitors at Luxor in 1997. In June 1995 they attempted to assassinate the Egyptian President Hosni Mubarak, but failed. This group operates mainly in the Al Minya and other governorates of Southern Egypt. This terrorist group has a worldwide presence with the United Kingdom and Afghanistan. The Egyptian Government speculates that Iran, Sudan, and other militant groups support and supply this organization.

C. HAMAS (Islamic Resistance Movement). This elite faction in 1987 was the Palestinian branch of the Muslim Brotherhood. Elements of HAMAS have been used to advance terrorism to pursue an Islamic Palestinian state in place of Israel. Strength of the party subsides in the Gaza Strip. HAMAS operates in Israel. It receives funding from expatriates, Iran, and private benefactors in Saudi Arabia and other Arab states.

D. Harakut ul–Mujahidin (HUM). This is an Islamic group that is based in Pakistan but operates in Kashmir. The leader, Fazlur Rehman Khalil, has been linked to Bin Laden and has signed his fatwa in February 1998. He operates terrorist camps in Eastern Afghanistan and has suffered casualties when U.S. missiles struck Laden–associated camps in Khowst in August 1998. HUM is dying for revenge against the United States. Numerous operations have been conducted in Kashmir. He has several thousand located in this region. Supporters are mostly Pakistanis and Kashmiris, who use all types of hideous weaponry. The HUM trains its militants in Pakistan and in Afghanistan.

E. Hezbollah (Party of God). Islamic Jihad, Revolution Justice Organization of the Oppressed on Earth and Islamic Jihad for the Liberation of Palestine are called "The Party of God." There is a band of radical Shiva formed in Lebanon that has led to an Iranian–style Islamic republic. Anti–West and closely allied and directed by Iran, there efforts are not closely followed and are not approved by Tehran. Involved with numerous terrorist attacks against the suicide truck bombing of U.S. Embassy and U.S. Marine barracks. Additionally, the group was held responsible for the kidnapping, detention, and killing of American people. Their cells are many; Europe, Africa, South and North America. They receive info, political and financial support, and they get tons of needed weapons from Iran and Syria.

F. Al–Jihad. From the late 1970s this faction has appeared divided into two warring parts; one is based in Afghanistan and is a key player in that Bin Laden is the new World Islamic Front. One important goal here is to overthrow the Egyptian Government and keep targeting U.S. targeting interests there. Of interest is the 1981 assassination of Egyptian President Anwar Sadat, which appears to concentrate on high–level officials. Operating in the Cairo area, this group has many networks.

G. Mujahedin–e Khalq Organization (MEK or MKO). Formed in the 1960s with a college–educated Iranian faction, the MEK sought to counter this excessive pull in the Shah's regime. This has developed into the largest and most active armed Iranian opinionated group. Worldwide, it preys on propaganda and prefers terrorist violence. With takeover and fanatic attacks on the U.S. Embassy in 1979, three explosions in 1998 which killed 3 persons, and other senile events boosted this party to oversee the several thousand fighters gain oversea support.

H. Popular Front for the Liberation of Palestine–General Command (PFLP–GC). This unit split from the PFLP in 1968 because it was time to focus on more fighting vice politics. They carried out many attacks during 1970–1980. They used hot air balloons and motorized hang gliders, especially when crossing the border into Israel. Currently, there are approximately 200–300 men employed in this organization.

I. Al–Qaeda. Bin Laden established this group in 1990 to bring together the Arabs who fought against the Russians. Afghan resistance was also aided and it was the duty of Muslims to kill U.S. citizens and their allies. And still the terrorists raised havoc by bombing U.S. Embassies in Nairobi, Kenya and in Tanzania, shot down U.S. helicopters in Somalia, three bombings against our flag in Aden, Yemen, and were plotting the assassination of the Pope. This is a fantastic umbrella organization that plans and executes. Bin Laden and his key lieutenants reside in Afghanistan and the terrorists maintain a camp there. So for external aid, Bin Laden with all his money will apportion $300 million to keep them solvent.

In the Naval Undersea Warfare division, Bandar Abbis was assigned to the torpedo development division. Normally he got a picture badge, which he wore each day at his office.

Order of business was to report at 0730 and leave work after eight hours of timely worthwhile service. The first week of training was to orient all of the history of projectiles during the almost fifty years of service. Back in the uprising of Japan and Germany the particulars were predicated on producing a weapon that would sink the submarine. Principally, what would happen if the U.S. submarines used a faulty system and that mechanism didn't attack the enemy sub? In 1942 this was documented by both sailors on board a U.S. submarine when their torpedoes came around and sunk their own boats.

Numerous lectures capitalized on the multitude of torpedoes since the end of WWII. Each had a different operative, a different depth, but that changed with the specific parameters of each elusive deterrent. That particular day they went into the buildings behind the chain–link fence where they were highly guarded. They showed the MK–28, which was in turn stolen from the German brand. Bandar was impressed with the knowledge of his mentors. A wake, for example, was solidified in the MK–30, was exhibited to the trainer. The next display showed the inside of their weapon, it's firing mechanism and the depth while running to the target.

By the end of the week we were into the MK–37. This was the sub–launched underwater threat of the 1960s. Interesting, but a glimpse of the future, the MK–37 has a 20+ knot range and works down to 330 meters (1,000 feet), which makes it a more productive weapon. This brief inspired many questions that Bandar brought forth the load in solving these paltry details.

An active/passive homing torpedo was big at the start of the second week. MK–46 was to combat high speed/performance targets being launched from aircraft. This was a two–speed, mono–propellant fueled, and used reciprocating external combustion. This led to the MK–48, a thin cylindrical self–propelled underwater projectile. Bandar was amazed at this quantum fire power. He noted that the power came from an axial flow pump jet propulsion that revolved about twin propellers, in addition to a combustion piston engine. The MK–48 had an excellent anti–submarine warfare mission. ASW was the name of the game, and, thusly, the submarine force was outfitted as soon as possible.

Torpedo and Unmanned Underwater Vehicle Engineering was the division he was to export to in the main office. He met Mr. Bob Franks, the section head, with five other members of this engineering group. He, unfortunately, was the junior man, starting at GS–14. Coffee and donuts, the meeting began with each man's review of his assigned duties. He learned what each man was doing and the labs where the work was completed. Franks assigned Bandar to work with Dave Sprint, who was ascertaining the deep thrust of the MK–48 in the deeper water cut–off. Also, Mr. Franks mentioned that Bandar would travel to San Diego, California, to visit the facilities there in two weeks.

This was the short period he had off from the undersea facility. "Mary" was waiting for him at his apartment. They caressed and stripped each other's clothes off and made unending, slow and precise love making. This was the fourth of July and the U.S. government had Monday as a holiday. His wife, although they were not married, she dressed, fed and really needed Bandar. At supper they talked of many things, which they agreed on almost any subject.

Sunday was "all hands day" at Rafson's Place. They met with open arms and continued on until they reached the back plaza. Of course they spoke in their native language and a record player played these old songs. The food laid out was way too much. After eating Bandar met him and they went inside the den of the house and Rafson Bahi asked him how he liked the job. Well, Bandar wasn't impressed, but he needed to know the info should he be asked to solve a similar problem. Specifically, he chose words to describe what he had been briefed on. It appeared he and assistance were to travel to San Diego in two weeks to get a full spectrum view of what was going on.

"How is Mary?" He quickly changed the subject.

"I would like to marry her, but I assume that is all right with you," he said.

On Monday he took Mary to the Navy Exchange. He had a pass, so they let them in. Mary liked a particular dress, which Bandar bought for her. They picked up several things and drove all over the base.

The first of August Bandar took a flight from Providence, Rhode Island, to New York, transferring to San Diego. He lifted on Sunday morning and was due in San Diego at four o'clock local time. The movie was idiotic, about a murderer killing several victims. He had reservations near the facility where he was to check in on Monday morning. After getting his two bags, he hired a taxi and arrived at the motel.

As usual, the Holiday Inn was magnificent, with a swimming pool, and the rooms were of high quality. After checking out his room, hanging up his clothes and everything out of his toiletries, he went down to the bar. It was crowded, so he made his way to the bar. Since he was sweating profusely, he ordered a draft beer. He looked at the clock and it was six o'clock in the evening. On his right he noticed with his field of right–hand vision a man sat down beside him. "Good evening," he said. He turned and acknowledged. His name was Rabbit Khanjani and he looked like he was a native Iranian. He reported he had left the country ten years ago and attended the University of California. He came from Zarand, which was about 600 miles southeast of Tehran. They chatted about being in San Diego and he had met Rafson back east in Providence. Eventually, he and Bandar had supper in the adjoining restaurant.

San Diego's weapons branch was a consolidation of buildings that were heavily guarded. With his security badge and current identification he went through the gate. Dr. Paul Ferris met him and he followed the doctor to an office inside the activity. Without reference to formality, he preferred to be called Paul. He came to this place when the Japanese signed the peace accords. He worked in development, weapon acquisition, and post–analysis problems. Paul outlined the schedule for that day, which included particular backgrounds of present–day weaponry.

MK–44 was the starting point of our briefing. A self–propelling projectile, the MK–44 was an active homing torpedo that used a salt water–activated electric battery for movement purposes. Once the torpedo was launched, the torpedo commenced a special search for the target. HBX–3 was the high explosive, weighing 75 pounds, which was set to run only 6 minutes. These parameters, coupled with 30 knots actual speed, 1,000 yards acquisition range, and minimum/maximum attack depth setting, made for a good threat in the Neptune and the P–3 Orion aircraft.

Questions were entertained with Bandar unloaded on several points. That afternoon we went further into the laboratory, where we saw several tests of this underwater missile.

At an Iranian restaurant, he met Rabbit for supper. They shook hands and wanted the waiters to seat them out of the way in the back of the facility. After being seated, they ordered wine, that of Iran's finest. They spoke in their native language. Bandar spoke of his childhood, with particular interest to soccer and educational experience. He was given a scholarship to Harvard University, where he received top honor in his class. His new friend came the opposite route, landing in the curriculum of the University of California. Rabbit was a superior and leader of his class in mathematics and chemistry. Although he was resistant, he worked with Rafson to establish upcoming students for granting them upcoming scholarships.

The menu was scrumptious, with vegetables, rice and lamb with pilaf. The wine kept flowing, making it a night to recall. The bubble burst and Rabbit asked about the terrorist bands in Iran. Suddenly I had been warned of this very subject. On Iran I talked of our MEK organization, of which I am a follower, being the largest party in Iran. My friend broke up my chatter by agreeing with my conclusions. We decided we would meet one more evening before I left.

For the next three days the tour continued with the major subject, the MK–46 torpedo. This superseded the latter starting in 1966. Essentially, this was a missile that was self–propelled, operated underwater and was designed to explode on contact or with close proximity to a theater target. This weapon was designed for submarines, surface ships, helicopters and for fixed–wing aircraft.

Switching around various components led to augmenting the warhead whereby the Captor mine was invented. Another advantage was the ASROC (Anti–Submarine Rocket), which could be fired from a ship after a fix had been obtained. The MK–46 was indubitable that it sought out high performance targets. Another side issue was improving the performance in shallow water. By the dense if this two–speed mono–propellant fueled, was the ability to select active or passive/active acoustic homing to sever the threat.

Traveling back to Providence, Bandar was thinking over his events of the past four days. After communicating the daily happenings, he zipped open his flight bag, which contained his notepads, pens, and other necessary note devices. Key of these instruments was a recording set (cassette), which was a plastic cartridge containing magnetic tape, with the tape on one reel passing to the other. On these tapes, Bandar had recorded secretly all of the lectures, labs and even Mr. Rabbit Khanjani's recent expressions. Additional taped reports were neatly catalogued and kept banded by a rubber band. Not know by and large, all undersea warfare studies, lectures, had been documented and turned over to Rafson. This had to be something big, but to my duty in support of jihad, or holy war, against the United States, this was a terrorist act that would explode the world back to the pre–Cambrian era.

CHAPTER 11

CENTRAL INTELLIGENCE AGENCY/ NATIONAL SECURITY AGENCY

Bush lied? Could Bush admit that there were no Weapons of Mass Destruction in Iraq on January 29, 2004? The ball is in his court when it comes down to brass tacks.

Possibly President Clinton came forth and said, "One way or another, we are determined to deny Iraq the capacity to develop weapons of mass destruction and the missiles to deliver them. That is our bottom line." February 4, 1998. And again, quoting him again, "If Saddam rejects peace and we have to use force, our purpose is clear. We want to seriously demise the threat posed by Iraq's weapons of mass destruction." — President Clinton, February 17, 1998.

This started the swing of the batting ball followed by the Clinton clan. Madeline Albright, who was Secretary of State, cited, "The leaders of a rogue state will use nuclear, chemical or biological weapons against us." A day later Sandy Berger, who was in charge of the Clinton National Security, stated, "He will use those weapons of mass destruction again, as he has ten times since 1983." — February 18, 1998.

Finally the power play from democratic senators Levin and a cast of others wrote a letter to the President that proclaimed, "We urge you, after consulting with Congress, and consistent with the U. S. Constitution and laws, to take necessary actions (including, if appropriate, air and missile strikes on suspect Iraqi sites) to respond effectively to the threat posed by Iraq's refusal to end its weapons of mass destruction programs." — October 9, 1998.

Throughout the end of 1998 and up to December 1999 there was constant bickering about the "destruction and palaces for his cronies," as well as the impending danger associated with this usurper of sovereignty. Saddam had his two sons who controlled power, money, and could eradicate men, presumably for pleasure.

Saddam Hussein was waging a "classical guerilla–type campaign," said a general of the U.S. Central Command, which is "getting more organized" every day.

What could the disposed dictator hope to accomplish? How could he, with a waging ragtag force of criminals and imported killers with nothing to do, nothing to lose, possibly defeat 170,000 occupying troops?

Saddam outfoxed one President and intends to outfox and outlast another. They saw the likelihood that his army would disintegrate under direct assault, he probably decided that the mother of all battles against democracy is a war of attrition. He may assume his current strategy to be based on these assumptions:

1. Our troop losses drove Clinton out of Somalia, Reagan out of Lebanon, Johnson and Nixon out of

Vietnam. In occupied Iran only 1 death a day sustained for months with pictures of bereaved families on TV would, in Saddam's thinking, not only demoralize the occupiers but also increase political pressure in the US and Great Britain to bring the troops home.

2. European and Muslim opinion, incensed at being ignored by a superpower, will continue to deny cooperation to the victors. Saddam assumes this would force Bush to turn over control of Iraq to the United Nations, in which this should not be imposed from the outside or the blue helmets would run at the first Sunni uprising.

3. Patience is not an American virtue. Saddam anticipates that the anti–war majority — furious at the unexpected ease of the US victory and struggling of mass graves of Saddam's doing would turn a steady attrition of casualties among occupiers into dread visions of "Quagmire."

4. Saddam's guerillas, aided by Syria and Iran, would hold out the fierce impossibility of a return to power of Saddam. A series of murders would continue to intimidate Iraqi scientists and officers who knew about weapons of mass destruction and links to Al Qaeda.

5. He presumes that British and American journalists after the obligatory mention that the world is better off with Saddam gone, would, by their investigative and opposition nature, sustain the credibility firestorm.

6. Inside Iraq with the Americans on the way out, the Shiite majority would split and when the Sunni

majority sees its power in Baghdad, the troublesome Kurds would separate, thereby triggering a
Turkish invasion of the north.

That's his comeback strategy. Is it a homicidal maniac's dream? If
the taped voice is Saddam's even as we believe, it means that he has
worked out means of a secret production and clandestine trans-
mission to cooperative broadcasters just as cunning as the concealment of damaging documents or recent traffic across the borders.

Our best to deny Saddam's putative return from Elba and to
put the summer of discontent behind us.

Drop the premature conclusion that we can't find proof of the
destructive weapons. Really, they never did exist. That's like saying
because we haven't found Osama Bin Laden or Saddam, those
killers never existed. Put sacrifice in perspective. A loss of one soldier's life is individual tragedy, but the loss of thousands or more
by a vengeful dictator would be a national tragedy. This purpose
of our armed forces is to protect us and that's the costly mission
our volunteers carry out every day.

Remember which nations had the right to do in a timely
fashion the centers are free to argue about the hard to read
intelligence, but few will deny that the world is indisputably
safer with the overthrow of a proven mass murderer and a financier of suicidal bombing.

This, above all: to end guerilla war in Iraq, find Saddam
and his ghostly crew. Saddam Hussein was a Renaissance man
— a genocidal pervert with a collection of hideous samples of
bubonic and anthrax specimens, who married his cousin. And
now, he is a prisoner in Cell Block X — which is the last place
he will breathe.

Hussein was born in Iraq in 1937 where he joined the Ba'ath
party at an early age. By the mid–century he was in turmoil when
a coup declared the country a Republic, but his party seized power
in 1963. Saddam married his cousin and fathered two sons.
Throughout 1960 and 1970 Iraq repeated the cycle of coup and

countercoup which led to bloody iterations. Interestingly, the Soviet Union took notice in this country's actions.

In 1979 Saddam became a launcher of war against Iran. He also authorized poison gas on his enemies including the Kurds. For this he was known as the "Butcher of Baghdad"! In 1980 Reagan launched a special envoy to dine with Saddam — Don Rumsfeld. Interesting!! The talk was of chemical weapons which lead to numerous U.S. companies shipping chemical and biological agents to Iraq. Additional samples had stains of anthrax, bubonic plague, and later improved toxins were delivered, such as ricin and sarin gas.

Torture was another tool in his bang of tricks. Public awareness slowly turned on Hussein when he cleverly marched on Kuwait. As the Clinton era became faded into a sex–soaked afterglow, George F. Bush administration started rumbling about Saddam, but did not have support until September 11, 2001.

The crises bloomed again in 2003 when the U.S. planned to invade Iraq. U.S. forces took the country by storm and his two sons were missing. Evidence of Weapons of Mass Destruction was the primary cause of this invasion.

On Sunday December 14, 2003, while hiding in a tiny dirt hole, Saddam Hussein was captured alive by the 4th Infantry Division of Army Special Forces. Those he terrorized must be assured the tyrant will never come back.

In 2001, a letter sent to President Bush, signed by Senator Bob Graham and others, pointed out that, "There is no doubt that…Saddam Hussein has invigorated his weapons programs. Reports indicate the biological, chemical and nuclear programs continue apace and may be back to pre–Gulf War status. In addition, Saddam continues to redefine delivery systems and is doubtless using the cover of an illicit missile program to develop longer–range projectiles that will threaten the United States and our allies." — December 5, 2001.

The dam is just about to burst at the seams! Soon, just about all of the constituency of the Democrats were upset with the "secret supplies of biological and chemical weapons." Al Gore, Carl Levin and Ted Kennedy gave interludes during the interpretative time. Senator Robert Byrd was furious with the fact that "intelligence reports indicate that he is seeking nuclear weapons," mentioned on October 29, 2002. Senator John Kerry wrote that "I will be voting to give the President of the United States authority to use force — if necessary — to disarm Saddam Hussein because I believe that a deadly arsenal of weapons of mass destruction in his hand is a real and grave threat to our society." Within reach this is building up the crises of where the President will gear this country to attacking Iraq.

"Without question, we need to disarm Saddam Hussein. He is a brutal, murderous dictator leading an oppressive regime…He represents a particularly grievous threat because he is so consistently prone to miscalculation…And now he is miscalculating America's response to his continued deceit and his consistent grasp for weapons of mass destruction…So the threat of Saddam with WMD is real." Senator John Kerry, a democrat, sealed the decision of the President with these words in a speech given on January 23, 2003.

To solve the mysteries of problems after their theories have been surmised, has been the bane of the public's existence. A decade ago, what were the Central Intelligence Agency's findings in definite counterintelligence with the Federal Bureau of Investigation asleep at the wheel. The President, numerous responsible terrorist/defenders of justice, Secretary of Defense, and numerous authors have slammed their pages with stories about whom and what — with all are at blame. September 11, 2001 will go down as a crude awaking of horrific incidents that were initiated by terrorists. Bin Laden had forecast even back in 1995 that there was something in sports, unusual transmissions, or closeting traits that had to be pieced together. The major ingredient is the hijacking of an airplane. This technique was tried before, leaving an airplane in a momentous crash in Scotland. On September 9th, 2001, my friend and I caught a flight from Portland, Maine. We were returning from Brunswick, Maine, because of a reunion. Two days later I was writing checks when the phone rang. It was my traveling friend who asked me to turn on the television set.

So after all is said and done, the Democrats say that the office of the president, namely George Bush, has pulled the carpet over millions of American citizens by prevaricating that there were no weapons of mass destruction in Iraq. Now the outgoing head of U. S. Army inspections, David Kay, has said that inequitably that the United States has not found stockpiles of the mass destruction of weapons in this country. And now Colin Powell agreed with this assessment which the administration line now believes Saddam has intended to build these weapons, therefore that was right or reasonable. So, let's take the case of the United States laying siege on Iraq, not by destroying WMD. If you are attacking with that intent it is best not to announce six months in advance, you have blown your cover, which gives the enemy to use weapons before you strike.

Then, on strike three, Kay was right, or we the troops were wrong if our read of the origin of the war was unaltered. The question remains unanswered; how the CIA and U.S./foreign intelligence operations made this blunder. Maybe there are two factors that will clarify this "walk through the tulips." One, Hussein had chemical weapons during the 1980s, and two, the French sold him a nuclear reactor that the Israelis destroyed in 1981.

The second point is Hussein, during the escalation of this war, the U.S. Security Council in November 2002 — March 2003, acted as if he had nuclear weapons. Saddam prevented inspections, for which Hans Blix harshly criticized his unwillingness to be forthcoming.

Thus, if Saddam ended his nuclear program, why didn't he open Iraq to detailed inspections? Another perspective is to undercut the rationale of war by cooperating with the inspectors to draw the conclusion; no military hardware. This is quite nerve wracking, thereby, his reasoning is difficult to fathom.

Operation Desert Fox in 1998 was an intense campaign to punish Saddam for failing to comply with U.N. inspections. Kay, however, did have an explanation during the 1990s because the Iraqis did not want to tell him that all arms were being produced. By and large, they were stealing the money allocated for their development. If the theory is correct, it is an intelligence failure for him as well as most of the world's intelligence agencies.

This testimony finds fault and leaves the cloud of dust overall. The first conclusion is that Hussein, including himself, had no nuclear weapons. Second in this roundabout discussion is that Iraq scientists rounded up at the end of the war revealed nothing of this miraculous course of flurry.

Either Kay's theory is bogus, logical or blasphemous, making Washington look good or sinuous is wrong. My gut tells me that this speculation is inhospitable and yet it provides Iraq the particulars of death.

In Langley, Virginia, west of the Potomac River, is the Central Intelligence Agency, which gathers information about foreign governments, certain non–government agents, or those that engage in terrorism. The majority of work that the CIA entertains is secret and above which pertains to economic, political and the like. Intelligence, which is collected by the president, Congress and other federal bureaus, is derived by counter or covert data that is collected through spies, spy satellites or collected by other means.

Principally, the covert actions include satellite picture analysis, side by side or special military operations, and secret aid that supports U.S. interests. Counterintelligence prevents loss of intelligence when such info is gained about our status of forces and military plans.

The CIA is an executive branch responsible to the president, National Security Council, Defense Intelligence Agency, and to the National Security Agency, which handles the secret communication devices using cryptography.

Some critics question whether a democratic government such as the United States should ever have a veiled agency. However, most elected leaders around the world believe intelligence powers are essentials to the security of their nations. Furthermore, many scholars understand that the United States has benefited from such work.

Being a Military Analyst in this agency is important to get top rate statistics from military studies, foreign party affairs and other sources makes the backbone of this country. To make a notch in this field of study dictates an unquestionable broad field, which necessitates travel to assess the relevant sources of data. All language opportunities are strongly advised to keep abreast of the vocalization problem.

More than a job, the clandestine service that challenges the recourses of intelligence, self–reliance and, above all, responsibility is paramount. Unbelievable quickness, ambiguous unstructured episodes fabricate a lead to work beyond national level. The final task is the counterintelligence threat analyst. His charge is to assess the U.S. through advice, analysis, clandestine operations, and produce strategic overview.

The National Security (NSA) is the largest, most decorated with secret devices, and is the most powerful intelligence agency on earth. It's wealth of manpower dwarfs the Central Intelligence Agency in all endeavors. Recent headlines tell of many episodes it can overcome, including the ongoing hunt of terrorist leader Osama bin Laden. Starting with collection of signal intelligence, which is "Signet", it is simply reading someone's mail. The other end is communications facts (COMINT), eavesdropping or language and snatching signals from other things like radar are known as (Elint).

At the heart of this invisible city is the NSA's massive operations building. Sixty–eight acres promotes many cubicles of floor space. A boxy structure with many floors of dark glass, this resembles a complex of any stylish building. Secretly, it gives one a thought of disseverment.

Hidden under this protective glass is a real building with a skin of copper and unique windows made of bulletproof glass. This method was to permit all sounds and signals (electromagnetic) from escaping the compound. The code word "Tempest" is used throughout the city and prevents electronic spies from capturing these emissions.

Another tall glass office belonging to the Technology and System Organization (NBP–1) is the ultra Mecca for NSA's highly sensitive crypto–industrial complex. Hidden from all eyes is a compound of buildings that encompass the contractors who are the inventors of the most compartmentalized satellite eaves-dropping equipment. According to sources, the NSA regularly listens to the INMARSAT, which uses, transmits and receives over spacecraft owned by the International Maritime Satellite Organization. It is obvious that Bin Laden is aware of a U.S. presence. On the other hand, NSA often plays tapes of his mother talking to her son over the INMARSAT connection.

Another example of this was in the summer of July 1997. NSA had concluded, based on several instants, that Iran was interested in the C–802 missile from China. This near–super-sonic weapon had created cries from America that it would cause danger to sailing in the Persian Gulf.

This sparked numerous events, which seem to advocate the Iranians to buy another version of this weapon, commonly know as the Generator 4203 mini–jet engine. By September, the Chinese handwriting was on the wall. The C–802 missiles were stymied, but there were no technical problems.

The problem of an interrogating problem gave fathom with vast hush boxes with the nomenclature of the CIA/NSG hung in effigy. Nowhere is the essence of secrecy obvious in Iraq. This reminds one of a terrorist encamp as it was explored in the Northern Africa desert. The camp is suspected to have men in training doing various things that make them qualify as candi-dates to be deployed as subversive agents. Unfortunately, this satellite was coming overhead, thus all training was stopped and the recruits went into the tents. Many unseen camps had been stopped and are noted on a special secret chart.

CHAPTER 12

IRAQ

Expectations of hoped–for scenes have not risen to the forefront — at least not yet. The arrival of coalition forces or troops have not sparked honor in Iraq to rival the response that guided the liberation of Afghanistan from the active hostility of the Taliban.

Many of the Iraqis most likely cheered Saddam's fall, but they have the most vivid memories of 1991. In the aftermath of Desert Storm, the Shiites rose among all others. Shiites, like all followers, are cautious to embrace the coalition too soon. They, undoubtedly, were to be sure that Operation Iraqi Freedom meant what it said.

Just prior to the summit meeting of the United Nations, the French and the Germans were against us leading a force into Saddam's palace. Against argument and more compliance, the three leaders of this about–to–be–war were the U.S., Spain and England. The controversy wrangled on to a surprise engagement on the 21ˢᵗ of March, 2003. The intelligence force, or intell (intellist), nebula, trailor, emancipate, lapse and loyal, found evidence that the ruler of Iraq and his sons were to be in a certain place outside of Baghdad. The super intell finding saw the President of the United States jumping and, therefore, the skies were filled with Tomahawk missiles and laser guided munitions. Thus led the breakthrough by Marines, Army and the British forces into Iraq, which started the road to Baghdad.

The public face of President Bush at war is composed and particularly restraint. Usually surrounded by military

Iraq

personnel, his is always in a particular mode, but those choreographed glimpses of the Commander–in–Chief's persona don't reveal all that is happening. Yes, the strain of this was palpable. Hard on himself, and yet, he is frustrated when generals who are not in direct dealings or members of his team of elite express doubts about our strategy. Some vehemently concerned on sticking with the planned was the plan.

Will the infamous 16 words from President Bush's State of the Union message spelled finis? The best answer is Iraq. The controversy exists because of airwaves from Iraq convey news of American soldiers ill–killed in ambushes and assassinations. The frank admission that the US finds itself in a guerilla war may have surprised Americans, or even policy makers. Now, there is a lot of reading going on into scenes of Iraqis cheering the arrival of the US in Baghdad. Saddam clearly retains significant numbers of loyalists to make life miserable for the occupying forces. He probably will not succeed, but the intervention in Iraq is proving more and more difficult and expensive and the intervention in the bulk ants.

Now that's the political problem. If every day's front page included stories of the smooth transition to democracy and conveyed happy announcements from the Secretary of Defense on down, this would be good news. Now the President's January words would attract little scrutiny. If the Americans and the British were to find concrete evidence of Saddam's weapons of mass destruction, programs from Iraqi scientists, military officers and government officials, explanations of what happened to the weapons of mass destruction, and then the uproar would disappear.

The news from Baghdad remains far from dire. The reports are not, however, as the images appear as though Baghdad's liberation. Pictures of Saddam toppling to the ground and the tearing up of posters threatened to become vague memories. Our forces could be experiencing abut that inevitably would be anticipated by the public and policy makers alike — if it were anticipated by policy makers, then it would be easily explained. Or, if the US would be settling in for a protracted struggle. There is a reason many distrust nation building.

Neither congressional probes nor partisan gameship on neither side, nor even columns of print will hide Bush's fate. Events on the Iraqi ground will, as they should.

The President receives a detailed brief from his aides every morning. Throughout the day he gets glimpses of the nearest TV, with heavy bombardments in the south or elsewhere. As he consumes big pictures of the war, Bush has confronted criticism coming from people he believes are his friends. Brent Scotcroft, for example, is questioning the necessity and wisdom of being at war. Similar complaints occur on the TV from many retired Generals or Admirals who ran over this adversary in 1991.

The first of worry is the Defense Secretary and his unequivocal view on the subject of troops. Army Commanders have erupted to complain that there are not enough men to wage the war they want to fight. Many saw nerves were buoying the balls as officers compared Department of Defense counterfactual Rumsfeld vs. Robert S. McNamara who failed to quantify the gross military and political realities of the Vietnam War. One colonel believed he wanted to fight a cheap war. He got what he wanted. As the Army V Corps Commander once said, "The military faces the likelihood of a stronger war than anticipated."

The comments plus the strong tension in the bumpy relationship of Mr. Rumsfeld and Gen. Shinsiki, the Army Chief of Staff, have led to such arguments as:

1. What is the Rumsfeld design for war or, more specifically, what is his approach to transforming the military?
2. The quality of its troops and technology leaves the defense secretary emphasizing precision weapons to fill the bill.

3. 100,000 coalition forces are doing the job with 100,000 all in reserve. This approach was agreed without turnover from the Bush Administration's diplomatic efforts.

4. Several months ago the Secretary of Defense wanted to cut the army standing forces to 8 versus 10 active divisions. Also, the brainless hypocrite wanted to cut back the Navy's carriers to ten. This was as precocious as President Reagan cutting the armed forces by fifty percent after Russia pulled out of the Cold War.

From the day the 1st Marine Expeditionary Force, the 3rd Infantry Division, and the Amtrek force set forth on Iraq, they moved ahead with vigor. In the eyes of Saddam's head that "America can't take casualties." His strategy is to use guerillas — Booth Party Vietcong — to harass our troops and to demoralize our image. Saddam's use of "paramilitaries" are those contained in U.S. military uniforms or civilian clothes; when they let their guard down these Iraqi, Shiite Bosra fling off their masquerade and there appears an AK–47 blazing.

So in the first week of fighting, it has cast a shadow over this forecast. Southern Iraqis have shown our troops that the Shiite majority is especially excruciating gain, pain and harassment on our troops. This is not planned on the trip to the capital of Baghdad. Paramount in the batter is the showing of the convoys' progress. The rapid advance of American forces has left the spearhead of the troops over 300 miles from its base — the convoy filled with precious fuel and ammunition started to resupply them and due much needed maintenance on their M–1 tanks and broadly fighting elements. The convoy had reached a flow point because they were stymied due to Iraqi soldiers who had provided incessant ambush. For the most part, the Iraqi attacks have been carried out by small bands of soldiers who capitalize on blitz–type tactics. The only thing remaining was to call in the Cobra gun ships as they raced to counter attack and fly back for more missiles. The Army's service ground command and similar commands had stated that in the second week of operations the overextended supply lines had stalled the U.S. drive toward Baghdad. For now, it could take weeks before any additional combat force joins or replenishes the force. What was unanticipated, not planned or even thought of — demoralizing.

Other reports are the lack of toxic news that had not been employed on our troops the soldiers have gone through training, know what to do, and their equipment works if we get hit with chemical or biological weapons. The U.S. military savvy, protective gas masks, protective clothes, and boots with gloves, atrophine as well as pralidoxime are carried with them as they must be injected immediately for exposure to gas.

Baghdad was a target that was surrounded by many hospitals, and many mosques. The center of town is the Tigris River that is mounted by buildings of many of Saddam's loyalists and by government buildings interspersed with military buildings. Our airplanes have bombs that are laser–guided as well as the Tomahawk missiles, which are launched from submarines or ships.

With the United States in triumph over Iraq, the concept of lighter, highly mobile weaponry is the key to success of the 21st century. Although the critics of the Pentagon have ripped into the Department of Defense this scene was eventually repaired as the supply coup caught up with the tanks. Yes, there were blemishes on this victory. The allied forces were short of success at the outset. Law and order in Baghdad would have been more orderly offense. But mainly this was a greatest triumph for the U.S. It was the first time that the maximum potential of the "electronic battle" since the Internet was invented by an obscure Pentagon organization called The Advanced Research Projects Agency in the 1960s. This is not what the White House calls "one gunmanship" as the President starts up the ladder for next year's election campaign. Iraq is in a state of dear debauchery or anarchy. Just at the moment when the President has factions learn of being a statesman, everything is going the wrong way in the world's most combustible regions. Who has the blame?

Dilemma in this country has caused the Bush administration to fail to play for enough for the postwar period. The Pentagon palace has succeeded in bringing about the fighting of the war, but then what? Apparently, the Defense whiz kids and aides think that Iraq will emerge from the war ready to take on the democracy led by American officials. Inter alia, a month after fighting has subsided, this country remains a lawless law without the basic needs of sustenance such as electricity, fresh water and lack of medical need or Care — Iraq is headed for a symbol of U.S. maladministration. By and large, the President will have to think this one out, or a longer time will be required to alleviate this bungle. As if the field goal was not good since the upright left goal knocked the ball away, what has happened to the hunt for the weapons? Case in point, Senators said that hundreds of suspected weapons sites are still being investigated. The area covered in this sandy space is equal to the size of California — after being there for seven weeks, at least 100,000 troops are standing guard or breaking up Arab factions. There are several blow–ups that make a man break glass. Maybe the speed of invasion causes them not to use or even to bring them.

Three days later the search for weapons will shift to new sites. A newest blast of sound coming from Secretary of Defense will move a new team, U.S. team, which will shift the focus away from previous sites before the war. According to a Major General, the Army has this task and he will land the 1,400 experts who will take over from a smaller military team. So, in essence, the search for weapons, biological, etc., will continue with only 200 of 900 "suspect sites" without finding any combative devices.

Of all of the mechanisms sent to Iraq for convoy protection or any other reason is a "troop killer." With more than 130,000 men spread between central and northern Iraq, the insurgency is having a field day holding roadside attacks on predictable convoy routes. The increase of sophisticated tactics in guerrillas attacks have made mince meat out of the use of armored or "heavy" Humvees.

A report by the 101st Airborne Division recommends the use of a .50 caliber machine gun in the rear. However, U.S. Intelligence and other convoy commanders were to provide a machine gun mounted inside a protective turret.

Virtually all escorts must be considered possible targets. The first sign is when they spot an Iraqi speaking on a cell phone as they transit along the road. Guerrillas tend to attack the rear vehicle, or shoot for the front windshield or the thin–skinned side doors of the non–armored Humvees. In another case, the attack of small arms fire normally leads to rocket–propelled grenades from the opposite side of the road. Another favored tactic involves a device called improvised explosive devices (IED) made of artillery rounds, plastic wads of hospital reaction or a mixture of fertilizer and diesel fuel.

In view of this the following has been recommended:

- Once an attack begins, speed up and maneuver and return fire.
- Install improvised protection on the sides and floors, i.e. sandbags.
- Trucks and Humvees remove doors and make it easy to shoot back.

"Why do we soldiers have to dig through local landfills for pieces of scrap metal and compromised ballistic glass to up–armor our vehicles?" a soldier asked when the Secretary of Defense visited Kuwait on December 9, 2004. This true statement has left the Army and the Secretary of Defense flat on their behinds. This commercial company has not done what should have been done in the past twelve months. The 278th Regiment Combat Team is going to drive north inside of Iraq for a year, but he put it so bluntly in a prominent forum. It is a fact that soldiers almost daily are maimed or killed by this fallacious unarmed Humvee without extra defensive cover.

CHAPTER 13

SECURING THE HOMELAND

Our nation has suffered a painful dilemma on September 11, 2001, and the immunity or self–centered evil enemies have led us to the openness of the terrorist. The worst of these is target number, one which any of the factions can reap deviation. A new wave involving weapons can and will affect our great country.

Today's terrorists are geared to strike anywhere, any time or any place. The terrorist threat to America takes all kinds or many ways a CIA agent can derive. We can never be sure we have them, but we cannot be over–confident in our views. Al Qaeda is not just the answer, but a combination of evil groups is the correct answer.

There are two inescapable identities about the violence in the 21st century:

First, our freedom, our openness, our beautiful cities
and skyscrapers, or our transportation systems cause
our mass system to be vulnerable to the masses.
Second, the ability to launch destructive attacks
that curtail populations and critical infrastructure
increases more with each passing year. In essence,
this is a problem Americans should adjust to.

Homeland Security has received higher priority as it has
begun to ripple through our country. Our nation has come to
the conclusion that we must involve the Federal Government
to plan and initiate new programs to make our homeland more
secure.

After the first plane demolished the World Trade Center,
every American citizen was up in arms. Lives were lost, some
flew combat patrols over our cities, and others boldly wore an
American flag in our lapel. Financially, a settlement of $10.5
billion was allotted to homeland security, which caused the
Federal government to:

• Increase the number of sky marshals on domestic
aircraft;
• Increase anthrax or other bacterial medication;
• Stop bioterrorism and other emergencies related
from additional terrorism;
• Patrol the approaches to our ports and harbors;
• Find a way to sort out and destroy anthrax bacteria;
• Employ National Guard at 420 major airports.

Since September 11, 2001, we have found other potential tar-
gets for which we must provide additional safeguards.
Airports, sea and water ports, nuclear facilities, dams, electric
plants, and biological and chemical units bring up the list.
High–profile events, such as the Olympics and the Super
Bowl, are candidates for terrorists. Finally, the President

ordered the Director of the Office of Homeland Security to develop and activate this wide–ranging as soon as possible.

Backed by giant boulder infusions, the cold Northeast keeps the monster waves of the Atlantic Ocean at bay. With the monies allocated and watching for new highly revised ideal systems that protect our Homeland Defense. Granted, we are banking all our assets on the armed forces, but the United States Coast Guard will take the leading edge. From being on watch of the Brooklyn Bridge or the thousands of representatives who comb the missions across 4 million square miles of waterways which stretch from Maine to Texas. The U.S. Coast Guard is vital to America today as it endeavors to protect against terrorism. "What we do for the nation is for every citizen now…It's a lot more focused on national security (and) very rewarding," said the leader of the Coast Guard, Vice Admiral Vivian S. Crea.

In the immediate days after the destruction of the World Trade Centers and the mighty Pentagon, 2,600 reservists were recalled. Reservists work hand in hand with active duty Coast Guard to provide cleansing efforts in New York, as well as redouble efforts to establish the implementation of "sea marshals." The bottom line: eliminate terrorism from happening in America.

The missions are many, but these are the primary charges:

- Wartime intervention
- Deployed port operations
- Peacetime engagement
- Environmental operations

The Coast Guard is a viable component in peacetime, crisis, or in conflict.

The physical assets, for example, cutters, aircraft and land facilities, have been put up with for the last decade. Deepwater Capabilities Replacement Project that develops a system of orderliness to ensure effective and cost–efficient of all its Deepwater assets. Eventually, these systems will achieve and will maintain an integrated level that can maintain its task of the future.

In major ports run major tasks depending on the status of the cities. For example, more than two dozen vessels were turned away from the Atlantic seaports. Check points are accessible if time is not available to verify intelligence and recant or identify hostile threats. Major gaps in security in and around U.S. waterways have been pronounced "safe."

The future of today's underwater vehicle is the readiness of each soul onboard the ship. Today's submarine builders are reaching into an SSGN concept that carries SEALs within concise weaponry that quells the adversary. No way can today's force defeat our MK–48 ADCAP torpedo. Either in the littoral or at the depths of the sea, we have the stronghold of the world.

Future submarines must face threats that would drive them to transform to today's power of the now and beyond 2008. These builders will be asked to use the level of technologies to carry forth their capabilities throughout the world.

With unbound proliferation of alien weapons, future enemies will attempt to deny our security forces in areas of Homeland Defense. With enemy weaponry and low cost technologies we can counter their advance. Examples are mines, improved diesel subs with maximum endurance, and with massive critical nuclear capability.

Submarines operate in a hostile and dangerous habitat. All future systems will be tested in new accelerated missions. Future missions of the submarine are:

- Communications/Networks
- Sensors
- Mine Warfare
- Unmanned Undersea Vehicles
- Special Operations Forces
- SSGN
- Communications/Networks

Submarine communications are limited to that of mission support information, which lessens minimal command and control of the sub's commanding officer. Network Centric Warfare gives the answer of the total force by networking systems and weapon control, and leaves way for other systems to be generated.

Future missions will require an increase in band width and connectivity. The report is that subs, inter alia, communicate without depth/speed restriction with broad band to maximize the realness of data. Real–connection and reach–back is available in the modem.

Advanced data are realized with the use of narrow band systems. With higher data rate antenna with a wide band based and finally a buoyant cable antenna solves the two–way communication dilemma.

SENSORS

Submarines need a wide range of acoustic and electromagnetic collection data. Future underwater vehicles need advanced sonar to affect their missions. Several studies will insist that future carriers will again defeat the multiple mass of each threat that they encounter.

SSGN

The United States is presently taking four old ballistic missile subs for the purpose of making each into an SSGN. This type of boat can operate in unknown areas where it can strengthen other U.S. forces. The capabilities are amass with this operable system. It has 154 cruise missiles, 66 Special Operations Forces, and a SEAL Delivery System. This fortuitous system provides a higher degree of firepower and virtually undetectable underwater.

UNMANNED UNDERSEA VEHICLES (UUVs)

UUVs can permit the sub to enter and exit an area with danger is paramount. This system provides extremely shallow water, a thing of the past, while the "reach" is extended without the risk of the SSN.

Unmanned vehicles will first support Mine Warfare. Its covertness makes it a candidate for Intelligence, Surveillance and Reconnaissance (ISR) and undersea/environment mapping.

ACOUSTIC RAPID COTS INSERTION (ARCI)

Modernization effort is capitalizing on the Commercial off–the–shelf processing performance. The cost, applying it to the acoustic sensors of the submarine, will induce rapid gain in sonic detection. While using similar arrays, ARCI has demonstrated significant gain in our subs' ability to detect our adversary. Incidentally, this is the baseline sonar system for the Virginia class, which can be retrofitted to existing submarines.

What do U.S. submarines do routinely? Very quickly, let's look at the missions which are classified beyond belief:

- **Intelligence, Surveillance, and Reconnaissance.** Submarines employ multiple sensors and across the spectrum can give a who, what, and where an exposure of what's going on.

- **Mine Warfare.** In covert offensive mining this is the platform that will convey. From Underwater Undersea Vehicles, these offer all those collectibles that give an element of surprise.

- **Landing Special Operations Forces.** Clandestine insertion of SEALs is the way to foster stealth and endurance. Precise insertion and extraction of the force makes mission accomplishment seem simple.

- **Power Projection–Conventional Land Attack.** 16 Tomahawk land attack missiles, with 16 backups, pave the way for a submerged launch.

- **Control of the Seas.** A nation that controls the sea through power protection, it opens up 90% of ocean transport, which unlocks our strategic lifeline. In World War II less than three percent of naval manpower sunk over five million in Japanese ocean shipping. For a time this bombing was considered to be a deathbed of the Japanese state of armed conflict. Almost at the same time, German U–boats pressed the Allies to increase exceptional large forces to defend our sea lives of transmitting.

Modern U.S. submarines are vastly superior to any in the world. They possess the skill to detect, hunt and strike on the high seas or in the littorals. From its work in the Arctic Ocean, it is ready, yet able to combine areas with others, specifically the P–3C world, to sail freely on this circular planet.

- **A Survivable Strategic Deterrent.** A strong deterrent of strategy, our Trident submarines (SSBNs) now carry 54% of the nuclear firepower. Submarines are striving for more littoral battle space, which will improve tactics that will locate, engage hostile subs in the twenty–first century. Likewise, we seek avenues of being elusive and still being as quiet as stealth.

In the fall of 1998, a board published a directive called the "Submarines of the Future." This report tarnished the perception of cutting or downsizing the amount of U.S. Nuclear Submarines. A force level of 50 is not enough to "cut the mustard." We must lambaste those who clearly advocate that this favors what we intuitively call for the rise of a rival competitor.

CHAPTER 14

MK–48 ADCAP MOD 6

Anti–submarine warfare tactics are necessary in combating the littoral shallow water areas. Numerous steps have been employed to stop deepwater threats, which ended abruptly in 1992. Without a doubt, there is a need to test or verify that the present torpedo accepts this as a pertinent viable sortie. Stepping back to 1941, the Japanese used a wooden device to stabilize the depth of their torpedoes to sink the armada of the U.S. Navy at Hawaii on December 7, 1941.

The work at the Undersea Warfare Center was tasked to undertake this particular problem; shallow water. Bandar was the man chosen for the job, since he had accelerated since he joined the center. He and designated engineers went to the Pentagon in May of 2001. Many robust Commanders and Admirals attended the initial meeting, which set the stage for testing, evaluation, and final testing at sea. Clearly, the podium was primed, which meant the actual "dirty work" would be experimented/planned at Undersea Center in Newport, Rhode Island. Bandar presented the obvious factors that had to be analyzed before the follow–on tests should be undertaken. He emphasized that all recourses for testing, pre–run analysis would be tested in an onshore trainer that he and his clientele would arrange prior to at–sea trials.

The Director of Test and Evaluation had the last say, in which he hoped the test plan would be out in six months. Overstated, he insisted the future or present ADCAP testing be done in a collective side–by–side manner. The meeting suspended with many handshakes and futurities awakenings.

As cited in previous meetings since the Pentagon, several of the men had developed a computer program that would transfer to a computer image that could handle this open–ocean shallow water exercise. His secretary raised him and she had Rafson on the phone. Although not normally called by him, he answered. Apparently the family had gone to visit his sister. Would he be free to see him after work? "Yes, of course," Bandar said. "I will see you at 6:30 pm."

The door opened and there was Rafson. They exchanged greetings and spoke Iranian. It had been almost 13 years since they had known each other. Rafson poured him a glass of wine so they celebrated the words of Almighty God who justifies "holy war," or "jihad," against the Americans. Rafson asked Bandar what he was working on.

"MK–48 torpedo is having some problems in shallow water techniques. I will investigate, recommend, and test these techniques within 2 or 3 years," he related.

Rafson smiled, but he quickly stood up and checked behind each picture, lamp, and telephone. At last he investigated the phone with which he immediately turned on the stereophonic sound system.

"Since you graduated from Harvard," he said, "you have been programmed to fit in with the Undersea Warfare Division. Bandar, you are a brilliant technician who has won all including the leaders of the torpedo world. Your leadership and personal integrity toward your peers is notable. No one will dare your faith in God is blessed with the anger of the fatwa against the United States that you carry within your soul."

A smile spread over his face as he toasted Rafson. Then he began relaying the past as if working for a Gestapo; an unknown working in a surreptitious guise. He told Rafson that he must be a front–waver, not a terrorist by trade, but one who is deceptive. Right away, from the very start, his recording of tapes, which he handed over to him, one way or another, this could be an instrument that could bloom and foster into the hands of a hostile incendiary.

The conversation switched sides as the elder began to talk policy. Rafson began by detailing the sizable gang of Iranian terrorists in surrounding Newport, Rhode Island. Implicit in his tone, he had men in every key spot on the Navy Station. They were identified only by their job and the necessary functions of their ability. They were notified by a note, or something that would cause them to initiate a vital step in achieving their goals. They were novices whose steps began the ultimate terrorist attack. "Do you surmise me?" he asked.

"Yes, I realize what you are declaring."

Rafson again said, "You are the principle leader of this episode. I will need your plans for this project you are undertaking when you have that set. I would very much like you to lead all facets of the torpedo, including the actual dropping of the units east of Newport in the torpex testing area. I think this has been a flickering of light tonight, which will burn until doomsday occurs. But believe me again, no one of my family and yours is cut in to this connivance." Bandar nodded his concurrence.

Two weeks later the Iranian Secretary of Defense met in secret with Navy officials in Chan Bihar. Armed guards challenged all people going into this rapidly unannounced confrontation. The Defense leader was concerned about the operational readiness of the KILO submarine. The Navy Admiral justified that two of the ultra–quiet vessels were ready now as Tareq, 901, was undergoing updates to sonar and weapon fixes. Today the secretary proposed a task that would highlight the cause of Osama bin Ladin's terrorist attacks on the United States. The plan was to obtain the MK 48 ADCAP torpedo for use in Iran. Ultimately, this would provide a new threat to the submarine by making it a superior warrior in the shallow waters where the diesel submarine is dominant. The plans as of now are to:

1. Plan the elements of this fatwa.
2. Identify the submarine and make changes to carry one or two of these missiles.
3. Nominate a tanker, whereby it can fuel this submarine to/from this mighty trip.
4. How are the Swimmer Delivery Vehicles progressing? I want to know the distance, kilometers per hour, and, perhaps, how long two torpedoes will travel for two hours.

"That being said, let us meet six months from now and see the empty holes evaluate in this execution," the Admiral said. The meeting broke up and many were wondering if this could physically or actually succeed.

The Iranian Admiral set aside several statements that the board deciding the work loads for this operation. The first thing is readiness, something that should be paramount in any resolution. How should these missiles be placed aboard the KILO? This, plus a quadruplicate of unknowns left the situation inevitable. Within two months, the Admiral would be back for a brief.

These officers were led behind closed doors, which meant "High Security." Plans were listed on a bulletin board, with each detailing his individual scenario. After the chalkboard was full of suggestions, the Commander began queering the odd-ball ideas. In thirty minutes he cleared the vast ideas into one active meaningful list of what we had to accomplish.

Bandar and the members of his panel gathered around the conference table to find out what the pre–report of the shallow testing of the MK48 said. He set the stage by announcing that we were still here with recent security regulations set up in the building. It was November 2001, after the hellacious event of September 11, 2001. So let's make known this points the finger at all of us in this room.

Second in command, Mr. Mark Abernathy, discussed the general way one should affect a shallow hunting water depth. In a complex computer room we sorted out the remnants of the reduced envelope of the object with upgraded electronics. This parallels guidance and controls uplifting which gives us the approach we are taking to solve the intricate unsettled mystery. This brought about questions leaning toward additional expanded software that was needed for the fix. After two hours Bandar came up with helpful hints on how to solve the bits and pieces of computer lingo to surge forward to test this new technology.

A follow–up was a new idea brought up across the table. Mr. Hand believed that a new upgrade in the system, MOD 6, was a fully digital sonar capability that would help the torpedo operate in shallow water, but counter diesel submarines operating in the littoral.

CHAPTER 15

A NEW TERRORIST

Before the brief with the Iranian Admiral, the Commander wanted to hear the status of his superior mentality. This meeting was only six months ago and it had developed into a serious clearance edge. As we know, this is equal to top secret disclosure, with references pertaining to charts, etc, are brought into the guarded silent compound.

This first item to be analyzed concerned the plan or the route the submersible would choose. A chart was depicted on the hanging screen that detailed the true track of the sub as it left Char Bihar. It would then go up the Red Sea until it reached the Suez Canal. Each of the designated turn points were marked with geographic data and the kilometers to that point. The next chart depicted the Mediterranean Sea, where the sub would skirt the shore of Sicily and reach the opening

Iran

Iranian Kilo conventional submarine.

of the Straits of Gibraltar. The final chart showed the transits of the ship as it headed for 40–00 N, 060–00 W, which is off-shore of New England in America. This brought up a vast number of questions that were answered by the Commander. Initial tasking should be made with Russia in order to seem feasible. Plans to replace, fix, or new gear had to be finalized prior to launching. All legal info should be arranged with Egypt in regard to the canal. All sorts of lamebrain queries were brought up, but the majority of these ideas were fluff.

The second order was the identity of the silent ship. Yunes was the latest ship received from the Soviets. Although it got to Iran in January 1997, the crew was trained by top–drawer Russian crewmen. Many of the crew were still of the same caliber and were ready to go. All integrate systems were up and the Yunes had a new Commanding Officer aboard. It was feasible to fly the fly while in the Med. Once outside in the Atlantic Ocean at night, destroy all markings leaving it a no–nation enemy.

As for the ordnance onboard, the Yunes indicated that the size was excellent and the weight may be 200 kilometers more than our silver bullets. So, in conclusion, we found not a problem with one or two even more. The best way to take on the weapon was to sink the ship two feet so the men in the SDV vehicles could unload and pry the MK48 with men from the sub. This did not have any questions and the Commander congratulated the speaker.

The third ingredient of this important mission was the selection of a tanker. This was not a problem, but it would require sufficient fuel from refueling the submarine to/from the U.S. First the tanker should be ready to meet and fuel without any problem. The basic category is at sea in the Atlantic Ocean near the Azores. Analysis showed a nook near the northern volcanic island of Corvo that offered some pro-tection when fueling.

Last, but not trivial, were the Swimmer Delivery Vehicles (SDV), which would make or break this moment of terrorist completion. The SDV had been in existence for seven years and was still growing. We have several devices, plus one coming from the U.S. via Canada to us. Basically, the swimmer was designed in 1964 and was primitive at best. Improvement was attained when the two–man MK–9 with transportation space for two torpedoes. A pilot and a navigator plus four other men with individual underwater breathing apparatus were advised with weapons onboard. There swift and going skills were due to the silver–zinc batteries, which attained 4 knots to speed and an overall speed of 36 nautical miles.

In 1999 a new MOD–1 was developed that added the rising lithium–ion battery that promised an increase of 20–40 percent increase in battery capacity. So, splitting the derivation, we could rely on 46 nautical miles for round–trip compliance. The Commander was pleased with this assessment. He directed you to meet with him as compelling data deemed so.

At 0900 December 10, 2004, the KILO was about to set forth on the long journey to places unknown. Prior to the previous month, the Iranian government had sent a dispatch to Russia requesting several parts, including several engine replacements. The return was to go ahead and give estimates of arrival. The Yunes, 903, was prepared to go within a moment's notice. The boat had an arrangement of accessories covered and strapped down on the stern end of the sub. Also, just in case, additional sets of batteries (Indian) were tied down below decks.

On the fifteenth of December, the Commanding Officer called his troops together. He told his men in no uncertain terms that this was a highly secret mission and that they would know the significance of it when they were underway. At midnight December 16th, 2004, the 903 left its mooring. A fake camouflaged unit looking exactly like the 903 filled its spot.

With testing and all computer mythology complete,

Bandar Abbis set the Torpedo Exercise the fourth week of January 2005. All stages of the torpedoes were gone over time after time with 100% accuracy. The weapons had been brought to the Naval Undersea Lab by a Torpedo Retriever (YPT) from nearby Groton, Connecticut, about six months previously. Armed guards followed them with Coast Guard boats paralleling either side. After securing the boat just outside the facility, the MK–48s were loaded in separate trailers and towed into one of the massive warehouses guarded with sentries and big iron chain fences. Long shapes were brought in. Eight were to be dummy charged and the rest were to be treated with the device that regulated the depth of shallow water desired.

After detailed testing and computer simulation, on Monday Bandar went to the facility and showed his identification to the guard. He recognized the security guard and immediately started talking about Christmas. Bandar and elements of his team set up the weapons and worked basically on the dummy version first. They followed a checklist and soon they were staring at the culprit. Within two hours they fixed the first dummy war shot. An analysis from the Director of Test and Evaluation observed the whole evolution. By the end of the first day, they had the first two MK48 Mod 6s ready for testing.

The Commanding Officer came on the loudspeaker and briefed the crew as they went on battery. "We are on a secret mission and all hands will listen up to keep this a secret voyage. I am ordering that most of the trip will be on engines, 20 hours out of 24 hours, until we get to the Suez Canal. We will stay surfaced with the Iranian flag flying. Then, we will enter the Mediterranean; more on that area when we get there. That is all."

CHAPTER 16

BEHIND THE IRANIAN SKIPPER

During the planning of this test, Bandar investigated the large range east of Newport, Rhode Island. It was big and had several advantages over the Atlantic Undersea Test and Evaluation Center (AUTEC). Principally, there were some ongoing tests scheduled at the same time in the fourth week of January. After working with the Weapons Analysis Facility (WAF) located in Newport, a system was evolved to do the test without moving to/from the weapons test range in Florida.

The future of today's underwater vehicle is the readiness of each soul onboard the ship. Today's submarine builders are reaching into an SSGN concept that carries SEALs with a concise weaponry that quells the adversary. No way can today's force defeat our MK–48 ADCAP torpedo. Either in the littoral or at the depths of the sea, we have the stronghold of the world.

The WAF obtains data from the firing submarine over a wide area satellite link. WAF mirrors this data within a simulated background. The WAF initiates launch using the hard-wire–in–the–loop (HITL) torpedo and transmits telemetry data to the actual submarine. The sub launches the MK–48 along with the wire guidance commands, which may bring about evasive change.

When the player achieves contact, he initiates power–up, preset, and then launches the weapon. The submarine will have eight fish onboard, all set for 60 feet. The weapon is a dummy, but can be recovered after they have run out of time. This plan was approved by all concerned because of Bandar's valuable quality.

As the Yunes approached the entrance of the Suez Canal the sun was setting. Nowhere in their plan was the slowdown of the ships and tankers; they reduced speed to eight knots. The flag was flying and the skipper had been on the conning tower. Back inside, he called for his engineering officer, and in three minutes he reported. The Captain was interested in fuel, batteries and ECT. The Lieutenant said that the fuel consumption was good, and the batteries were excellent and in good shape. "It is imperative that when something suffers a delinquency you let me know. Understand?" demanded the Commanding Officer.

At sunrise the view was stupendous. The city was cascaded with multiple orange–red colors as ole Sol appeared. Finally, we could see the Mediterranean Sea. Clear of the harbor, after everyone had a chance to see the site, we dived and let the diesels rest.

Our first leg brought us South of Sicily and then we headed for the mouth of Gibraltar. The Iranian crew was sharp, left no stones unturned. After underwater, the Captain forewarned them that all stations would be manned according to regulations. Be on the alert.

Halfway across the western Mediterranean, the engineer had a meeting with the CO, XO, Operations Officer, and the Navigator concerning the modus operandi. Planner of power, he gave the status of the total diesel fuel to date along with the present battery reading. He concentrated on the upkeep of the battery when we were snorkeling. His maintainers were sure that the batteries would last until the Azores, where we would refuel. After, the Captain looked over the snort vs. battery, where he thought we should use our diesel power more to reach the Atlantic Ocean. "How are our swimmers holding out?" said the Skipper.

"They are exercising every day and have fabricated a running machine that keeps their calves and muscles in shape," added the Executive Officer.

"Down 'scope", ordered the CO. Just ahead, about one hundred and fifty miles, lay the entrance to the Mediterranean. The Captain just reviewed the darkness yet the number of ships that were passing in the night. There were many thoughts running in the massive brain and nervous systems of this man. He was running behind this intended track so he contacted engine control and he would snorkel to gain momentum. He began snorkeling on January 9, 2005 at 12:30 a.m. The ship was making 9 knots as she passed Gibraltar.

CHAPTER 17

PENTAGON 0900 HOURS LOCAL, JANUARY 10, 2005, WASHINGTON, D.C.

ooking at the other side of the world is the five–sided composition that beholds 17½ miles of walkways; in short, it's a 27–mile hike through the Pentagon. Heels of shoes decorated the wax of the floors, each moving toward the task.

On the fourth deck of the plant is the Command Center, which houses the Intelligence branch, which gives a brief at nine o'clock every morning. The principal coordinator of the staff was Rear Admiral Joseph Swain. He was in charge of a staff of forty–odd briefer, insiders (intelligence gurus), and plotters.

As the Rear Admiral reached the entrance way, a Lieutenant announced his presence. "Attention on Deck." "As you were," was the Admiral's reply and everyone seized a seat around the roundtable. Lt. Blevins started off by giving the normal status report on Iraq, the political drama, and the numbers of causalities, both Iraqi and American. The status of forces was displayed on the computer pen–pointer, which represented each fleet worldwide. This, plus other interruptions, carried the brief several minutes longer.

Admiral Swain then recognized a Lieutenant Commander Intel type whose name was LCDR Brown. "Admiral, I received a secret noforn message from the Gibraltar listening station at 0032 local time, where they detected a KILO Class submarine snorkeling at 270 true at nine knots. This contact was not noted until the operator reviewed the tapes."

"Commander, who sent us the message?" replied the Admiral.

"The message went to all NATO address and through back channel; the message was readdressed to us and Airlant facilities," he said.

"Have we got flak from anybody?" the two stars asked.

Commander Brown switched to the screen where the three KILO submarines that had been purchased from Russia to Iran. He showed the mechanics of a conventional sub that has less noise, particularly when snorkeling. LCDR Brown, who was a second tour in the Pentagon, remembered a brief during his fist tour regarding the KILO.

"What in the world is a KILO doing venturing into the Atlantic?" said the Admiral.

"I think he has an agreement with Russia to change/swap parts on this sub. I will find out after this brief," said the Commander.

"I want to know what the damn critter is doing! Let's contact CIA and NSG players to be here this afternoon for a rally–around–the–flagpole. Maybe they can analyze this more closely," said the senior officer.

At 1300 the room was filled with onlookers, especially the representatives from Central Intelligence and the Naval Security Group. Upon informed of this detection, the CIA used their spy satellite to focus on the submarine locations of the KILOs. According to the view, all three subs were in port. Additionally, one boat or more had been conducting operations off the Gulf of Oman; the deep waters of the Persian Gulf. By and large, these make this a watch over an area in the event Iran posed a severe threat to its homeland.

Naval Security agent said that recent tapes in the Middle East area explained a Russia–Iran agreement was to take place at the end of January 2005. The increase in tension was due mainly to the nuclear issue.

With that coming from the all–be–intellect, that introduced several academic problems the Admiral faced. "Who classified it as a KILO class submarine? He, our man–in–command in Iran, has he been notified of this scenario? What is the sub going to Russia for? And why, pray tell, is he snorting outbound the Mediterranean Sea? And finally, let's contact Ocean Systems Atlantic and see what stations might pick up this sub," he stated. These questions unanswered, the two stars walked out of the room.

The outgoing messages were sent regarding the use of the Torpedo Test Range on January 27–28, 2005. The precise coordinates of the range was delivered plus one U.S. submarine, a tow ship that would pull the extorp target and the ATF that was on scene commander of the range. Specific code names were involved with principal coordination via UHF satellite communications. Also included was the Weapons Analysis Facility, which coordinates with the sub for firing data.

The Newport facility would carry all of the leaders who were to view the test. Bandar Abbis, the head of the evaluation, elements of the MK 48 Mod 6 development, and

Commander, Operational Test and Evaluation Force would be onboard.

The submarine, based at Naval Station Groton, received eight MK 48s that were basically inert but handle extremely accurately, according to computer trails. The procedure would be followed before the weapons were fired.

At brief time the next morning, January 11, 2005, the charts were displayed showing the Gibraltar Strait and the guesstimated track northward, around the Norwegian Sea, and into Murmask. The briefer started with the position just outside the Med and calculated the course. At present, there had been no contact or any communication from the intruder at all.

The next brief confirmed the listening stations, of which one was manned in England. It was hoped that this station would gain contact. Most of the Atlantic stations would be monitored by Ocean Systems Atlantic.

The next intelligence chap was Commander Bud Higgins. Iran was displayed showing the three submarines moored side–by–side. "Admiral, our spy rode down to the Iranian submarine facility and, under darkness, he sighted with a Forward Looking Device, two, I repeat two submarines tied up," he said.

"Son of a bitch. Did they camouflage with nets, ECT?" he said.

"Our man in Iran said it was a skillful cream of the crop." the Commander noted.

Another Lieutenant sighted that the Yunes was the last KILO to be in place in Iran in January 1997. Soviet submariners were aboard, and they used this team until the Iranian crew was checked out. Problems concerning the battery and air conditioners were significant problems. According to the briefer, drumming up an abstract or an abridgement, a major refinement could be in progress.

The last man over the fence post gave a personal high confidence call to the analysis that made the initial LOFAR call.

We received this, a LOFAR gram that was flown to Norfolk and passed to Andrews at 0700 this morning. The writing was on the wall as the Admiral and the others present looked over the telling record.

Before the brief ended, the Admiral gave the following orders:

1. With CINCLANTFLEET approval, let's launch a P–3C to conduct a FLIR search based on the suspected track north of Portugal at night.
2. Trigger all access transients from Iran and query, if seen, marking anything unusual.
3. Naval Security keep monitoring for break of silence.
4. With the uncertain problem of nuclear plan, let's be cautious of this ship until we confirm it is headed for the Kremlin.

At midnight local time the skipper checked his orders. In one hour he was supposed to monitor a certain frequency. He was to listen after the broadcast. He conjoined with his communications officer and verified frequencies. The skipper wanted to listen in. At 0100 we heard the Iranian station giving the weather report. After finishing the weather, the radio reported, "39–00 N., 031–00 W." The skipper looked at the next point on his chart. The tanker would be in the Northern tip of Corvo, Azores. He submerged the communication mast and he passed this to the navigator for a quick change in his course.

Throughout, the transient from Gibraltar to the Northern Island of Corvo was tense, yet the crew withstood the hazards of being virtual slaves. The Commanding Officer of the 903 knew that they were extremely low on diesel fuel. Who knows when a battery link will explode with acid fuming from within its casing? According to the satellite fixing and the navigator's bug, we were fifty miles from our designated tanker. "Periscope depth," he announced. The sea was relatively calm, with the sun disappearing in the west. He saw Corvo at 338 degrees with little or no boats in the area. After declaring down scope, he made an announcement: "Attention crew, this is the Captain. In about two hours we will be looking for our tanker. We will be on the surface, but silent is the codeword. When we reach the ship I will pass further word. That is all."

The tanker was spotted by a flashing light coming from the bridge. The ship was at the northern end of the island, partially hidden by a sharp detached fragment of an island.

On the morning of January 16th the Pentagon clairvoyants had come up with nothing. The patrol force had spent 180,000 pounds of JP-4 flying the P-3Cs searching for the KILO, which entailed absolutely zero. The surveillance network had no contact and now these encounters would be postponed until the Iceland sonar stations could save the day.

Finally, out of the blue, a commander started talking about fuel for the KILO. That turned some heads. The analysis took into consideration that the KILO must be driving on fumes and, with their poor battery performance, they must be desperate. After drawing a radius of six to seven knots, this curve passed through the islands of Azores. This made sense to the intelligence crowd.

A large black cotton linen was draped over much of the submarine while it was taking fuel. The tanker employees carried the Indian batteries below decks as the crew remained quiet as they transported fresh food into the bowels of the sub. Guards were watching both front and aft of the ship for unseen disclosures. The swimmers were happy with their SDV on the back deck. It took some water, but that was immediately cleared up. The Captain of the tanker was amazed the SDV got this far. He gave another message that the submarine captain needed; the rendezvous point.

CHAPTER 18

A VIEW FROM THE SATELLITE

Amid the puzzlement of the Pentagon, the dare of the advancing terrorist as silently as the fallen snow and the light of the new day launched a P–3C from Lajes, Azores, where it had been operating for the past two days. The brief was to fly along the radius depicted to detect and take pictures of any suspected tanker. The first stop was the Flores Island, where no ships were sighted. The forward radar was cut on again and off after two sweeps. The contacts were marked and the pilot received the contacts as fly points one and two. The pilot altered heading to the first contact. It was a type that evolved into a freighter, apparently headed west. The next fly point was east of Corvo, Azores. Finally, this looked like a tanker. "Set Condition three," said the Pilot. With cameras on board, the plane descended from 2,000 feet to 500 feet above the water. The tanker was flying the Dutch flag, at ten knots, and she was on a heading of 140 true. This ship was reported direct to CINCLANTFLEET. The name was blotted out and was at least two–thirds full of oil.

At the Command Center the report of a tanker January 17, 0500 local that was at or near the Azores islands provided many assumptions:

- The tanker fueled the submarine.
- Where is the KILO headed now it has got oil?
- Is this some sort of terrorist activity?

Admiral Swain was prompt at the brief, which began about what/where/when is the KILO. The discussion unfolded about the tanker, which embellished many conclusions. In essence, we had answers that equated to Carter's Liver Pills.

USNS Loyal J-AG05, an advanced small water hull.

Finally the Admiral spoke: "This incident has boiled over to the point where we must contact Moscow in order to settle this matter. I will coordinate with the State Department, Homeland Security and CINCLANT to enhance a careful scrutiny of the east coast during the next several days."

Onward, the Yunes slipping thru the water made it across the Atlantic. The Captain was talking to the navigator with precise time of arrival. Batteries were again performing with expediency, making the sub right on course. January the 20th, we will gladly meet those missiles of honor.

The report from Moscow was informative, as the sub would be ready on January the 25th. This was as expected, but there was no sighting along the coast of Norway. If the projected speed of 6 or 7 knots was plotted from the Straits of Gibraltar, the United States boldly appears.

At 1200 local January 26, 2005, Bandar Abbis and the compliment of men from the Undersea Systems plus the representative from Commander Operational Test and Evaluation Force were aboard the Discovery Bay. This boat, which was only 186.5 x 40 feet wide, was a Torpedo Trials Craft that estimated and analyzed this particular exercise. This ship had onboard SHF (super high frequency), satellite communications, covered radio air teletype, and UHF covered systems. This ship was delivered in 1992 but it had been improved considerably. Also, two Torpedo Retrievers, YPT, were all ready on station, marking each of four geographic points of the exercise area. They were to tow the sled for torpedo firing and the other was for recovery of the missile. The submarine was a fast attack type that would be positioned at 41–00 N, 067–00 W. Also to cover the operation was a P–3C from Brunswick, Maine, to report any shipping, whales, and which may be used to locate missing torpedoes.

The morning of the exercise was chilly at best. A low pressure area had passed to the northeast the previous night, leaving a slightly bustling day. Connections were made with the retrievers and the submarine. Finally, the P–3C arrived on task. "Commence the exercise," stated Bandar at 1100 local time.

Cleverly, the Captain raised his periscope and noted that the Discovery Bay was still there. He made an additional sweep of his scope. "Down Scope," he ordered. The ship was near the sub, so the Commanding Officer ordered his team to embark. The special team went into a room, closed the hatch, whereby seawater was let in. When the room was saturated with sea water, the leader opened the outside door and the swimmers went out to the aft deck. They disengaged the sled and were off to the vicinity of the boat. It was 1230 local time by the navigator's watch.

The Weapons Analysis Facility was in charge of making the new mod of the MK 48 do its function. After three hours, the YPT had all but one torpedo. Finally, the attack submarine fired the final fish. At 1430 local, Bandar broadcast finex and congratulated all hands. The P–3C gave an off station report and headed to NAS Brunswick, Maine.

By 1440 local time the logs, charts and other digital data had been transferred. Bandar looked up and the Captain of the ship plus other crewmembers had drawn their guns. In Iranian, they said it was time. Bandar agreed. A soft knocking was heard on the aft side of the ship. The Captain and the crew shot all that remained on the ship except Bandar. Two swimmers came aboard and hugged them. The leader plus the Captain opened up the long hatch and found two MK 48 Mod 6 torpedoes. The two men, plus three others, lifted the long giant to the sled. Easy, however slow, the claps closed on one locked in the left side. Finally, each giving a hand, the mission was consummated. SLV was set, and the MK 9 headed off on a reciprocal course. Bandar was pleased and praised all of the Captain's workers. At 1500 local time the Discovery Bay exploded into many fragments.

Admiral Swain had spent several nights tossing and turning. After CIA and NSG collaboration, he finally decided that a torpedo testing range could be the target of this submarine riddle. Homeland Security and all of the Navy's assets were inventoried at 0900 January 27, 2005. The only ships/submarines were the fish–tester on the range and a Small Water Plane Twin Hull (SWATH), which is a second generation SURTASS ship.

So the Admiral contacted CTF 84 and CTF 12 to direct these ships to the given arc of this circle covering the exercise area. Operational Immediate messages backed up the acceleration of this action. Satellite messages were used to alert the VP–10 P–3C aircraft and the SWATH ship to be watchful at all times. The fast attack participating in the Operational Test should proceed to this outlined arc when the test was completed. Finally, when all had been done, the C–130 aircraft launched with the Navy SEALs from Norfolk, Virginia.

Back in the Central Intelligence Agency, one of the satellites was homing in on the torpedo range. The viewer noticed 3 ships and one P–3 flying in the assigned sector. After watching daydreams for two hours, the exercise was terminated at 1430 local time. At times, the submarine and the aircraft were to follow other orders, switching to new frequencies. While looking from the satellite, it noticed something developing on the stern of the Discovery Bay. After homing and enlarging in on this vessel, the instrument disclosed four men offloading a weapon into the water. This was radiated to all concerned via flash traffic at 1452 local time. At 1500 Eastern Standard Time, a calamitous event causing a blast of energy resulted in complete annihilation of the vessel.

From the C–130 eyes the detonation; what was left scoured the water. Additional tasking was being forwarded by Operational Control. First, the C–130 marked on top the wreckage and went reverse course almost backward to the suspected sub. At ten miles and 300 feet the SEALs departed the aircraft. The aircraft continued on and climbed to 2,000 feet to send the necessary message. The team was in place for the six Iranians. At 30 feet of water, the SEALs had every piece of gear known to humanity. Commander Ben Foster was their leader. Before launching from the aircraft, he briefed the team to form a barrier of 30 feet apart of the intended track. Eventually a fine sound of an SLV was heard. Lights flashed and the Commander brought in the team. They sighted the sled with four men trailing the two riding the sled. The Commander gave the signal and all the doors of hell were released. Silver arrows filled the sea as, in one fell swoop, the Iran SLV was doomed. Teams of two removed the pilot and navigator and drove the sled to the surface.

The USNS Loyal T–AGOS was returning from the North Atlantic from an OPEVAL test. She had the reduced Diameter Array streamed to gain contact on the KILO. By this time, 1630 Eastern Standard Time, the USS Shark was rapidly slowing down as it approached the datum. The P–3C, not forgotten, had deployed sonobuoys in the area without contact.

Admiral Swain was faced with a problem. Should he light off the SWATH? A quick call to the CNO and he was ecstatic with the resolution. Shark coordinated with the SWATH and requested a ping. Loyal replied and the noise was bellowing. The contact was eight miles from the U.S. submarine.

The Captain aboard the Iranian sub was wondering what that excruciating noise was. The men should have been back by now. Fifteen minutes more and…

The President had been informed, he granted the attack, and the attack left only an oil slick after the water erupted.

Diplomatic correspondence was unleashing either side when Iran failed to steal away with the new MK 48 ADCAP Mod 6 torpedo. Granted the SWATH ship had been denied the use of active information because of the damage to whales and the like. This action was waived to keep our country free from terrorists, self–governing and free democracy.

As the plot wound down to an abrupt standstill, there was John, the grandson of George A. Chartier, who triggered the Julie–like device that obviated a subversive attack.

EPILOGUE

Rafson Bahi was a proficient craftsman who mechanized and put on the assembly line a force that was capable of taking the MK–48 torpedo. Bandar Abbis was his stalwart agent, but carried out his allegiance to Jihad. His leadership in Newport, Road Island, reveals a chilling effect on the homemakers of this town. Rafson Bahi was sought by the Federal Bureau of Investigation and was caught by one of his kind who got drunk in a local tavern. Who is Rafson Bahi's replacement?

An attempt at a terrorist invasion was extinguished by the expertise of a Navy Command Center Admiral who believed it was prudent to pursue this happening. Yet, even as we paraphrase this topic, Homeland Defense force was not needed. Iran's terrorists sought the MK–48 weapon and were to deliberately take this object at sea and return it to their homeland. Why was the overhead satellite viewing the aborted takeover?

Numerous times the U.S. contingency forces were submitted to ambush attacks, leaving many casualties and dead,

191

adding up to 1,400 personnel. The Central Intelligence Agency was to protect these convoys but their hunt through satellites were pointed elsewhere. If the view from the sky sorted out the hiding place of Saddam Hussein, this operation would have been a turkey hunt.

Weapons of Mass Destruction are a total brouhaha when it arrives at Saddam Hussein's doorstep, despite disobedient actions of the United Nations. Nevertheless, he did not principally have nuclear intentions but he did have an ongoing chemical program, a biological warfare, and did maintain a series of Scud — variant short–range ballistic missiles (SRBMs) with ranges out to 800 kilometers. Dating back to 1999, Hussein has rejected the return of inspectors relevant to the previous disarmament.

Iraq's weapons of mass elimination are a vigorous concealment effort which has kept this argument at a peak. Standing in our own way, the numbers, quantity, etc. are buried in the sand. We have recognized this by watching Baghdad over the past fifteen years, redirected the United Nations approved trucks for military purposes into weapons facilities which were encountered during 2001–2003. Military vehicles were used to transport essential components to harvest an outcrop of venom. Some of these so–called, "wagons of death" have been found on the side of the road heading west from Baghdad with traces of biological/chemical residue. What happened to the twenty personnel whose doctorates in microbiology, microorganisms and chemistry that were on the leading edge of doom?

Even since the gathering of evil doers in Syria several months ago, the stream of subversive followers has brought a great increase in insurgent manpower. As we ink this parcel, men that are trained, wearing uniforms in some cases with protective suits, are exhibiting elite primed for the rendezvous in the battlegrounds of Iraq. This haven included the border of Syria and the desolate region to the northwest of the capital city. Before the outset of ripping Iraq wide open, these trucks carrying oil or some other provisions were moving strategic elements or pieces that form weapons. At night, when these trucks reached Syria, they dumped their contents into the sand for future use.

From World War II to the present time we have shown an egotistical, cocky view that we should not let happen. Hawaii, the surprise attack that crushed our Pacific Fleet, no ships were upgraded or were even built prior to the Korean episode, the Viet Nam catastrophe, and the status of affairs today leaves a veil of interrogation. The 567–page report rewrote the myths and accusations of the September 11, 2001, which was not needed in July 2004. Who was this and that, always deplores and instigates the wrongdoers. And from this date, we are three years behind the power curve.

The horrific number of deaths accumulated in any country where our Armed Forces participate should not be compared to the able–bodied men who fight for the Red, White and Blue. And yet, the Federal officials deny such a scheme, but swipe Army's Ready Reserve who still had some period of obligation remaining.

Back as far as August 2000, Dick Cheney pointed out that the military has been "overextended, taken for granted, and neglected." The Vice President and Senator McCain, plus a list of Congressmen, have spoken against "running down the military" when one triples our commitments while cutting force levels by one third. The Army today cannot meet monthly recruiting levels.

Unequivocally, an answer to decaying military strength would be to institute a Universal Military Program. Once an 18–year–old completes high school, he or she will be sent to military training for eighteen months to learn esprit de corps–inspiring enthusiasm, devotion to duty, honor, regard for others and teamwork. At the end of 18 months duty to their country, they could continue in the active or reserve forces; those who desire can pursue a college degree. Another imperative item is this repetitive Base Closure issue, which has already closed many bases that have adequate quarters and facilities which would handle this new style of training.

In summary, neither the Democrats nor Republicans will budge on this service bill in Congress. So today we are striking at the heart of the Armed Forces which, as directed, has withdrawn troops from Korea to replace men in Iraq and Afghanistan. Unless the manpower keeps falling by the wayside, we shall find the Defense Department in hot water with a thin force with no one to solve tomorrow's problems.

"How many roads must a man walk down,
Before you call him a man?
How many seas must a white dove sail,
Before she sleeps in the sand?
Yes, how many times must the cannon balls fly,
Before they're forever banned?"

"Blowin' In The Wind"
A Bob Dylan Lyric

READERS, TEXTS, TEACHERS

READERS, TEXTS, TEACHERS

Edited by

Bill Corcoran and Emrys Evans

BOYNTON/COOK PUBLISHERS, INC.

UPPER MONTCLAIR, NEW JERSEY 07043

Library of Congress Cataloging-in-Publication Data

Readers, texts, teachers.

   Bibliography: pp. 251–262.
   Contents: Introduction / Bill Corcoran and Emrys Evans —
Readers, texts, teachers / Clem Young — Readers recreating texts /
Emrys Evans — Teachers creating readers / Bill Corcoran — [etc.]
    1. English literature—Study and teaching (Secondary)
2. Youth—Books and reading.   3. Reader-response criticism.
4. Creative writing—Study and teaching (Secondary)   5. Language
arts (Secondary)   I. Corcoran, Bill.   II. Evans, Emrys (W. D. Emrys)
PR37.R43   1986   820'.7'12   86-17556
ISBN 0-86709-187-8

For information address Boynton/Cook Publishers, Inc.
52 Upper Montclair Plaza, P.O. Box 860, Upper Montclair, NJ 07043

Printed in the United States of America.

87   88   89   90   10 9 8 7 6 5 4 3 2 1

Acknowledgements

The editors would like to thank the following for their parts in helping to produce this volume: Ken Watson, of the University of Sydney, who had the original idea and has stood behind us and encouraged us constantly; The University of Birmingham, Mitchell College at Bathurst, New South Wales, and the British Council for fostering Emrys Evans's six months' exchange in 1983 with Jack Thomson, of Mitchell College, which enabled him to meet many of the contributors and thus make the book a more unified collaboration than it might otherwise have been; and Brenda Cox, for word-processing most of the manuscript and typing half the correspondence.

Permissions

Excerpt from "The Jaguar" from *New Selected Poems* by Ted Hughes. Copyright © 1956, 1957 by Ted Hughes. Reprinted by permission of Harper & Row, Publishers, Inc. and Faber and Faber, Ltd.

"Small" from *Voyage into Solitude* by Michael Dransfield. Copyright © 1978 by University of Queensland Press and reprinted by their permission.

"Ulysses" from *Selected Poems* by Cesare Pavese. Translated by Margaret Crosland. Published by Peter Owen, London, and reprinted by their permission.

"The Projectionist's Nightmare" from *Notes to the Hurrying Man* by Brian Patten. Copyright © 1969 by Allen & Unwin Pty. Ltd., North Sydney, NSW, and reprinted by their permission.

Excerpt from "The Black and White" by Harold Pinter. Copyright

Contents

Introduction

BILL CORCORAN and EMRYS EVANS

In the Preface to *Literary Theory: An Introduction* Terry Eagleton (1983) points to "a striking proliferation of literary theories" over the past twenty to thirty years, which has meant that "the very meaning of 'literature,' 'reading,' and 'criticism' has undergone deep alteration" (p. vii). The same period has seen both progress and uncertainty in the approaches to literature in schools. Till recently, most specialist English teachers have themselves been educated in a literary critical tradition stemming from Cambridge and the New Criticism. Classical literature has been taught through practical criticism, often with a strong view to the textual bias of literary examinations. In the context of an expanding comprehensive system of schooling in English-speaking countries, teachers have come to feel a major responsibility for the literary experience of all students of all ages and abilities. Simultaneously, the available range of children's and adolescent literature has widened and deepened enormously. What is needed, therefore, is a revised basis for offering and encouraging the experience of literature in schools. To this end, the essays in this book represent an attempt to explicate the range of theory known as reader-response criticism, to argue its distinctive relevance to the needs of young, developing readers, and to indicate how classroom practices might be changed to accommodate the insights offered by reader-response theorists.

The argument is immediately joined in Clem Young's opening chapter which provides a historical overview of the roles of both readers and teachers in classrooms dominated by particular critical stances. These stances, in turn, define the discursive practices of the classroom, and more particularly the status of the literary text within a triadic relationship of "readers, texts, and teachers." To

1

see the text as part of Leavis's Great Tradition, or as Eliot's autonomous artifact, is to cast the teacher in the roles of custodian or informed explicator, and the student-reader as a sort of cultural *tabula rasa* or embryonic critic. Within the major variants of reader-response criticism, the focus shifts (in Culler's (1975) terms) to "Stories of Reading," where readers are seen as active cocreators or recreators of text. Deprived of the teachable "content" of a text, the teacher's role expands enormously. She must focus (with Iser and Rosenblatt) on the reader's reported transaction with the text; she must recognize (with Bleich and Holland) the validity of subjective recreations or the tantalizing evidence of individual reader's "identity themes"; she must see in the text (with Culler and Riffaterre) the structuralist blueprints or story grammars which cast her in the role of "readability" expert and provider of increasingly complex text; and she must accede (with Barthes and Eco) to the perhaps worrying prospect that the very institution of "literature" as she has known it is under threat, reduced to "readerly/writerly" or "open/closed" documents which will be read quite differently by students with unique intertextual histories.

The specialized focus for Emrys Evans in "Readers Recreating Texts" is a personal interpretation of the writings of two key reader-response theorists—Wolfgang Iser and Louise Rosenblatt. His overriding argument, shared by all contributors to this book, is that the practice of literature teaching must be based on a coherent theory of the reading of literature, and be addressed to all readers, not to an elite of candidates for the university. Evans pays particular attention to the relationship of literary reading to the life of the reader, and elaborates in detail the implications of constructs such as "blanks" in stories and novels, the "wandering viewpoint," "negation," and the role and status of the common reader. He is particularly careful not to elevate unduly the status of either reader or text, since Iser and Rosenblatt "leave the way open for the world of the reader to relate itself to the text, whoever the reader, and whatever the text."

In "Teachers Creating Readers" Bill Corcoran insists that forms of teacher intervention must be based on four overlapping types of mental activity which seem to be involved in an aesthetic reading: picturing and imaging, anticipating and retrospecting, engagement and construction, and valuing and evaluating. Most classroom reading events will involve a four-stage sequence: (1) foregrounding and introducing the text; (2) encountering and reading the text; (3) the provision of "meaning space" for the student's initial response; and (4) collaborative explorations and the refinement of response. Corcoran is particularly concerned with the teacher's role in enhancing an oral reading, with the provision of alternative forms of response (the reading journal, setting personal questions, response graphs, diagrams, and visual representations), and with sharpening student awareness of readerly practices through interrupted readings, literary cloze procedures, sequencing, and providing beginnings, middles or endings for texts which have been tampered with in constructive ways.

Through "The Stories That Readers Tell" Robert Protherough assembles further evidence of the ways in which reading goes on in classrooms. His purpose is to illustrate a proposition advanced by Culler (1975) and empirically tested by Purves, Foshay, and Hansson (1973) in *Literature Education in Ten Countries*—that "telling stories about stories is a form of learned behaviour." Through some response-centred activities, "once seemingly original, now conventional enough" (writing an ending, describing "where you are" in a story at the climax, rewriting a story from the point of view of another character, and providing private evaluations of stories), particular light is shed on how responses seem to develop in classroom communities of storytellers. "All that is required," according to Protherough, "is a new way of looking at what students tell us." We may, for example, see in his characterization of "active" and "passive" readers degrees of reflexiveness which allow students (and teachers) to recognize productive "misreadings" and to jointly find ways of capitalizing on them.

How do teachers go about organizing their classrooms to put into practice the ideas and approaches outlined thus far? For Lola Brown the problem of "Rendering Literature Accessible" comes down to the question of "what is ours to control?" Most pressingly there is the issue of *resources*—how to provide for student access to a wide range of texts, and how to assist students in the selection of appropriate texts. We can also control *physical space*, and perhaps more importantly *airspace*: "We decide whose voices are heard, and by whom." Brown offers particular advice for the treatment of a shared class text employing the following phases: how to capture, preserve, and extend the individual response; how to develop initial responses collectively; and how to represent conclusions about a shared text. Her dissatisfaction with genre- or theme-based curricula forces her to a final question: "How can we design in advance a course which will reflect the notions of reader-response criticism, yet still have coherence and continuity?" The tentative answer is a reading/writing program which has as its constant reference point the "literature" that students write. Such a program would acknowledge a need for extended periods for shared reflection on reading, the provision of student choice in the literature to be read, and the development of criteria for teacher-selected texts based on a close examination of student reading and writing.

Peter Adams documents the conclusion of Lola Brown's chapter by focusing directly on "Writing from Reading." His central notion of "dependent authorship" goes some distance beyond the perenially popular, but still unexplained process known as literary modelling. To read in reader-response ways is to know that "not only can no story ever tell all that there is to tell, it *must* not." So Adams's active, creative, and engaged readers move into authoring, into rewriting their reading, as they imaginatively reconstruct a gap in *A High Wind in Jamaica*, add an episode to *The Sword in the Stone*, a continuation to *Z for Zachariah*, an epilogue to *Lord of the Flies*, a dream to the conclusion of *The Slave Dancer*, or rewrite the ending of *The Owl Service*. His teacher-reader's commentary on these "dependent" narratives constantly returns to issues such as their "revelatory power" and a mastery of conventions which Adams maintains was not readily apparent in much of his students' previous writing.

Clem Young and Esmé Robinson, in their treatment of "Reading/Writing in the Culture of the Classroom," provide accounts of the cultural and institutional histories of samples of student writing. After revisiting the notion of what it means to read with a sense of the writer, and write with a sense of the reader (Smith, 1983), they provide brief accounts of three reading/writing projects "which aimed to sensitize students to the problems that authors face in creating writerly texts." Young and Robinson's purpose, of course, is to challenge a series of assumptions apparently left unexamined in restricted versions of reader-response theory. The "shoebox narrative" and the constructed characters "Terry Wright" and "Thomas Albury" address directly conventional accounts of the boundaries of "literature," the notion of genre as unproblematic, and the issue of the "author's" immediate visibility.

When Leslie Stratta and John Dixon confront traditional questions associated with "Writing and Literature: Monitoring and Examining," they unearth three effects or assumptions of formal literary examinations: "(a) they carry presuppositions about the kind of knowledge to be derived from reading literature; (b) they require, and indicate in detail, the narrow forms of discourse which are authorized; and (c) they express a limited ideological position about the kind of world to be found in most canonical literary texts." The outcomes of the tradition are exemplified in a capable student's timed, distanced and generalized response to

Gulliver's Travels. We are left in little doubt about those qualities of the formal analytic essay apparently most valued by examiner/readers. But Stratta and Dixon's more constructive purpose is to lay "the foundations for an alternative tradition." To this end, therefore, they focus on emerging alternatives to the fossilized argumentative essay—on journals, on recreative writing where the student chooses an appropriate form, on a director's narrative commentary on a scene from *A Winter's Tale,* and on forms of constructive retelling which provide evidence of engagement with a text. They discuss, as well, emerging alternatives in the form of the literature question which will allow students "their own interpretations of what's going on, and their own reflections on the significance (of a scene) for the ideological meanings they are constructing." Finally, Stratta and Dixon argue for changes in approved texts and materials for literary study, acknowledging in particular that the discourses of radio, film, and television have as much claim to be "set texts" as the institutionalized, academically approved products of the heritage of print.

For Molly Travers, the case for poetry is seen as continuously problematic. In "Responding to Poetry: Create, Comprehend, Criticize," the reading/writing thread is further spun out through a consideration of the ways in which writing poetry (creation) is seen as a necessary prerequisite to reading and understanding it (comprehension and criticism). What, then, is to be gained from the writing of poetry in schools? From Travers's sources there are at least five outcomes: (1) "as a way of releasing one's emotions and increasing mental health"; (2) "as a method of developing one's own personal language and increasing self-esteem"; (3) to enable "less articulate pupils" to use "the language conventions expected in prose"; (4) to use "the structures of poetry" in the service of "appropriate ways of writing to meet audience expectations"; and (5) to learn poetic conventions, "through writing from great poetry as a model, including pastiche." Certainly the central part of Travers's discussion is a reassertion of the value of allowing thirteen- and fifteen-year-olds a free response, since this provides the only basis for identifying projective readers and the grounds on which adolescent taste and discrimination are likely to rest. We are left with a composite view of "the adolescent poetry reader," and a portrait of one "poetry teacher," whose furious attempts to counter contemporary neglect of poetry in the classroom leave him feeling that he is merely "piddling in the Pacific."

Roslyn Arnold's "The Hidden Life of a Drama Text" documents, in a specialized way, the reader-response issues raised in all of the preceding chapters. The process of "sub-texting" engages readers in productive re-constructions of a drama text so that their initial, idiosyncratic responses follow more closely the demands of the text itself. Arnold illustrates the process first with well-known extracts from *King Lear* and *Romeo and Juliet*, and later with some more elusive dialogue from Pinter's *The Black and White.* Her conclusion is compelling and to the point: "Knowing how to mean (in some of life's most important exchanges—like marriage proposals) means knowing how to sub-text." And for a drama teacher in particular: "Dialogue has become triadic (reader-text-teacher) or "trialogue" with webs of meaning interlacing all participants and all the language functioning in the reading experience —this includes the language used by the participants in establishing the context for the reading experience."

While the transactive criticism of Iser and Rosenblatt occupies pride of place for most of our contributors, we have acknowledged, as Susan Suleiman (1980) does, the vast range of audience- or response-oriented criticism, and consequently various ways of defining "readers," "texts," and "response." Pam Gilbert tests this proposition in her coda, "Post Reader-Response: The Deconstructive Critique." After a brief historical placement of reader-response theory, she grants three emerging and useful consequences of reader-response in the English classroom: a plurality of meaning; a plurality of response forms; and a focus on the reading process. Yet Gilbert is particularly wary of the largely unexamined practices of "teacher-readers" and the taken-for-granted assumptions underlying the student's "personal response." Her deconstructive warning is that private responses to texts and notions such as "personal voice" and "ownership" run the risk of ignoring the status of literature as "an ideologically constructed field of discourse," and that the "means of production of this cultural construct is what should engage students and teachers of literature."

These essays, then, affirm the explanatory power of reader-oriented theory, and in their range of concerns invite teachers to conduct their own explorations of the transformation of real texts by real readers in their own classrooms. We need to know much more about the reading process, about how certain texts guide the reader into advancing hypotheses and alternatives as she reads. We need to know how context affects reading and re-reading and how responses build up over time. We need to know much more about the production of "literature" as reading/writing within the cultural contexts of classrooms which see no disjunction between the activities of readers and writers. We need, above all, to know what further sorts of redefinitions of "readers," "texts," and "teachers" are needed so that "literature," however defined, can maintain its central place in the English classroom.

1

Readers, Texts, Teachers

CLEM YOUNG

Literature in the Classroom

From the beginning, our encounters with literature are facilitated, stimulated, supported, and shaped by those others who share them with us. Our first literary experiences are made possible by competent readers—parents, older siblings, relatives, and friends—who aid us in the realization of the literary experience. They are our first teachers of literature, and as they focus on our unconscious enjoyment of the experience, they share our joy. At school, they will be replaced by others—parent surrogates who have other, more explicit goals for our literary encounters, and quite firm ideas about how these goals are to be achieved. In time, they, too, will be replaced by other voices which will in their own ways and with varying degrees of authority and influence continue to influence our readings of texts—reviewers, librarians, critics, publishers, as well as those with whom we share the experience.

In schools, our readings of texts are monitored and modified by the presence of an *other* in the person of the teacher, and it is this triad of relationships involving readers, texts, and teachers which is central to an understanding of the ways in which readers are made and modified in classrooms.

Literature and the Liberal-Humanist Tradition

The establishment of English literature as a reputable study in schools owes an enormous debt to the work of Matthew Arnold—schoolmaster, School Inspector, poet, and critic. Through a series

7

of Inspector's "Reports on Elementary Schools" between 1852 and 1882, and in a number of essays of literary criticism, Arnold argued that

> We should conceive of poetry worthily, and more highly than it has been the custom to conceive of it. We should conceive of it as capable of higher uses, and called to higher destinies, than those which in general men have assigned to it hitherto. More and more mankind will discover that we have to turn to poetry to interpret life for us, to console us, to sustain us. Without poetry, our science will appear incomplete; and most of what now passes with us for religion and philosophy will be replaced by poetry (Arnold, 1888, p. 2).

English literature was carried into the school curriculum on a sea of faith, a faith that great works of literature could have a civilizing influence on the nation, could do for the masses what the classics had apparently failed to do for the privileged, could provide a bulwark against rising materialism, could compensate for the failure of religion to socialize and to humanize the nation. Culture was to be represented by literature, and English teachers were to be its missionaries.

The kind of classroom envisaged by Arnold's liberal humanism was one which emphasized the centrality of the text. Literary texts were to be regarded as cultural artifacts which exist as repositories of knowledge about ourselves and the world around us. The role of the reader is that of the acolyte, the uninformed yet earnest and studious individual desirous of coming into contact with the great minds of the past through their writings. The model for the reader is the Scholar-Gipsy, who rejected the class-divided world created by modern industrial capitalism for the imaginative, mystical insights of the gipsies, with their understandings of "the workings of men's brains" and their powers of social healing through art. The alternative, to Arnold, was awful to contemplate, the alternative to "culture" ("a pursuit of our total perfection by means of getting to know, on all the matters which most concern us, the best which has been thought and said in the world") (Arnold, 1969, Preface) was "anarchy."

The Reader as Critic

Arnold's view of the roles of reader, teacher, and text represents a model of cultural transmissiveness. The text, as the repository of human wisdom, presents "a criticism of life under the conditions fixed for such a criticism by the laws of poetic truth and poetic beauty" (Arnold, 1888, p. 4) and is placed at the centre of the experience. Teachers are charged with helping their reader-pupils become true scholars, "acquainting [themselves] with the best that has been known and said in the world, and thus the history of the human spirit" (Arnold, 1873, Preface).

The literary critical movement which came to be known as the New Criticism took as its starting point the autonomy of the text and its centrality to the literary experience. The New Critics so refined this perspective that elements considered to be external to the text (such as the "author's intentions" or the "great thoughts" of the minds that in Arnold's view created the classical works) were seen to be extraneous or irrelevant. The central question was to be "Is it in the text?" and in classrooms this question would be asked by teachers and answered by their pupil-readers.

Essentially, the New Criticism postulated a universal reader, an "everyreader," who can call the text into being but is freed of the human characteristics of personality, social background, and a life lived in time and space. In the role of the critic, the reader is regarded as behaving in an objective, if not scientific, way towards the text as cultural artifact. The reader as critic (and the pupil-reader as critic in embryo) must learn to examine and re-examine the text so that the "true" reading can be arrived at.

In an examination of the reader as critic, the work of I. A. Richards must be regarded as seminal. As a critic, Richards helped to develop and popularize the techniques of the new criticism: a concern for the primacy of the text, a more objective and scientific approach, and a system of close textual analysis. More significant for our purpose, however, was the way in which Richards focused his attention on the reader's responses to the text, and it is in Richards's work that both the notion of the reader as critic is best articulated and the problems of the model best understood.

In *Practical Criticism* Richards (1929) published the results of his examination of the responses of a group of undergraduate students to eight poems. Richards found an extremely wide range of responses to the poems, remarking that "sometimes when widely different views are expressed we receive the impression that, through some twist or accident in communication, different poems are being discussed" (Richards, 1929, p. 55).

From a new-critical perspective, Richards was concerned about the incidence of "incorrect" readings and judgements made by a number of students, and on the basis of his examination of student responses Richards set down those factors which seemed to inhibit a "true" or "correct" response. Richards, however, was also concerned with applying new knowledge in psychology to provide an understanding of the process of response, and in this sense he stood in two intellectual camps:

One camp was New-Critical: that is he believed in the funda-mental purpose of learning to read literature faithfully because he believed in the enduring integrity and autonomy of the work of art. The other camp was much more psychological, and in his earlier work, *Principles of Literary Criticism* (1925), Richards went to great lengths to describe and demonstrate the subjec-tivity of aesthetic value judgement. He believed in the necessity of developing a psychology of literary judgement. Thus, while recognizing for the first time that real readers' responses must be studied in order to develop such a psychology, Richards im-plied that such a psychology is normative, and that different responses and different readings can be corrected on the basis of that norm (Bleich, 1975, p. 111).

To regard the reader as acting in the role of the critic does, of course, have several real advantages. "Good" readers of literature, that is readers who take what Margaret Early (1960) calls "con-scious delight" in literary works, do behave remarkably like critics: they choose with discrimination, and rely on their own judgements; they are aware of the potential narrowness of their own perspective, and strive for a more universal view; they under-stand the need to willingly suspend disbelief, and postpone critical judgements; they participate as equals in the dialogue of response that the universe of printed criticism offers.

There are, however, other important ways in which readers in responding legitimately to texts do not behave in ways appropriate to the role of the critic. Readers are first of all people who bring their own individual histories to the experience of the work: if reading a poem, as Coleridge suggests, involves the very soul, then the responses of readers to texts are by definition unlikely in prac-tice to be accompanied by the kind of dedicated objectivity that the reader-as-critic role requires. Moreover, reading is a language act, and as all language functions within a context (social and his-torical as well as linguistic and situational), response to the text as language will be affected (even created) by the whole context. We may speculate on the responses of the Elizabethan audience to a play by Shakespeare, but we cannot experience it: the experience is rooted in the context. Readers also encounter texts not only in differing circumstances but for vastly different purposes: the reader reading for unconscious enjoyment, for revision, or for the purpose of writing a literary review is likely to respond in qualita-tively different ways.

The reader-as-critic explanation of the relationship between reader and text is ultimately a theory of deficits. Once the possibility of perfect response ("correct meaning") has been postulated, we are left with the certainty of failure. Since no actual reader will respond to the text in the same terms as the best critics (let alone "as well as" our hypothetical universal critic), all response is by definition inadequate. It is this sense of inadequacy of personal felt response that has been the unintended but nevertheless inevitable effect of four decades of teachers' emphasis on the reader as critic as an appropriate role for pupils in school.

Richards himself was aware of the problems posed by the literary critical perspective as a means of explaining the relationship between reader and text. He observed that readers would sometimes move from "a high level of discernment to a relatively startling obtuseness" and concluded that

> "Making up our minds about a poem" is the most delicate of all possible undertakings. We gather together millions of fleeting and semi-independent impulses into a momentary structure of fabulous complexity, whose core or germ only is given us in the words. What we "make up," that momentary trembling order in our minds, is exposed to countless irrelevant influences (Richards, 1929, p. 317).

As Allen (1977) suggests, when the normative position of the critic is abandoned, these "countless irrelevant influences" become important phenomena in our attempts to understand and explain the complex process that is any individual's response to a work of literature.

Responding to the Text

The perspective of New Criticism, while placing the text at the centre of the classroom experience, also provided the teacher with a position of considerable power and authority. Less concerned perhaps with guarding the culture, the teacher would become an explicator of the text's meanings and would offer a powerful role model to pupils by regarding the work as an objective cultural phenomenon. The pupil-reader would be offered the role, not of scholar, with its connotations of contemplation and retreat, but of critic, learning the techniques of unlocking textual meanings and internalizing the canons of literary judgement and taste. The metaphors of academic journalism would succeed Arnold's ideal of pastoral scholarship.

At the same time, however, a number of alternative theories of education were beginning to influence the teaching of English in schools. What they had in common, despite their differences, was a sense that it was the individual that mattered, and that education should account for the needs of and differences between individual children in school. The educational debates of this century have confirmed the centrality of English, but it is the children and their needs (rather than "the culture") that have been placed at the centre.

A shift in emphasis from text to pupil presages a shift in concern from the gap between performance and norm to a concern for felt response. The important questions become not "Why are students failing?" but "How do students respond? How might we be able to help their responses to grow? What are the factors that cause them to respond in these ways?" James Britton, in commenting on the nature of the reader's response to fiction at the Dartmouth Conference in 1966, put it this way:

> . . . a naive writer and a naive reader may share a satisfaction in circumstances which would only infuriate or at least disappoint a more sophisticated reader. Is this naive response different in kind from that we desire for literature, or merely different in intensity of feeling or complexity or comprehensiveness or verisimilitude? In other words, are such responses (and children must make many of them) the bad currency we seek to drive out, or are they the tender shoots that must be fostered if there is to be a flower at all? (Britton, 1968, p. 3)

The origins of this shift in emphasis from text to reader may be found, paradoxically, in the work of I. A. Richards. Richards, drawing on his critical insights and his experiences as a teacher, concluded that there was a need to develop, through a study of the responses of actual readers, a psychological theory of literary judgement. Such a system would be normative, and Richards implied that its value would lie in its application to the "correction" of "wrong" responses. We now know that such a system cannot be constructed. Definitive readings of literary works are simply not possible: what we find within a text depends not only on what we are capable of finding (or apprehending once someone else has found it for us) but on our purpose for looking in the first place.

The systematic study of the reader's response during the half century since Richards's historic work has emphasized the active contribution the reader makes to the literary experience. A number of writers emphasize the creative aspects of the reader's behaviour in relation to texts and see the reader acting in the role of co-creator, with the author, of the literary work.

While the New Critics were arguing the possibility of naive or innocent encounters with texts, that is, readings which denied the existence of reader experience, Rosenblatt (1976) was expressing the view that the process of literature is fundamentally a negotiation of meanings between reader and writer. She sees defects in both the interpretational model (the reader acting on the text) and the response model (the text acting on the reader) because each implies a single line of action. The relation between reader and text, however, is not linear but situational, an event occurring in a context of time and space.

Rosenblatt argues that this "transactional" model of the reading process

... underlines the essential importance of both elements, reader and text, in a dynamic reading transaction. A person becomes a *reader* by virtue of his activity in relation to a text, which he organizes as a set of verbal symbols. A physical text, a set of marks on a page, becomes the text of a poem or of a scientific formula by virtue of its relationship with a reader who thus interprets it (Rosenblatt, 1937, pp. 43-44).

Bleich (1975) summarizes the position when he argues that

The history of criticism in modern times says that explication is the primary act of criticism. Critics must concentrate on "translating" literature into some other more intellectual language in order for the literature to be publicly received. This more or less "scientific" attitude has created the dangerous and false impression that a work of literature is objectively independent and that it somehow functions apart from those who write and read it. The fact is that a work of art or literature must be rendered so by a perceiver. If Max Brod did not read and publish Kafka's work, it would have no existence, even if it remained indefinitely in some vault. It is not just the "message" or the expressive essence of a work of literature that is created by the reader. The work itself would have no existence at all if it were not read. This is not simply a formulaic application of the old "if a tree falls in the forest . . ." paradox; with regard to symbolic works, *all* aspects of their existence, function and effect depend on the processes by which they are assimilated by an observer. These processes are different in each individual, making the act of assimilation of special importance. To say that perceptual processes are different in each person is to say that the nature of what is perceived is determined by the rules of the personality of the perceiver (Bleich, 1975, p. 3).

The role model for the young reader that is postulated by Rosen-blatt, Bleich, and others is that of co-creator of the literary work. Indeed, Bleich has developed an extensive curriculum framework through which students can learn (again) to make their own sub-jective responses to texts, and learn (again) to trust the validity of these responses.

Bleich argues that the discipline of this subjective criticism is gained through the objective treatment of the subjective response. His course of study proposes four incremental phases which work outwards from an examination of the uniqueness of the reader's personal feelings towards a developing notion of the shareability or dialectic of communal or public interpretation. During the first phase, "Thoughts and Feelings," the aim in class is to understand how people respond emotionally and then translate these re-sponses into thoughts and judgements. When the readers are ready for the second phase, "Feeling about Literature," the focus shifts to an analysis of the characteristic styles of perception of each reader, the ways in which readers differ in their co-creation of lit-erary texts. Through an analysis of a number of response papers analysed according to the readers' perceptions, affective responses and associative responses, Bleich indicates how the classroom dynamic can shift from a conformist criticism of the text itself to a diversity of personal readings of the text.

In the third and fourth phases of Bleich's program, "Deciding on Literary Importance" and "Interpretation as a Communal Act," the teacher's singular authority is in effect replaced by the "social authority" of the class, which is an "aggregate (of the) values that are held by virtue of the group's existence in the first place" (p. 94), and which ensures that the audience for response statements is the reading community of the classroom rather than the teacher as cultural guardian or arbiter of quality and taste.

As cocreator of the literary work, the reader is regarded as inter-acting cooperatively with the writer in the joint process of literary creation. However, this cooperation should not be seen as implying a perfect or complete harmony between reader and writer. As Slatoff (1970) has argued, even the most tightly constructed liter-ary works can exert only a limited degree of control and guidance over even the most docile and sympathetic reader. Texts are read by human beings, and the reader's response to the work is also a response to the presence of the author in the work, an instance of human interaction that, like all such interactions, will be charac-terized by tension and discord as well as by concurrence and harmony.

The case for a full, active, complete participation in the creation of the text by the reader is also a case against the "detachment" so often recommended as essential to mature reading. Distance, argues Slatoff, *is* more likely to make objects and events in life as in art more orderly and more beautiful—"to obliterate discordances and blemishes." However, what we achieve through detachment (rather than involvement) is to blunt the edge of the literary experience:

> Insofar as we divorce the study of literature from the experience of reading and view literary works as objects to be analysed rather than human expressions to be reacted to; insofar as we view them as providing order, pattern, and beauty, as opposed to challenge and disturbance; insofar as we favor form over content, objectivity over subjectivity, detachment over involvement, theoretical over real readers; insofar as we worry more about incorrect responses than insufficient ones; insofar as we emphasize the distinctions between literature and life rather than their interpenetrations, we reduce the power of literature and protect ourselves from it (Slatoff, 1970, pp. 167-168).

The Reader as Recreator

In some ways Rosenblatt stands in two similar but different positions in regard to the role of the reader. On the one hand, she stresses the transactional nature of the activity, thus suggesting that she regards the literary process as a negotiation of meaning and the reader's role as essentially that of a cocreator. Elsewhere, she speaks of the process as one of recreation:

> Every time a reader experiences a work of art, it is in a sense created anew. Fundamentally, the process of understanding a work implies a recreation of it, an attempt to grasp completely the structured sensations and concepts through which the author seeks to convey the quality of his sense of life. Each must make a new synthesis of these elements with his own nature, but it is essential that he evoke those components of experience to which the text actually refers (Rosenblatt, 1976, p. 113).

The difference between a perception of the reader's role as essentially cocreative or recreative is essentially a difference in degree of responsibility to the text. Many would see in the notion of cocreation the abandonment of responsibility on the part of the reader to the text, an acceptance (if not an encouragement) of self-indulgent impressionism and "mnemonic irrelevancies," and ultimately the failure of an essential component of the literary experience, the transcendence of the particular and the personal.

The concept of the reader as recreator, on the other hand, suggests that "something" exists before a person becomes a reader through the act of giving meaning to printed symbols. The effect of this perspective is to suggest that the reader has a responsibility to transform symbol to language ("text" to "poem") in a way that does justice to the work: literary works are not puzzles, but neither are they inkblots.

The notion that each reader recreates the work leads us to a different perspective on the role of retelling in the literary process. Historically, "mere" retelling has been seen as an inferior response —a failure to come to grips with more difficult or more abstract concepts, perhaps a lack of sophistication or experience or even intelligence. Evidence put forward by Bleich (1975) suggests that this is not so and that retelling may involve a more complex response than we had hitherto suspected. To Bleich,

> . . . the essence of a symbolic work is not in its visible sensory structure or in its manifest semantic load but in its subjective recreation by a reader and in his public presentation of that recreation (Bleich, 1975, p. 21).

Recreation for Bleich includes the action of retelling: it is not so much a recreation of the authorial conception as a resynthesis and restatement in terms of the reader's personality.

Bleich's stress on individual perception leads to a shift in responsibility for response to the respondent. Readers must learn the features of their own characteristic styles of perception; that is, they must learn, through examination of their own subjective responses, to look at their own recreations deliberately and objectively. The discipline of subjective criticism is gained through the objective treatment of this subjective response.

A different view of the reader as recreator is offered by Stratta, Wilkinson and Dixon (1973). Starting from a language functions perpsective, they see the reader as being engaged in recreating "imaginatively the experience expressed in the abstractions on the page" (p. 70). Recreation, in this sense, is not restricted to Bleich's notion of retelling ("public presentation") but may be achieved in a variety of ways: rewriting from a different point of view, changing the literary form (say from novel to radio play), rewriting in another context, and so on. The aim is to provide a rich variety of experiences, a wide range of ways in which readers can exercise their rights and responsibilities in making texts mean.

The perspective offered by Stratta et al. is valuable in helping to define more closely the role of the student-reader within the transactional model of the reading process, and the role of the teacher in helping readers develop and mature in their responses to literary texts. As with Rosenblatt, the text provides the raw material from which readers, acting individually or collectively, create literary works. In Stratta's terms, all texts are scripts, and readers become producers of literary works using these scripts as raw material. The nature of these productions, the imaginativeness of their recreation, the uniqueness of the rendering of the experience of the text, will depend on the suggestibility of the text, the sensitivity of the reader to these suggestions, and the insightfulness and skill of the teacher in helping young readers give form and shape to their imaginative recreations. Texts need readers to bring them into being as literary works, and young readers need teachers to help them explore the range of possibilities in shaping their responses to the text-script.

The Reader as Spectator

The emphasis given by Stratta et al. to reading as the recreation of the author's experiences (rather than as a kind of idiosyncratic reaction to a symbolic stimulus) reopens the issue of the relationship that exists between reader and author. Harding (1963) proposed that a "quasi-social link" exists between the "maker" of an object and the "onlooker" who regards it. Harding's onlooker, or spectator, is not, however, to be regarded as being uninvolved, but rather as being a non-operative observer to the action. In the role of the spectator, the reader may be engaged intellectually and emotionally in the experience of the text, but nevertheless has no direct physical participation in its events.

Harding suggested that the notion of the reader as spectator might have important implications for understanding the process of literary response, and his ideas were taken up by Britton (1970) in the development of a functional model of language. Britton proposed a model consisting of three broad functions: the expressive function, in which language is used in an intimate, personal and unrehearsed way with a supportive audience; the transactional function, in which the individual acts in the role of participant and uses language to operate on the world; and the poetic function, in which the individual acts as a spectator and uses language to operate on the represented world.

Britton, like Harding, finds the origins of the spectator role in anecdote and gossip, elements of the expressive function. Gossip, in fact, can be seen as a less highly wrought form of literature: it involves a narrator and a listener, characters and plot. There is also a sense of shared experience, of enjoying "that it was as it was and not otherwise," in Harding's words. More importantly, the persons concerned are not using language to operate on the real world but stand rather as spectators to the action: they are involved, interested, surprised, amused, or disgusted, but they are not expected to take any action as a consequence of these feelings, nor do they have powers of intervention in the events they observe.

Britton's model is developmental, in the sense that the transactional and poetic functions grow out of the expressive. Expressive language is very much first language: it is the function in which children first learn to operate. As children's understanding of themselves and their world and the degree of their control over their world grow, their ability to use language grows out from the expressive towards the transactional and poetic functions. The origins of complex literary forms such as the novel are thus to be found in the relatively unsophisticated stories of children. Similarly, the responses which are made by young, inexperienced, or immature readers are seen to be "naive" rather than "wrong":

> Kate Friedlander . . . noticed the tremendous satisfaction young children derive from reading stories related to an Oedipus situation . . . but she sharply distinguishes this satisfaction from "a literary response," which she seems to feel must somehow have to do with art rather than life. I am sure she is wrong; these responses are unsophisticated . . . but they are the stuff from which, with refinement and development, literary responses are made. Again, at quite a different level, teachers using the "practical criticism" method sometimes introduced passages of literature paired with sentimental or otherwise second-rate writing, inviting comment leading to a verdict. Is not this an attempt to drive out bad currency? If, as I believe, satisfaction with the second-rate differs in degree but not in kind from the higher satisfaction, teachers should surely be concerned to *open* doors; as the pupils advance, other doors will close behind them with no need for the teacher to intervene (Britton, 1968, pp. 3-4).

Hardy (1975) offers a similar view of the literary process. She represents the narrative act in terms of "tellers" and "listeners." The reader in the role of the listener can be seen to be behaving in ways very similar to the Harding/Britton notion of the reader as spectator. For Hardy, too, the origins of what we choose to call literature are to be found in everyday language behaviour.

The man in the street who says that he could write a novel if only he had the time isn't necessarily a laughing-stock. Like everyone else, he is telling stories and scraps of stories every day of his life, assembling and revising the stories of his days into an informal autobiography (Hardy, 1975, p. ix).

In the poetic function the spectator operates not on the real world but on its representation. Hardy's contribution to this position has been to elaborate on ways in which narrators self-consciously represent and explore the process of narration: characters, like readers, must be "good listeners," lest like Don Quixote they cause the story to stop.

Audience-Oriented Literary Criticism

This recognition of the essential role of the reader in the process of literary meaning-making has in recent years shifted beyond the school classroom, with its pedagogical emphasis on developing young and inexperienced readers, to the more general level of literary critical theory itself. As Suleiman (1980) has observed, "the words *reader* and *audience*, once relegated to the status of the unproblematic and obvious, have acceded to a starring role" (p. 3). Although not overtly concerned with teaching and learning, a number of these modern audience-oriented critical perspectives do have implications, direct or indirect, for classrooms. Two emphases or preoccupations of audience-oriented criticism would appear to have particular relevance for teachers: the concern for the interactional relationship between reader and writer, and the ways in which this interaction is mediated through the structure of literary texts.

The contemporary view of the reading of literary texts as involving a dialogic relationship between reader and writer may be traced to the pioneering work of Bakhtin (1929). Bakhtin started from the view that language, as a system of social signs, carries within it the means of both conformity (through the narrowing of meaning to make signs "uniaccentual") and diversity, disruption, and liberty (through the capacity of language structures to promote multiplicities of meanings). Bakhtin's stress on multiple meanings may be compared with the later work of Derrida (1976) and the notion that multiplicity is inherent in the nature of language itself (rather than something "outside" the text that is "brought in" by the reader). Similarly, his valuing of the most open texts, namely those which permit the most diverse responses, and whose authors subordinate their voices to the "multiple voices" of the characters of the text, echoes the later work of Barthes on "readerly" and "writerly" texts, and Eco's (1979) "open" and "closed" texts.

Booth (1961) has described the process of reader-writer interaction as one which occurs between an "implied reader" (which is a role offered to the reader by the author through the text) and an "implied author" (who represents the presence of the author in the text). In practice, each real reader is invited to take on the role of the particular kind of reader "required" by the text—the kind of person who would find these things interesting, or amusing, or shocking—who would, in Harding's words, enjoy the fact that they were so and not otherwise. And in reading the text, the reader constructs an image of the kind of person who is telling the story, the text's "implied author." Booth's distinction between real and implied readers and authors is reflected in Prince's (1973) studies of the role of the "narratee" in fiction and in Iser's (1978) theory of textual blanks, both of which have important implications for teaching students to respond as readers of literary texts, because of their emphasis on reading as participation.

S/Z, Barthes's celebrated study of Balzac's story, *Sarrasine*, is usually cited as the archetypal example of the reader responding to the text through its structural organization. According to Barthes, literary texts are organized according to a system of five interrelated codes. The *hermeneutic* code is the system of puzzles and mysteries that invite the reader to hypothesize a track through the text. Balancing this process, and running counter to it, is the *proairetic* code, which the reader uses in retrospect to organize textual events in a logical order. The *semic* code is used by the reader to construct an image of characters through the use of various qualifiers, adjectives and adverbs, just as a mosaic is constructed from an assortment of individual impressions. The *symbolic* code is the code of antithesis, in which literary "meanings" are worked out through the juxtaposition of a series of opposites or oppositions. The *cultural* code is the system which is built into the text that allows it to be linked to a social and cultural context, and is used by the reader to contextualize the text.

The question of whether (as well as how) these ways of "deconstructing" the conflicting discourses of literary events, of identifying the voice of the work and the ways in which the reader makes that voice speak, are new and exciting challenges for the teacher of literature. Their place in the process of reader-response criticism will be questioned by those teachers who regard a concern with the form of the text and the ways it works on (and through) the reader (real and implied) as a return to that very formalism they have striven to overthrow. But reader-response criticism properly involves a study of the processes of involvement and participation, as well as of reaction, and, sensitively treated, leads to the development of readers who are neither left gazing at their novels, awaiting some text-inspired personal illumination, nor are they to be transformed into literary mechanicals, rudely learning to "cough in ink." Rather, it represents the means whereby young readers learn to respond, learn to trust those responses, and come to understand the processes whereby those responses are both required of and required by the structures of literary texts.

2

Readers Recreating Texts

EMRYS EVANS

Who Are the Readers?

This book is concerned with all readers of imaginative literature. Its authors also believe that that should really mean everybody. But as we go on, in this chapter, to consider what happens when readers meet texts, there are four points about readers to bear in mind. First, we need to be thinking of all the children and young people in the schools and colleges where we teach, at their present age and at their present stage of interest and sophistication as readers. The very first need—never mind the future—is that they should be able and happy to read for their own satisfaction and enjoyment in the present time.

Secondly, we are concerned with those same young people as they grow up, and with their older and younger relations. We are concerned with the whole population as readers.

Thirdly, we are concerned equally with both those who do and those who do not go on to higher education. The bias of attention in schools has sometimes bent one way or the other. Sometimes we find syllabuses which are obviously geared to the "high flier"; at other times the "average" or even the "less able" dominates to the detriment of the would-be university student. We need a middle path, with opportunities for diversion to either side, which will enable us to provide for the needs and interests of everyone.

Finally, we must certainly not neglect those who develop a strong preference for literature and see themselves as potential writers, critics, or scholars. As teachers of English, we are likely to share their enthusiasms, and it is perfectly reasonable that we should encourage them, acknowledge and draw on their interests and increasing knowledge for both their own sakes and for the

22

benefit of the other people they are working with. But we should not plan so as to forget that these will always be a minority, or that our wider responsibility is to the greater body of people, for all of whom books can be a pleasure and a challenge.

How Do Readers Read?

The idea, implied in the title of this chapter, that what any reader does in reading an imaginative text is to "recreate" it, has been suggested by many recent writers. Wolfgang Iser writes: ". . . the meaning of the literary work remains related to what the printed text says, but it requires the creative imagination of the reader to put it all together" (1978, p. 142). And in the same passage he quotes John Dewey as saying, of art in general, that "without an act of recreation the object is not perceived as a work of art." In yet another context, discussing the teaching of language and literature in schools, Stratta, Dixon and Wilkinson speak of "recreative" teachniques in the study of novels and poems (1973).

The basic argument is that, contrary to the assumptions of many ordinary people and some earlier writers, no work of art is fully "made" when it leaves the chisel, brush or pen of its original maker. It depends, in every setting, in every period of time, and in the mind of each individual viewer, hearer, or reader, on a re-making, in which that viewer's or reader's own experience of life is related to it, interprets it, and is sometimes altered temporarily or permanently by the encounter.

Of course, this recreative process is much affected by the context in which it takes place. The context in turn is affected by whether the reader is alone or in a group. I may, for instance, re-member that I first read *Othello* sitting on some rocky cliffs in the west of Wales, or the time when the gloom of the final chapters of *Jude the Obscure* was made even heavier for me by the fact that I was reading it on my own, in a very solitary house, while I was suffering from influenza. All readers will have their own special recollections of this kind, which will affect their memories and their future encounters with those particular texts.

But although we will read many books alone, others we will meet in company. Students may read a text with their whole class, and then the work becomes a communal property, so that both the first reading and later rereadings are coloured by the comments of other class members and recollections of how the reading was done.

In the 1960s, for example, when political satire first strongly invaded the British public consciousness after the Second World War, with stage shows like *Beyond the Fringe* and television programmes like *That Was the Week That Was,* a lively class of thirteen-year-olds in a London school was finding all this very funny and very fascinating. So we went back in class to some of the more accessible classics of the genre, like Swift and Orwell. It was also expected that we would read one Shakespeare play at this stage— probably not their first, but quite early in their experience of his work. Usually it might have been *Julius Caesar* or *Twelfth Night* or *Henry V.* But because of this lively enthusiasm for the political, we chose *Coriolanus.* Of course, we did not study the play in great detail, but they thought they recognized Caius Marcius, Menenius and the Tribunes, and, if they did not make much of the deeper implications of the struggle between Caius Marcius and Volumnia, they enjoyed the play, reconstructing it largely in their own terms and in terms of their own times as they saw them.

Three years later some of the same students found *Coriolanus* again set as an examination text for their studies in the final years of their secondary schooling. The new recreation was, of course, much more subtle, grappled more firmly with the problems of the text, questions of staging, all the relationships presented by Shakespeare, and the possible implications beyond those obviously applicable to the present day. And so, for members of that group of students and their teacher, who happened to be the same person at both levels, *Coriolanus* remains a special experience, referred to whenever any of them meet again, though the students are now in their thirties and the teacher is feeling retirement is not too far away! For any of them actually to revisit the play now, whether on the page or in the theatre, would certainly be to discover yet another experience, different from that of the third-year or the Sixth Form, but still partially informed by both. And so our reading, and our possibilities for recreation, grow.

Whatever our emphasis on the importance of the reader and the power of the recreative experience, we still have to account for the text as a focus for whatever we are doing. The critics and theoreticians of the twentieth century who have emphasized readers and their activity rather more than texts and their authors vary greatly in the standing they accord to the text and its writer. A reading of Jane Tompkins's collection, *Reader-Response Criticism,* will show something of this diversity of attitudes. Tompkins's collection and her bibliography are indispensable to any serious student of literary theory and criticism in the mid-twentieth century, and such students, and teachers who want to go beyond what we can offer here, will certainly turn to *Reader-Response Criticism* for further study.

Iser and Rosenblatt

Here, though, two writers and two books in particular will provide a broad framework for the study of readers recreating texts. They are Wolfgang Iser's *The Act of Reading* and Louise Rosenblatt's *The Reader, the Text, the Poem,* both published in 1978. Iser, though he has worked in America, is a European; his book was first published in German, and is rooted in the phenomenological viewpoints of Husserl and Ingarden. Rosenblatt is an American, though she has studied in Europe. Her first book, *Literature as Exploration,* was published in 1937, and the later volume is a very consistent successor to it. Yet for all the disparities between their backgrounds and history, there is much in common between these two writers, and we will go on to look at some of this common ground and try to draw out its implications for reading and teaching.

Before taking up the first of these points, though, two further reasons for asking our own readers to take reader-response criticism seriously ought to be offered. Firstly, in looking for a theory of reading to help us to teach other people to do it well, we need to find writers who seem to describe as accurately as possible what we think actually happens to us when we read a book. Here the writer of this chapter must throw up anonymity for a moment, admit his own individuality, and say bluntly: "I find that Iser and Rosenblatt describe, more accurately than anyone else I have read on the subject, what I feel I do when I read. And so I hope that it may describe what some of you do, too."

Secondly, there are many parallels between the observations Iser and Rosenblatt offer on the process of reading literature, in fairly experienced readers, and what other people have told us about the processes of learning to read in general. Among these are, in particular, Frank Smith, Margaret Clark, and Margaret Spencer/Margaret Meek.

What Is the Text?

Louise Rosenblatt, in her Preface, states most clearly the attitude to the text which is basic to her writing and to most critics who belong, in one way or another, to the reader-response field.

"The premise of this book," she writes, "is that a text, once it leaves its author's hands, is simply paper and ink until a reader evokes from it a literary work—sometimes, even, a literary work of art" (1978, p. ix). This puts the novel, poem, or play in the reader's hands into a rather different perspective from that in which it was seen by critics of many earlier schools. A sort of mystique which used to surround the book is removed, and so the constant and narrowing question, "Is it in the text?" becomes less restricting. The education of readers, particularly in the discipline known as "practical criticism," often appeared to assume that authority for a reading lay in the text alone, not at all in the reader, nor in the society inhabited by either reader or author, nor in the relationship of reading to all the other activities with which readers occupy themselves.

And yet, as I have said earlier, we must not play down the text too greatly either. Both Rosenblatt and Iser pay attention to the proper status of the text in the reading process. Rosenblatt's title, *The Reader, the Text, the Poem,* says something about her view. She discusses in her first chapter who *The Reader* is and how the reader's position has been viewed by different critics in different periods. *The Text* she has described in the sentence just quoted. *The Poem* is the product of the interaction between the reader and the text. The reader has to make the poem for himself or herself out of the text, bringing to the reading also the particularity of the world in which they meet. "The reader's creation of a poem out of a text must be an active, self-ordering and self-correcting process" (1978, p. 11).

Iser sees similar relationships, governed by similar processes. He agrees with Rosenblatt that there are three things involved, two of which they agree in calling "the reader" and "the text" (and their attitudes to these two are very similar) and one which for Rosenblatt is "the poem" and for Iser "the work itself." But Iser goes further than Rosenblatt in both mentioning and stressing what he calls "the virtuality" of the work. It is a term he shares with the aesthetic philosopher Susanne Langer, to whose work he refers from time to time in *The Act of Reading.* To call something "virtual" seems to be at the same time an acknowledgement that it is not altogether "real"—it lives somewhere outside the world of things we can touch and smell and measure—and a claim that it has some special power, some "virtue," beyond what the matter-of-fact words of the inert text can offer.

Rosenblatt has a little more to say about the text, which might help teachers to see how it could be approached in the classroom and in discussion with their students. She suggests looking at it as a *constraint* on the reader's activity, rather than as a *norm* which everyone should try to approach in the same way. "To speak of the text as a constraint rather than a norm . . . suggests a relationship rather than a fixed standard. Instead of functioning as a rigid mould, the text is seen to serve as a pattern which the reader must to some extent create even as he is guided by it" (1978, pp. 129-130).

So a text can be seen as a sort of starting point, which gives every reader an idea of the lines to pursue in reading it. But since every reader will bring to the text a different experience of life and different pictures of the scenes, characters, and activities which are being realized in a particular reading of it, the blueprint will never produce exactly the same experience twice.

To adopt this view of the reading process is obviously to put difficulties in the way of examining and assessing students' progress as readers of literature. If we cannot exactly agree just precisely what it is that each reader *should* take away from his or her encounter with a particular text, how can we judge between the performance of different readers? This is a point we shall come back to in Chapter 8, but here it is perhaps worth saying that, if subjective attitudes, both of the student and the teacher as readers, are an essential component of any real "reading," all we can try to do is to teach ourselves to judge the honesty and validity of different subjective attitudes, and record those judgements in our assessments.

What Happens While We Are Reading?

Another emphasis which is common to both Iser and Rosenblatt, and of interest to teachers, is on the reader's activity *while* actually reading. This is at least as important as what the reader thinks about the book when it is finished; indeed, it is perhaps even more important. In the second chapter of her book, Rosenblatt describes an experiment in asking readers to comment on a text while reading it. Their comments revealed something of their processes: phrases like "on second thoughts" and "at a second look" were common, and the move towards a realization of the metaphorical language of the text was a gradual one. Iser, as usual, puts it more densely: "reading itself 'happens' like an event, in the sense that what we read takes on the character of an open-ended situation, at one and the same time concrete and yet fluid. The concreteness arises out of each new attitude we are forced to adopt towards the text, and the fluidity out of the fact that each new attitude bears the seeds of its own modification" (1978, p. 68).

This attitude to the importance of what is going on *while* one is reading, not merely what one can say about a text *after* reading it, is gradually gaining strength among teachers of reading and literature. A recent article by Lola Brown called "Do I Teach as I Read?" (1982), suggests techniques for helping children examine the process of reading, and we shall have more to say on the subject in later chapters. John Dixon, in *Education 16-19*, gives an example of an English Sixth-form boy recording his first reactions to a reading of Blake's "A Poison Tree," while David Jackson, in *Continuity in Secondary English,* shows similar processes in action at different levels of the school. In experimental inquiries, other teachers have tried to make it possible for children of various ages to record what is going through their minds as they read books. Tony Martin, at the University of Birmingham, interviewed two children, of around twelve years old, daily for a short period while they were reading particular books, including Philippa Pearce's *Tom's Midnight Garden.* This is a book in which the gradual realization of the relationship between the young Tom and the elderly Mrs. Bartholomew, mediated through Tom's nightly journeys into the past of the garden at Mrs. Bartholomew's house, can proceed very differently for different readers. The final recognition that Mrs. Bartholomew is indeed the Hattie whom Tom has met in the garden can be a total surprise to some readers, a delighted confirmation of earlier suspicions for others, or a partial modification of different expectations for others. In any case, the young people in this study each showed their own course of thought, none of which could be called "wrong," though each was different (Martin, 1985).

Relating Our Lives to Our Reading

Sharon, in Donald Fry's book *Children Talk About Books* (1985), calls reading "experiencing something but you haven't actually lived through it." Another way of looking at what goes on when you are reading, which interests most of the reader-response critics, is to consider how we relate this experience which we have not actually lived through with what we have actually lived through in our lives. Up to a point, it must be true that we make sense of what we read partly through a comparison between what the text is proposing to us and what we know directly from our own living. The failure to take full account of this vital element in a full reading experience has often been a weakness in the attitudes of teachers who take their view of reading from the so-called

New Criticism and the Cambridge school of F. R. and Q. D. Leavis and their followers. Both these schools of criticism seemed to start from an assumption of a commonality of experience in readers, as if we must all have led much the same sorts of lives as they themselves chanced or chose to lead, shared their views on most things, and read the same books. Quite obviously this cannot be true of children, and only rarely will it be true of adults, unless they too happen to be literary scholars of a rather special kind.

Rosenblatt and Iser leave the way open for the world of the reader to relate itself to the text, whoever the reader is and whatever the text. Rosenblatt shows how reading "[builds] into the raw material of the literary process itself the particular world of the reader" (1978, p. 11). Iser sets out to balance "the reader's own disposition" with "the role prescribed by the text," and says: "if [the former] were to disappear totally, we should simply forget all the experiences which we are constantly bringing into play as we read—experiences which are responsible for the many different ways in which people fulfill the reader's role set out by the text. And even though we may lose awareness of these experiences while we read, we are still guided by them unconsciously, and by the end of our reading we are liable consciously to want to incorporate the new experience into our own store of knowledge" (1978, p. 37). And this obviously takes us a step further, too, into the realm in which the experience of the world which we derive from literature plays a part in the totality of our knowledge of life, alongside what comes from "actually living through it."

This relatin' of our own world to the world of the text partly accounts for some texts being easier and some more difficult for us to read. A child brought up on a narrow coastal plain closely backed by mountains, where the rivers all run rapidly to the sea, will find it difficult to imagine the slow-running Thames of Kenneth Grahame, where "messing about in boats" is the thing to do on the river. But the same child, who can watch each day as he walks to school the changing patterns of the clouds on the mountains, will relish the experiences of Bilbo and the dwarves in the Misty Mountains of Tolkien's *The Hobbit* even more powerfully and directly than his lowland contemporary.

Meanings and Images

We suggested earlier that one reason for asking teachers to take an interest in reader-response criticism was that it often agreed in its view of reading with authorities on the reading process itself.

One of these, Frank Smith, has often stressed that too much emphasis on the ability to decipher individual letters and words is counterproductive in teaching non-readers how to read. In a list of "Easy Ways to Make Learning to Read Difficult," he includes the tendency to "insist on word-perfect reading" (1978, p. 139). And elsewhere he writes a sentence which Iser quotes: "Meaning is at a level of language where words do not belong" (1971, p. 195). What both Iser and Rosenblatt make clear is that in the successful reading of imaginative literature one thing which has to happen is that words turn into images in the reader's mind. It is a transformation with which some readers seem to find no difficulty at all right from the start, but for others, perhaps over-concerned with the mechanics of the reading process, it seems to provide great problems, and for them we need to find ways of helping.

And we must not assume that all images are necessarily visual. Good writing will summon up images of sound, smell, and all the other senses, as well as of sight, and some more strongly for some readers than others. That our own imagining is never identical with other people's is evident to everyone from the experience of seeing a film or a television version of a book we have read for ourselves. Occasionally we may find the experience satisfactory; at other times we wish we had never looked at it, but stuck to our own version. In either case, it will not be the same: how could it?

Besides, as Donald Fry says, the imaging is "for ever being revised." This is a major consideration in Iser's account of the reading process. "The reader's communication with the text," he writes, "is a dynamic process of self-correction. . . . It is cybernetic in nature as it involves a sequence of changing situational frames; smaller units constantly merge into bigger ones, so that meaning gathers meaning in a kind of snowballing process" (1978, p. 67). Enjoying reading and obtaining the fullest value from what we are offered in major works of literature depends very much on our ability and willingness to revise one set of impressions constantly in the light of what we learn as we read on. If a reader comes to a work with strong prejudices for or against some particular point of view expressed in it, he may well either not notice or reject its invitations to modify that point of view. Iser illustrates this by reference to the character of Thwackum, in Fielding's *Tom Jones.* Thwackum is an orthodox theologian in terms of the Anglicanism of Fielding's day, but he comes to represent "the human mind as a sink of iniquity." However, if a reader comes to the novel with a strong bias towards orthodox Anglicanism, he will find it very much more difficult, perhaps even impossible, to accept this reading of Thwackum. Aidan Chambers seems to suggest that the child reader finds it more difficult than the adult to make adjustments of this sort (Chambers, 1985, pp. 36–37), but this is not necessarily so at all. If in certain simple moral areas children tend to be more narrow-minded than adults, where other matters are concerned they are often much more open and less subject to prejudice. So both in our sensuous imaging and in our reading of the moral and other implications of a text, the willingness to rethink and revise is essential. The fully aware and adult reader does that at least partly consciously while reading: as Rosenblatt puts it, "the reader contemplates his own shaping of his responses to the text, a far from passive kind of contemplation" (1978, p. 31).

The Reader's Activity

Writing about the relationship between author, text, and reader, Iser quotes Laurence Sterne, in *Tristram Shandy*: "'. . . no author who understands the just boundaries of decorum and good-breeding, would presume to think all: The truest respect which you can pay to the reader's understanding, is to halve this matter amicably, and leave him something to imagine, in his turn, as well as yourself. For my own part, I am eternally paying him compliments of this kind, and do all that lies in my power to keep his imagination as busy as my own'" (1978, p. 108). And, Iser continues, "thus author and reader are to share the game of the imagination, and, indeed, the game will not work if the text sets out to be anything more than a set of governing rules." "The reader's enjoyment begins when he himself becomes productive, i.e., when the text allows him to bring his own faculties into play." The teacher's object all the time, whether working with very young children, older students advancing in their appreciation of literature, or even adults who have returned to evening or day classes in the hope of improving their knowledge and enjoyment of poetry, novels, or drama, is to make it possible for them to play this game as well as possible. And the object of the game itself is not to win—there is no way of winning—but to make the experience as rich as possible each time one plays.

Rosenblatt develops the side of this argument which assumes that the role of the reader is a very active one in a most interesting way. You will remember that she wanted us to see texts, not as norms, but as constraints on the reader. What happens when a reader reads she sees as a "transaction" between the reader and the text—John Rowe Townsend, among others, has described it as a "collaboration." In any case, the process is a very dynamic and vital one, about which she writes: "the reader's attention constantly *vibrates* between the pole of the text and the pole of his own response to it. The transactional view of the mode of existence of a literary work thus liberates us from absolutist rejection of the reader, preserves the importance of the text, and permits a dynamic view of the text as an opportunity for ever new individual readings, yet readings that can be responsibly self-aware and disciplined" (1978, pp. 129–130). This notion of a "vibration" in the process of reading compares interestingly and suggestively with a use of a similar term—"oscillation"—which occurs in R. W. Witkin's *The Intelligence of Feeling*. Witkin is writing about education in and through the arts generally, and is perhaps more concerned with young people as producers of artistic objects than with their reception of works of art already completed. Nevertheless, for him the vital activity is often controlled by this "oscillation" which takes place between an individual's creative impulse and the medium in which that individual has chosen to work. The impulse seeks to control and shape the medium: the medium in turn constrains and controls the impulse. The result is the disciplining of impulse through the attempt to express it in an appropriate form and through that medium. Witkin stresses the importance of this activity in education generally, and particularly in the education of subjectivity and the emotions, as opposed to objectivity and the intellect. For any teacher working in the arts, the biggest challenge is to start this oscillation, or vibration, where it is not occurring, to maintain it when it is, and to make it as productive and as valuably disciplined as possible (Witkin, 1974, pp. 23–24).

"Blanks" in Stories and Novels

At the beginning of this chapter we discussed the kinds of readers we were talking about and emphasized the need to take a very general and non-elitist view of the pleasure of reading. Rosenblatt emphasizes this view strongly, and sees her own arguments as tending towards this sort of attitude to reading. But before we return to this point, there is one major aspect of Iser's theory which needs to be considered, and this is his account of the role of what he calls "blanks" in the construction of narrative literature.

The idea of the blank comes from the field of social psychology. Wherever people meet and act together, there exists between them a realm of uncertainty and unpredictability. I cannot experience your experience, nor you mine. I form an idea of your idea of me, and that is what I act on, at least in part, when I meet you. You cannot know precisely what my idea of your idea of me is. So all the time there are "gaps" in our relationship, which we fill according to the situation and the conventions of our society. But it is the gaps that make us need to communicate at all. To fill these gaps in our face-to-face contacts acceptably, let alone constructively, means taking account of other people and what we believe they are thinking. If we fill the gaps entirely with our own projections, we become isolated, and communication fails.

Texts, says Iser, have a similar effect on their readers. It is of the nature of literary texts, in particular, that they are full of— deliberately riddled with—these gaps, which he calls blanks. Some of the gaps are in obvious places—between chapters or longer sections of novels, for instance, or between the scenes and acts of plays. More subtly, some authors require us to read, as we say, between the lines.

When a reader's mind works on the blanks in a text, an "act of constitution" takes place, and the text comes to life in the reader's reading of it. It is essential to this point of view that a work, as we have already remarked, is not so much the object we hold in our hands as we read, but the living experience that grows in our imaginations as our lives interact with the author's written instructions. The most important of these instructions, moreover, are found not in the words so much as in the blanks between them. And what these blanks call for is not so much *completion* (which could lead to all sorts of false and over-subjective interpretations) as *combination*. Novels are presented to us in segments—sentences, passages of description or dialogue, chapters. In each segment, while we are actually reading it, lies the theme of our reading. From each theme we try to predict the future course of the narrative, and to build up horizons for our view. Then we move on to the next segment, and the one we have just read becomes part of the receding background. We correct our reading as we move on, and so gradually build up the whole imaginative experience which comes from the meeting between our own lives, including our lives as readers, and the text in front of us.

Children Use Blanks Well

I do not think there can be any literary text, however simple, which does not offer the reader blanks to operate with in this way. Even language is not essential: picture books make the principle very clear, because each gap between pictures is an invitation to propose the next picture—an invitation which is quickly confirmed or modified by what the artist actually gives us. The effect of this is especially obvious when we turn the page, whether the book is like one of Raymond Briggs's, with lots of small pictures on each page, or like *Where the Wild Things Are*, in which expectations are vitally excited by a controlled turning of the page, as many teachers and their classes know.

In a rather more complex text in words, we have already mentioned Sally's reading of *Tom's Midnight Garden*. Early in the book she thought she began to see clues to what was going to happen. One clue was the village that Tom sees in the distance, outside the wall of the garden; another was Hattie's calling herself a princess. As Sally read on, it appeared that neither of these two clues was as important as she thought at first, but the fact that the clock belonged to Mrs. Bartholomew, and the inscription, "Time No Longer," began to point in various more fruitful directions. It is not, of course, the "clues" themselves that constitute the blanks, but the pauses one has in which to reflect on them. In this case these were tightly controlled and perhaps unusually extended, because by agreement Sally was only reading two or three chapters each night and coming back to discuss them with her teacher in the morning. All the same, there are chapter endings which provide the pauses, and the invitation and the need to think (Martin, 1985).

Sally was eight. Emma, aged twelve, read several novels, including Joan Aitken's *The Wolves of Willoughby Chase* and Peter Dickinson's *Heartsease*. Before she began, she was asked what the covers of the Puffin editions suggested to her. Of the Aitken she wrote: "It looks exciting as though it has deep down sources of evil hidden inside it," and she thought it was going to be about "the wolves trying to capture some people, but children set the people free and send the evil away for ever." She "knew" *Heartsease* was about children "because it has a picture of a horse on the cover."

The blank between a book's cover picture and its text is not a strictly literary one, perhaps, and yet it is instrumental in affecting many people's reading, as paperback publishers know only too well. Emma's predictions here are not quite accurate, of course, but her *combining* of the cover with the text would undergo many modifications as she read on. In fact, we see these combinations and modifications happening in her notes. She writes about Marge, in *Heartsease*, when she has moved some way into the text: "Marge is getting more used to machines. She is still uneasy about them and still thinks them a bit wicked, but as she has no choice but to go on the voyage, she is forcing herself to like [the tugboat] Heartsease."

In certain modern novels the blanks themselves become the theme, and the reader is confronted by his own projections in attempting to combine them. Iser's example here is the work of Ivy Compton-Burnett, in which the highly complex dialogue, whose words tell us "not only what would have been said [but] what would have been implied but not spoken [as well as] what would have been understood though not implied," obliges readers to ask many questions about all their own preconceptions of human behaviour. Perhaps one would not expect to find complexities of this kind in children's literature or in the books used in school below the most advanced classes. And yet the relatively recent field of Young Adult literature supplies a number of examples. Robert Cormier's *I Am the Cheese* contains in its basic structure a tension between the apparently directly told narrative on the one hand and the psychologist's tapes on the other. From very early in the book the reader is invited to ask how these two are related, and the answer is not given till the very end of the book— if then. Alan Garner's *Red Shift* uses several techniques to invite the reader's necessary participation. Even in what seems the most obvious area of the novel—the twentieth-century story of Tom and Jan—the dialogue is often so taut that we have to think twice about who is saying what and when, and considerable gaps of time between utterances are often left entirely unmarked. Like an actor preparing his part, we have to find them for ourselves and understand their significance. If we add to this the shifts, at first entirely unexplained, between the three historical stories and the invitation to try to understand what connection there is between them, we have a novel of very considerable complexity indeed.

Two other ideas of Iser's and one of Rosenblatt's need to be considered in this chapter. From Iser we take the idea of the reader's "wandering viewpoint," and the proposition that, complementary to the blanks we have already discussed, fiction also works partly through the "negation" of the reader's expectations. Rosenblatt stresses that the reading of literature is not an elitist activity, and this must be an argument of special significance to teachers in schools, where our aim is to teach everyone to read as well as they can.

"Wandering Viewpoint"

Very early in *The Act of Reading*, Iser reminds us how eighteenth century writers compared the reading and writing of a novel to a journey in a stage coach. He cites Scott and Fielding, and indeed the first chapter of the last book of *Tom Jones* has Fielding saying goodbye to his reader "like fellow-travellers in a stage-coach, who have passed several days in the company of each other" (1978, p. 16).

Iser's reader, however, is rather more independent of his author than Fielding (and many other authors, perhaps) have tended to allow. His argument hinges on the fact that a literary text, like, say, a painting or a piece of sculpture, can never be perceived entirely at any one time. We build up our impression of the work from "a moving viewpoint which travels along *inside* that which it has to apprehend." And, in Iser's view, "this mode of grasping an object is unique to literature" (1978, pp. 108–109).

The wandering viewpoint of the literary reader is very different from the kind of attention the same reader would give to a non-literary text. Instead of checking the author's work against the real world to see if we have an accurate or an inaccurate account of what is actually going on, literary readers have to build up the object for themselves. The work has to be recreated each time it is read, and the wandering viewpoint adds to the richness and the diverse possibilities that lie behind the process of recreation.

As we would now expect, Iser later stresses the function of blanks in the text as an aid to the wandering viewpoint. At each individual moment as we read, we see the characters, places, and implications of the work from one single vantage point. Our perspective may be that of the hero, of a minor character, of the author as narrator, or of the author as detached and ironic observer of his own work. But as we read on, the varying perspectives intertwine with each other, sometimes supporting, sometimes challenging the assumptions we are making. Blanks, as empty spaces between the segments of the text, give us a chance to link them and so gradually to build up our increasing grasp of the work as a whole.

The more viewpoints we are offered, and the more effective blanks we find to coordinate them from, the more complex, and so the more thought-provoking and significant, the text and the work become. Young readers will need help to understand and use the challenges offered them by major literary works. So it becomes important for teachers of literature to understand the complex workings both of major texts and of good readers. The years of adolescence are certainly not too early for reasonably competent readers to be asked to reflect on where they stand at different moments in their reading of a text. David Jackson has given us an excellent example of this in his account of a 15-year-old girl's reading of the novel *Nancekuke* through the journal she kept: some of the techniques he offers are well worth trying with other students and other texts (Jackson, 1980). David Bleich's record of seven different students' readings of Robert Frost's "A Drumlin Woodchuck" demonstrates how even a lyric poem can be seen from so many different points of view that the richness of a group interpretation should be far greater than any individual could produce alone (Bleich, 1975).

Negation

Iser's view of the quality or technique in novels which he calls "negation" depends on his analysis of the history and function of novels since the earliest examples of the form. The novel is concerned with society and history, but "though [it] deals with social and historical norms, this does not mean that it simply reproduces contemporary values" (1974, p. xii). The norms of social behaviour are set in a new context so that they can become the subject of discussion and be questioned rather than tacitly accepted. Unusual behaviour of any kind negates the reader's expected norms and so leads to active participation in the making of the novel, with new meaning leading to new insights and the criticism of old attitudes.

Iser takes his examples of the effects of negation from classical novels: *Joseph Andrews, Vanity Fair,* and *The Sound and the Fury*. Children's novels, however, are not different. In some ways, the scope for negation is wider, since most children have not developed the narrow range of expectations which the majority of adults come to accept. It is essential to much "fantasy" literature, for example, that conventional expectations in the wide areas of time, space, and the range of possible beings should be negated. Time can "slip" between centuries and decades; space can be traversed by means not usually available, and there is room for unknown animals and intelligences which inhabit non-human bodies.

We do not need to go to fantasy, though, to look for negations in children's novels which will lead to the questioning of norms. There are many "realistic" novels which set out to challenge the assumptions of different societies about the relationships between people of differing sexes, races, or beliefs. Joan Lingard's *Across the Barricades* and its companion books introduce their readers to the sectarian divisions of Northern Ireland, and, through the challenging relationsip between Kevin and Sadie, invite a rethinking of the balance between prejudice and love. Patricia Wrightson's *The Rocks of Honey* takes a very conventionally brought-up white country boy as its central character, starts by showing us his

stereotyped reactions to the arrival in his neighbourhood of an
Aboriginal boy and a little white girl, and gradually educates him
(and its readers) towards a wider receptivity to human behaviour.

In general, I think that the recent developments in children's
fiction show us that its scope for challenging stereotypes and
broadening intelligence and imagination is very considerable
indeed. Some novels for older readers—in the area sometimes
labelled "Young Adult"—have explored questions which even
adult fiction left alone till very recently, such as homosexual love
(in Aidan Chambers's *Dance on My Grave*), state "security" and
its implications for individuals (as in Robert Cormier's *I Am the
Cheese*), and the effect of history and locality in the shaping of
personality (as in Alan Garner's *Red Shift*).

Reading and the Common Reader

Perhaps it was Samuel Johnson who first used in print the
phrase "the common reader"—rejoicing to concur with him in his
understanding of Gray's "Elegy." But it was Virginia Woolf who
took it up as a title for her collection of literary essays. In any case,
two major critics in different periods, both aware of their own
special privileges and responsibilities as writers and as experienced
and subtle readers, nevertheless stress that the ordinary person,
reading literature, has views and can express them. Virginia Woolf
emphasizes the way we can grasp a work as a whole: "Wait for the
dust of reading to settle; for the conflict and questioning to die
down," and after that "the book will return, but differently," and
we can grasp it "as a whole" (Woolf, 1932, pp. 290–291 as quoted
in Rosenblatt, 1978, p. 133).

Louise Rosenblatt quotes this passage from *The Second Common Reader* in the last chapter of *The Reader, the Text, the
Poem*. But Rosenblatt's own attention is mainly on what she calls
the "transaction" which takes place between the reader and the
text, in order to produce "the poem." "The intrinsic value of a literary work of art," she writes, "resides in the reader's living
through the transaction with the text" (1978, p. 132). Where the
New Criticism's insistence on "close reading" was firmly centred
on the text, above all considerations of author or reader, Rosenblatt's "transactional" view of reading, while it still requires close
attention to the words of the text, also "assumes an equal closeness of attention to what that particular juxtaposition of words
stirs up within each reader" (1978, p. 137).

Modern critics have sometimes disagreed about what term they should use to describe the sort of reader who can make the most of a literary experience. The "informed" reader, the "competent" reader, and the "ideal" reader are all terms which have been used. Rosenblatt dislikes all these adjectives. To her, their use suggests an unjustifiable condescension towards the ordinary reader. She is not the first person to suggest that the full aim of the reading of literature is to bring us into possession of the work we are reading. John Dixon has pointed out that the word "possession" here, as in certain other contexts, has an appropriate ambiguity: if I read *King Lear* well, I gain possession of Shakespeare's text for myself, at my age and in my setting, but at the same time such great works *possess* me. Lines of *Lear* roll around my mind; I alternate as Lear and Fool, Gloucester and Edgar, Kent and Edmund, Cordelia and her sisters. Rosenblatt puts very clearly indeed the dilemma that faces the teacher of literature: "If readers are . . . to be helped to be 'in possession of the literary work of art,' the real problem is the maintenance of . . . spontaneity and self-respect while at the same time fostering the capacity to undertake rewarding relationships with increasingly demanding texts" (1978, p. 140).

Notice two points in particular: first, "to maintain spontaneity and self-respect." This is not easy, as many of us must have found, when children move from picture-books to text, from junior school to high school, from children's literature to examination texts. Yet somehow it must be done, in the long run if not always from day to day. And secondly, "rewarding relationships." Relationships, note, not one relationship. There is no one right way to read any literary text, nor will any one relationship be perfect or beyond reconsideration. Sometimes it is quite right for us to say "yes, this student has got as far with this book as is possible now," and not to pursue it further, and so perhaps kill whatever relationship, whatever spontaneity, there was.

The argument is not that all critics of all periods before this were self-conscious snobs or elitists. But very often the belief seems to have been that there was in society a certain group of people, privileged perhaps by birth or upbringing, but certainly specially prepared by education and choice of career, to read with peculiar subtlety and to share their readings within their special circle. Rosenblatt concedes that the critic is a specially sensitive and devoted "fellow-reader," but then insists that the one thing a critic cannot do is to "read the text for us." Teachers of literature are critics both before and whilst they are teachers: they must be, at whatever level, or they will skimp their job and be no help to their students. But their object is to help their students make their own transactions with the texts. Rosenblatt's plea is for criticism to "reflect more of the dynamic of a reading, reporting it as an event in time, in a particular personal context." If we will do this honestly and thoroughly for our students, we can help them to do it for themselves, as Bleich shows in the individual examples both of students' writing and of his own thinking and teaching, in *Readings and Feelings* (Bleich, 1975).

Still, in the last chapter of her second book, Rosenblatt offers one new way of looking at literary texts which may help us as we go on to consider the teaching of different literary genres and forms in schools and colleges. "We are used," she says, "to thinking of the text as the medium of communication between author and reader. . . . Perhaps we should consider the text as an even more general medium of communication *among readers*" (1978, p. 146). Taken this way, we can understand more clearly how interchanges of views about a text will reveal different temperaments, different literary and lived-through experience, and how these can lead to increases in insight and perhaps sometimes to consensus. Above all, we must not try to force consensus, since this would be false to the very nature of the reading experience, which depends as much on the individuality of the reader as it does on the common availability of the text.

3

Teachers Creating Readers

BILL CORCORAN

In continuing the argument of the first two chapters I want primarily to consider some further accounts of the act of reading offered by student-readers and theoreticians. Without an understanding of the reading process, teachers will never understand how their interventions are meant to assist students as they learn to read literature. From the relatively secure footings of knowing about the activities of experienced and inexperienced readers, we should be better placed to suggest a set of enabling strategies which characterize the effective teacher of literature.

What Counts as Reading? Some Conflicting Evidence

As an immediate way in, we might consider Tolkien's (1964) well-known account of the way in which reader and writer initially meet in a shared world of their joint making:

> Children are capable, of course, of *literary belief,* when the story-maker's art is good enough to produce it. That state of mind has been called "willing suspension of disbelief." But this does not seem to me a good description of what happens. What really happens is that the story-maker proves a successful "sub-creator." He makes a Secondary World which your mind can enter. Inside it, what he relates is "true": it accords with the laws of that world. You therefore believe it, while you are, as it were, inside. The moment disbelief arises, the spell is broken; the magic, or rather art, has failed. You are then out in the Primary World again, looking at the little abortive Secondary World from the outside. (p. 36)

There is plenty of evidence that young readers are frequently more articulate about their experience of reading, and more convincing in their validations of the secondary world, than rules of adult scepticism might allow. Witness this language story related by Robert F. Carey (1982).

"Is That for Real?": A Language Story

Katie, nine, and her five-year-old sister, Allison, were having a discussion about a book Katie had read. Their father was driving the car in which the discussion was taking place and at first was only half listening to Katie as she summarized the story she had just finished.

The book, *The Borrowers*, had been an enjoyable reading experience for Katie and her summary was of considerable interest to her admiring younger sister. The story involves a fanciful family of tiny people who live in the walls of a large old house. They take what they need from the belongings of the "normal" family living in the house. Because of the small family's size, they are necessarily creative in their use of the articles they borrow. They might use a pocket watch for a wall clock, for example.

In the midst of this summary, Allison suddenly asked, "Katie, is that true?"

It was at this point that the father tuned into the conversation, monitoring the older sibling's response. "Yes," Katie answered, "That's true."

For the father, an experienced teacher, the response was a red flag. In his eyes, Allison was clearly being given misinformation. Assuming his finest teacher-type demeanour, Dad lapsed into a good impression of a self-righteous educator. "Now Katie, you know that's not right. No, Allison, of course that's not true. You know there aren't *really* any little people like that."

Allison, as usual, remained thoroughly unintimidated. "Oh, Daddy, I know it isn't *really* true. I meant, is it true *in the story*? Did those little people really do *that* in the book?

"Yes," Katie added, nodding. "That's what she meant."
(p. 324)

Allison is well on the way to becoming a reader. From her five-year-old vantage point she is able to puncture her father's adult version of the rules of reading. In acknowledging the storyteller's right to manufacture and maintain illusions, she knows, of course, that "it isn't *really* true," and demands only to know if it is true *"in the story."*

Unfortunately, this episode could be the first in a series of damaging encounters which will go unchallenged as the child trades the playful world of the home for the serious regimen of Margaret Donaldson's (1978) "disembodied" school contexts. Perhaps initially the nursery rhymes, picture-books, fairy tales, and the oral lore of childhood will be replaced by the diminishing, linguistic poverty of the basal reader. And perhaps later still the boisterous name-calling, joking, jeering, gossipy world of the adolescent subculture will be silenced in the quest for distanced, abstract, detachable knowledge about the teacher's books.

At the secondary level, in particular, the distinction that Louise Rosenblatt (1978) draws between *efferent* and *aesthetic* stances to reading may help both teachers and readers understand what happens in some classrooms. To regard reading as an efferent activity is to focus attention on the information a reader is expected to take away *and use* during or after reading. One of the potential dangers of thematic teaching is that literary texts, or more often disenfranchised fragments of whole texts, are read merely as sociological documents intended to add to accumulating evidence about "Old Age," "War," or "The Comic Spirit." Worse still is the premeditated assault by worksheet on the student's first journey through the text. To ask readers to slow their gallop with *Children of the Oregon Trail* to punctuate a passage of pedestrian dialogue, or to hunt up the dictionary definitions of six unfamiliar Americanisms, is just a little less inconsiderate than insisting that they hold a mock debate on the subservient role of frontier women, *before they see how the story ends.*

Such procedures have their natural, and unfortunate, culmination in the eventual loss of reading faith by many examination candidates. They meekly submit to imposed critical judgements, leaving their teachers to solve what have become a series of cryptic crossword puzzles. Since they need only approved phrases to satisfy the examiner, they willingly anaesthetize any feelings of empathy or enjoyment they must indeed have had in private, initial encounters with the set texts.

The hal'mark of aesthetic reading has little to do with these experiences. It involves, instead, those aspects of remembrance, speculation, and association which are evoked in the process of creating a story or poem. This act of creation depends intimately on our store of past experiences and our previous encounters with spoken or written texts. We need constantly and confidently to reassure our students of the validity of their personal reconstructions, and of the importance of analogies and anecdotes embedded in their primary world. Teachers simply cannot read *for* students, not even the weary examinee, since "the reader's primary goal as he meets the text is to have as full an aesthetic experience as possible, given his own capacities, and the sensibilities, preoccupations, and memories he brings to the transaction" (Rosenblatt, 1978, p. 132).

Tracking the Reading Process: A Surer Path

We can isolate at least four basic types of mental activity which seem to be involved in an aesthetic reading: *picturing and imaging, anticipating and retrospecting, engagement and construction,* and *valuing and evaluating.* What evidence is there of these processes in the following accounts of "What Reading Is for Me" offered by Gill Frith's (1979) students, and what sort of expansions can we make from other sources to develop a set of classroom implications?

A Hundred and One Dalmatians

The last book I read was *A Hundred and One Dalmatians.* It was a very good book and when I was reading I got a mental picture of what I was reading in my head. It was as if I was watching tele, the figures moved. Like one of the pictures was of the dogs climbing into a house by going through the coal cellar. I could see the back of the van with the flap down and the dogs jumping in. The van was all dark inside so when the dogs got in I could not see them because they were covered in soot. If I am reading and I want a mental picture I can not get one. If I am reading and I take no notice of a picture I get one.

Tracey, aged 11

As I Read a Book

As I read a book my imagination pictures the scenes of the book as if I was actually there and the people in the book I really know. Even as far as the people are myself but somehow I am always looking at the people even if I know their feelings as well as mine own. It seems as if I am somehow detached but my feelings are very much involved.

The books I most prefer are novels or imaginative books like *The Hobbit* or *Weirdstone of Brisingamen.* These books may be classed as children's books but I could read these books over and over again and still awaken the same interest. I find I have great problems in analysing books because I am too involved in the book and I have to concentrate in order to stand aside.

Ann, aged 17

What Enters My Mind When I Read a Book

When I read a book, the things that go through my mind are whether I can understand the characters, the way in which they act and why they act in a certain way. Whether the plot is moving fast enough or whether there is not enough action but too many descriptive passages. I often guess as to what will be the outcome of a certain scene and whether the scene will greatly influence other scenes. If I find a book particularly uninteresting I read but my mind is thinking about other things such as what would I rather be reading or what has happened at school. I mechanically read the page but my mind is not taking in the words or the meanings. The meaning reaches my eyes but doesn't enter my brain.

If I find the book interesting I will tend not to take in what I am reading at that moment but think about what will be happening on the next page or in the next chapter.

Julie, aged 17

1. Picturing and Imaging

Tracey is quite explicit about the "mental picture" she gets from her reading of *A Hundred and One Dalmatians*. As she says, it is almost a television or cinematic eye that sees "the dogs climbing into a house by going through the coal cellar," but the back of the van is so dark that the soot-covered animals disappear from view.

With all three readers, on the other hand, there is evidence of what happens when the role of mental images is expanded to take in the possibility of committed and uncommitted readings, or the stances of relatively active or acquiescent readers, a distinction that Robert Protherough pursues in Chapter 4. Ann's imagination ensures a positive introjection, as she "pictures the scenes of the book as if I was actually there and the people in the book I really know." She knows the characters' feelings as well as her own, but recognizes as well that "analysis" of favourite books will always remain problematic, "because I am too involved in the book and I have to concentrate in order to stand aside." Things are much worse for Julie, as she painfully and honestly recounts what must be a reasonably familiar experience for most of us—the dutiful "reading" of a teacher-chosen text: "I mechanically read the page but my mind is not taking in the words or the meanings. The meaning reaches my eyes but doesn't enter my brain." And finally, according to Tracey, the whole picture is so natural, so dependent on the unique transaction of the moment, that it pays neither to try too hard nor to worry if the pictures fail to materialize in an engrossed reading.

This issue is worth labouring if we are to understand Iser's (1978) insistence that "mental images do not serve to make the character physically visible; their optical poverty (in Tracey's terms) is an indication of the fact that they illuminate the character, not as object, but as bearer of meaning" (p. 138). The temporal dimension of the act of reading, combined with the individual temperament of the reader, ensures the fluid development of a set of superimposed and successively modified images. The strength, significance, and permanence of these images depends, as always, on the reciprocal engagement of sense, emotion, and intellect as reader encounters text and text directs reader. It is therefore simplistic to confine this definition of meaning to picture stills on a movie screen. After the *whole* movie has been run, what is more likely to claim our attention is a desire to share consideration of how the combined images affected us emotionally and intellectually.

Given the importance of picturing and imaging, we can honour those individual and shared elements of reading by asking students to say what they see in their mind's eye during or after reading. Such an approach legitimizes the place of anecdote and suggests that analogies and fantasies are constructive ways of rendering the picturing/imaging process more explicit. The student who seems restricted to paraphrase has not been let into another of Iser's secret reader behaviours. As Emrys Evans has illustrated in Chapter 2, it is the gaps in a text, its very indeterminacy, that allows the reader to picture and image.

2. Anticipating and Retrospecting

Depending on the type of reading we are giving a text, we are always a little ahead or a little behind the position of our eyes on the page. The process of prediction works so well with non-literary texts because our need for information will be satisfied provided we simply read to the end of the text. With literary texts, however, retrospection assumes an added importance. As sentence succeeds sentence, our short- and long-term memories play havoc with what we had carefully read before. We may even have been exhorted by well-intentioned teachers to look out for "foreshadowing," which they should know by their repeated rereadings is yet another shifting illusion. According to Coleridge (1817 [1949]) the motion of reading is like the oscillations of a snake, or of sound waves through the air: "At every step (the reader) pauses and half recedes, and from the retrogressive movement collects the force which again carries him forward" (p. 150). There can be no literary reading without a retracing of our mental steps in order that we may proceed again.

Julie, in particular, is aware of the anticipatory needs of the engrossed reader: "I often guess as to what will be the outcome of a certain scene and whether the scene will greatly influence other scenes." And if the book is particularly "interesting I will tend not to take in what I am reading at that moment but think about what will be happening on the next page or in the next chapter." Apart from the activities of guessing or thinking through, she will also be engaged in speculating, hypothesizing, and extrapolating. With adults, as well as children, the label of reader is undeserved until we are found guilty of skipping the occasional page (or ten) to get the current problem resolved.

Too often, perhaps, when a teacher reports frustration with a particular class "discussion" of literature there is a lack of recognition that the teacher's *present* reading has been cumulatively enriched by a repeated series of more or less satisfying rereadings. Those continued opportunities have built-in pauses for retrospection, especially where the text is richly constitutive, as in a Shakespeare play, or a novel by Alan Garner or Jane Austen. The disappointment could be turned to advantage by helping students involved in an initial reading adopt a more reflective stance. Julie's almost classical definition of boredom, "whether the plot is moving fast enough or whether there is not enough action but too many descriptive passages," betrays an unreflective impatience with anything but the most unadorned of narratives. So strong is her desire to see the story resolved that its landscapes seem intrusive aspects of authorial indulgence.

3. Engagement and Construction

These processes are joined in order to capture not only the reader's emotional reaction to the text, feelings of identification, empathy, involvement, admiration, or one of a thousand other psychological states she may be able to name, but also to suggest that texts, because of their inscribed ideologies, have at least the potential to change readers.

Ann comes closest to describing those elements of identification or projection which help to illustrate the concept of engagement:

[It is] as if I was actually there and the people in the book I really know. Even as far as the people are myself but somehow I am always looking at the people even if I know their feelings as well as mine own. It seems as if I am somehow detached but my feelings are very much involved.

This familiar tug between detachment and involvement has further echoes of Harding's (1937) spectator and participant roles, which Young has dealt with in Chapter 1. But as a clarification of the interplay of engagement/construction, we should turn to Britton's (1977) concepts of "piecemeal" and "global contextualization." The process of "piecemeal contextualization," like Rosenblatt's efferent stance, involves selective reading, where we pass over the unacceptable or incomprehensible and settle for those things of immediate use in the primary world—fixing that leaking tap, increasing that insurance premium, or joining that cinema society. On the other hand, "global contextualization" demands that we bring the sum total of our literary and life experiences to a complete verbal construct. We shape the reading, and in a direct way the reading shapes us. We are offered one of those glimpses into alternative worlds which enable us to "read" ourselves better, to expand the growing circle of our day-to-day living.

There is a simplistic view that when we teach reader-response ways of reading, our sole aim is to elicit engagement responses from the very heart and soul of a student. But as Rosenblatt (1985) reminds us, we need to see the act of reading "as an event involving a particular individual and a particular text, happening at a particular time, under particular circumstances, in a particular social and cultural setting, and as part of the ongoing life of the individual and the group" (p. 100). This emphasis on particularity underscores the existence of culturally produced texts and readers, and points to transactive reading events which are structured by the placement of readers, texts, and teachers in a unique set of social, ideological, and institutional relationships.

Unfortunately, there is insufficient space here to take anything but a few faltering steps down some of the paths that this view of engagement/construction might imply. Having said that the text creates us to the exact degree that we apprehend it, we need to retain a healthy scepticism as Arnoldians or Leavisites take advantage of our vulnerability. By collaborating with and even denying assent to authors, we deliberately forge rather than find a cultural capital in *what* and *how* we read, not *who* we read. The teacher's task, after all, is to make accessible to students those institutionally sanctioned and empowering ways of talking about the literary productions of the culture.

Again (with some wrench of the metaphor) we can address the question of the teacher's role in selecting what is to be read. Some literature, like some medication, may even be good for us, but the image of the teacher handing out prescriptions from a moral or psychological dispensary is a dangerous one. In the absence of a degree in literary pharmacology, we might be best advised to allow recognition of the ways in which students are personally and socially constructed by the literature they read. They *will*, for example, gain access to lives other than their own; they *will* become more self-aware; and they *will* be left with a capacity to critique themselves and the culture in which the text is embedded. It is presumptuous, however, to suggest that the teacher can guarantee the nature of that critique, or even that it will be exercised.

4. *Valuing and Evaluating*

Valuing is that stance we all employ when we make judgements about whether a text is worth beginning, or if it is worthy of our persistent effort. Evaluating involves those sets of more specific criteria, based either on personal experience, or on formal, structural elements "of the text" which appear to be institutionally endorsed.

Some sense of this range of evaluative reactions can be gauged from the following student responses to William Carlos Williams's "The Use of Force." (The story centrally concerns the conflict between a family doctor and a young girl who is suffering from diphtheria. In order to confirm his diagnosis, the doctor must forcibly insert a wooden spatula into the girl's mouth so that he can examine her throat. He eventually succeeds in the face of violent resistance from the girl and a bemused lack of co-operation from the parents.) An admittedly extreme example of the meshing of an untimely, teacher-imposed reading experience is clear in this thirteen-year-old's response:

> This thing is not what I would call a story. My brother just died of cancer 3 weeks ago, which changed my attitude towards doctors completely. I now understand them. No human doctor would do what that (damn) doctor did. Furthermore I think the story I just read was the worst, meanest, and dumbest story I've ever read or heard about!!! P.S. I shall never read another thing that William Carlos Williams ever writes.

Even at grade twelve, there is a lingering refusal to grant literature its virtual existence. Most teachers will recognize this sixteen-year-old's evaluation of the actions of the child and the doctor in the same story.

If the child had acted in an orderly manner the situation would have been a lot smoother, but wouldn't have altered the final outcome, as the doctor gets to see her throat anyway. . . . If he had talked to the child alone and explained that diphtheria was a serious illness but it could be cured if discovered soon enough then maybe she would have submitted peacefully.

Alternatively (to our chagrin?), the press for detached evaluation will produce the textbook accuracy of this abstract, judgemental account of the story viewed as exemplar:

Williams wisely introduced no distractions such as background information, irrelevant characters or descriptive passages. This results in the intense unity of action which builds up till the climax which is also the conclusion.

"The Use of Force" displays the characteristic features of the short story quite admirably. It is concise, has a centre of interest, it involves the reader immediately in the story, has no irrelevancies, and creates a single impression. Williams combines these techniques with an interesting plot, well used language and life-like characters, resulting in a well-structured, well-developed and entertaining story.

Perhaps most of us would settle for this less pretentious attempt by a sixteen-year-old to grapple with the use of dialect, uncertain of the exact place of personal, rhetorical, or aesthetic criteria as benchmarks for evaluating his experience of the story:

I believe the story could have been much better. The dialogue is staccato; it's choppy; it doesn't flow. The lines are strictly comic books like something out of "General Hospital." The author slaughters his own feeble attempts at colloquialisms as a stylistic device. The mother and father speak well most of the time. On occasion they say "ain't," "her throat don't hurt her," or "we tho't you'd better take a look." From this, the family shows structure and accent traits belonging to either a backwoods Tennessee farmer or a Cockney flower girl. At times the mother even sounds Jewish! How does one decide!

Of the four psychological processes described here, it is necessary to accord valuing/evaluating a superordinate position. As Applebee (1978) suggests: "Not only are most things evaluated, but the way in which they are evaluated becomes a more or less permanent part of our memory of the response" (p. 90). To place the experience of reading clearly in the context of the experience of living is to address quite directly the question of individual tastes and motives for reading, to revisit Britton's (1970) "legacy of past satisfactions" (or past frustrations). The value our students place on reading is based as much on the informed decision of engaging in a pleasurable act as it is on subsequent judgements of how this book measures up to "other books I have read." Experienced readers will be committed, discriminatory, yet catholic on the question of taste. Both Harold Robbins and Tolstoy will have their day (or hour) as the mood takes them.

Experienced and Inexperienced Readers

From these accounts of the psychic processes of reading, and from the evidence of writers such as Richards (1929), Squire (1964), Purves (1969), and Meek (1982a) we can build up a reasonable picture of good/sensitive/experienced/perceptive readers, the possessors of what Jonathan Culler (1975) calls "literary competence." These delightful paragons, when they exist in our classes, combine linguistic and psychological abilities, literary insights and experience, and general attitudes to reading in something like the following ways:

- They can comprehend verbal ambiguities, regularize complex syntax, and discriminate among verbal rhythms. In their potential literary progress from *The Three Little Pigs* to *Ulysses* they have responded knowingly to irony and metaphor, and, with an appropriate sense of intertextuality, they delight in recognitions of allusion and parody.
- They constantly predict how a story will unfold, and have powers of inference which enable them to catch immediately the nervous atmosphere of the opening scene of *Hamlet,* or to realize that Swift didn't really want the babies eaten. They will suspend judgement until they have tested tentative interpretations.
- They expect to *help* the author *make* the story, and in their willingness to collaborate in a search for meaning, questions like "what happens next and, why?" are matters of considerable curiosity. They even *skip* sections *without guilt,* casting back and forward to check the validity of their predictions.
- They can evaluate an author's point of view, and tolerate the many resonances that a work may have through time, knowing that their responses will be partial, cumulative, complementary, and even contradictory.
- They fuse emotional and intellectual responses, refusing to recognize any artificial distinction between what happens in the

heart and in the head. At the same time, they are vitally concerned with the ways in which authors achieve their effects.

- They know, finally, that they could be authors, and they often are, enjoying in turn the power of providing texts to be read by someone other than their teachers.

By way of instructive contrast we could consider a more comprehensive listing of factors that Raleigh (1982) considers to be characteristic of poor/unwilling/inexperienced/imperceptive readers. After reflecting on his own experiences with a class of fifteen-year-olds, and considering the evidence of a range of reading surveys, Raleigh follows the non-reader through a series of unproductive reading encounters at home, and through primary and secondary school. The following composite picture emerges:

- You are a boy.
- There isn't much book-reading at home or among relatives and friends.
- You were initiated into reading by methods which highlighted the techniques rather than the functions of reading and which communicated to you a narrow sense of what reading is and what it's good for.
- At your primary school there was a heavy emphasis on reading aloud to the teacher from "scheme books" (perhaps taking up to a term to finish a book in this way) and little opportunity for extending silent reading from self-chosen material.
- You tended to be slow with your other work in class and so missed most of the opportunities that were there for silent reading "after you've finished."
- You haven't talked much about books in school or elsewhere.
- You don't own any books yourself.
- You don't belong to a public library.
- The secondary school you go to doesn't have a decent library, or if it has one, doesn't encourage you to use it.
- The school doesn't have adequate class library provision.
- Subject teaching in your school makes limited use of texts (i.e., limited as to type of text and kind of use); where it happens, reading is guided and frequently interrupted; the teaching stresses the demonstration of competence (literary and otherwise) over the development of interest and purpose in reading.
- You've been offered a series of inappropriate books by adults who are keen that you should do some reading.
- You see a considerable gap between the kinds of books legitimized in school and the kinds of books you might choose to read yourself if you could find them.

- You haven't developed your own reliable criteria for choosing a book so you have made a series of bad choices yourself.
- You don't think you're much good at reading.

Whilst some of the problems in Raleigh's list are outside the immediate sphere of influence of the English teacher, there are enough signals in these accounts to ground a set of teaching strategies which will both help the experienced reader and unlock doors for the inexperienced. We will acknowledge a range of readers, with immensely different literary and experiential schemata they can bring to bear on a text, with a range of abilities which allow them to see the text as an aesthetic object, and with degrees of reflexiveness which will permit analysis of their transactions.

How Does the Teacher Intervene?

Having considered what the reader does in an unaided reading, we need to shift attention to forms of teacher intervention which reflect an informed attempt to enhance the quality of naturally occurring processes. But as a prior issue, we pay heed to Margaret Meek's (1982c) daunting admonition: "Whatever comes out, let nothing we do stand between reader and author, for we are parasitic middlemen when all is said and done" (p. 291). We acknowledge, therefore, a range of occasions when we have acted as unusually altruistic brokers and have extracted no fee for introducing our reading clients to a novel, short story, or poem which adds to their reading capital. Nevertheless, there are specific things to be done, specific questions to ask of ourselves, if we are to pursue "the new pedagogy" to which Meek (1982b) referred in another context:

> The essential feature of what I call new pedagogy is that, as it proceeds, both teacher and pupils *come to know* what they are reading in ways they may help each other to define. There is no one-way transmission of traditional literary wisdom from the older to the younger. Nor is there a false assumption that the younger reader is as experienced as the older one. The pupil meets "new" text, the teacher rereads "known" text. Their responses extend each other's seeing. The teacher needs a reflexive awareness of the younger reader's stage of development and of her own (p. 92).

In the reading community of the classroom, the teacher will naturally be concerned with a sequence of activities and questions, some preplanned, but most resulting from a series of emerging negotiations, which allow for the following stages: (1) foregrounding and introducing the text; (2) encountering and reading the text (especially a novel) to allow the aesthetic interplay of picturing and imaging, anticipating and retrospecting, engagement and construction, and valuing and evaluating; (3) providing sufficient time and space for the individual to express, in a variety of ways, the essence of an immediate and unique transaction; and (4) creating subsequent opportunities, after the expression of an initial response, for teacher and students "to extend each other's seeing" through a series of collaborative explorations, allowing as well for revisitings and reflections of a primarily personal nature.

1. Foregrounding and Introducing the Text: Context and Pretext

It has been stressed, both here and in other sections of this book, that there is a unique set of life experiences and encounters with literature that each reader brings to each new reading experience. Since the classroom can never be considered an entirely neutral arena, it is important to acknowledge that the notions of context and pretext have ideological as well as pedagogic implications. Why has the teacher chosen *this* text, for *this* class, at *this* time? How potentially problematic are the embedded contexts in which the reading is to take place? To acknowledge the significance of such questions is to acknowledge Ian Reid's (1984) summary view of literature as "semantic transaction," as *situated discourse*, shaped by interpersonal and institutional contexts" (p. 56).

Before the class engages in the task of filling in the gaps of the text, the teacher may find it necessary to construct a series of paths preparing a way into the text. The possibilities are virtually endless, and range through open discussion, role plays, focussed writing, explicit connections with previous reading, and a set of procedures aimed at creating a mood.

To point up the incomplete treatment of this issue here, we might simply ask what importance we will accord to biographical information or textual categorizing. As Purves (1972) has suggested, does it affect our understanding of "The Pit and the Pendulum" to know that Poe drank? How does it affect our understanding of "La Belle Dame Sans Merci" to know that Keats died of tuberculosis? Does it affect our understanding, appreciation, interpretation, judgement, or involvement to know whether *The Tempest* should properly be called a romance or a tragicomedy?

What, at a more precise level, constitutes an approach to *Wuthering Heights*? How much do students need to know of the social context of the novel? Is it possible to provide a literary context by looking at some ballads of the supernatural, especially stories of the changeling and the fairy being of human form, like "The Daemon Lover," "Barbara Allen," "La Belle Dame," or A. D. Hope's "The Walker"? Again, is there any information about Emily Brontë herself that can be regarded as essential, anything about her narrative style which might help the student understand the milieu in which the novel was written?

2. Encountering and Reading the Text.

At the simplest level we are concerned here with the issue of whether the initial reading is to be silent or potentially enhanced by other voices—the teacher, the students themselves, the author, or readers in the school and its immediate community. What, then, constitutes a good oral reading? What is to be learned from careful listening to a group of students preparing for a rehearsed reading? To pose such questions is to realize immediately the inadequacy of a set of written exhortations or guidelines. It is also to acknowledge what Peter Abbs (1983) has called "the neglected oral charge of literature" (p. 36).

A. The Teacher Reading Aloud. This time-honoured celebration of stories and texts is built on a tradition of performance. It derives its magic from the spellbinding power of the tribal storyteller and the rousing recitations of the wandering balladist. Further, virtually every study of so-called "reading readiness" stresses the importance of parents reading aloud to children and thus sensitizing them to the structure and nature of literary language.

Rowan Cahill (1979), from Bowral High School in New South Wales, takes us down an autobiographical path which should trigger off our own personal stories of how we became "hooked on reading and writing":

Pooh and Other Things

I can remember primary school—being read to in the afternoons by Miss S., who brought the words to life from the page, and showed me that books are enjoyable. . . . I can remember my father who read to my brother and me once each week, on Sunday night; his voice brought to life for us the traditional boys' classics of Stevenson, Ballantyne et al. . . . I can remember high school, which started for me in 1958, where poetry came to life from two teachers who never presented a poem to us without vocally interpreting it (admittedly they had rich voices, were sure of themselves, and one had theatre experience); unforgettable was the voice of Dylan Thomas (on record of course) narrating *Under Milk Wood,* introduced to us during the old Leaving Certificate 4th Year. . . . Then at Sydney University during the sixties, hearing the incredible and legendary *Winnie the Pooh* readings by a group of staff members showed me (upon reflection) that people like being read to, even when they are in their late teens, or are adults . . . (p. 19).

Cahill goes on to quote approvingly some observations of Jack Schaefer, who presents the novelist's view of the restrictions and invitations of print:

> Literature is a maimed act, crippled by being printed in books. It began as a vocal art—the writer "speaking" directly to his audience. . . . The writer has tried with the words he has used, with the way he has used them, the calculated progression of them, with their management on the page, with the limited typographical tricks available to him, with the aid of the few expressive punctuation marks custom and grammarians permit, to suggest what his voice would be doing when speaking directly. He has tried to indicate how he wants his words to reach the mind's ear of the "listener." He has done his best to embed the "sounds" in print. And there, alas, for all he can do about it they remain unless and until a reader, a "listener" makes the mental effort to summon them forth (pp. 20–21).

But Schaefer has only hinted at the complexity of the problem. The writer's deliberate patterning of words on a page presents not only a challenge to respond to a unique clustering of linguistic signifiers, appropriately punctuated and following a finite set of grammatical rules and conventions. The reader must discover how the symbolic system of the text invites her to recognize who is telling the story, where the story takes place, how the plot or story line is developing, who the characters are and how they relate to one another and herself, how fantastic or real their world is, and most important of all, whether she is absorbed or bored by the whole process.

On one level, then, a good oral reading should allow the student to act more like a Sherlock Holmes than a Watson. What is "elementary" to Holmes, but invariably unclear to Watson, is that there are elements of the Moriarty-Holmes relationship in all types of fiction. In their search for knowledge or "truth," the characters are involved in an intricate process of laying false clues, of deliberately dissembling or misrepresenting, of passing through stages of ignorance, illusion, and imaginative constructions of one another.

The teacher's voice must dramatize this intricate web of relationships so that the student can hear the voices in texts and possess, in turn, the "implied dialogue among author, narrator, the other characters and the reader," which Wayne Booth (1961, p. 155) describes.

As Hayhoe and Parker (1984) and Protherough (1983a) have suggested, the need to keep an oral reading on the move may involve the teacher in decisions about large- or small-scale editing of the text. Large-scale editing involves value judgements about the likely effects of omitting the laboured beginnings of some novels (like *Tom Brown's Schooldays*), the secondary plots of others (like so much of Dickens), or the lengthy descriptions and musings of the author of his characters. In adopting the role of "authorized" commentator, the teacher may also decide to engage in small-scale editing which would involve such moves as encouraging students to guess at the contextualized meaning of difficult words, or to provide, in appropriate parentheses, a useful synonym or a brief paraphrase of a difficult passage. Such techniques leave the decision of what might be gained from a silent, slower, more contemplative reading up to the individual student.

Since many potential teacher-readers still suffer from diffidence and a lack of confidence in their ability to read aloud, a few brief reminders of practical issues related to physical space and manner of delivery may be in order. Two images will suffice to remind us of what, after the vagaries of weather and timetabling have been taken into account, we can materially do to create and maintain a space for reading. The first picture is that of a group of primary school children sitting at the feet of the teacher while enjoying a shared-book experience. Somehow we have to approximate that conspiratorial setting by demanding that desks, at least, be rearranged. There needs to be a signal from the physical grouping of class and teacher of a promise of shared pleasure, that something special is to be enacted. The second image is that of Coleridge's grey-bearded narrator who "holds [them] with his glittering eye." We need to constantly monitor the reactions of our "reading guests." By lifting our eyes from the page we can detect the glaze or glow in their eyes and react accordingly.

Some basic theatrical considerations will allow a sensitive teacher to decide how a reading is meant to enhance the development of those mental images evoked by the text. From mime, we can explore the possibilities of somewhat less exaggerated physical movement, the arching of an eye, the raising of a hand, the slumping of the shoulders and so on. From vaudeville and the impressionists, we can see the value of caricature, of the sheer vitality of combining physical movement with a repertoire of exaggerated voices. The purpose, after all, is to allow characters, whether real or fictional, to take on a life larger than their own.

While none of us will pretend to be a Sir Laurence Olivier, his objection to what he called "the singing of Shakespeare," provides clues of how to deal with pace, pitch, tone, and tempo. All need to be either slowed or quickened as the demands of dialogue, or the effects of humour, sadness, or feverish action demand. For a properly prepared reading, we need to see the book as an actor's script, awaiting our own directions for staging. Above all, we need to be committed to the notion of rehearsal, whether into the private audience of a tape recorder or the sympathetic yet critical audiences of the home or teacher training institution.

B. The Student Reading Aloud. What is needed here is a substitute for those stuttering and embarrassing unrehearsed readings around the class. To institutionalize this activity is to create unnecessary guilt or frustration for the good readers as they indulge a natural process of scanning ahead, and to confirm the felt insecurity of the poor reader. Where this procedure appears to work, and undoubtedly it does in some classes, we are dealing with a majority of students who have already been well taught and who show an obvious respect for one another and the text. It continues to possess them, and they possess the text and their peers, despite the occasional blemish in delivery.

On the whole, however, there are more productive alternatives. Most students will accept the opportunity to engage in performances that have been properly rehearsed. A natural but little used extension of involving students in their own readings is "Readers' Theatre." At the level of the text itself, one would need to look for passages of particularly evocative description, of absorbing action, or of dialogue mixed with overt hints about characters and their relationships. *The Pinballs* or *Great Expectations* could stand as examples of the types of novels possessing all these qualities and appropriate to different age groups.

The readings may be live or taped, intended for the students' own class or for younger groups of students. Importantly, there is as much to be learned for both teacher and students in the processes involved in deciding how to read a story or poem as there is enjoyment to be gained from the actual performance. Listening in on the rehearsal will provide teachers with immediate evidence of the ways meaning is negotiated in private and social encounters with texts.

In animated discussions of how to deal with a particular piece of dialogue, how to convey the atmosphere of a suggested passage, how to capture the rhythm, tone, or texture of a poem, students will reveal all of the qualities of an experienced reader. In the end they may even shed that deferential stance so characteristic of teacher-dominated classrooms, where students, mere apprentices in the art of reading, dutifully wait on the words of the teacher as master-reader to unlock the secrets of the text.

C. Other Readers: Other Voices. It seems axiomatic that teachers should invite other voices into the classroom to complement their own. At one level, there is the increasingly wide range of commercially available tapes and records where authors themselves, or professional readers, present interpretative renderings of particulat short stories, novels, or poems. There will be some occasions when these oral performances will be made available to the class as a group, and others where individual students can make use of "listening posts" with individual headphones. There is potential enjoyment here for one group of students who need the guidance of a slower reading with less demanding materials, or for another group who are off onto their own private and frenzied excursions into the world of a particular poet, or of a specific genre like science fiction.

At another, perhaps more important level, there is the largely untapped resource of voices in the school and local community. There might be an opportunity for groups of English teachers to indulge themselves in a bit of professional play by combining their voices for mutual benefit in tapes that can be used with a range of classes. Student teachers, and even teachers from other subject areas, might be prepared to either practice an art or reveal a suppressed and lately unexercised talent for reading. Parents, as well, can be especially helpful, either reading to small tutor groups or acknowledging through their unique voices the multicultural world of texts. In any of these ways, the school and its community can celebrate a cultural community of readers, as a necessary complement to organizational practices like wide reading schemes and Uninterrupted Sustained Silent Reading.

3. The Provision of "Meaning Space"

The "problem" with so much literature "teaching" in the past was a refusal to allow students the opportunity to express a provisional, holding response. In the indecent haste to render a public, formal statement of theme, structure, or imagery, there was never enough time to make an entirely interim statement through a range of forms: immediate jottings, drawings, or exploratory, taped monologues of what the student has made of the text. Much less, that entirely natural phase of "thinking about it," of savouring in silence, was rudely foreshortened to accommodate the teacher's public interrogation along paths determined by her confident re-reading of known text.

There are clear and obvious strategies, in a reading journal, in the posing of student-initiated questions, or in reactions to open-ended statements provided by either teacher or student, to provide those spaces where, because the intial response is seen as person-ally valuable, the students come to see themselves as readers.

A. The Reading Journal. Instead of chapter summaries, students could be asked to keep a journal or log of jottings, reactions, and questions which chart their own reading processes and reactions. The plot summary is a pernicious form of the self-fulfilling proph-ecy, because it denies the validity of what Britton (1968) sees as the essence of active response to literature, "an unspoken mono-logue of responses—a fabric of comment, speculation, relevant autobiography" (p. 8). How do I feel about this character? Does anything in the story remind me of things that have happened to me? Is there anything in the story that is putting me off? Is that the way things happen in real life? Surely the author doesn't expect me to believe *that*? Such questions need to be valued by students and teachers to make "unspoken monologues" articu-late, and thereby provide a basis for talk among a community of readers.

About the worst thing that can happen to the journal is for it to be viewed as yet another assessable piece of writing. If this hap-pens, it is because teachers and students have failed to negotiate the form and purpose of this particular activity. In the absence of such discussion very early with one's class, what is likely to turn up is a series of carefully drafted and redrafted statements in re-sponse to the types of questions raised above. It may take some time, given the background experiences of the class, for students to see the journal as personal and exploratory, as an immediate means of getting down their thoughts and feelings, as an opportun-ity to engage the teacher in forms of written exchanges where she becomes a trusted sounding board, or as an essential seedbed of ideas to be drawn on in later group discussion.

The following entries from one thirteen-year-old's *Z for Zach-ariah* response journal can serve as a reminder of all of these possi-bilities in practice:

Two good
questions.
Can you guess
the answers?

Chapter 2. What is the Man doing? Why is he
coming? Zachariah, if she is called that, is
a pretty smart kid. She knows what to do to
survive, and is doing it well. She may be a
bit vain, but we all are.

Good. You're the
only one to
wonder what the
significance of
the title is.

Chapter 9. How long are they going to survive? Will they have any children? Will
John Loomis live? I am not going to guess
what is about to happen, or what type of
relationship is going to develop between Ann
and John.

This book, changing the subject completely is
very much like the one the Science Fiction
(writer) John Wyndham wrote though I can't
remember what it is called. Both books are
about what happens after an atomic war and
the rebuilding of earth.

See if you can
remember. I'd
like to read the
Wyndham book.
(The Chrysalids)

Chapter 11. I now know who Edward was, and
it is sickening to think of John Loomis
killing him. I feel like throwing up.
Edward had family and wanted to see if they
were alive. It must have been a terrible
quarrel. I'm now not so sure I want Mr
Loomis to live. A murderer! how terrible.
I want Mr Loomis to live for Ann's sake but
for nothing else.

Imagine
how Ann
feels then!

Chapter 26. So the book finishes as it
started, but the people have changed. I hope
Ann does find life, and I'm pretty sure she
will. I don't hate Mr Loomis any more only
feel terribly sorry for him and for his mistakes. Life is so precious, why must we
always destroy it, maim it, or try to control
it? I hope there never is another atomic
war. Mr Loomis has now become a better man
though the circumstances are terrible.

Better in the
sense that his
gratitude to
Ann for saving his life
prevails over his impulse to shoot her?
When she leaves, she robs him of one thing he really wants,
immortality, and he relinquishes that deliberately,
if reluctantly.

To provide one more piece of evidence, here is a brief extract from the journal kept by a sixteen-year-old as she recorded her first encounters with the poetry of Michael Dransfield, especially "Small," which is reprinted here:

Small

watching the ants,
making a road through the sand to
help them. watching clouds what they become.
holding court in a circle of
grave dolls.
under the leaves it never rains.
spider pie for tea.

Michael Dransfield

Shortly after reading "The Card Game," I read "Small." Wow! I thought it was terrific. The words literally jumped off the page and hit me. The poem reminded me of when I was a child, and how every little thing amazed me, especially the clouds and I could make them anything I wanted.

Also the vivid description of the ants was startling as I could just imagine the ants, as small as they are, moving through the dirt like tanks do through scrub, to make it easier for the following infantry. Likewise, when Dransfield says:

"holding court in a circle of grave dolls."

I got the image of a circle of toadstools or mushrooms, formed in such a way that they appear to have their heads bowed in conference over some serious matter concerning the running of the garden.

However, I felt that these were merely descriptive lines to suggest a routine, established existence, whereas the guts of the poem is to be found in the last two lines:

"under the leaves it never rains. / spider pie for tea."

That is, when we live in a sheltered environment, be it our childhood or otherwise, we only see a small portion of the total picture of life. As such we can not hope to broaden our horizons, unless we are prepared to take a step and leave our small haven of security, even though this could mean getting engulfed by the emensity of it.

All of the primary movements of mind, the psychic processes of coming to grips with a poem are here on a small scale. Pictures give way to images, and in turn to hypothesizing and ideation. The focus of reading is on the pattern of words, their power to evoke remembered childhood fantasies ("how every little thing amazed me, especially the clouds as I could make them anything I wanted"), to force analogies with ants and lumbering tanks, or of toadstools with a ponderous boardroom, and finally to make a forceful statement about trading "a sheltered environment," a "small haven of security," for the uncertainties of a life beyond. There is still, however, a lingering doubt that this student feels some pressure to "produce the goods," to embark somewhat prematurely on the task of delivering a detailed, evaluative statement.

What has yet to be thoroughly documented is how readers' and writers' journals provide evidence of the symbolic relationship between comprehending and composing, between Holt and Vacca's (1983) reading with a sense of the writer and writing with a sense of the reader. Martin (1983) and Dixon (1984) have plotted some of the paths, and some of the contents, in what should be construed as literary journals or commonplace books. What might appear first is a fragmentary record of reactions, a spilling of thoughts and feelings on the page as the reader engages in a tentative dialogue with the text. These first impressions become, in turn, the focus for later reflections on aspects of that dialogue. For Nancy Martin's students the form of the journal entries "gives the challenge to perceive and utter beyond the (relative) commonplaces of ordinary speech," so that the stories these students eventually write "carry strongly the sense that the literature they have read has made writing their oyster" (p. 51). As John Dixon absorbingly rehearses his own reading of "A Slumber Did My Spirit Seal," or traces the efforts of a seventeen-year-old trying to imagine how Polixenes and Camillo might behave, what they might be thinking and feeling, as they utter their lines in Act 1 Scene ii of *The Winter's Tale*, he underscores the significance of journal narratives, or other forms of "transitional writing," to provide tentative answers to some fairly weighty questions:

- What are the precise stages by which the reader moves from the verbal signs to a dynamic, imaginatively present contact with people in action?
- What expectations are generated, as the cultural codes for construing reality are recognized?
- How is the reader's stored experience affected in the process of imaginative reconstruction—and reflection on it?
- What does the reader make of harmony and dissonances in the "discussion" with the author? and what precise forms may this take? (p. 23)

Especially in later years, the journal should be seen as providing sufficient space for initial reactions, repeated reflections, a repository for copying and illustrating favourite passages, and as a springboard and permanent home for more personal, literary, or academic writing. The sheer scope and necessary interrelatedness of its concerns allow for synthetic pauses where the student shapes a personal and intertextual history of her own stages of growth as a reader/writer.

B. Setting Personal Questions. Given the opportunity to pursue their own lines of inquiry into a text, students show a remarkable ability to engage in what Moffett (1968) called the process of "expatiation":

> The heart of discussion is expatiation, picking up ideas and developing them; corroborating, qualifying, and challenging; building on and varying each other's sentences, statements, and images. Questioning is a very important part, but only a part, and should arise out of exchanges among students themselves, so that they learn to pose as well as answer questions. For [his] part, the teacher should be relieved of the exhausting, semi-hysterical business of emceeing (p. 46).

We have been in possession of the evidence for some time, especially in the accounts of small group discussion of literature offered, among others, by Barnes, Churley, and Thompson (1971), Phillips (1971), and Dixon (1974). The eddying, sometimes passionate, and never perfunctory posing of the personal question in small groups shows students pursuing negotiated debates into issues which bear little relationship to the hierarchical questions of reading comprehension theorists.

One concrete example should serve to underline the validity of what Vernon Hoffman (1982) called the personal "problem question." Each of the twenty-two students in his matriculation class was allowed one problem question on *The One Day of the Year.* (This play, by Alan Seymour, explores the conflicting attitudes of two generations of Australians to the public holiday which "celebrates" the defeat of Australian and New Zealand forces at Gallipoli during World War I.) Here is a sampling of that interpretive community's "reading" of the play expressed in the form of sixteen questions: (1) How does Hughie's family react to Jan? (2) Why does Seymour introduce the character Jan? (3) Why do Hughie's parents resent Jan at times? (4) Whose moral values are greater, Jan's or Hughie's? (5) Did Jan influence Hughie in any way? (6) Is Jan just polite to Alf when she listens to him, or does she respect his ideas? (7) Do you think Alf is as sure of himself as he thinks he is? (8) Will Hughie ever change Alf's attitudes toward Anzac Day? (9) What do you think was Wacka's attitude to Alf, and why? (10) Why do you think Wacka was so quiet about expressing opinions on Anzac Day? (11) Does Mum remain on the outside of the battle between Hughie and Alf? Does she take sides? (12) Has the idea of an attitude towards Anzac Day changed over the years? (13) Should we accept the traditional idea of Anzac Day? (14) Is *The One Day of the Year* an analysis of Australians in the 60s or is it a picture of all Australians? (15) Would the outcome of the play have been different if its setting had not been on Anzac Day? (16) When reading the play it is noticeable that there is a recognizable generation gap. Do you think this gap will remain or narrow in times to come?

C. Response Graphs, Diagrams, or Visual Representations. After students have listed the most important and least important events in a story, they might be asked to plot these points on a graph from "least interesting" or "boring" to "highly interesting" or "gripping." What becomes open for inspection, then, is a sense of one's own story in retrospect, and possible ways of defining story structure. Drawings and diagrams, carried to various stages of "artistic" rendering, provide a visual form of character relationships, a time chart of significant events, or resymbolizations on a different canvas. As always, the teacher will be left with a difficult decision in principle as to how far she will press the artist, collage-maker, or poster-designer for a definitive commentary on the product. Connecting art with art may be just as problematic as connecting it with life.

Since this chapter concludes with a range of activities which involve the use of texts that have been tampered with in some way, for some real purpose, it may be sufficient for the moment to note the potential of activities such as underlining, labelling, or annotating texts. Marking up a text in this way, highlighting matters of significance and pattern, providing interleaved commentary, questions, and reactions, provides established forms for meeting the close reading demands of Barthes's (1975b) "writerly" texts.

This form of "reading with the writer's pen" leads inevitably into construction of key statements or issues which represent the reader's global response. Justification of these response statements may, and perhaps should, lead directly back into the text. Yet opportunities always exist for transformation into recreative written responses (such as documentaries or diaries), translations into another medium (such as radio plays or interviews), rewritings for a younger audience, or as extensions into improvisation or role play.

4. Collaborative Explorations: Refining Responses

Given the provision of time for the individual response, this phase provides an opportunity for extending, refining, and sharpening the forms of the initial response. Drawings and visual recreations may assume the status of art. Initial jottings may, through a series of reflexive, expanded rehearsals and reconsiderations, develop into a range of deliberately shaped statements. The product itself may be called "literature" (as Peter Adams argues in Chapter 6), or exist at the level of equally powerful expressive/discursive forms of documentation (as Clem Young and Esmé Robinson argue in Chapter 7). In either case, it is important to acknowledge the potency of those continuing opportunities to amplify an initial set of reactions.

It may suffice at this stage to refer the reader to Lola Brown's more specific treatment, in Chapter 5, of the procedures she uses to capture initial responses, to develop these responses collectively, and to represent conclusions about a shared text. Her emphasis on teachers and students as active collaborators is seen as an alternative to the limiting discourse of classrooms dominated by teachers' questions and teacher-chosen texts.

Tampering with Texts

All of the procedures dealt with thus far insist that the text, and the reader's evolving transaction with it, be left intact. But a strong case can be made for the occasional tampering with texts in order to focus a sharpened attention on readerly processes. In spite of their comparatively recent rediscovery and enshrining as "D.A.R.T.S." (directed activities related to texts) by *The Effective Use of Reading* (Lunzer and Gardner, 1979) team, or "scaffolding" by Moy and Raleigh (1984), these activities, or variations on them, have long been in the repertoire of inspired teachers who have played with, distorted, and cut the texts to shape their students rather than contorting their students to the shape of the text. Indeed, anything that deflates the spurious authority of the text so that it becomes the object of engaging play is preferable to the silent, reverent encounters at the altar of literary religion. No matter what their initial appeal, we should take care that the following activities carefully match the occasional needs of some students as they encounter some texts, that they don't degenerate from overuse into another orthodoxy.

1. The Interrupted Reading

The most obvious strategy for drawing students' attention to processes of prediction and anticipation is to arrest the act of reading at significant points in the text. With short stories this may mean literally presenting, piece·by piece, a text that has been taken to with a pair of scissors. Alternatively, a poem can be revealed line by line on an overhead (provided it is not one of Hopkins's linguistic *tours de force*). Of course, students need to feel completely free of pressure to provide a "correct answer," for this procedure simply underlines the process of forming and testing hypotheses which is the basis of all learning. The realization that all student readers must come to is that writers provoke a range of expectations, only some of which will be verified in subsequent lines, paragraphs, stanzas, or chapters.

As students progress through a series of short- or long-term predictions, or of retrospecting on their prior, incomplete readings of the text, they actively engage in questions like the following: (1) Why is this action, form of words, or event important? (2) What is likely to happen next? (3) How does this alter my understanding or interpretation of what has come before? (4) How is all this going to turn out? (5) Do I anticipate a happy or sad ending? (6) Why is this character here at this time? (7) Why is the author concerned so much with presenting this character's point of view? (8) Where am I located, where am I standing in relation to the characters and events? (9) How has the author made me feel antagonistic or sympathetic to his characters? (10) Can I accept the view of the world that the author appears to be offering by all that has happened? (11) Why should I bother to persist with this to the end?

Through all these phases, students are trail-blazing explorers, meticulously mapping their individual paths through the world of text, circling and recircling, guided and sometimes productively misguided by the landmarks they think they see in the text. All the while they have been attracted by Coleridge's [1871 (1949)] "pleasurable activity of mind exerted by the journey" (p. 150). They certainly feel no need for the teacher as informed tour guide.

2. Literary Cloze Procedures

In this activity, which can be infinitely varied, students are given a copy of the text from which key words are deleted. Usually in pairs, or groups, they have to provide replacements for the missing words. Interesting questions can be asked, both of ourselves and the students. Is it necessary, for example, to know *about* metaphysical poetry to complete the following gaps in George Herbert's "Virtue"? Or will it suffice to pay careful attention to syntax and mood?

> Sweet day, so cool, so calm, so bright,
> The bridal of the earth and sky:
> The dew shall weep they fall tonight,
>   For thou must die.
>
> Sweet rose, whose hue _____ and brave
> Bids the rash gazer wipe his eye:
> Thy root is ever in its grave,
>   And thou must die.
>
> Sweet spring, full of sweet _____ and _____
> A box where sweets compacted lie:
> My music shows ye have your closes,
>   And _____ must die.
>
> Only a sweet and virtuous soul,
> Like seasoned timber, never gives:
> But though the whole world turns to coal,
>   Then chiefly lives.

What identification and accommodation to the writer's style is necessary to complete the following passage? (Two unhelpful clues for those who do not immediately identify the source: (1) The receptacle omitted at the end of the first sentence contains gin, and (2) Mrs Harris is entirely a product of Mrs Gamp's somewhat inflamed imagination.)

> Here Mrs Prig, without any abatement of her offensive manner, again counterfeited _____ of mind, and stretched out her hand to the _____. It was more than Mrs Gamp could bear. She stopped the hand of Mrs Prig with her own, and said, with great feeling:
> "No Betsey! Drink fair, wotever you do!"
> Mrs. Prig, thus _____, threw herself back in her chair, and closing the same eye more _____, and folding her arms tighter, suffered her head to roll slowly from side to side, while she _____ her friend with a _____ smile.
> Mrs Gamp resumed:
> "Mrs. Harris, Betsey—"
> "_____ Mrs Harris!" said Betsey Prig.
> Mrs. Gamp looked at her with amazement, _____, and indignation; when Mrs Prig, shutting her eye still closer, and _____ her arms still _____, uttered these memorable and tremendous words:

"I don't believe there's no _____ a person!"

After the utterance of which expressions, she leaned forward, and _____ her fingers once, twice, _____; each time nearer to the _____ of Mrs Gamp; and then rose to put on her bonnet, as one who felt that there was now a _____ between them, which nothing could ever bridge across.

The shock of this blow was so violent and sudden, that Mrs Gamp sat staring at _____ with eyes, and her mouth open as if she were gasping for breath, until Betsey Prig had got on her bonnet and her _____, and was gathering the latter about her throat. Then Mrs. Gamp rose—morally and physically rose—and _____ her.

Clearly, this procedure which recognizes the continuities between reading and writing can be productively applied in writing workshops. Either student or teacher can deliberately remove words or phrases which are somehow causing difficulty in the developing piece. Both reader and writer are involved in a drafting process that involves a conscious striving for the most appropriate word or construction.

Variations on this activity involve the interpolation of a piece of alien text. In picking out the intruding piece of Tennyson from the following poem, students might be expected to comment on features such as line length, tone, and vocabulary:

The Projectionist's Nightmare

This is the projectionist's nightmare:
A bird finds its way into the cinema,
finds the beam, flies down it,
smashes into a screen depicting a garden,
a sunset and two people being nice to each other.
The wrinkled sea beneath him crawls;
He watches from his mountain walls,
And like a thunderbolt he falls.
Real blood, real intestines, slither down
the likeness of a tree.
"This is no good," screams the audience,
"This is not what we came to see."

Brian Patten

Finally, the extract below is an adulterated version of the first half of Ted Hughes's poem, "The Jaguar." The italicized words are substitutes for those in the box beneath. In approaching the task of putting Hughes's words back into the poem, students will again be engaged in shared justifications of their choices with reference to images, form, and a series of personal understandings of what Hughes is trying to do.

> The apes yawn and *scratch* their fleas in the sun.
> The parrots shriek as if they were *quite mad,* or strut
> Like *proud peacocks* to attract the stroller with the nut.
> Fatigued with indolence, tiger and lion
> Lie still as the *earth.* The boa-constrictor's coil
> Is a *circle.* Cage after cage seems empty, or
> stinks of sleepers from the *seething* straw.
> It might be painted on a nursery wall.

fossil	on fire
sun	cheap tarts
breathing	adore

3. Sequencing

A number of jumbled segments of a story or poem are presented to students. Their task is to confer a sensible or aesthetic order on what appears to be an incoherent text. It may be better to start with simple narrative sequences with no more than four to six parts, or with poems containing a similar number of stanzas. The number of decisions involved in determining the "correct" sequence for this simplified version of "Cemetery Path" by Leonard Q. Ross is a reasonably sophisticated form of this activity. Perhaps just as importantly students should read the original version, just to see how much has been lost of the story's rivetting atmosphere, how a deliberately crafted artifact has been emasculated. (The original story follows this version.)

"Cemetery Path"

(a) Maybe it was the liquor. Maybe it was the temptation of the money. No one ever knew why, but Ivan agreed to cross the cemetery.

(b) He saw the large tomb. He kneeled, cold and afraid. He drove the sword between his knees into the hard ground.

(c) Late one snowy, windy night a young lieutenant in the bar said to Ivan, "You are a pigeon, Ivan. You'll walk around the cemetery in this cold—but you won't dare cross it."

(d) Ivan started to get up from his knees, but he could not move. Something held him. Ivan pulled and tugged and tried to get away but something still would not let him move forward. Ivan cried out in the darkness. "Oh, God, help me! Help me! Please help me!" Still he could not move. He cried out again in terror. Then he made senseless noises.

(e) Ivan was a timid little man. The villagers called him "Pigeon," or sometimes "Chicken." Every night Ivan stopped in at the bar near the village cemetery. Then he walked a mile around the cemetery to get to his lonely shack on the other side. The path through the cemetery would save him many minutes. But he had never taken it—not even in the full light of the moon.

(f) The people in the bar couldn't believe it. The lieutenant winked to the men. Then he took his sword, "Here, Ivan. When you get to the middle of the cemetery, in front of the biggest tomb, stick the sword into the ground. In the morning we shall go there. And if the sword is in the ground—five gold rubles for you." Ivan took the sword. The men drank a toast and laughed at Ivan.

(g) The lieutenant said, "Then cross the cemetery tonight, Ivan, and I will give you five gold rubles."

(h) The wind howled around Ivan as he closed the door of the bar. The cold was as sharp as a knife. Ivan buttoned his long coat, which almost touched the ground. He could hear the lieutenant's voice, louder than the rest, yelling after him: "Five rubles, Pigeon, if you live!"

(i) Ivan said, "The cemetery is nothing but earth like all the earth."

(j) The next morning, they found Ivan on the ground in front of the largest tomb, in the middle of the cemetery. His face was that of a man killed by some terrible horror. And the lieutenant's sword was in the ground where Ivan had pounded it— through the back of his long coat.

(k) Ivan pushed the cemetery gate open. The darkness was terrible. He was afraid. The wind was cruel and the sword was like ice in his hands. Ivan shivered under the long thick coat and started to run toward the middle of the cemetery.

Cemetery Path

Leonard Q. Ross

Ivan was a timid little man—so timid that the villagers called him "Pigeon" or mocked him with the title "Ivan the Terrible." Every night Ivan stopped in at the saloon on the edge of the village cemetery. Ivan never crossed the cemetery to get to his lonely shack on the other side. The path through the cemetery would save him many minutes, but Ivan had never taken it—not even in the full light of the moon.

Late one winter's night, when a bitter wind and snow beat against the village saloon, the customers took up their familiar mockery of Ivan. His mild protests only fed their taunts, and they laughed when a young Cossack lieutenant flung a challenge at their quarry. "You are a pigeon, Ivan. A rabbit. A coward. You'll walk all around the cemetery in this dreadful cold, to get home, but you dare not cross the cemetery."

Ivan murmured, "The cemetery—it is nothing to cross, Lieutenant. I am not afraid. The cemetery is nothing but earth."

The lieutenant cried, "A challenge, then! Cross the cemetery tonight, Ivan, now, and I'll give you five gold roubles—five gold roubles!"

Perhaps it was the vodka. Perhaps it was the temptation of the five gold roubles. No one ever knew why Ivan, moistening his lips, blurted: "All right, Lieutenant, I'll cross the cemetery!"

As the saloon echoed with the villagers' derision and disbelief, the lieutenant winked to the others and unbuckled his sabre. "Here, Ivan. Prove yourself. When you get to the very centre of the cemetery, in front of the biggest tomb, stick my sabre into the ground! In the morning we shall go there. And if the sabre is in the ground—five gold roubles to you!"

Slowly Ivan took the sabre. The villagers drank a toast: "To Ivan the Hero! Ivan the Terrible!" They roared with laughter.

The wind howled around Ivan as he closed the door of the saloon behind him. The cold was a sharp as a butcher's knife. He buttoned his long coat and crossed the dirt road. He could hear the lieutenant's voice, louder than the rest, calling after him, "Five roubles, little pigeon! Five roubles—if you live!"

Ivan strode to the cemetery gates, and hesitated, and pushed the gate open.

He walked fast. "Earth, it's just earth . . . like any other earth." But the darkness was a massive dread. "Five gold roubles . . ." The wind was savage, and the sabre was like ice in his hands.

Ivan shivered under the long, thick coat and broke into a limping run.

He recognized the large tomb. No one could miss that huge edifice. Ivan must have sobbed—but that was drowned in the wind. And Ivan kneeled, cold and terrified, and in a frenzy of fear drove the sabre into the hard ground. It was hard to do, but he beat it down into the hard earth with his fist, down to the very hilt. It was done! The cemetery . . . the challenge . . . five roubles . . . five gold roubles!

Ivan started to rise from his knees. But he could not move. Something was holding him! He strained to rise again. But something gripped him in an unyielding, implacable hold. Ivan swore and tugged and lurched and pulled—gasping in his panic, sweating despite the knife-edged cold, shaken by fear. But something held Ivan. He cried out in terror and strained against the unseen imprisonment, and he tried to rise, using all his strength. But he could not rise.

They found Ivan, the next morning, on the ground right in front of the great tomb that was in the very centre of the cemetery. His face was not that of a frozen man, but of a man slain by some nameless horror. And the lieutenant's sabre was in the ground where Ivan had pounded it—through the dragging folds of his long and shabby coat.

4. Beginnings, Middles and Endings

Asking students to provide their own versions of stories from which beginnings, middles, or endings have been removed involves not only the sense of an ending, but also the sense of initiating actions, complications, and consequences—a whole arsenal of structures in the reader or the text currently being detonated by schema theorists and story grammarians (Durkin, 1981; Bruce, 1980). While the smoke settles on this battlefield, our attention might be better diverted to the student-writers' accounts of why they chose to introduce certain characters, to provide this or that type of resolution, or to experiment with point of view, style, or atmosphere.

There is an underlying tension through most of this chapter which should at least be acknowledged. For the moment, it seemed more important to pursue a range of provisions and strategies for extending responses to intact texts or to play with texts in order to see how they were made than to align the developing argument for intervention in martial array under either reception aesthetics or structuralist and post-structuralist banners. The very notion of "teachers creating readers" is bound to be problematic within the frameworks of these (overlapping) theoretical positions. No doubt the crisis in literature teaching will continue to be furiously debated. This text stops with an invitation to its readers to construct their own texts by continuing to observe the activities of experienced and inexperienced readers, to clarify their own positions about the place of literature in the classroom, and above all to reflect on their emerging needs as reading-created-teachers.

4

The Stories That Readers Tell

ROBERT PROTHEROUGH

When we talk or write about our experiences of reading a book, our accounts themselves normally take on a narrative form. Just as when we want to share the seeing of a film or play, we find ourselves telling stories about stories. The relationship between these stories is the subject of this chapter.

Most English teachers have long recognized that no clear division can be made between what one does as a teacher of writing (or talking) and what one does as a teacher of literature. Writers are always reading and readers are always writing. What we read offers the chief source of insight into how we ourselves might write; the awareness of ourselves as authors increases our sensibility to what we read. A crucial activity, then, is when a child produces a written (or spoken) "reading" of a text, uniting the two activities in a single process. I want to examine some examples of this happening—children deciding what *kind* of story to tell—drawing on some lessons taught recently in a large comprehensive school near Hull.

i

We know from describing our own "readings" of a text that sometimes we try to condense the original into an impersonal summary, a kernel narrative. On other occasions, we may prefer to offer an autobiographical episode, in which we describe what happened to us while we were reading or listening. Although text-centred stories differ from response-centred ones, they are both creative acts of interpretation, and there is little point in trying to separate out, as E. D. Hirsch (1976) does, concern for *meaning* "in" the text from concern for *significance* "to" the reader.

75

Readers make meaning *and* significance, and they come to understand both better by the stories they frame.

Younger secondary children usually keep these two narrative modes separate. When they had been read a short story ("The Killing" by G. Bosley) and were asked to write about it, eleven- and twelve-year-olds saw the invitation to describe the story to a friend, saying what was going on in their heads during the reading, as proposing two quite separate topics. Typical examples of their reactions are:

1. "The Killing" was about a man named Mr Powell who killed a farm pig in front of a few people. One of these people was a boy who was holding a matchbox with a secret in. Near the end, after the pig had been killed, it was hung up and all its insides were taken out and shared among the people.
2. When the story was being read I felt ill. It is cruel to the animal and I am not very bloodthirsty. I thought how horried it would be to see a pig being cut up and all the insides being taken out. Then to blow it (the bladder) up and play football with it, I think it is very unfair to the animal.

The apparent choice of whether to tell an "objective" or "subjective" story has been established for them by concentrating on that part of the teacher's suggestion which has appeared dominant to each individual.

As students develop as readers, they are more likely to see the two activities as complementary and interrelated. Asked in the same terms to write about her reaction to Doris Lessing's "Flight," for example, a fifteen-year-old girl starts by describing what are apparently the "facts" of the story, but almost immediately introduces personal interpretation (recognizing the symbolic links between the two "flights," judgement of character, explanation of implied attitudes, personal response to the situations, links with actual experience, and tentative evaluation).

> The story was about the feelings of an old man when all his grandchildren have reached adulthood and "deserted" him. This situation is related to and compared with the flight of the pigeons. The grandfather feels bitter because his life is over but he is too selfish as he is not prepared to let Alice "live" as he must have done once. He has forgotten how he felt and acted at 18 and thinks that "attention" in old age is all that he is left with. It was interesting for me as I thought about how both of the main characters never tell and how often similar situations must occur in real life. At the conclusion of the story both

parties seemed to realize how they must make an effort to bridge the age-gap and understand, for me, this was particularly touching and enjoyable.

Descriptions of stories like the three quoted are important for teachers because they provide virtually the only way in which we can examine and discuss responses to literature. The intense reaction which we cannot put into words may be real enough for us as individuals, but it cannot be shared if it remains locked inside us. When we talk with children about their reading, we are not—as some adults conveniently seem to imagine—reacting directly to their experiences of the book, but to the way in which those experiences are mediated through language, to what children are willing and able to verbalize. Examinations in English Literature are largely tests of candidates' ability to write (Protherough, 1986; Dixon, 1984). Just as the story we enact from the text may not match the story of other readers, so the story we tell may not match the one we have created in our minds.

Telling stories about stories is a form of learned behaviour. What kind of learning is involved? The basic activity of literary education could be defined as guiding students about what kinds of information to include and what to omit when they tell stories about their reading. Teacher questions like, "What is this text about?" or "How did you feel about this text?" or "What did you like or dislike about it?" exercise a powerful control not only over the immediate reply but over students' developing perceptions of what kind of commentary is perceived as being appropriate. The methods of discussion that are practised, the explications that a teacher offers, the kinds of written assignments that are set all act out models of literary storying, which exert an influence over the students' responses. Indeed, one basic problem in "teaching" a story is that teachers tend to have formulated *their* story—often after repeated readings and rehearsals—and expect that children will, on demand, offer stories which match the teachers' (and are liable to be called "wrong" or "irrelevant" if they don't).

An example will show how this kind of literary learning goes on without any explicit instruction. Sixteen-year-old readers of Heller's *Catch 22* were asked to jot down brief reactions to the book after their first private reading, and then again after a period spent studying the novel. A comparison of the two versions shows significant differences: a tendency to move towards consensus judgements, an increased emphasis on social satire, greater awareness of structure. The chief difference, though, is a swing away from personal, groping reactions ("I think the book is about . . . ," "it seems to me," "seems hard to grasp," "I like the way . . . ," "I could hardly understand any of it") towards describing what Heller, or the book, "is saying" ("Heller writes in a manner which . . . ," "shows how war corrupts," "not just a book about war," "the points put over by Heller," "Heller shows how corrupt the world is," "the plan helps bring out the meaning of the book," "the book is about . . .") and towards judgements ("one of the best modern novels," "cleverly constructed," "a book to admire from a distance," "the book is brilliant . . . totally ingenious"). To use alternative terminology, the second responses use the *spectator* (rather than the *participant*) mode much more than the first. Two complete examples may help to give the flavour.

1. **First response**: Very shocking—something completely new to me that sometimes I didn't know how to react to it, whether to laugh or get upset about it. I thought that there was an immense feeling of being trapped and of things being very repetitive. So many things made no sense. Somehow I would think that Youssarian was the only sane person but then when some madness happened it would be explained so that it almost made sense which was ridiculous—such as the things that Milo did for the syndicate!

Second: I realize now that it is not simply an "anti-war" novel. I think Heller is a very caring man and this shows in the book. He cares about the people who are bullied and punished by those in power. He shows us that those in power are the ones with money. So you can't get anywhere in life without money—not just in war. This shows the injustices in life which we have to face. Therefore, I can "relate" to the characters in *Catch-22* as they are very real and could appear in everyday situations in the reader's life. Heller has been very clever as he has created all of these people in a wartime situation to show us how they appear in our lives and we recognize them.

2. **First response**: The book begins rather slowly as the reader is trying to work out what is actually happening and when. Certain points do tend to go on endlessly and, even boring, despite all the satire and humour. It is very difficult to keep track of all the characters, and most of the time I try and remember who is who, and who did what. It is certainly a book which needs to be read and re-read a number of times to fully appreciate its contents and understand the role of each of the characters. It is distinctly humorous, and enjoyable, although long!

Second: After finding difficulty in reading the book and trying to enjoy it, I found that studying it changed my attitude towards it completely. I feel that I understand the characters better and, particularly, I am able to sympathize with Youssarian unlike before.

I think I can see now what Heller is trying to put across to us through his use of satire and instead of finding certain parts of the novel just funny, I now find that I understand the meaning behind it. Therefore, the book to me is no longer a book simply to laugh at, but a book to recognize and develop Heller's meaning and understand it.

In these two pairs of responses, the shock, the emotional impact, the uncertainty of how one "ought" to feel, the confusion and the puzzlement are replaced by a more confident stance in which the students assure themselves and the teacher that they can now "understand," "see," "relate to" what Heller has "shown," "put across," "created." Their concern to show, for example, how Heller's caring is revealed in the novel, or what the theme of the book "really" is, or the function of the satire, demonstrates how they are learning to abandon some stories in favour of others. In higher education they will be pushed still further to believe that *interpretation* is the reader's supreme form of storytelling, only successfully practised by specialists called critics, who are to be imitated by undergraduates.

ii

There is a continuum between the child's earliest retelling of the familiar picture-book story and the critical article in a learned journal. The stories which children tell in school enable us to understand something of that continuing developmental process which we call "learning to read." In that process there are two key phases: learning to behave as a reader and becoming conscious of being a reader.

Children learning to read act the part of readers in different ways. When Alex, aged 3, sat beside Adam, aged 2, turning the pages of a familiar book and "read" to him the text accompanying the pictures, both of them were engaged in early stages of learning what readers do. Throughout the school years, pupils are discovering—among other things—how to transform themselves into readers, how to become individuals who have certain kinds of experience from a text. We know (Protherough, 1983a) what seem to be the most common of these experiences when reading fiction: how to project themselves into a character whose feelings and adventures they share, how to enter a situation close to the characters, how to establish links between their own lives and the people and events of the story, how to become a more distanced watcher of what is described. And we suspect that these different kinds of reader behaviour are incremental: that children extend their repertoire and are therefore progressively able to enjoy a wider variety of texts which make different demands on them. There seems no evidence that modes of reading are like Piagetian stages, one more "mature" mode replacing a more "primitive" one.

Stories of reading provide one way of discovering which pupils will be capable of responding to certain kinds of literary effect. Older students enjoy Thurber's odd fairy story, "The Princess and the Tin Box," in which the princess turns down the handsome but poor prince to marry the one who brought her the platinum and sapphire jewel box. Thirteen- and fourteen-year-olds are likely to be divided between those who respond to the story and those who do not. Eleven- and twelve-year-olds are generally less enthusiastic. When the members of one such mixed-ability class of these younger students jotted down their responses, they revealed a tension between how they *wanted* to read the story and how the conclusion indicated that they *ought* to read it. They transferred their irritation at the reading *experience* into comments about the unsatisfactory nature of the *story*. Only one boy thought that it had a good ending. Four pupils could see the point but were disappointed nonetheless. The remaining twenty were angry in different ways at a conclusion that seemed to them "stupid," "silly and irritating," or "queer" because it "led you up the garden path," "because it was obvious she was going to take the fifth one but it didn't come true." The clash between convention and reality was hinted at by just two or three of the children:

> The ending was clever but you usually find fairy tales have happy endings and I was disappointed by the way this didn't.

> The ending was what anybody normal would have wanted but I thought that she would have chosen the last prince because that's how most fairy stories end.

Significantly, when presented with Roald Dahl's updated version of *Cinderella*, in which the Ugly Sisters lose their heads, and Cinderella chooses to marry an ordinary jam-maker instead of the Prince, the same pupils showed none of these reservations. The ending was "good, clever," "brilliant," "very funny," "much better than the original" despite the occasional "awful" or "gory" bits. The difference would seem to be that Dahl signals from the beginning that his version is to be different and mildly "shocking," with Cinders revealed in her undies and the shoe flushed down the lavatory. They were accepting a new set of conventions throughout rather than having a conventional set abruptly challenged at the end.

With a group of thirteen- and fourteen-year-olds, those who rated the Thurber story below average (13, mostly boys) all expressed their dislike of the ending in similar terms to those of the eleven- and twelve-year-olds: it was not a "proper" ending for a fairy tale, endings should be "predictable," this one was "a shock and I don't like shocks!"

I think the ending spoilt the story.

I prefer logical kinds of story endings that leave you contented.

I think the ending that would have suited this story would have been the princess falling in love with the last prince and choosing the tin box.

I like endings which you expect to happen.

I like predictable endings to books so you don't have to do too much thinking.

The rather smaller number (7, all girls) who rated the story above average described the ending as a "refreshing change," and "interesting twist," "unconventional," "more true to life."

I like it when you can't predict the ending.

I liked the story ending with a twist. I thought it was very clever to have made the listeners believe and continue the normal ending. I thought the story would be the usual soppy one, but instead it was a good idea to change the ending.

In the second phase of reading development, children come to a growing awareness of what other readers beside themselves (and eventually that abstraction "a reader") might understand and feel. In the examples quoted at the beginning of this chapter we can see the shift, between 11 and 14, from direct transcription of a reading experience to the attempt to analyse and interpret it. The farther that development goes, the more likely it is that stories about response will become—in effect—statements about how a text *ought* to be read.

iii

Secondary pupils who are entering this second phase, at what-ever age, can be characterized as "active" (or "conscious") readers as opposed to "passive" (or "automatic") ones. The distinction can be seen in terms of the stories they tell about their reading. Active readers demonstrate an awareness of themselves *as* readers, conscious of the kind of reflective enactment which they practise in the act of reading. This awareness—one aspect of what is now termed metacognition—appears to be much more common in suc-cessful comprehenders of text than in less successful ones (Robin-son and Schatzberg, 1984). They are active in constructing mean-ing, bringing to the text their knowledge of the world, of language, and of literary conventions. They reflect upon the text as they read it, anticipating and retrospecting, querying why the narrative works as it does, relating parts to the whole. By contrast, the pas-sive seem relatively incurious about the text; they behave as though reading is simply converting print into sounds, word by word, sentence by sentence. They allow print to carry them along at a relatively superficial level, reading each successive passage with little attempt to relate it to what has gone before or to contem-plate its significance. Active readers are more likely to think in terms of cause and effect, of consistency of character, and of the expectations aroused by particular conventions or story grammars.

The distinction cuts across ability levels. It is true that the major-ity of active readers are also able pupils, but some highly intelligent children seem unable to operate actively in constructing meaning, and some apparently less able ones can be very perceptive in bring-ing texts alive. Nor is there a neat correlation between reading styles and what is being read. The *Effective Use of Reading* team (Lunzer and Gardner, 1979) seem, in some of their latest work (Lunzer et al., 1984) to be disseminating a misleading impression that whereas informative texts demand active reading, narrative texts only require passive reading.

Indeed, when one is reading a gripping story for pleasure, understanding does come without effort. This style of reading is often called "receptive," and what this means is that the reader does not pause at frequent intervals to reflect about the overall sense. The story carries him or her along and stimulates the right questions without any conscious effort (p. 14).

The same simplistic notion that "Reading in science . . . is more demanding than reading in English" is argued at some length in the accompanying volume, *Reading for Learning in the Sciences*

(Davies and Greene, 1984), where again it is suggested that fiction only requires "receptive" reading, in which the reader is "carried along by the text . . . so involved that s/he is likely in fact to be unconscious of what s/he is doing" (p. 42). The largely unexamined assumptions are that the "reflective" reading appropriate for "information processing" in science and elsewhere involves "conscious effort," pausing "at frequent intervals," and that because the reading of narrative is apparently not marked by these indicators it is somehow "less demanding."

The Hull enquiries into the reading of fiction (Protherough, 1983b) offer no support for this viewpoint. Children's story reading is often reflective and perceived by them to be so. They may not pause frequently in reading (though some do), but this is largely because they have "naturalized" (internalized) the particular conventions which are required to bring order and significance to the text. (The same process, of course, is seen in readers of science texts as they mature.) The kinds of reflectiveness which are revealed—to very differing degrees—in their spoken and written responses to story indicate their relative ability to see whether the story is likely to lead to a "point" or moral; to recognize what holds the different parts of the story together; to interpret character, discern motivation and "read" relationships; to distinguish between likely and unlikely outcomes; to establish connections between narrative and its sub-text or thematic content; to distinguish the key episodes or incidents in the text which are most significant for an understanding of the whole. Some of these abilities can be illustrated by comparing the responses of active and passive readers (*reflective* or *receptive* in the terms of the Schools Council project) in a mixed-ability class of thirteen- and fourteen-year-olds to a story by Roald Dahl.

The story, "Parson's Pleasure," describes Mr Boggis, a trickster who deals in antique furniture and—disguised as a clergyman—discovers a Chippendale commode in a remote farmhouse. He convinces the crafty farmer that he only wants the legs, in order to make a coffee table, and with a show of reluctance offers £20 for a piece that might fetch £20,000. At the point where Boggis goes to fetch his car, pupils were asked to write down how they thought the story would end.

Of 24 pupils, eleven had apparently failed to pick up any of the hints in the story that Boggis might be in for a rude shock or any of the suggestions that cheats should not prosper. They did not respond to the fact that the viewpoint in the story was shifting for the first time from Boggis to the three countrymen, and that the reader therefore anticipates some action from them. Rather than expecting that the fable would lead to some moral point, eight of the pupils simply assumed that the story would end with the success of the dealer's plan:

> He'll give the farmer his money and they'll load it into the car.

> He will sell it for a very good price in his shop.

> He'll buy it and he'll tell them how much it is worth then drive off.

The last of these seems particularly implausible in view of what we have been told of the character concerned. Three suggested equally flat endings, but ones which also conflicted with what had gone before ("He doesn't want to pay for it so he won't come back"; "he will pretend to get his car from the road but he won't he will quickly drive off home.") In none of these cases are the issues raised in the story concluded by the proposed ending.

Thirteen more "active" readers realized that there was "going to be a twist in the ending," "a catch at the end," "some sort of a twist," which they predicted with varying degrees of perceptiveness:

> Maybe they'll con Boggis somehow if they realize what he is doing.

> The farmers will try and load it in car but drop and break it up.

> As they carry it out they drop it and it all smashes into tiny pieces and Boggis starts to cry or chop it up for firewood.

> It won't fit so they insist on sawing legs off here and now.

Three of the thirteen, it is true, predicted additional complications which might seem out of key with the tone of the story (the farmer also being a disguised antique dealer, Mr Boggis producing a gun) but at least were aware that the narrative predicted further development in order to *be* a story, that it could not just peter out.

The way in which these 24 pupils later evaluated the story (and especially the ending) seemed very closely related to whether they belonged to the "active" or the "passive" group of readers. All but one of the 13 who anticipated a final twist recorded that they thought it was a "really good" or "excellent" ending, which "leaves you to imagine what Boggis said" and was appropriate because "it was his own lies that caused it." All eleven of those who predicted a "flat" ending thought the actual conclusion "bad," "disappointing," or "stupid" or "not what I expected" because "you do not know what will happen," "it should of gone on," "it just stops."

How do we explain this marked difference in attitude? It seems reasonable to suggest that those who have constructed an uncomplicated story for themselves, and have failed to pick up the advance clues which Dahl scatters in the story, are taken aback when their expectations are frustrated. The twist is not seen as clever but only irritating. On the other hand, those who anticipate that the dealer cannot be allowed to get away with his trickery and that he will be frustrated by some turn of events are pleased with the conclusion, regardless of whether or not they anticipated the actual outcome. Unlike the other group, they like the fact that the story ends with Boggis just returning to find the priceless commode chopped to pieces. They are able to imagine his reactions without needing to have them spelt out in the text.

A related difference appeared when students were asked to re-read the text, and to comment on the differences between the second reading and the first. Those who had anticipated a twist found interest in picking out the "clues" which they had passed over the first time:

A few things you notice which could have made the ending more obvious than it was.

You could go over parts you didn't fully understand the first time.

You get more into it and find more about the characters.

One girl wrote:

When I read a story for the first time, I'm just looking at the story line. I'm held in suspense, and am not particularly interested in beauty of words or phrases. When I read it for the second time, I can see the plot building up, and all the twists the author has put in. I usually read it more slowly and thoughtfully (sounds pompous but it isn't).

Those who had been disappointed by the ending also tended to see a second reading negatively: "it is not as exciting," "you already know what's going to happen next," "it's more boring" are repeated over and over again. For them, the story is seen purely in terms of events; once those events are known, the story has nothing left to offer. For the others, however, there is significance and interest in the *way* that those events are presented in words.

iv

The chief strategic problems for a teacher are to decide how far it is desirable to preempt certain responses to a text, and to decide on ways in which pupils can be encouraged to formulate their own versions of the story in a narrative that is more than a plot summary. Creating an appropriate *expectation* about what is to be read seems to increase the chances that students will respond actively to it, thinking about the experience of reading. The suggestion that repeated encounters with a given kind of ending helped pupils both to anticipate and enjoy such conclusions more (Protherough, 1979) has been developed by a number of enquiries in the U.S.A. Graves (1983) found that students who were given a brief synopsis of complex stories before reading the full texts understood and remembered the stories better. Pearson and Tierney (1984) have similarly found that reading of analogous texts improves students' ability to comprehend and retain information.

On the other hand, to guide too closely, to point to vital clues that might be missed, to elucidate "what the author means here" all tend to short-circuit the responsive process. If readers are not given enough to do, they lapse into passive reading. There is much to be said for holding back and letting what seem to us "inadequate" versions of the story be formulated first and refined in discussion. It is through making their own narrative patterns and comparing them with others that children develop the power to become "active" readers of increasing sensitivity. Teachers also learn what they can easily miss—how varied the reactions and the "stories" within a group can be. Consider, for example, pupils' reactions to a story with a simple sub-textual element.

"Woof" by Jan Dean centres on a boy, Kevin, who gains a certain notoriety in his school by behaving like a dog and barking rather than speaking. He is introduced in the act of irritating two teachers, being dealt with by a relatively understanding headmaster, and pursuing girls at break. At the climax of the story the metalwork master, Jack Crockett, determines to teach the boy a lesson, forces him to "fetch" a metal bar covered in grease in his mouth, and drives him out of his assumed role. "Now Kevin was just like all the others." The story ends by recounting how, some months later, there is a spate of fires in the school, in one of which an explosion throws Mr Crockett twenty feet across the room. When the head greets Kevin with his usual "Woof-woof!" we are told that Kevin looked blank. "I don't do that any more, Sir," he said, and smiled. Most adult readers will assume the implicit interpretation, never directly stated, that Jack Crockett's treatment has driven Kevin from the relatively harmless dog performance to incendiarism and revenge.

If teachers ask classes questions which lead them towards this interpretation (What did Kevin do to get his own back on the metalwork teacher? What do you think Kevin was doing at the end instead of behaving like a dog?), they may easily assume that everybody has "received" the same view of the story. If they ask pupils to tell a story about their reading, though, the apparent agreement swiftly evaporates. When a mixed-ability class of four-teen-year-olds were asked to explain which of the teachers in the story had the best way of handling Kevin, several replied that "none of the teachers dealt with him very well." Of those who opted for one, a number said that Mr Dalton, the headmaster, had the best idea because "he kept his temper" and "took Kevin's be-haviour as a joke." The greatest number, however, said that they thought Mr Crockett had the right method:

> He was the one that made Kevin behave sensibly and brought him back into reality.

> He solved the problem of the barking . . . when Mr Crockett deals with Kevin they both know that Jack Crockett had won.

> He made Kevin realize that he must grow up. He played Kevin back at his own game.

> When Mr Crockett dealt with him, he never wanted to do it again.

These students thought that Crockett's punishment "really sorted Kevin out":

> He needed a firm, harsh punishment so that he would know that he was just behaving stupidly and would not behave like that again.

> Kevin needed to be taught a lesson and Mr Crockett was the only one who did that.

> Humiliating him was the only solution.

> He couldn't go on all his life making silly noises, people would think he was potty and eventually he would get put away.

The notion, expressed by these pupils, that Mr Crockett has somehow "sorted Kevin out," "taught him a lesson," "made him behave sensibly," "solved the problem," or "brought him back into reality" shows how different the story is which they have con-structed from the one in their teacher's mind. Indeed, when they were asked how they would have treated Kevin, a number of these pupils simply said they would have acted like Mr Crockett. One said that it was a good story because it offered "a few points on how to handle" such a situation in real life.

> If I was a teacher in that school I would have kept my temper but made sure that Kevin had to act like a dog thoroughly which

means that he would have to be taken out on a lead for a walk, have dog meat as a school dinner, and just act everything he does like a dog would have to do.

We can only assume that their emotional reactions to Kevin and their punitive desire for his behaviour to be checked made these readers pass over the ending of the story without considering its significance. It is not surprising, then, that they were the ones who —when asked to evaluate "Woof"—said that it was "far-fetched," "boring," or "weird." Those who approved of Mr Dalton's treatment of Kevin, by contrast, were more likely to say that the story was "a good one" and to see the point of the conclusion.

It has to be said that a preference for Mr Crockett's treatment is not a *misreading* of the story, but a *misinterpretation*. The pupils who held this view had understood the literal meaning of the text, but their interpretation of the events failed to take into account the unstated implications of some of these. Assessing a story is very much like assessing events in the "real" world: we judge in terms of our knowledge, our experience, our personalities, and our standpoint. The importance of the last of these can again be shown in narrative terms.

The same story was read to two classes of thirteen-year-olds, both of which covered the ability range. The pupils, who had done some previous work on viewpoint, were asked "where they were in the story" at the climax. About half said they had realized the scene from inside the imagined consciousness of a single character. Most of them had imagined themselves as pupils in Mr Crockett's class; only a few had projected themselves into Kevin or the teacher. A slightly smaller number reported that they were more detached, or that they had shifted from one viewpoint to another during the scene. One boy said that during the reading he had been "all around the place being different people at different times." The detached viewers described the experience in such terms as "I was outside the action, watching down from above" or "I was just imagining the scene, and not really being in a person. An outsider." Two girls used images of composing the scene drawn from the cinema or television. One said, "I was like a television camera, just watching the whole scene, not being anyone." The other commented similarly, "I was outside like a camera man, moving wherever the voices were. When Kevin spoke I closed up on Kevin."

The feelings which pupils had were related to where they had "placed" themselves in the story. Those who imagined themselves as Kevin naturally felt "scared, frightened," "worried and scared because I didn't know what the master would do next," and "angry with Mr Crockett." They empathized with the character: "I could almost taste the grease myself." "I felt as if the pain was in me." Most of those who were other pupils in the class recorded that they were sorry for Kevin and that the episode made them "feel sick" or "horrified," but there were some interesting variations and ambivalent reactions:

> I felt Mr Crockett had to teach him a lesson, but not as mean as he'd done.

> This made me feel scared because he might pick on someone else (like me).

> I felt sorry for him having to pick up the bar in his mouth but it was best to get Kevin to stop behaving daft.

> I thought the teacher was right to stop Kevin's behaviour, but not in the way he did. He was too tough.

> It made me feel that Mr Crockett was very cruel but was doing the right thing to Kevin.

A boy who imagined himself Mr Crockett reflected "I felt a bit cruel but then I felt happy that I had got it through to him." A girl who also said that she "felt inside this character" said "I was in a mean mood and I acted like it."

Those who shifted the position from which they experienced the events had accompanying changes of emotion:

> I felt a bit frightened when I was in Kevin but when I was a pupil I felt amused.

> First of all I was laughing at Kevin when he was doing his dog-act, then when Mr Crockett got Kevin back and made him pick up a bar covered in grease in his mouth, I felt frightened for him.

> When I was in the class I was eager for Kevin to be made a fool of. When I was in Kevin . . . I felt reluctant and wished I'd never started the whole idea, and sick with grease.

> I was at first one of the pupils in the metalwork class but when Mr Crockett got nasty I changed to be just an onlooker. The story made me feel uneasy.

Another method of estimating the range of ways in which individuals have realized the implied meaning of a text is to ask them to rehandle it from the viewpoint of another character. "Phone Call" by Berton Roueché is a convenient, brief story for such a purpose. It is told in the first person by a young driver whose truck

breaks down on a remote road by an isolated house. He calls there
to make a phone call to the market which employs him, and is ad-
mitted by the music teacher, Mrs Timothy, who lives there. He
fails to understand her mounting suspicions of his motives, and is
bewildered when she suddenly produces a knife. As she approaches
him, smiling strangely, he panics, seizes a clarinet, and strikes her
arm with it. The story ends at this point, with the words "Then
she began to scream."

There are only the two characters in the story, and Mrs
Timothy's thoughts and feelings have to be realized through the
imperceptive commentary of the young man. When 55 twelve- and
thirteen-year-olds were asked to retell the story, but imagining
themselves to be Mrs Timothy, starting from the youth's knock on
the door, only five found the task too difficult to undertake, or
were unable to sustain a consistent viewpoint. The stories of the
others can be divided into four main categories.

Seventeen pupils shifted the viewpoint mechanically from the
man to the woman, using the same events and speeches but changing "I" to "he" and "she" to "I." In these versions, there was no
real attempt to suggest the woman's thoughts and feelings: they
were doing an exercise rather than telling a story. Eleven added an
occasional stage direction or indication of feelings to make the
narrator's behaviour clearer: "I slipped a knife into my pocket just
in case the man tried anything," "trying to act puzzled," "I eyed
him nervously," "he looked at me in a funny manner," "I looked
at him bewildered."

Eight also added occasional phrases to indicate what the woman
might be thinking at particular moments in the narrative:

> I thought it kind of suspicious, so I had second thoughts on let-
> ting him in. I'd heard all about young men raping or attacking
> women.

> I didn't like the look of him. I knew about these funny young
> men from the paper but I let him in anyway.

> He started making up many excuses but he couldn't find one.

> I don't really trust him, and he does look a bit scruffy. But
> maybe I'm coming to the wrong conclusion.

Fourteen fully reinterpreted the experience, imagining themselves in the woman's role, rather than simply treating it as an exercise in manipulating text. All fourteen were girls. Elizabeth, for
example, begins her narrative:

I opened the door and there stood the young man. He used my correct name, but how did he know? He said I had written my name on the mailbox. I was wary at first as he seemed like all the other boys on the news—vandals. Then I told myself that I was letting my imagination run away so I let him in. As soon as he stepped in I knew it was a mistake the way he was looking at me, letting his eyes go up and down my body. He said he wanted the telephone but I knew what he really wanted it was me. I gave him the phone and kept calm. I told him I had a husband who was due home any minute. Feeling scared I went into the kitchen to get a knife—it was extra protection but he probably had something worse.

Rachel gave her woman a rather different character. When the young man replies that he knows her name because it is on the mailbox, she thinks:

It was. I realized that it was. Silly me accusing this poor boy!! Just to make myself more at ease I said—"What market?" "Lester's market." "Oh yes I see." "And my truck has broken down and I should like to use your phone," he continued. "Well . . ." I said worriedly and looked intensely at him for some time. Was his story true? He looked as though he thought he was tough. Perhaps he should attack me as soon as the door was closed after him. Maybe he was the rapist which was in the area. Silly thoughts. I'd let him in. ". . . the telephone's in the living room." I stuttered. He stepped in. Oh my god why did I let him in.

Julia presents the final part of the story like this:

I told him to hurry with the call and I went into the kitchen. What if he is a mugger? I thought. I took a sharp knife from the drawer and put it in my pocket. I felt safer now. I went back in, he was on the floor and he looked as if he'd been going through my things. I questioned him about it. "What are you doing?" He gave an excuse of knocking an ash tray over. If he did surely it would have broken? I asked him if he'd made the call. He lied, he told me there was a party line. I picked up the receiver, it buzzed. I told him to forget any ideas he had. He tried to fob me off with excuses so I took out the knife. The worm had turned! His attitude changed he was frightened. I got him up against the piano and was about to stab at him with the knife when he grabbed the clarinet off the piano and swung at me.

The knife flew from my hand and a terrible pain struck my wrist. I just stood there and screamed.

V

The response-centred activities described in this chapter, once seemingly original, are now conventional enough. However, if we see successive sets of jotted reactions, prediction, shifting the viewpoint, and other creative rehandlings of story elements simply as a few among many equal "things to do with" a book, then we may not realize their true importance. They do, of course, exist in their own right as "English" approaches that may be more productive than comprehension tests and formal essays. Their particular significance, though, as we are coming to realize, is that they can also be the means of throwing light on a particular community of storytellers and on the way in which responses seem to develop. What might be called, at a critical level, "inadequate" or even "wrong" readings of texts can be seen, at a pedagogic level, as invaluable indicators of what kinds of learning need to go on, as well as providing essential raw material for discussion within the group. All that is required is a new way of looking at what students tell us. There are endless questions to which teachers would like answers: In what ways are the stories we tell about poems different from those about novels? How does a second reading differ from a first? How does the context of a reading affect our response to it? Does the speed of reading make a significant difference? In what ways does our private reading differ from hearing a story read to us? Only now, though, are we becoming aware that the answers will not come from research projects, which distort the circumstances they seek to investigate, but simply by teachers looking at their own work in a new light:

> To think of teaching and research as the same activity and to use response statements towards this end . . . converts the classroom from an exchange point for information to a research site at which new knowledge is developed and proposed (Bleich, 1980, p. 366).

5

Rendering Literature Accessible

LOLA BROWN

Everyone else in the house has been asleep for hours. I sit here stretched out on the carpet in front of the fire in the lounge, my third cup of tea beside me, absorbed in the world of "The Scarecrows" (Westall, 1981), which I picked up some time earlier—about 11:30—to banish the pieces of the day which refused to fit neatly together, and to settle my mind for sleep with half-an-hour's reading. Nothing—not even the thought of the irresistible lethargy that will, I know, descend on me around mid-day tomorrow in my classroom—nothing has the power to wrench me from the world which I inhabit for this moment—until the last page is read and the covers can be closed, their contents escaped and jostling, in a myriad of images, sharp, disturbing new awarenesses, memories of England, for places in my mind. I shall think more about this book. I shall also sleep now, because I am satisfied that I have it; it is mine, stored away for reordering, reconsideration, remade by me alone in this free, comfortable silence, to be remade again when I talk about it to a friend or try to get a student to read it, though I wouldn't want to do that just at this moment.

Tomorrow, the classroom, where reading can never be quite like this. To begin with, there are thirty other people present, and all thirty-one of us, even if we're reading "silently," are aware of those other human presences in subtle, if not overtly disturbing, ways. The environment carries messages about the serious nature and shared common purposes of the reason why we share this space: there's a blackboard covered with mathematical wisdom at one end; we sit on metal chairs (mine is wooden) at desks (mine is bigger than theirs, as a token of my relative power and status); notices about applications for university entry, school assemblies, school rules, are pinned on regulation State-Supply notice boards.

There aren't any cups of tea. We're all together for an exactly-measured amount of time: in forty minutes a bell will tell us that we have to stop reading and disperse to diverse destinations for a variety of other communal experiences. And we're all reading the same book, which none of us "chose," in an absolute sense: I decided on it after consulting the list of possibilities on the Public Examination syllabus.

These ordered elements were not at all troublesome to the conscience of a teacher of literature when I began teaching over 25 years ago. On the contrary. They reinforced the focus upon the authority of the text, the whole text, and nothing but the text that dominated teaching practice at that time. Further, my big desk invested me with a level of borrowed glory, as one who held the key to received critical opinion *about* text. The prime concern of students then was to learn to read me. Some did it so well that they didn't need to read the text at all. And yet, even then, there was often joy and delight in discovery, even though, in the end, written responses had to be pushed and pulled into a shape acceptable to teacher—or public—examiners at every level of secondary school.

It's the system in which I made first acquaintance with many works of literature of great significance to me, ones to which I return as reader and as teacher. Its power in shaping me as reader is difficult to anatomize, but absolutely undoubted. I flourished, enriched; many—most—of my school contemporaries did not survive, as readers.

The fundamental disharmony between my behaviour as an independent reader and the behaviour of student-readers apparently dictated by classroom conditions is, for me, the starting point in addressing the problem of rendering imaginative literature accessible to *all* young readers. It's the problem that is, as Emrys Evans indicates in Chapter 2, at the heart of this book. For me, as for him, reader-response criticism, with its descriptions of what probably happens for most people when they read literature, closely reflects my own experience. Teachers who engage in honest reflection on their behaviour as readers generally reach similar conclusions. In my work as a secondary English adviser in South Australia, I have found that this personal reflection, supported by descriptions of the process in print in the work of such critics as Iser and Rosenblatt, constitutes the most powerful imperative to consider ways of using those features of a classroom that are under those teachers' control to the end of helping *all* students to be or become independent readers.

What is ours to control? What is it that we are able, despite the obvious institutional constraints, to "organize" in a classroom? Far more than my earlier glance at such a situation would suggest, I believe. For the purposes of this chapter, I'd like to examine four of them, all of which carry extremely powerful explicit or implicit messages about reading.

Firstly, and most obviously, we control **resources**—we are responsible for what students read, and for what they are to understand as the purpose of that reading. Certainly, we work within constraints of book stock, of examination syllabuses, of what a school or the community it serves accepts as "literature," of the past and present state of each student's experiences as a reader, of assessment systems to which we are required to conform. However, these do not relieve us of the responsibility for decision-making about all matters relative to resources: they make this even more imperative.

Secondly, we control **airspace**—talk. We decide whose voices are heard, and by whom. We also decide what it's legitimate to talk *about*, publicly, in our classroom, in relation to literature. The same is true of writing.

We also control our **space**—the four walls of our room, the deployment of people and furniture in it.

Fourth and finally, of course, we manage the **structure and sequence of experiences** that add up to a year-long literature-based curriculum.

At this point, I want to reaffirm the bases of my own beliefs about teaching literature, although I have already indicated something of them, because they inevitably colour all that follows. In a recent publication by the Education Department of South Australia called "A Single Impulse," a group of teachers with whom I worked in a coordinating role, identified this as the central principle that must inform our work as teachers of literature:

> . . . the principle of OWNERSHIP of a work of literature by whoever reads, watches, or listens to it (South Australia, 1983, p. 18).

We went on to say that we felt there were three factors on which such "ownership" was based:

1. Choice over material and response to it.
2. The life experience brought to the work.
3. The cumulative experience of literature brought to the work (Ibid., p. 18).

The metaphor of "ownership" has been criticized in some quarters as denying the notion of interaction between reader and text, or reader and reader. No such meaning was intended; we were simply concerned to place the individual student's experience of the text, rather than our own, at the centre of the classroom study of literature, and to suggest that the end purpose of our teaching, always, must be to enable each student to take profit from his/her encounter with whatever text is presented in the classroom.

This is the position I occupy. It does determine my selection of examples and the questions I raise in discussing the organization of resources, airspace and space, and time in the literature classroom.

I. Resources

Independent, autonomous readers choose what they read. The self-correcting process of prediction and adjustment is not, for them, fraught with fear of error-making. During their reading, and when they leave a text temporarily or permanently, they value their own conscious or subconscious selection of what is significant in it. They often share reading experiences in talk usually, with friends.

The issues of readers' choice and confidence are at the core of such behaviour. As teachers, we cannot ignore them. In terms of organizing classroom resources, I want to deal with two aspects of those issues:

a. providing for choice of material to read
b. providing for, encouraging, and extending individual response to shared teacher-chosen texts.

A. Student Choice of Material

Class libraries made their first appearance long ago. Often, however, they were a kind of optional extra. The committed readers liked the convenience of having books on hand for borrowing without a trip to the resource centre. The uncommitted readers took one book now and then so that their "borrowings" did appear in the record book, even though they had no intention of reading them. Little or no class time was allocated to the reading of these books; little or no class time was offered for students to share their independent reading and their responses to it. Consequently, in the minds of many, it didn't count. It wasn't what mattered, as reading, by comparison with the teacher-directed study of a class set.

Now, in South Australia, one compulsory section of the Matriculation English examination for students aged seventeen to eighteen requires extended self-chosen reading. It has become legitimate; the system values it. The alternative Year 12 syllabus also specifically requires evidence that students have chosen and read for themselves at least four novels during the year. There is, then, no problem in terms of external pressures in the acknowledgement of choice over material as crucial to the development of readers.

The fact remains that many teachers find it extraordinarily difficult to make independently chosen reading a cornerstone of their classroom practice. It's hard to make the move from seeing ourselves as teachers of literary texts to teachers helping students become better readers. Once that shift in role-perception is achieved, however, we can begin to develop appropriate strategies for managing resources and helping students take control of their selection from them. One comprehensive example must serve.

Nigel Howard, an adviser in senior secondary curriculum, described how he worked with the English Faculty at Parafield Gardens High School in developing a series of reading programmes for students aged thirteen to fifteen "which sought to develop them as readers and responders to literature." At the time, Nigel was working as a Reading/English teacher. He writes:

> The philosophy on which the programmes were based was that all students want to read and that our job as teachers is to encourage those who do read to read more and those who don't read to begin reading.
>
> All students in secondary school are developing adult readers, and all have a right and a need to be assisted in that development, not only in what they read and how they read, but also in developing their responses to their reading.
>
> No matter what year level or structure was used, the basis of the programme rested on improving students' access to:
>
> • a wide variety of books
> • information to aid in selection
> • time in school to read the books
>
> One without the others will not work in encouraging *all* students to read. A programme of Silent Sustained Reading without support in aiding students' book selection from a wide variety of books will inevitably lead to continued frustration in those students who do not read. This may in turn lead to complete disruption of a lesson or the whole program.
>
> Helping students find books that are both appropriate and enjoyable will have little effect on those students who do not

read if provision is not made to give them time in school to read those books.

At Parafield Gardens High School, we employed a range of strategies to help all students as readers. In order to increase students' access to a wide variety of books, we:

- made full use of the resource centre and participated in the choice of adolescent fiction;
- started a bookswap table with books donated by teachers and students which was kept replenished with books from fêtes, student swaps, and donations;
- had individual class libraries. I started one for my class with books I bought for ten and twenty cents from fêtes and second-hand book shops. These were added to by the students with books brought from home. The whole library was given away at the end of each term;
- had 700 books in the reading area which were literally "there for the taking." The books were the remainders of the Public Libraries Book Sale.
- publicized commercial book clubs;
- gave books as prizes and frequently lent books to students from our own collections;
- "published" and openly displayed the students' own writing in book form alongside commercially published books. (These student productions were avidly read by all students from all year levels.)

In order to increase students' access to information to aid in book selection, we:

- read a great deal of young adult fiction ourselves. The teacher-librarian provided invaluable assistance in helping our reading and matching students to books; [the year levels and ages of students in this school are as follows: Year 8 (13); Year 9 (14); Year 10 (15); Year 11 (16); and Year 12 (17–18)];
- ran library shuttles in association with Silent Sustained Reading. Students in Year 9 usually had Silent Reading one day a week. When it was possible, we would make sure there was a teacher in the library for this period. Small groups of students who needed to get a book would be sent to the library to select a book and then return to class. The result was ten minutes of chaos at the beginning of the lesson while the teacher and librarians ran around asking "what do you like?" "what do you want to read?"; then a period of calm in which all the students returned to their class with a book which they might find enjoyable;

- had a "book review wall" in the centre of the open space, on which students wrote, on art paper, short reviews of books they had read. These were stapled onto the wall to resemble "bricks" (by Term III the reviews were lengthier and told prospective readers more);
- had a policy of reading aloud to students of all year levels to involve them in, and extend, literary experiences;
- encouraged students to talk about their reading to each other, to share and build on their responses to reading;
- spent time with students who didn't read, talking about what they had liked reading, hadn't liked reading, and their reading behaviour;
- had students write about themselves as writers and about what they had written, and connected that with the displays of their own writing;
- brought films and Theatre in Education teams into the school to extend students' experience of literature;
- produced a book for the Year 8 reading programme with a star rating system; a reading diary; postcards to send to other readers;
- arranged a visit to Year 11's by a writer during Writers' Week and had a local semi-professional storyteller talk to the Year 8's about Story Telling to broaden their literary experience;
- set up displays in the open space unit on Australian Authors, Writers' Week and Shakespeare.

In order to increase students' access to time in school in which to read books, we:

- made full use of the time I had to work on the reading programme by working in the class with the students' English teacher. This gave a good student/teacher ratio and enabled the students' English teacher and myself the freedom and time to work with students who did not read, at the same time catering for the complete range of readers in the class. This usually happened in two-week blocks and was most effective in those classes where it was repeated every term;
- team taught at Year 10; two English teachers were put together for three weeks in order to extend reading and to work together on a common programme of response to literature;
- developed an elective system at Year 10; during Term II two weeks were set aside in Year 10 for electives. Students would choose a "topic" and work for two weeks with the teacher of this topic. Most, but not all, topics were based on literature; amongst these was extension reading with the teacher-librarian;

- developed a reading programme for *all* Year 8 students. Once a fortnight, all the Year 8 classes were combined and were given the choice of attending sessions for silent reading, or of being read to. A library "shuttle" service was carried out at the beginning of the lesson and every student was given a reading programme book which included a reading diary, bookmark, "book-of-the-week" page and other activities which were related to books. As part of this programme, we had a section on Story Telling which involved inviting the storyteller to talk to the students, teachers talking about anecdote and folklore, and involved a lot of Story Telling by the students;
- had time for Silent Sustained Reading in all classes. Some classes were once a week; in others a whole week of English lessons once or twice a term was set aside for reading;
- in many cases gave up free lessons to support the reading programmes of other teachers. This included making ourselves available to set up displays, take students down to the library, supervise Silent Reading, and spend time talking to individual students.

B. The Shared Class Text—Preserving and Extending Individual Response

There are compelling reasons for using a shared class text if we want to help children become better readers. There are practical ones, too, such as the constraints of book stocks and public examinations. What is absolutely critical is that we use them in such a way as to capitalize on the diversity of readings we will inevitably get from any class of thirty different people. What we have to avoid is that set of assumptions underpinning the classroom practice I described on page 94—that all students read at the same rate; that all students will arrive at the same conclusions about "the meaning" of a given text; that ours is the only ultimately valid interpretation. If we assume diversity, we may be able to turn what appear to be problems in this context to positive use.

For many years now, English journals have carried articles by teachers describing ways in which they have done this. I want to offer particular examples of practice in four phases of the shared study of a text: (1) getting the book read, given the fact that people read at vastly different rates from one another; (2) capturing initial personal responses; (3) developing initial responses collectively; and (4) representing conclusions about a shared text.

1. Organizing for Different Reading Rates. In an article on teaching in a mixed ability context entitled "Mick Stability and Gnome Arks," Brian Bates (1984) writes:

> To always teach in ability-grouped classes can produce the deadly flame thrower technique—you may recall the scene from the film *All Quiet on the Western Front* where a soldier, operating a flame thrower, tries to "reach" all members of a group. Knowing that he is unable to do this with the primitive weapon (or methodology) he is using, he aims for the middle. He misses the few quicker ones in the front—and those trailing at the rear were not quite within range anyway—so he aims for the middle —and does a great deal of damage.
>
> But to teach with an awareness of the truly *mixed abilities* of a class can be very daunting—too many targets, moving in different directions, you say! The flame-thrower methodology does not work! The teacher, I admit, can at times feel more like a mad arsonist, darting around the scenery, lighting little fires in the imagination of individual students . . . and sometimes being scorched by the flames on occasions—very exhausting, yes, and not perhaps an attractive analogy. But if you want your students to read a novel, should it always be the same one? And does it have to be read by Friday? And they don't all *have* to "write this," do they? If you truly taught to *mixed ability*, you would never knowingly set a student a task that you felt sure he/she would fail, would you? And if you're not marking and grading the finished written products, you might find time for these before-writing and during-writing and after-writing activities that you read about in "A Single Impulse" (South Australia, 1983). You might help a wide range of writers to think, plan, and edit —rather than merely grade final copies.
>
> The more I work alongside the writer, the more carefully I explore the *range* of individual abilities within the class, the easier and more rewarding it becomes to plan lessons which may sometimes *start* with a common novel/shared reading, but which develop from that point to provide a range of experiences which cater for a variety of interests, talents, and perceived needs. (An outline of this approach is attached.) To be free of having to mark a class set of same-topic writing is the first step in this exciting, liberating, personalized approach to helping kids make meaning. If you've not made that step, you won't understand my enthusiasm, or the possibilities.
>
> So, if you're in a system that fosters bad teaching, and the system needs changing, change it; and if you can't, at least teach

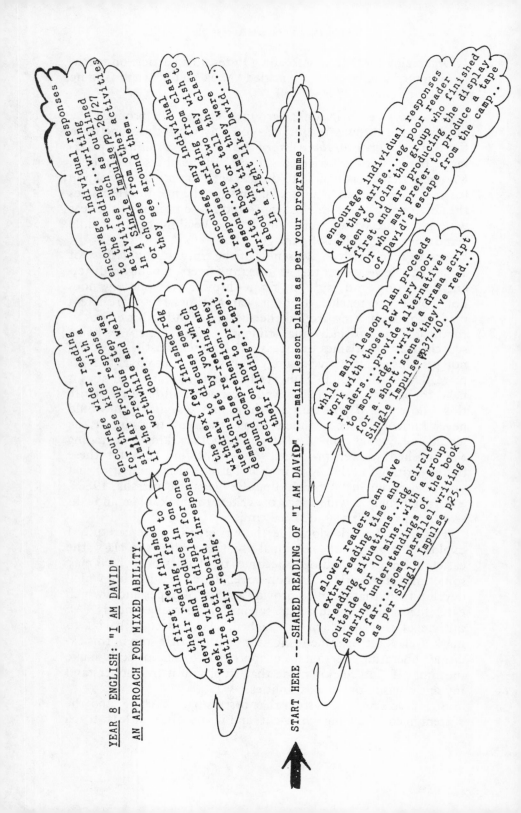

with a determination not to allow the system to distort what you know is good for kids and kids' learning (Bates, 1984).

2. Capturing Initial Personal Responses. We've grown quite good at this. Response journals, taped monologues by students in response to an initial, then a second and third reading of a poem, writing about the episode in a novel a student most enjoyed, a most-liked/disliked character, all these practices are part of most teachers' repertoire now. Why is it important? Several reasons. The best one is—to keep us quiet; to make us listeners to (or readers of) their writing first, and to ensure that our subsequent intervention is shaped by what we hear (or read). As well as this, though, it is part of the message-giving about which I wrote earlier (page 93). It is one way of demonstrating that each reader does indeed recreate the text for him/herself, using his/her life and reading experience to make sense of it. It's a reassurance to students about the processes readers will and must be using.

The examples I listed at the beginning of the previous paragraph are, I suppose, open-ended questions in disguise, some determining the *form* of written or spoken expression (journal, monologue), some determining the *focus* (an episode, a character). After we'd read a good deal of Donne's love poetry, I asked my present matriculation class of sixteen- to eighteen-year-olds to choose some lines and/or a poem they found memorable and to tell me why these lines, or the poem, seemed significant to them. Before the inevitable practice for exams, I wanted a writing task that left the pinpointing of personal significance and the links with individual experience to the individual student, within the common frame of reflective writing.

Here's Tanya, writing about the lines:

> All other things to their destruction draw,
> Only our love hath no decay;
>
> (John Donne, "The Anniversary")

Love is presented as it should be and that is the one basic thing in life that is immune to all the disintegration around you. The subject is memorable because it is so relevant to society nowadays which is a world full of people destroying themselves or others by murder, suicide, fighting and rape. The lines suggest the lasting loyalty of one person to another. This aspect of life is again disintegrating and becoming non-existent in our modern society.

The changing values in our society are leading to a greater number of marriage break-ups and divorces and so it also makes me wonder where the notion of true, lasting love has gone and if it will ever come back.

Julie told me about Auntie Hazel and Uncle John, who have been married for forty or more years which, as she remarks, "says something in itself."

Theirs is not merely a physical love and I feel the part of the poem which reminds me most of their love is:

"Our two souls, therefore, which are one,"
(John Donne, "A Valediction Forbidding Mourning")

because I see them as one person, one soul, together. One is not complete without the other; it is as if there is an invisible bond holding them magically together which merely stretches when they are apart, and never breaks. My uncle is often in hospital as he suffers from a heart complaint. At these times, even though they are apart, you can feel the other standing there next to or somewhere close to the other; one never seems to be without the other.

I suspect Robyn is having some hassles at home at present. She writes in response to these lines from "The Canonization":

'Alas, alas, who's injured by my love?
What merchant's ships have my sighs drowned?
Who says my tears have overflowed his ground?
When did my colds a forward spring remove?
When did the heats which my veins fill
Add one more to the plaguey bill?'

I remember as I first read this how it crystallized some thoughts I have had; parents seem to put obstacles in the path of a relationship; they do this because they think it is in your best interest but I think they should read this opinion of Donne's. Parents often blow things out of proportion. I think they could at times take one step back and view things in this light; coming in late one night won't sink any ships.

Merodene wants the real John Donne to stand up! She writes of the song "Sweetest love, I do not go, . . ."

It is emotional and very sincere. It brings up my opinion of Donne. From his other poems I got the impression that his view of women was that they're only good for one thing and that he didn't know the meanings of the words "faithful" and "relationship." After reading the poem it made me think that I may have been hasty in my judgement. Maybe he does know the meaning of faithful. Perhaps he is a caring person.

Charlotte says of

> Thy firmness draws my circles just,
> And makes me end where I begun

I also feel this kind of what I term love, with my fiancé who lives in Melbourne, and it was nice to read exactly as I feel in 17th Century poetry. In this way I found it memorable and of great impact to read.

All of these students are connecting, comparing, contrasting, and recreating the text for themselves from their own stock of resources. Tanya seeks reassurance in her bleak, pessimistic view of the world. Julie finds lines that sum up her perception of a relationship. Robyn finds lines that crystallize her present frustrations. Merodene can't reconcile the opposite views she hears Donne expressing. Charlotte finds that some things don't change in three centuries.

It's important that *I* am aware of this diversity. It's important that *they* are aware that this is as it should be.

3. Developing Initial Responses Collectively. As I implied a little earlier, I suffer from the disease that plagues most English teachers —I talk too much. Many of the strategies I have tried in recent years have been intended to remedy that. Early last year, I determined that the collective study of two novels by Ruth Park (*The Harp in the South* and *Poor Man's Orange*, Penguin, Australia) in this same matriculation class would evolve from their initial impressions after reading them. Importantly, they were novels I hadn't read or taught before. So, when nearly everyone had finished the first book, and before another word had been said by anybody *about* the books, we all spent a lesson speed-writing our impressions of

- the character we most admired/sympathized with
- the character we most despised/condemned
- the places vividly imprinted on our memories
- episodes that stuck in our minds

This is, of course, another variation on the notion of open-ended questions. I took all this writing and collated it. To start with, I simply transcribed every comment made about a particular character, indicating the relative frequency with which each observation was made.

Those lists often revealed quite contradictory views of the same person. The books are set in Sydney in the post-World War II years and trace the history of the Darcy family, Irish Catholics living in conditions of extreme poverty in the slums of the city. Hughie, the alcoholic and usually ineffectual father, evoked extremes of response, from bitter and violent scorn to sympathetic appreciation of his generosity of heart and frustrated gestures of defiance of his circumstances. The same was true of Mumma, who aroused the ire of the committed feminists in the class while evoking feelings of unqualified admiration for her staunch and self-sacrificial dedication to her family in others. I copied these lists for us all, and we set about examining these apparent contradictions, drawing on the text for confirmation, trying to reconcile one with another and to understand why we held the positions we had taken up—what it was we were bringing to the text that accounted for some of our reactions: we all told our own stories. In the process, we speculated about Park's intentions in inviting such an ambivalent response. The class numbered 22. They chose to do the talking as a whole group on this occasion—fearful, I suspect, that they might miss something if they were in small groups!

As we discussed, from my summary lists, the places and episodes people found memorable, we began to discover patterns in the novel's structure: deliberate juxtapositions of trivial and profoundly significant events, of contrasting places, of funny and tragic happenings. As a page reference guide for myself, I had earlier noted the chapter contents throughout the first book: this then became the check point for such theories.

It was a good experience: one of those rare occasions when I felt reasonably satisfied that I *had* vacated centre stage, that we were genuinely and collaboratively engaged in making meaning from a text, accepting our personal perspectives but expanding them through encounters with other readers. My own reading of these novels was very greatly enriched by that sharing.

4. Representing Conclusions about a Shared Text. If there is diversity at the beginning, in the pace at which people read in a classroom; if we try, by some means, to give varied individual response status, and to capitalize on the variety in order to enrich our understanding of a shared text; what, then, at the end? How can we organize classroom activity to allow for diversity at that point of departure from the text for the time being?

In this situation, where we have chosen the material to be read, our objective must be to give students as much control as possible over the development of their responses to it, and the expression of those responses. The examples to which I have referred have all sought to do that. We need to maintain that principle to the end, offering students a range of possibility, in terms of *focus* and *form* of expression, to crystallize their thinking before they leave a text. Furthermore, if there is such a range of possibility, and if the products are shared publicly, all students have access to new ways of reacting to literature, to different ways of representing response which may otherwise not become part of their repertoire either as readers or writers. The implied message here is important too, in the general context of studying literature: the covers close, but the contents are now possessed by the reader and capable of generating further reflection in her, and through her, in others.

One illustration must serve to suggest the kind of thing we might do at the conclusion of a class study. I will refer again to those students studying Ruth Park, and to an idea I stole from a fellow matriculation teacher, Elizabeth Butler. At the end, I demanded from them an item for display, representing what they most wanted to present to others about their experience of these novels. It could be a poster, a collage of relevant pictures from newspapers or magazines, a simulated diary extract from one of the major characters, a collection of relevant anecdotes, or a number of other things.

One student, an irregular attender, a not-very-committed matriculation English student, came and chatted to me about the stories her grandmother told her of the Depression days on a farm in the Riverland. I said, "Write about them," and she did—about the beggars who came to the door, about the indignities of collecting dole rations, and so on. Another produced thirty pages of diary entry by Dolour, the central character, complete with coffee stains and finger marks. When I read this one, I was disappointed: very little seemed to have been added to the original text in terms of thought: much of it was virtually word for word except for the change to first person narrative. So much time and effort with so little advance in perception, I thought. But then Charlotte said to me, "This has really changed my view of Dolour. Writing from inside her mind makes it different. I realize how much she's like me."

A third student produced the poster on page 108, and made these notes on it:

Rose bush—hardy plant & can survive in hardy conditions (represents the people of Surry Hills).

Roots—represent how the people in S. Hs. are firmly anchored to their habitat (their home).

There are thorns and flowers growing on the tree—saying "there is no rose without a thorn"—i.e., there are good & bad sides to people & life. There are no favourable conditions without

a drawback (some unpleasantness). So the flowers & thorns represent life & its irregularity.

The diff. coloured flowers—represent the multi-cultural society.

Picked a rose bush because some parts, like the leaves & flowers, wither & die & some branches break off—represents the theme of the cycle of life.

Rose bush is growing from a crack in the footpath—respresents the poor, crowded conditions in S. Hs. & how there isn't much room for growth or development.

The foot-path is there because it is something that people walk on—represents that the people of S. Hs. are stepped upon & treaded down by others (higher-class people—their oppressors).

Foot-path is crooked—means that the path of life doesn't head in one definite direction—not all plain sailing—it deviates back & forwards.

Factories in background—represent how the people are lower-class & poorly educated because they work in such places. Also that S. Hs. is a dirty, polluted area.

Sun shining between the factories—indicates that the people will survive where there is a glimpse of hope (representing God) & things are always brighter on the other side.

Three different focusses; three different points of distance from the text; three different forms of response. We shared all of them in class. I think that was an exercise in shared meaning-making; that the range of things the book caused us to reflect on was certainly expanded; that we saw new possibilities in different forms of expression.

Readers can recreate texts even within the most confined of spaces, a core text to be prepared for a public examination. And, in fact, matriculation students will seize such opportunities with gratitude when they're offered. These products were not for grading, yet all but two or three people in the class set about constructing them with a high degree of enthusiasm.

Most English teachers would subscribe to a theory of literature teaching which sees the reading done in English classrooms as performing the function of expanding students' perspective on existence. Most of us, however, are very prone to seeing the whole, and not the parts: at the end of the study of a work, we collect in our heads all the insightful comments made by individuals, all the sentences, paragraphs, or whole pieces of writing that carry the marks of discovery and delight—all the posters, or their equivalents —and measure the success of this particular study by such gathering of gold. It's a survival tactic, a salve for egos bruised daily in classrooms, which are difficult and demanding places to be at the best of times.

Primary or elementary teachers, on the whole, don't talk of their classroom experiences in whole-class terms to the same degree. They are trained to track the progress of each individual. I think we secondary teachers are beginning to learn how to do this. The point is that if we believe the role of literature in education is as I described it, we need to organize our classrooms so that *every* student has an opportunity to profit from reading, individually chosen or shared, and to have access to every possible resource to enable that to happen. This means, in turn, that we cannot rest in those isolated manifestations of "success" we tend to muster at the end of a shared reading experience to persuade ourselves and others that it was all worthwhile.

If each reader must recreate the text for him/herself; if such recreation is heavily dependent on the life and prior-reading experience brought to the text; if at stages during that process, sometimes during the reading, sometimes during a rereading, that recreation can be enriched by access to others' perspectives on the text, then it stands to reason that a classroom must be organized to provide far richer and constant interactions among all readers present. This brings me to a consideration of the next two elements I said I would deal with—space and airspace.

II. Space and Airspace

Every feature of a classroom carries messages. In a classroom whose inhabitants are engaged in reading literature,

- Who talks to whom about texts?
- Who writes to whom about texts?
- Who listens?
- Who reads what other people present write?
- Does some of that writing become "text" to be studied?
- What is the talk and writing about—the text, the whole text and nothing but the text, or about the processes and personal information individuals are using to make sense of it?
- What has sufficient status to be displayed?
- Is it only the kind of material I described at the beginning of this chapter?
- What do the walls say about literature and who writes and reads it?
- What about the nature and deployment of the furniture?
- What does its arrangement say about the relative, and fixed importance of individuals' voices?

• Taking all the assignments set over a year, what assumptions about reading, readers, and texts predominate? Are they consistent with what we believe/know about these?

These questions are fundamental to a teacher of literature who believes the process of reading approximates those descriptions of it in Iser and Rosenblatt's works. Some teachers I know who operate from these basic beliefs are beginning to find imaginative modes of organization to answer them.

"Operation Share," carried out in a Year 12 class studying the South Australian alternative to matriculation English, is one such enterprise. To satisfy one part of this Senior Secondary Certificate, students must read four novels of their own choice. The teacher is left to devise appropriate means of checking that this has been done. Lois Martin at Para Hills High School arranged for a small group of parents to read one each of the works of adolescent fiction chosen by the 19 members of the class. Then, one afternoon, each adult sat with the student who had read the same book to talk for over an hour about their responses to it.

No student was with one of his/her own parents. In fact, there were very few parents of members of this class in the group. All the chosen books were, in some way, concerned with the process of growing up. Students and parents were moved by the experience. They exchanged views openly, after the initial ice-breaking, and left with new perspectives on each other and the novel they had talked about.

This movement beyond the confines of the classroom in sharing responses to literature was developed dramatically by the late Vernon Hoffman, an inspired and inspiring teacher in a school with more than its fair share of problems in an industrial area of Elizabeth. At the conclusion of their study of *The Great Gatsby* and *Tender Is the Night*, his matriculation students created The Gallery, an exhibition of posters symbolizing their individual concepts of Fitzgerald's preoccupations. The Gallery was first displayed within the school. The English Consultant and other teachers were invited to inspect the exhibition and to question each student about his/her creation. These students find writing difficult: they are, however, vigorous and entertaining speakers, and, as their work indicated, capable of finding sophisticated and dramatic symbolic modes of representing their thought visually.

The exhibition and its creators then travelled to Wattle Park Teachers' Centre in Adelaide to a State conference of English teachers, where, again, visitors were astonished at the insight into the books these students displayed. Finally, this company attended the national conference in Adelaide with Vernon, once more providing local, and this time interstate, participants with a memorable, and in a sense, disturbing experience. Their skill in this context called into question the means we commonly employ for assessing a student's understanding of a work of literature—the literary critical essay. The walls of Vernon's classroom, in this instance, would have conveyed unequivocal answers to the questions I raised at the beginning of this section, as would the talk involved in each successive presentation. There, readers were their own "experts"—confident, clear-headed, and imaginative.

Display is, of course, an enormously powerful influence in our 1980s lives. This alone is a sufficiently compelling reason for us to capitalize on it in teaching literature.

One further illustration of material ways of demonstrating that we place reader-response at the heart of our teaching of literature must suffice to conclude this section.

Each year, the South Australian English Teachers' Association produces a collection of poems written by students and teachers in the state. In 1983, we decided to make a set of posters to accompany this anthology, together with an accompanying booklet offering suggestions for their use. Most of them are intended to be written on, literally, by students. They are incomplete. That in itself is really saying something about reading.

We took lines or phrases, snippets of poems from the collection, which we hoped would trigger connections: memories of past life-experiences, heightened awareness of present ones, associations with books students had read or films they'd seen. That reordered, connected experience might prompt some new "reading" of some aspect of the world.

So, for instance, with one poster we suggested that they

"Think of a range of situations in which someone might be listening, watching, waiting . . ."
Who listens?
In fear?
Hope?
Malice?
Where?
Why?

We ask:

Have you met any characters in stories or poems you've read or films you've watched who listened, watched, waited?

. . . and so on.

With another poster we said:

- Is dreaming thinking forward . . . or thinking backward . . . ?
- Imagine what it was that caused each of the poets above to think of dreaming. Compare your ideas with the details in the poems.
- Write about:
  a wonderful dream
  an unlimited dream
  a dream you will thaw when you are old

With both of these posters and with a number of others in the collection (for examples, see pages 114 and 115), we've ended by suggesting that students make another incomplete poster for other people in the class to use in the same way. At the time, that suggestion was meant to be a way of placing students' writing alongside that of published authors as another source of learning. It was meant to show how, if you begin by offering them literature to read, then what *they* write can become the next literature to be attended to in the classroom. Literature generating literature.

I now see further potential in this concept of incomplete posters for a purpose I want to return to in my next and final section, but will foreshadow here. Produced and used at various points throughout a year, such posters could perhaps become *one* means by which the accumulated insights into human experience were encapsulated and shared—the student-created, progressively-written, shared "class text." They could become one public means of displaying learning through literature. A new text each year for each class, even if the set books remained the same, because no two groups could ever write exactly the same one. I should add what must be fairly obvious I suppose, that I believe in the power of display both as incentive to and as recognition of student endeavor.

The poetry posters, then, seek to have students connecting what they read and experience, what they read and what they write, to make connections in many dimensions and to make those connections public. The desire to make those connections possible, and to find some sort of continuity in a year-long literature-based course, is the subject of my final section.

III. Organizing a Literature-Based Curriculum

I don't believe we've ever had much of a vision of how to organize a year-long literature-based curriculum. There are, to my mind, considerable problems with the most popular current ways of doing it. What are they?

The Five Cent Piece.

The five cent piece lay on the footpath
dropped there deliberately by a boy
he couldn't be bothered pocketing it.
Many people saw it
but of course, no-one would pick it up.
'What's five cents anyway?' they thought.

The boy........

The five cent piece smirked in the sun.

... by ALISON HOGARTH....

Down the cellar dark and deep
Lies a dark and dusty heap
Of long forgotten things.......

.... I could fossick here all day
Amongst the stuff that's thrown away.

ELLIS SMITH.

First, there's an author-based syllabus, which our current South Australian matriculation syllabus purports to be—and is, in some highly significant ways. It *does* invite an approach that sees works of literature primarily as expressions of a person's view of the world, rather than primarily as manifestations of a particular genre. This seems to be a distinct improvement in emphasis, since it comes a lot closer to what I think is happening when people read. It also reflects the way most of us behave in making choices of *what* to read: we find a book we like and then seek another by the same author.

However, while our new syllabus does seem to reorientate the study of its literature, it hasn't escaped its genre-bound origins in terms of its structure. Given the reqiuirements that students read the words of one dramatist, one prose writer, two poets, and a Shakespearean play, it's evident that we haven't moved very far from where we were before in our conception of a literature-based curriculum, except perhaps in the "Extension" section of the course, to which I referred earlier.

A third approach to the organization of such a curriculum is the old favourite of themes. I think we've generally tended to cluster literature from different genres in pursuing a theme: to gather some poems, a play, and a novel together as a basis of enquiry into prejudice or love or war or whatever. Not always, of course, because it's not always possible.

At the present time, there are further demands placed on us in terms of balancing the ingredients of the literary diet we feed students—the literature, that is, which *we* choose for them to read, or watch. I'm not suggesting that these needs to include specific elements are imposed willy-nilly by some external authority. I'm saying that if we take seriously the notion that much literature is powerful and persuasive in its representation of aspects of "reality," then it's incumbent on us to exercise the choices *we* have responsibly. For example, we need to ensure that a female perspective on existence is included in our literature curriculum; we need to consider both male and female role-models represented; we need to look at the range of cultures represented—and if, indeed, there *is* a range! All these issues are vitally important. How on earth can we fulfill all these demands and still retain some kind of coherence in an English curriculum?

The answer to that has to be "we can't," if your ideas about readers and reading are anything like those that underpin this book. Whatever connections *we* make among successive literary texts we choose for students to read are ours, and the danger is that the name of the game becomes "guess them." In one way, author-based study is a lot less susceptible to such dangers: at least the "connections" can emerge from within the texts and must be inherent in them rather than being imposed from outside by one teacher-reader.

Given this multiplicity of demands and the dangers or inadequacies of the traditional ways of organizing literature-based courses, how can we design in advance a course which will reflect the notions of reader-response criticism, yet still have coherence and continuity?

Here are my half-formed (perhaps misshapen) thoughts: the conclusions to which I have come, at this time, about a literature-based curriculum.

1. The basic and recurring reference point for such a course, the means by which coherence and continuity were made and made apparent by and to students, would be the literature they wrote rather than the literature they read or saw or heard.

I see this writing in three dimensions:

- for public consumption and public on-going use would be the kind of product I was hinting at before in talking about the South Australian English Teachers' Association posters: the displayed or circulated commentary, reflection, invitation, with its "connections" explained by its author.
- for private reflection: the journal writing in which the flux and flow of experience, real and literary, can be captured.
- for me, the teacher—and other peer "teachers": writing in which we all, teacher and students alike, experiment with a range of forms, choose a range of focusses, and then share our writing, so that what I and others know about writing can be placed at the disposal of each growing writer.

I'm coming to believe quite strongly that students' literary products—and, of course, they don't all have to be written—have to become the reference point we look to if there is to be any real sense of continuity in English courses. The students are, after all, the only fixed and constant factors, apart from ourselves.

2. My course would have built into it periods of time at regular intervals—perhaps twice a term—for personal and then shared reflection on those connections they perceived—the likenesses and differences among the works of literature they had encountered in the intervening period. *Their* connections—*their* expression of them—*their* selection of significant issues emerging from the literature they and I had chosen. These periods of time, maybe four or five days, would be the periods during which those special products for public consumption were made and shared. I can see some

ways in which the writing done for themselves and the teacher during those periods could become the means by which they monitored their own learning, their own added or changed perceptions, as the year proceeded.

3. Students would be required to choose a good proportion of the literature they read. They would be required to share their responses to it with other people.

4. Given these three elements, and the orientation of questioning I've illustrated earlier, I could, I think, use the literature I had at my disposal in a school's stock with profit to the students. I could choose a work of literature because of its intrinsic power, not because of its relevance to a theme or because of its genre or for any other reason. I could, certainly, aim at a diet varied in all the dimensions I listed before because I would be freed of the need to give the *appearance* of order and preplanned sequence through connections *I* made explicit. But I could take great care in deciding the sequence in which I presented texts for shared consideration, and in this respect, the recent work of Protherough 1983b) offers some interesting directions to consider.

I think it's possible to preplan, in broad terms, all four of these elements. I'm not describing anything new; just a recombination and reorientation of what we already do. But it *is* important, because what exists in our heads as purposes most certainly determines the perceptions students have of what's happening in our classroom and why.

And so I have come full circle, to the point where I began. The task facing us is to discover those methods of classroom organization that give all readers access to the kind of literary experience we have grown to value profoundly, the kind I represented by my reading of "The Scarecrows." I believe we have far more power to change things than we realize: it is up to use to use it wisely.

6

Writing from Reading— "Dependent Authorship" as a Response

PETER ADAMS

Analysis and criticism (of literature) does have an important part to play in English studies, but it is in no way a substitute for, nor is it synonymous with, creative appreciation. The latter requires that realized form be closely related to the pupil's creative expression and that he express his feeling response in a direct and personal way. It requires that he make an "artistic" response to the "artistic" work of others.

(Witkin, 1974)

Intuition is an invitation to go further—whether intuitively or analytically.

(Bruner, 1974)

Six years ago, a quiet, serious, and rather withdrawn fourteen-year-old boy walked up to my desk, handed me the following piece of writing, and went back to his seat:

After the Rescue

Jack[1] strolled across the lane, kicking pebbles into the grassy ditch where water gurgled. Rain drizzled, the stone wall draped with moss dripped, and further on, a frog croaked. He stopped to listen to the frog again, and became Jack the hunter. The air was quiet, apart from water trickling and the sound of the road a few blocks away. The frog croaked again, and Jack swept forward, his satchel swaying under his arm. The thought of catching his bus to school did not cross his mind. He was hunting again

---

[1] Jack, of course, is Jack Merridew from William Golding's fable, *Lord of the Flies*, imagined now as being back in England after having been rescued from the burning island by the cruiser. The students had been asked to choose one of the survivors and show how he reacted to being returned to "civilization" after his experiences on the island.

and that was all that mattered to him. All his senses were sharp, his eyes missed nothing under the grass where his prey might sit. The hunter's hand skilfully delved beneath the mossy bank of the ditch and he grinned at what lay underneath. A pair of moist beady eyes peered up at him from a fat little body; its fat stomach heaved up and down as it puffed air in and out of its mouth. Jack frowned and grabbed at the ball of fat. The frog hopped into the stream and kicked away. Jack watched it come to rest on a stone. The feeling of being bettered by such a small animal angered him. He breathed in and leapt after the frog. Water splashed his trousers and soaked his shoes. He stumbled on, bending and grabbing at the hopping figure ahead of him. At last he knelt in wet moss, grasping the billowing frog in his fist. None of his anger had subsided. He had power over the fat little frog. Jack rose slowly, his front dripping, his breathing heavy. All the frustrations of the past few days in school, in strict civilized society, were let out at once as he hurled the frog at the stone wall. Its head opened and blood oozed out. "I meant that!" uttered Jack.

James Farmer

The moment I read that, I knew that something important had happened, although it took me some time to begin to appreciate the full significance of James's achievement. Here was a depth of response to the novel, an intensity and seriousness of engagement with it, that I suspected would have remained largely (or even wholly) unglimpsed if I had not followed my instincts and asked for "After the Rescue" rather than the essay I felt I ought to set. I had hoped for some lively and interesting writing, but this was startling in its unexpectedness and its power. Although James was an intelligent boy and a more fluent writer than many of his classmates, nothing he had previously written had suggested to me that he might one day produce something like this.

What, I wondered, had happened to produce writing like this? Was it possible that other students were capable of work of this calibre? Were there other ways of writing that might tap a similar depth of response to other novels? It was with questions like these that the work on which this chapter is based began, and the chapter itself might best perhaps be regarded as a kind of report on work-in-progress.

Dependent Authorship

Like James's epilogue to *Lord of the Flies*, all of the pieces of writing which appear in this chapter are examples of what I have come to think of as "dependent authorship." What I intended by that might perhaps be most readily demonstrated by a brief synopsis of the contents of the chapter:

- Imaginative reconstruction of a gap in a text (*A High Wind in Jamaica*)
- Adding another episode to a text (*The Sword in the Stone*)
- Writing a continuation of a text (*Z for Zachariah*)
- Adding an epilogue to a text (*Lord of the Flies*)
- Adding a dream to the conclusion of a text (*The Slave Dancer*)
- Rewriting the ending of a text (*The Owl Service*)

In each case, the task has required the student to take on *the role of the author*, and to write from "inside" the world of the text. In the most obvious sense, what the student has written is "dependent" upon the original because it cannot stand alone and be self-sufficient; it requires a knowledge of the original in order to assume its full significance. But there are more significant senses in which the student's writing is dependent upon the original. In contrast to what we might call independent or fully-fledged authorship, where the writer starts from scratch, as it were, in dependent authorship the student's own imaginative activity is sustained and supported by a prior creative activity—the author's—and the original work not only provides the student with a repertoire of resources upon which to draw, but just as importantly, it provides a powerful set of constraints to be observed. The original work, therefore, supports and constrains and amplifies the student's imaginative entry into the life of the text *in the role of author*. It is my experience that dependent authorship not only enables a surprisingly wide range of students to write about literature with an unusual depth and power of response, but that it is the means by which they can discover and explore elements of their response to the work that they could not grasp or articulate in any other way. Why this should be so is a question I will take up in the conclusion of this chapter, after I have sketched in some of the possibilities that are opened up for students by dependent authorship.

1. Imaginative Reconstruction

Every story, as Harold Rosen has recently reminded us (1983), contains within it the seeds of other potential stories, the ghosts of narratives that have given up their lives for the sake of the tale in which they are embedded—for stories exact a ruthless economy.

This is perhaps inevitable. We can never tell all. But not only can no story ever tell all that there is to tell, it *must* not. Its existence as a story—and not something else—depends on that.

For example, in Colin Thiele's *Blue Fin*, the exact fate of the
tuna clipper *Dog Star* is deliberately left unresolved, her disappearance serving both to emphasize the treacherousness of the sea and
to prepare the reader for *Blue Fin*'s own battle for survival. Although, in the economy of the novel, Thiele is undoubtedly right
not to describe the sinking of *Dog Star*, a good deal *is supplied* for
the reader's imagination to work on:

All through Monday night people worked and waited, watching for flares, listening for radio news, checking facts. There was
not much to know. *Dog Star* had gone out on Saturday night,
and arrived at the tuna grounds a hundred miles south sometime
on Sunday. She'd taken a catch of eight tons before nightfall,
and added another twenty or thirty early on Monday morning.
She'd answered the regular radio call at 8:15 saying she'd be
back with a full cargo by midnight, or early Tuesday morning.
But that was the end of the story. After that, silence.

Later, after a coastal search has failed to find any trace of the
missing boat, the episode is brought to a close in the following
way:

"Could have saved all this trouble if they'd used their heads,"
said an old-timer categorically. "*Dog Star* didn't get to within
cooee of the coast."

"How do you make that out?"

"Well, she was down on the shelf at eight in the mornin'—still
fishin', and she didn't answer the sked call at twelve. Figure it
out for yourself."

"That's right, she probably didn't leave till ten. Only had a
couple of hour's sailing at that rate."

"Fifteen or twenty miles. That's all she could have done before she went down. And that still leaves her a hell of a way
from the coast."

"You reckon she's down? Definitely down?"

"What else?"

"Could be driftin'—no engine. Or radio out, or sheltering
somewhere in the islands. Old Bob was a funny coot."

"'Course he was. I bet he took her straight across the Patch!"

"You reckon?"

"'Course I reckon."

"And she didn't make it?"

"What do you think? Old *Dog Star*? With thirty ton o' tuna?
She'd be down in the water like a wet bag. And that ruddy great
bait tank up stern too. No, she just went under."

"Short seas and rips."

"Big seas you mean. Stand up out of nowhere. Great green walls. Fall straight on you like earthquakes. *Dog Star*'d never climb out from under."

"Poor old Bob. He was a nice bloke in his way."

"They're always nice blokes. But the sea gets 'em."

This seems a particularly clear example of the mutually constructed "game of the imagination" that Wolfgang Iser regards as being central to the activity of reading:

> If the reader were given the whole story, and there was nothing left for him to do, then his imagination would never enter the field. The result would be the boredom which inevitably arises when everything is laid out and dried before us. A literary text must therefore be conceived in such a way that it will engage the reader's imagination in the task of working things out for himself, for reading is only a pleasure when it is active and creative (Iser, 1975).

"Figure it out for yourself," says the old-timer, and then proceeds to provide the reader with an example of the kind of activity to which this incomplete story should be prompting him.

This is a useful example to discuss with students because of the unusual amount of prompting that the text provides, but, even so, it is important to note that the speculations of the two old fishermen do not, at this point in the novel, actually reduce the indeterminacy of the narrative. If some possibilities seem to be excluded—for example, that *Dog Star* has not gone down—even they are only provisionally ruled out, for *Dog Star* could still come chugging into Port Lincoln in the next chapter . . . or the next. But the longer she is away, the more convinced we become that she has indeed sunk: the field of indeterminacy shrinks to the question of *how* she met her fate, and this we feel no compulsion to pursue. This may partly be the reason why asking students to imaginatively reconstruct what happened to *Dog Star* (by writing an additional chapter for the novel, for instance) does not, characteristically, produce writing that is particularly concentrated or powerful. But where there is a high degree of indeterminacy, where the text is particularly teasing and enigmatic, then imaginative reconstruction comes into its own. Such a case is afforded by the episode in *A High Wind in Jamaica* in which Margaret Fernandez takes up residence in Otto's cabin.

When Jonsen and his drunken crew made their way down into the forehold, it was Margaret, of course, who most clearly understood the nature of the danger they were in, but her subsequent behavior remained incomprehensible to the rest of the other children:

> But what interested (Emily) more was the curious way Margaret had gone on, those next few days.
>
> For some time she had behaved very oddly indeed. At first she seemed exaggeratedly frightened of all the men: but then she had suddenly taken to following them about the deck like a dog—not Jonsen, it is true, but Otto especially. Then she had departed from them altogether and had taken up her quarters in the cabin. The curious thing was that now she avoided them all utterly, and spent her time with the sailors: and the sailors, for their part, seemed to take peculiar pains not only not to let her speak to, but even not to let her be seen by the other children.
>
> Now they hardly saw her at all: and when they did she seemed so different they hardly recognized her: though where the difference lay it would be hard to say.

Thereafter, the novel only affords us a couple of revealing glimpses of Margaret. When Emily is injured by the marlin-spike, Jonsen immediately carries her down into the cabin:

> There sat Margaret, bending over some mending, her slim shoulders hunched up, humming softly, and feeling deadly ill.
>
> "Get out!" said Jonsen, in a low brutal voice. Without a word or sign Margaret gathered up her sewing and climbed on deck.

Where Margaret goes, we do not know, but she is the first on the scene after Emily has murdered the Dutch captain:

> ... and the first witness of the scene was Margaret, who presently peered down from the deck above, her dulled eyes standing out from her small, skull-like face.

What has wrought so terrible a change in Margaret? Apart from showing us what Margaret does after she has been dropped overboard, the novel leaves us to work it out for ourselves.

Robert, a fifteen-year-old, began by rehearsing the evidence and reconstructing Margaret's motives and feelings in the following way:

> When Margaret took up her sleeping quarters with Otto, she took a step into a kind of adulthood, leaving her childhood behind her. This step, she thought, would be good, in that she was separating herself from the rest of the children, and it was a sort

of "growing up," leaving the others behind. But this "good" step was to turn out to be a tragic step, and Otto continued to use her, she had started to earn a reputation from the captain, and probably the other sailors, as a slut or a tool that was used by Otto. She was no longer that innocent enquiring little girl, and how she learnt to miss that innocence.

When she looked down through the skylight of the cabin and saw the tragic thing Emily had committed, the murder of the Dutch captain, I bet she had felt like weeping for the end of innocence, like the boys in *Lord of the Flies*, weeping for the end of innocence for Emily and herself. First Margaret lost her innocence of childhood through intercourse—then Emily lost her innocence of childhood through murdering the Dutch captain. Which sin was worse for a child, I have no idea!

As she was dropped overboard into the sea, I think the face Otto may have seen was the face of an indignantly hurt child. A child!

When she took up sleeping with the other kids again, she was trying to take a step backwards to childhood again—but it isn't at all successful as the others isolate her and she can't have her innocence again, once she has lost it.

I wondered whether Robert would get any further with this exploration if he changed tack and wrote about Margaret from "inside" the novel, imaginatively reconstructing what might have taken place in Otto's cabin. That night he wrote this:

Margaret sat on the bunk, gently rocking from side to side with the head swell, a downcast look on her face. She never ever really got sea-sick, but right now she felt decidedly queasy. As the stern once again shot into the air, and her stomach was forced down into her boots, the boat gave a melancholy sigh. Then, as the stern plunged down again and her stomach was eerily transported from her toes to her ears, she felt sure she was going to be sick.

It was dark in the cabin, and musty too, but the sun was shining outside. She could see the light coming through the crack in the door. The thin sliver of light pierced the darkness of the cabin, and she reached out and put her hand through it. It felt warm, which made her realize she was cold. She wished that she could go out onto the warm deck. But she remembered what Otto had told her, and she knew, of course, why she wasn't allowed to go on deck with the other children.

With that idea gone, she turned her attention to the doll lying on the bunk beside her. She had made it from a rum bottle and wrapped some old rags around it. Onto the neck of the bottle she had pushed a large potato (which she had scavenged from the galley) and had pushed some splinters into it to serve as eyes and a mouth. Otto called it her "spudhead," but she called it "my child" and nursed it as if it were. Right now, her thoughts wandered over her own lost childhood, and she found herself absent-mindedly nibbling the doll's head with her neat fine teeth. Raw potato wasn't that bad.

As Otto opened the door and stepped in, she was suddenly brought back to the present.

"Get up," he said to her, and then sat on the bunk, and she stood up and went over to the door and, with one arm holding the doll to her chest, she ran her fingers down the crack where the sunlight was shining through.

"Come here," Otto said, and she turned to see him starting to undo the buttons on his shirt. Margaret turned back to the doll and started rocking it. She looked up at the roof of the cabin, where patters of little feet and squeals of delighted laughter showed that the children were engaged in their endless game of Consequences. She turned her back to Otto and looked at her feet, the laughter of the children echoing in her head.

"Come here." Otto's voice was flat and peremptory.

Margaret shook her head and bit her lip, still with her back to Otto.

"Hey?" he said, a little puzzled. "Come here."

The children's laughter reached Margaret's ears again, then a single tear splashed on her foot. Her frail body was shaken by a wracking convulsive sob, and the doll fell, hitting the floor and breaking off at the neck. The potato head rolled up to Otto's feet and lay there, looking up at him.

Robert Paterson

So moving and so assured a piece of work almost defies commentary. Clearly, it represents more than an exemplification of the kinds of understanding it revealed in the first piece—it seems, in fact, to be integrating what he consciously knows about Margaret with other and less consciously articulable levels of understanding. (In this connection, it's perhaps significant that Robert handed up this piece of work saying, with a grin, "It's got ironies in it even I don't understand.")

The whole thrust of the piece, indeed, is away from the discursive statement of meaning and towards its poetic evocation through image and symbol. Even what he borrows is transformed in this direction. The hint thrown out in Hughes's apparently casual remark that Margaret was feeling "deadly ill" is taken up in the opening of Robert's piece and developed in such a way that one world, the objective world of the violently heaving cabin below decks, becomes a metaphor for another, the inner world of psychological dislocation and disorientation, in which Margaret is compelled to endure, with a dispirited resignation, what she feels powerless to alter. The ship itself seems to partake in Margaret's condition, its melancholy sigh an expression of the resigned weariness with which it, too, endures what it cannot change, heaved sickeningly from stem to stern on the rise and fall of the head swell. And Margaret, seated on the bunk, absorbed by her growing conviction that she is indeed going to be sick, can only regard the way in which all things in her world have taken on an oddly fluid air of instability with a gravely composed surprise that it should have turned out so.

Even where the connections with the earlier piece seem most apparent, we are aware of differences. The sunlight outside and the children's laughter overhead obviously represent the world she has lost, her "innocence of childhood" as Robert called it. But these images carry a range of felt suggestion and sympathetic insight that the earlier phrase cannot convey. In the contrast between the upper world of light, warmth, irrepressible gaiety and heedless freedom, and the lower depths, dark, cold and musty, in which Margaret remains confined, we not only feel the poignancy of her loss and the impossibility of her return to that other world,[2] but we come to understand more fully what exactly it is that she has lost. It is not just sexual innocence that has been lost; it is the living world of human warmth and motion from which she has been set apart. For Margaret, the "game of Consequences" is indeed "endless," and no game at all.

Nothing in the first piece, however, could have prepared us for the appearance of the doll in the second. No doubt, Robert took his cue from Rachel, who obsessively secreted her bundles of rags in odd places all over the ship, but the use he makes of Margaret's doll is highly original. In the pathetic object and Margaret's attempts to comfort it he has found the perfect symbol for her desperate need to be a child who is comforted by a loving and protective mother. Although it is unlikely that Robert could offer us an account of the psychological mechanism at work here, his

---

[2] The unobtrusive sexual symbolism of the crack in the cabin door not only serves as a reminder of how Margaret entered this world of mute and helpless suffering, but, when she wistfully runs her fingers down it, the gesture subtly emphasizes the impossibility of return. (Margaret's symbolic rebirth comes only after she has been cast overboard by the outraged pirates—out of death she wrings a provisional kind of restoration. "After such knowledge, what forgiveness?")

handling of it is nevertheless extraordinarily subtle and complex. For instance, when Margaret's thoughts turn to the past, she begins absent-mindedly to nibble the doll's head, as though, by incorporating the object that symbolizes the child she once was, she can recover what she has lost. Although there is a small comfort to be gained from it ("Raw potato wasn't that bad"), the attempt is, of course, doomed to failure, The result is that the doll is defaced, just as she has marred her own childhood through another, equally gnawing compulsion. ("The contempt the sailors felt for Margaret, their complete lack of pity in her obvious illness and misery, had been in direct proportion to the childhood she had belied.")

When she stands at the cabin door, cradling "her child" in one arm and ignoring Otto's curt command, she is, of course, both mother and child, but now a mother who is helpless to protect the child she still feels herself to be. When the doll smashes on the cabin floor, not only does the destruction of the doll recapitulate her original "fall," but it signals the collapse of the defense mechanism by which she sought to protect herself from those feelings of helpless vulnerability which are so powerfully focused in the image of the doll's head lying at Otto's feet, staring up at him in mute and inexpressive appeal.

2. Adding to a Text

In this section we cross a shadowy kind of border-line. The examples in the previous section were of stories that, in some form or other, were implicit in the original text. Of course, as *Blue Fin* makes so conveniently explicit, there are many possible stories about *Dog Star*'s disappearance, just as there must be other ways in which the gap in *A High Wind in Jamaica* could be filled— though the power of Robert's version makes it difficult to imagine alternatives. What is not in question, however, is that there *is* a story to be told—the story of *Dog Star*'s disappearance or the story of Margaret's suffering.

But in the examples that follow, the original text may not imply the existence of these additions, although the novel is enhanced or even challenged by what is added.

a. Reduplication, or "More of the Same." Some novels lend themselves particularly well to this kind of addition. *The Sword in the Stone*, for example, contains a series of episodes in which the Wart becomes an animal: perch, hawk, ant, owl, wild goose, and badger. These transformations form part of the Wart's education by Merlyn for his future role as King Arthur, and although they have a roughly cumulative structure, there is no particular reason why there should not be one more, or even one less. (In fact, White himself took some of the episodes from the later *Book of Merlyn* and incorporated them into *The Sword and the Stone*.)

To ask for an additional transformation episode for *The Sword and the Stone* is to place some very sophisticated and exacting requirements upon young writers, since White's writing in these episodes combines comic gusto with an astonishing ability to enter into "unknown modes of being." Yet, instead of the floundering we might expect, the result can be a kind of creative liberation, a release of unsuspected imaginative energy. Here is the opening of one such addition, written by a thirteen-year-old, in which the Wart is changed into an octopus:

The Wart All at Sea

"Oh, these pestering flies!" yelled the Wart, swatting a large blue bottle that had landed on his nose. "And these donkeys are so uncomfortable! When are we going to stop at the next institution, Merlyn?"

"Mmm," mumbled Merlyn, ignoring the question.

"Oh, how I wish I could go for a swim," moaned the Wart, looking out over the calm blue sea. "Couldn't you change me into a sea fish, Merlyn?"

"No," said Merlyn, "that part of your education is over. We came to France so that you could visit some of the monarchs here, and visit the great institutions, and if you ask me once more, I'll turn you into a . . ."

"A fish?" said the Wart hopefully.

"No, cabbage," snapped Merlyn, who wasn't in the best of moods.

The Wart settled into a more comfortable position on the donkey's back and decided to ask no more questions, not for a while anyway. Merlyn rode on, not seeming to notice the heat as he still had his winter cloak on.

After another hour of riding, the Wart had become quite sore from the constant jolting of the donkey and began pestering Merlyn, who at first was asleep.

"Merlyn, couldn't you change me into a sea fish?"

"Mmm? . . . No!"

"Just a teeny weeny one?"

"No!"

"Why?"

"You'd probably get eaten, and besides, I can't."

"Why?"

"Emugel, emugel, emugel!" yelled Merlin.

"I beg your . . . mm, mmm," mmmed the Wart, finding himself without a mouth. "Mmm, mmmm, mmmmm!" It could have been anyone's guess what he said!

"Emugelnu, emugelnu, emugelnu," chanted Merlin, and the Wart was himself again.

"Turn me into a fish!" yelled the Wart straight away. "If you can turn me into a cabbage, you can turn me into a fish. Do you hear? I want to be a fish, a fish."

"Emugel, emugel . . ."

"All right!" said the Wart. "I'll be quiet."

A quarter of an hour of silence followed before Merlin said, I suppose I could turn you into a sea creature . . . not a fish though."

"What then?" questioned the Wart.

"I'll need some help from a friend though," said Merlin. "What is his name? Supotco Siragluv? No, no. Ah, Siragluv Supotco? No, that's not it. Ah, let's think, what is his name?"

"Don't say you've forgotten, Merlin," said a faint voice from all around.

"No, no," said Merlin, "how could I? Gnik fo eht aes, Gnik Supotco Siragluv—or, as I knew you, Luflliks."

"I didn't think you would forget," said the still faint voice. "What is it you want?"

"Esaelp ekat eht Traw ot ruoy modgnik, sa eno fo uoy, dna tcetorp mih. Uoy ewo ti ot em," said Merlin.

"Tell him to walk," said the voice.

"Walk," said Merlin.

The Wart obediently walked into the water up to his neck.

"Carry on," said Merlin.

"B-but . . ."

"Just carry on walking," said Merlin.

The Wart kept on walking along the seabed, blowing bubbles every now and then. Still nothing happened!

Suddenly a shark appeared, and made a pass. Snap!

"Whew!" said the Wart in relief, but his relief changed to panic as he had just blown out the last of his air. He took several gulps of seawater, coughed, or rather, vomited it back up, and began striking for the surface.

How I wish I were an octopus, thought the Wart, as the shark made another pass, just missing the Wart's nose. Almost at once, the Wart found he had eight legs and his body had been pushed back behind his head and, best of all, he could breathe, although the air tasted funny. . . .

Shaun Wakeford

How neatly the transformation is accomplished, Merlyn's magic and the Wart's own panicked wish intersecting just at the crucial moment!

Adroit and amusing it certainly is, but how are we to approach writing like this? We would be mistaken, I believe, to think of such work only in terms of its success as pastiche. There is a good deal more going on here than mere imitation. Indeed, the word *imitation* itself sets up the wrong kind of expectations. Although the Wart and Merlyn are, by and large, recognizably the same characters as those we know from the novel, they seem to have passed through a kind of sea-change. Merlyn, preoccupied, sleepy, and snappish, seems to have become rather more like one of those unpredictable elderly relatives we might expect to find in a Saki story, and the Wart, too, seems different, more of a child—demanding, strong-willed and even, at times, imperious.

I don't think we should see this simply as Shaun's failure to "get it right." The writing has its own independent vitality and "rightness." Writing like this, I'd suggest, represents a point of meeting between two sensibilities, the author's and the student's, and in this transaction something new comes into being.

We tend to think of imitation rather narrowly in terms of an intention to reproduce the features of an author's style, and so deprecate the practice as essentially uncreative. But, in this case, we might be better to think of Shaun as writing in the manner of T. H. White, and to recognize that this has been the means of a surprising creative release. Not only has writing in this way allowed him to open up and exploit a vein of humour that is fluently inventive and disarmingly good-natured, but it has provided the conditions under which he could create that gently effective, almost numinous moment when the King of the Sea, King Octopus Vulgaris, announces himself to Merlyn in "a faint voice from all around."

The conclusion of Shaun's story provides us with another instance in which considerations of simple indebtedness are not sufficient to account for what is going on. After a series of adventures in his new shape as an octopus, the Wart finally meets King O. Vulgaris:

> "Oh," said the King, "I have something for you from Merlyn."
> "Merlyn?" said the Wart. "You know Merlyn?"
> "Yes, we are acquainted. He asked me to give you this," said the King, handing the Wart a small carved piece of rock. "For your, er—how would you say?—your transportation."
> The Wart took the rock in his tentacle. It felt warm and smooth, as he traced the lines with his fingers, and finally dropped it to the sandy beach.

For a thirteen-year-old, Shaun is already a very accomplished writer, and in the imaginative coup by which he effects the Wart's "transportation" he has moved beyond anything we could account for in terms of simple imitation. He is as much emulating White as imitating him. Faced with this kind of assurance and control, it would not be unreasonable to conclude that writing in the manner of White has tapped a deep spring of imaginative creativity in this boy.

b. Continuations. Recently, an Adelaide newspaper carried the following brief review notice:

> *The Further Adventures of Huckleberry Finn* by Greg Matthews. If there is anything to be said for developing an author's idea long after he had died, then this is probably the book to say it. If you couldn't get enough of Mark Twain's original, you'll be pleased to know that Huck, Jim, and the others sound much the same in Greg Matthews' extension as they leave the Mississippi and head off to California to find gold.

The very terms in which the recommendation is made warn us of the dangers involved in such an undertaking. By and large, novels don't invite us to continue them, either as readers or as writers. We may wonder, as we finish a book, what happened to such-and-such a character, how things turned out for so-and-so, but we do not pursue such speculations very far, as a general rule. We are content with the sense of closure we have achieved with the text. Any addition, therefore, may strike us as unnecessary (and so trivial), or as an intrusive meddling with what is best left alone.

But, if we consider the ending of a novel like Robert O'Brien's *Z for Zachariah*, it is possible to see a role for continuations that does not involve that kind of impertinence or trivialization:

> Now it is morning. I do not know where I am. I walked all afternoon and almost all night until I was so tired I could not go on. Then I did not bother to put up the tent, just spread my blanket by the roadside and lay down. While I was sleeping the dream came, and in the dream I walked until I found the school-room and the children. When I awoke the sun was high in the sky. A stream was flowing through the brown grass, winding west. The dream has gone, yet I knew which way to go. As I walk I search the horizon for a trace of green. I am hopeful.

It is difficult to know quite how we are to take this. Is the appearance of the stream the morning after her dream a sign that

Anne will find what she is seeking, or is her conviction that the stream points the way ahead as much a wish-fulfillment as the dream? It seems unlikely that there is any irony present here (and even if there were, what would it mean—that Anne is both deluded and doomed? too bitter a pill, surely), yet the more we consider the dangers of the journey that lie before Anne, the more slender seem the grounds for hope.

It is one thing to speculate about the possible outcomes of Anne's quest; it is another entirely to take up the story at this point and follow Anne further into the deadness. We cannot know, of course, what will happen to her—and the continuations below envisage very different outcomes—but it is possible to imagine developments which do not fulfill the promise held out to us in Anne's last words and yet which do not only leave us with a sense of waste and defeat.

In the following example, Anne has decided to return to the valley. On the way back she has accidentally punctured the safe-suit and injured herself. Aware that her life is in danger, she makes her way back to Burden Valley, hoping that Mr. Loomis will look after her in her need as she looked after him in his. At the point where the extract begins, Anne, ill and weak from exposure to the radiation, has just reached the valley and has made her way back to the house:

> When I opened the door, I saw that Mr. Loomis was not there. I figured he was picking up supplies. I fixed up my cut and lay down in my father's chair. I waited and waited.
>
> Finally I got the strength to go upstairs and look out of the window. From here I could see the whole valley. I got the binoculars that were on the mantelpiece in my room. I got up on my bed and looked out. Firstly, I looked at the store. I saw nothing. Then the fields. There was one more place. The corn crop on the side of the hill. A cold shiver went down my spine. I was right. I saw the tractor on its side.
>
> I fell back on my bed.
>
> This is my last entry in my diary. I grew up in the valley and I am pleased I can die in the valley. I hope someone will find my diary and see what we really went through.
>
> I am afraid.
>
> Sam McClure

The voice we hear in these words is recognizably Anne Burden's, and we feel that the way in which she meets the extremity of this situation is completely consistent with what we know of her from the novel. Part of the success of Sam's continuation, then, lies in the feeling of continuity it creates. Yet the ability of the writing to move us testifies to something more than that. We feel, in fact, that a particular kind of value is being brought to definition in the writing, a value or an attitude, moreover, which discloses itself only as the writer is able to enter into and dramatize Anne's consciousness from within, as it were. Here Anne confronts the defeat of all her hopes and the certainty of her own death, and yet the effect, for all its bleakness, is not finally negative.

What is striking is the courage and dignity with which Anne confronts her fate. The bare stating manner of the prose is not artless—it is the means by which powerful feelings are held in check. In the second paragraph, for instance, Anne's mounting dread as she begins to realize Mr. Loomis is never coming back is very powerfully conveyed by the pared-down terseness of the utterance. Reading the passage aloud, as it demands we should, we find we have to pause heavily after we have read "Then the fields," and in that pause we hear the silent expiration of Anne's last hope. When she turns to look at the corn crop, it is in the expectation of finding Mr. Loomis dead. The physical collapse that follows immediately upon her discovery of the overturned tractor suggests the almost insupportable strain involved, the strenuousness of the effort it required to confront what she had already foreseen. ("What heart heard, ghost guessed.")

But perhaps we come closest to saying what is being dramatized here when we note the absence of protest. The final section of Anne's diary moves into the present tense, as if, more important than her grief and despair, is the need to bear witness, even in a world in which there may be no-one to heed her testimony. There is also the need to find some fitness in the pattern her existence has assumed. What her diary testifies to, she now sees, is not only what she uniquely experienced, but what "we" went through. Momentarily, she and Mr. Loomis are held together in a vision of mutual suffering. Then, and only then, does she speak directly of her feelings of fear and vulnerability in the face of death. There is nothing else left to acknowledge after that—the rest is silence.

There is no bitterness and no repining—and nothing could be further from self-pity. There seems to be an absence of any consciousness of self other than as an experiencing centre. What Sam has given us in Anne's diary represents what we might perhaps call the achievement of a difficult kind of sincerity, which, in its disinterestedness and its vulnerable openness to experience reminds me, at least, of some of Lawrence's last poems.

If Sam's continuation sketches out one possible line of development, Robert's takes up another.

Close to death, Anne recovers upon hearing, with a rush of joy, "the harsh raucous cry of a crow" outside her tent. Realizing that there must be another valley beyond the next ridge, she is revitalized, and sets out upon her way. At the point where this extract begins, she has reached the ridge and has seen the valley about two miles further on below her, but darkness has prevented her from pushing on:

August 17

The crow woke me at dawn today. When I stepped outside the tent I could see the school building clearly. I am sure that when I get there, there will be two or three families of children waiting to be taught, children left behind by their parents, just as I was left behind by mine.

August 18

I reached the town an hour later. The sun shone a bright yellow, just as it should. I took out the geiger counter. It read 4rs, and as my valley had a reading of 5rs, I guessed it was below the danger level. I took off the safesuit. I took a hairbrush and a mirror from the cart and brushed my hair. I put the brush and mirror away and began to walk in the direction of the school. I turned a corner. The school stood at the end of the street. It consisted of only one building with a rainwater tank. There was no sound but the clickety-click of my shoes on the pavement. The school loomed closer and suddenly I had reached the school gate. I unlatched it and it swung open, creaking as it did. I stepped in, shutting the gate behind me. There was a church bell in the middle of the yard. I tolled it. The noise of it reverberated around the hillsides, completely destroying the silence. That would bring the children along. I waited. No-one came. I tolled the bell and again it echoed around the hillsides, and again I waited, and again no-one came. They had to be inside. I opened the door and walked in. The teacher's desk stood at the front, empty. The children's desks were lined up in rows around me, also empty. I walked over to the teacher's desk and the seat. I waited. There was no-one and nothing, nothing but foolishness. Z is for Zachariah and it always will be. I laid my head on the desk and wept uncontrollably. I cried for my foolishness, I cried for my disappointment, I cried for my hopelessness, and still I cried. I don't know how long I sat there weeping, but when I regained control of myself, I looked up. There in front of me stood an old man, with a little boy's hand in his right hand and a little girl's hand in his left, waiting for me to begin teaching.

One day the schoolroom will be full.

Robert Harper

Anne's dream of finding a schoolroom full of children who are waiting for her is fulfilled here in the only way I can imagine being imaginatively satisfying; and in bringing the story to such a conclusion, Robert makes us aware of something about Anne that may have escaped our notice . . . the remarkable and moving unselfishness of her dream. What the conclusion of her story emphasizes is that what matters is not the perpetuation of her individual existence, but the fact that the children represent a guarantee that human life itself will continue. As she has always been, Anne is the tender of life in others, and the hander-on of those values and those kinds of knowledge that make life more than brute existence. To have captured that so convincingly and so unsentimentally is a considerable achievement.

Both these continuations are imaginatively convincing, yet they envisage very different outcomes to the story— and it is possible to envisage still other outcomes. Yet, in one important way, Sam's and Robert's continuations of *Z for Zachariah* are remarkably similar. In each case, the way in which Anne's story is brought to an end brings a particular set of values sharply into focus, values which we can recognize as being potential in the original. Though there is development and change, Anne acts, essentially, as we would expect her to, and these continuations, therefore, cast their shadows backward as well as forward.

3. Epilogues

An epilogue, of course, is simply a specialized form of continuation, but one which warrants separate treatment here because it can provide students with an unusually powerful way of exploring and defining their responses to central aspects of a work.

Two features of the epilogue, in particular, seem crucial to its success: its brevity, and the time-lapse it usually involves. Together, they encourage the seeking-out of those events or situations, turning-points in a character's life, which are felt to be maximally revealing.

Asking students to write an epilogue to a novel like *Lord of the Flies* sets up a kind of dialogue between the author and the student, a dialogue in which the value-meanings imaginatively realized in the student's epilogue comment on the novel's vision of life in original and revealing ways.

Just how original will, I hope, become apparent from the following examples, both written by fifteen-year-olds:

Afterwards

Jack looked into the depths of the pool. It was clear, crystal clear, not a ripple creased the surface. Serenity filled it inviting him closer. A loud explosion rocked the dome, but Jack didn't even hear it. His body felt soft and fuzzy and he just wanted to sleep. Forever.

He was no longer the hunter. That had finished long ago. Strange that, he never had liked pigs, but there weren't many left now. Kneeling down, he touched the water, sending a crinkle across its flawless sheet. He wished only to slip into its depths, and sleep there, but a voice recalled him from his thoughts.

"General, we're ready for evacuation now."

Slowly turning from the pool, Jack nodded and said in a weary voice:

"Thanks Ralph."

Lisa Jarmyn

In contrast to the victoriously cock-a-hoop Jack we remember from the last pages of Golding's novel—all restraint thrown to the wind—the Jack we see here is defeated, and we feel as if what we are observing is a way of life which has just completed its trajectory. The defeat, of course, is both internal and external, the one being mirrored in the other. And, in defeat, the pool in which Jack contemplates the repose and self-forgetfulness which have eluded him quickly becomes an invitation to the peacefulness of oblivion. But (in a way that is reminiscent of Robert Frost's "Stopping by Woods on a Snowy Evening") the longing for death is checked by the call of duty: "General, we are ready for evacuation now."

Jack's rank and the role associated with it—artfully withheld until the end—subtly suggest the way in which he has sought to channel and control those aggressive and destructive instincts which were woken into clamorously urgent life within him while he was on the island. But, despite the strenuousness of his (lifelong) effort of sublimation, it has ended in defeat, and all Jack is left with is his weariness and the belated recognition that the inner drama was played out long before the outer one was over: "He was no longer the hunter. That had finished long ago." In its wake, there is only a curiously dissociated sense of calm and a blank emptiness.

Such a vision of Jack's end, such an extrapolation from Golding's novel, is imaginatively convincing and, in its turn, reflects back upon its original. What Jack stands for in the novel, the human potentiality he represents, has become subject to this girl's deepest intuitions and feelings—her moral sense, one might almost say. The result is not the imposition of a previously determined conclusion, but a recognition, imaginatively realized, that this is where the inner logic of Jack's "case" leads. Jack's solution, the restriction of an essentially unaltered drive within narrow boundaries, cannot ultimately sustain identity. The inner loss is not noticed until, prompted by the outer defeat, he looks inside and finds that his sense of who he is has leaked away long before, unnoticed and unmourned. In its absence he confronts an inner blankness. If this reminds us, in different ways, of both Conrad's Decoud and Shakespeare's Macbeth, that provides us with a clue to the nature of this girl's implicit criticism of Golding: the ultimate result of Jack's "choice" is a despairing awareness of one's own nullity. The writing leads us, therefore, to a heightened awareness of the human centrality of those values which Jack has attempted to set at naught, values without which life becomes meaningless and insupportable. There is no corresponding assertion of value at the end of *Lord of the Flies*: ironically, Ralph is saved only by the arrival of the naval officer, and we end with the vision of the cruiser at anchor off the end of the island.

Ralph

He walked along the beach, as he had done last night and the night before that. He idly kicked the pebbles which the sea had rounded in the decades gone by. He glanced out to sea. He could hear the waves crashing onto the reef, but he couldn't see them. Only the moonlight let him distinguish between the water and the sand, but sometimes even they merged together.

Little waves broke near his feet, making tiny bubbles which exploded into nothingness, only to be replaced by another line of bubbles. Life was like that, he thought. People were like that.

The waves licked at his feet. He spotted something glimmering in the water. It was a shell. He reached down and picked it up. It was pale pink, almost white, with a slight spiral twist, covered with a delicate pattern.

He cradled the shell against his chest, recalling the island: the waves pounding on the reef . . . savages . . . Simon . . . Piggy. He shut his eyes tight, trying to hold back the tears. He saw savages dancing, Piggy was falling, claws and teeth tearing, the noise beating in his ears. Piggy was calling him, he could see him falling, falling . . .

He took a step into the sea. The waves reached for his shoes, splashing his trousers. Water surrounded him He was slowly sinking deeper, deeper. Piggy was calling. He walked further out. The waves splashed on his chest. He shuddered. His feet were losing their grip; he could no longer touch the bottom.

He hardly noticed the water closing over his head.

Small waves crept further up the beach, touching a pale pink thing with a slight spiral twist, covered with a delicate pattern. The world was at peace.

Darren Gaunt

Like the opening of Lisa's piece, the beginning of Darren's epilogue foreshadows all that is to come. Night after night, as Ralph has walked the uncertain boundary between sea and shore, he has been treading another borderline, the shadowy boundary between being and un-being, which, in his brooding despair and deepening sense of anomie, has become increasingly difficult to discern.

The sea not only provides him with images in which his own nihilism is reflected ("Life was like that, he thought. People were like that."), but it is an active agent in his destruction. It licks hungrily at his feet and casts in his path the shell which now only serves to bring home to him, with an overwhelming vividness, the failure of ordinary, unheroic goodness—decent and rational—to contain the savagery and unreason which finally destroyed them. The shell is beautiful and delicate still, glimmering faintly in the water, like some ideal which Ralph still yearns for but which his experience has taught him has no habitation in the human world. That is the turning point—with that realization, there is no longer anything left to hold him to life. When he hears Piggy's voice calling to him, it represents not only his own powerful yearning for death but the promise of comfort, the promise of being reunited with the "true wise friend" for whom he had wept on that other beach.

But that is not all. After Ralph's death, there is a coda:

Small waves crept further up the beach, touching a pale pink thing with a slight spiral twist, covered with a delicate pattern. The world was at peace.

The sea is no longer hungry. It touches the shell gently and unquestioningly, as if its purpose were achieved, and the shell is just a shell, "a pale pink thing with a slight spiral twist, covered with a delicate pattern." Here is a world of things, devoid of human meanings, self-sufficient and at peace with themselves. It is as if a balance has been restored, a status quo reestablished. We are left to ponder a world that not only is unable to provide the meanings and values that make human existence supportable, but is indifferent or hostile to such human needs. The sea reaches out to Ralph in his anguish and despair and expunges him, merging his nothingness with its own. We are left with the uneasy feeling that human existence is surrounded by a mute world of things patiently awaiting those moments of human vulnerability which will allow them to reduce consciousness (being-for-itself) to its own condition of sheer facticity (being-in-itself). "Suicide," as Sartre remarked, "is an absurdity which causes my life to be submerged in the absurd."

This is a vision of man's place in the natural world that we might take as a corrective to the long lyrical passage which concludes Chapter 9 of *Lord of the Flies*:

> The water rose further and dressed Simon's coarse hair with brightness. The line of his cheek silvered and the turn of his shoulder became sculptured marble. The strange attendant creatures, with their fiery eyes and trailing vapours, busied themselves round his head. The body lifted a fraction of an inch from the sand and a bubble of air escaped form the mouth with a wet plop. Then it turned gently in the water.
>
> Somewhere over the darkened curve of the world the sun and moon were pulling; and the film of water on the earth planet was held, bulging slightly on one side while the solid core turned. The great wave of the tide moved further along the island and the water lifted. Softly, surrounded by a fringe of inquisitive bright creatures, itself a silver shape beneath the steadfast constellations, Simon's dead body moved out toward the open sea.

Not only does Darren reject that offer of metaphysical consolation, but he decisively rejects any view of Ralph's experiences that would see him emerging a "sadder but wiser" man:

> In Ralph weeping, we have an ordinary, decent human being almost destroyed by forces he cannot control but who, through struggling to comprehend those forces, gains something approaching heroic status.... With his "education," Ralph may go back to society a saner, wiser individual: one of those who are prepared to stop the world reaching those stages at which it throws up the dead airman and the trim cruiser in the distance (Whiffey, 1970).

4. Dreams

Since dreams are highly condensed symbolic representations of inner experience, not only can they provide a very useful way of focusing students' attention upon a character's inner response to the experiences he or she has undergone in the course of the novel, but they can encourage the poetic evocation, through image and symbol, of meaning and insights that could otherwise not reach formulation.

After a group of thirteen-year-olds had read Paula Fox's novel, *The Slave Dancer*, they were asked to write a dream Jessie Bollier, the slave dancer of the title, might have had after he was safely back in New Orleans, a dream in some way prompted by his experiences on the slave ship, *The Moonlight*. Here is what one student produced:

> I am at the bottom of a hill, a steep hill, which rises into a mist. At the top of this hill is a graveyard. The long grass stands still, silent, expectant. Around the hill I can see nothing. A deathly silence hangs in the the air.
>
> Somehow I know I must reach the top of the hill, reach the black gravestones, the proud gravestones that form my horizon. I take a step, and a sharp pain shoots up my leg. Another step, another jab. I know that I have to get there, have to take another step.
>
> Suddenly, on both sides of me, I can see the sailors. They are moving towards me. They all look old, wrinkled, and their clothes are the ones they wore on the ship, but torn, shredded, worn. Each sailor wields a stick, waving it above his head. I keep walking, step by step. As they come closer, I can see their faces, in the mist. They have no eyes, just pools of black, holes in their faces. I feel scared, but I keep walking. They get closer. Just before they reach me, Purvis and Ras appear on either side of me. They do not look like the sailors. The sailors stop, as if they are scared. Purvis, my protector. Ras turns his head and smiles at me. Purvis just stares at the top of the hill. Ras moves his hand, waves me on, towards the top of the hill, the graveyard. I look at the sailors again, and take another step. Simultaneously, Ras and Purvis take a step, a mirror of my movement. The sailors start to fade, disappear. At first I thought it was only a movement of the mist, but they all disappear. All, that is, except one, who I now recognize as Ben Stout. He moves towards us, as we move towards the top of the hill.
>
> Dark clouds are collecting in the sky, storm clouds. Purvis and Ras walk with me to the top. Ben Stout reaches us, from the side, and moves to block our way. He no longer has a stick in his hands, but a whip, a nine-tailed whip. He holds it in the air, and smiles a victor's grin. I hesitate, and again Ras motions me towards the top of the hill. I move on, walking straight at Ben Stout, and just before I reach him, he disappears, and a cry of anguish rings out, the first sound I have heard.

The storm breaks, and a warm rain starts to fall. As we move on, it gets hotter. A breeze picks up, and develops to a strong whistling wind as we near the summit. It is getting darker.

The ground levels out. We have reached the top of the hill. The graveyard is only about twenty steps away, but Purvis and Ras have gone.

The rain is almost unbearably hot, driven against us by the wind, and I have to fight to stay on my feet. It is almost as black as night.

I keep walking, and reach the graveyard. In front of me, between me and the first headstone, is the stub of an old candle.

I pick up the candle, and move to the nearest headstone. I notice, now, that all the headstones are in a circle, facing the middle of the graveyard.

I cannot read the inscription because of the darkness. Suddenly the candle flickers into life and the flame burns straight and steady, not offering a flicker against the force of the storm.

I read the gravestone. There is no name, no information, just a birthdate and a dash, then a space. I move to the next gravestone. It is the same.

For the first time I notice a bare patch in the middle of the circle. Everywhere else there is knee-high grass.

In the middle of the bare ground lies my old brown fife. I struggle over to it against the wind. The rain has become heavier, and hotter, scalding me. I pick up my fife and play as I have never played before. The music is not what I had played in the streets nor the broken jig on *The Moonlight*. It was a new sound: deep, resonant, but sweet. One by one, as I play, the dates of death appear in the spaces on the gravestones, one digit at a time, as if it is a struggle for them to appear. The moment the last digit on the last gravestone appears, I stop playing, and the wind and rain stop, as if the task is ended. The silence roars in my ears, and I look towards where Ras and Purvis stand. They both smile, and then they start to fade, and disappear. I am alone, with my old fife in my hand. Another breeze picks up, but this is cool, fresh and gentle, barely enough to bend the grass. Waves of grass bend, in unison, all around the hill.

Suddenly I take a tight grip on my fife, and hurl it out, and it moves in slow motion, twisting and turning, out of the graveyard, slowly tumbling down the hill, and disappears into the mist.

The sun breaks through the clouds and the whole scene becomes brighter. I know that my task is done. The mist begins to

disappear, and I look out, to see what lies beyond the mist, beyond the hill, but before I see, I wake. . . .

Andrew Young

In general, there's little difficulty in seeing what this is about: in
the central action of the dream, an act of atonement is performed.
When Jessie finally reaches the top of the hill and plays his fife, we
feel that in some way the spirits of the dead slaves have been laid
to rest, some kind of partial reparation has been made. The fife,
the instrument through which the boy became an unwilling and
appalled agent of the slaves' degradation, has become the means
by which some kind of reconciliation is achieved. All that is clear
enough. But what do the rain and the wind represent? What is it
that Jessie might fight against if the task of reparation is to be
completed?

As soon as Ben Stout's malignity is defeated (his cry of anguish
is that of a damned soul), the gathering storm breaks and a warm
rain begins to fall. Jessie is now alone. Purvis and Ras no longer accompany him, and he is about to begin his task. The nearer he
comes to the circle of headstones, the more he has to struggle
against the wind, and the rain, which has become unbearably hot,
intensifying all the while as he approaches the graveyard. Only at
the moment when he has finished playing his fife do they stop,
and the breeze that then springs up brings not only a sense of
peace and refreshment but, as the grass bends in unison, a feeling
of reconciliation.

It's not difficult to see the rain as tears, tears of anguish or re-
morse, but whose tears—Jessie's, or the dead slaves', and why
should they have to be fought against? The answer seems to me to
come with the playing of the fife:

> I pick up my fife and play as I have never played before. The
> music is not what I had played in the streets nor the broken jig
> on *The Moonlight*. It was a new sound: deep, resonant, but
> sweet.

"Deep, resonant, but sweet"—like the voices of Negroes lifted in
song, perhaps. There is a moment in *The Slave Dancer* when the
slaves do sing:

> At the increasingly harsh shouts of Ben Stout, some of the
> black men had risen, swaying, to their feet. Then others stood.
> But several remained squatting. Stout began to lay about him
> with the cat-o'-nine, slapping the deck, flicking the fangs to-
> ward the feet of those who had not responded to his cries with
> even a twitch. At last, he whipped them to their feet. The

women had risen at the first word, clutching the small children to their breasts.

"Bollweevil!" called the Captain.

Ned suddenly lit up his pipe.

I blew. A broken squeal came out of my fife.

"Tie him to the topmast crosstrees!" screamed Cawthorne. Stout, smiling, started toward me. I blew again. This time I managed a thin note, then some semblance of a tune.

The cat-o'-nine slapped the deck. Spark clapped his hands without a trace of rhythm. The Captain waved his hands about as though he'd been attacked by a horde of flies. A black man dropped toward the deck until Spark brought his heel down on his thin bare foot.

I played against the wind, the movement of the ship and my own self-disgust, and finally the slaves began to lift their feet, the chains attached to the shackles around their ankles forming an iron dirge, below the trills of my tune. The women, being un-shackled, moved more freely, but they continued to hold the children close. From no more than a barely audible moan or two, their voices began to gain strength until the song they were singing, or the words they were chanting, or the story they were telling overwhelmed the small sound of my playing.

All at once, as abrupt as the fall of an axe, it came to a stop. Ben Stout snatched the fife from my hands. The slaves grew silent. The dust they had raised slowly settled around them.

Through their song, the slaves' pain and suffering, their yearning for release, find expression and, as it rises above the shrill trilling of Jessie's fife, it represents a defiant refusal to succumb, mute and defeated, to the inhuman degradation that is forced upon them.

So, in the dream, as Jessie fights through the wind and the scalding rain, we are being shown that the dead want more than our pity, for pity alone cannot restore what death has robbed them of. In death they have been denied what *The Moonlight* could not take from them, their irreducible human dignity, and only when the living become the means by which that dignity again finds expression, can the fact of death be accepted. Then death is no defeat: the fife sounds,[3] deep and resonant, like the song of *The Moonlight*, but now sweet, and, one by one, the dates of death appear on the gravestones.

---

[3] It is appropriate that the fife, which had turned the slaves into shambling caricatures of human beings, should be the means by which their full humanity is rescued from oblivion. It is even more appropriate that it should be cast away.

It is a moving vision and one, we could quite reasonably say, that represents a remarkable intuitive understanding of the purpose and function of Paula Fox's novel.

5. Altering a Text: Rewriting the Ending

This is not something to be undertaken lightly or frivolously, as the examples of *King Lear* and *Great Expectations* may serve to remind us, but there are cases where the possibility of an alternative ending raises important critical issues. If, for instance, one finds the ending of *Huckleberry Finn* unsatisfactory, what other conclusion can one imagine for the novel, and from what point in the book would one have to begin rewriting?

The Owl Service, by Alan Garner, offers a particularly interesting case. The book is predicated upon the idea that the violent and mutually destructive relationship that began in the legendary past with Lleu Llaw Gyffes, Blodeuwedd, and Gronw Pebyr, has repeated itself in each subsequent generation, ending, every time, in catastrophe for the two men and the woman involved. This pattern of events threatens to repeat itself in the present through the lives of Gwyn, Alison, and Roger. But, in the last chapter of the novel, Roger, quite unexpectedly, transforms the pattern of destruction into one of reconciliation and forgiveness through a simple gesture of sympathy and caring that we had not thought he was capable of making.

A group of thirteen-year-olds who had read *The Owl Service* with close attention, and who had been introduced to the legend from *The Mabinogion* upon which Garner draws, were asked to rewrite the final chapter of the novel so that things turned out the way they always had in the past. This involved them in finding ways in which Gwyn, Roger, and Alison would each be "destroyed," just as in the legend Blodeuwedd is punished for her unfaithfulness to Gronw Pebyr by being transformed into an owl and each of the men becomes responsible for the other's death. In effect, the students were being asked to take up the novel at a point before Alan Garner deflected its trajectory, and to complete the pattern that had been looming throughout it.

Here is one boy's response to the task:

The Owl Service
Chapter 27

"Gwyn! Gwyn! Gwyn!"

Roger searched the garden as far as the wood, but he couldn't find Gwyn. He made his way slowly up the old peat road, slipping in the mud and cutting his hands and knees on the sharp pieces of slate embedded in the road. He stopped and turned around to look back into the valley. He was halfway up the road and had a good view. He could see the line of the river through the rain, the house, the bridge, and yes! Roger had just caught a glimpse of a figure standing on the bridge in a black mackintosh, staring bleakly into the rushing water.

Roger turned and ran down the slippery road, faster, faster, until his legs couldn't keep up with his body. He stumbled and skidded full length on the road, cutting his hands and chin. He got up and started running, stumbled, and ran again. He reached the river and began to run towards the house and the bridge.

"Gwyn! Gwyn!" Roger yelled through the thick wall of rain. Gwyn was still standing on the bridge, staring at the water.

"Gwyn, come up to the house. Halfbacon wants you. Gwyn, listen to me," Roger yelled, shaking Gwyn by the shoulder.

"Get lost," said Gwyn. "No," and gave Roger a shove.

"Gwyn, listen, Alison is in trouble. She needs you. Please Gwyn, come to the house."

"No," said Gwyn.

"Come on," said Roger, and he grabbed Gwyn's arm.

"Get lost!" yelled Gwyn, and gave Roger a hard shove.

Roger stumbled on a loose board on the bridge and fell under the railing and was swallowed up by the surging river. His head reappeared further along the river for a few moments before the surging torrent pulled him under again.

Gwyn thought he heard screams from the house, but it didn't matter. All he wanted was revenge.

He walked calmly away from the bridge and towards the peat road.

Alison screamed aloud as claw marks dragged at her flesh. Her face was scored with them, crossing over and over, but there was no blood. The marks were under the flesh. Huw stood there watching.

"Where is that boy being?" he mumbled.

A flying piece of wood smashed one of the panels of the kitchen window, sending glass across the room. The rain trickled in through the gaping hole and dripped off the sill, forming a puddle on the cold stone of the kitchen floor. The wind howled and battered at the door. Water dripped through the hole in the window. The puddle slowly grew in size.

Gwyn stood alone on the Bryn, staring down into the valley, lit at intervals by flashes of lightning. Rain flowed from the tip of his nose to the ground. His clothes, even the ones under his mac, were wringing wet and clung to his body. But he didn't care, he didn't care about anything—nothing mattered anymore. He just stood there for the sake of standing.

Something swished over his head and disappeared into the rain in the direction of the house. Gwyn looked down at his shoes. They were plastered with mud and stuck to the mud was a feather: an owl's feather.

The puddle now almost covered the whole of the kitchen floor but, because of uneven wear, odd humps of dry stone stayed above the water level. Alison lay still on the wooden table, breathing small shallow breaths.

"Always it is the same," mumbled Huw. "Always she sees owls, not flowers." He shivered. He realized that it was cold.

Carefully, he picked up Alison and took her through to the lounge room. It had changed since he had been in there many years ago. There was a new carpet on the floor, and new furniture.

He gently put her down on a sofa and propped her head up with cushions. It started to grow dark, so he drew the curtains across the two windows and flicked the electric light switch on. He looked at the bulbs, but they didn't light. He glanced around the room, then walked across to an oak cabinet in one corner of the room, fumbled with a box of matches, and light came to the room in the form of several candles in a gold candle-holder. Huw stood in the flickering light, staring at Alison.

"Always it is the same," he mumbled.

Gwyn coughed. The cold wind cut through him like a knife, and he began to shiver. His teeth rattled loudly.

He heard an engine down in the valley and saw two points of light slowly moving along the valley road.

"Huh, Lord Muck returning from his rounds," he thought aloud. "Won't he get a surprise when he gets back!"

Clive drove slowly along the narrow winding road. Never can be too sure in this weather. Tree might have fallen across the road, or something.

Gwyn watched the two points of light getting closer to the house. Suddenly something passed within inches of his face. He turned around, but could see nothing.

Swish.

He felt a cold jet of air rush past the back of his head.

Swish, again.

Swish, swish.

Gwyn shielded his face as the night air was suddenly filled with owls. Hundreds of them, silently travelling through the cold night air.

He didn't know how long it lasted, but it seemed for eternity. When he finally did uncover his face, the night air was calm, except for the steady beat of the rain and the occasional howling of the wind.

He decided to go down to the house.

It took him a good hour of crawling and slowly walking before he reached the river. He looked up the valley towards the house. Funny, no lights on. Power must be off.

He entered the house through the kitchen door. The floor was about an inch deep in water. He splashed through the kitchen to the passageway. The lounge room door was open and a faint light filtered out. He hesitated, then strode towards the door. Alison lay on the couch. Clive sat opposite in his favourite armchair, and Huw stood by the window.

As Gwyn entered, Clive said calmly, "Help her, Gwyn. Please help her."

"Why?"

"Please help her. Please."

"How?" questioned Gwyn.

"Comfort her, boy. Comfort her," whispered Huw.

"No," said Gwyn.

"Please."

"No," said Gwyn.

Clive sighed, and reclined in his chair.

"Where's Roger?" he questioned.

"Don't know," said Gwyn. "Last time I saw him he was in the river."

"What?" said Clive, sitting up quickly. "What do you mean, in the river?" By now his voice had risen to a shout.

"In the river," said Gwyn. "Didn't stand a chance, just got sucked under."

Clive grabbed Gwyn and shook him vigorously, then slowly let go and sat down. His face was pale.

"We should have left earlier," he said slowly. "What's going on in this accursed valley?"

"No, no," screamed Alison suddenly.

Clive, Huw and Gwyn all turned quickly towards her. She was beating at the air with her fists.

"Get away!" she screamed. "Get away! No, no, no."

Clive, still not able to take it all in, just sat there. Huw walked over to her. Alison looked at him fearfully.

"Get away!" she screamed, backing towards the door. "Get away!" She bumped into Gwyn, who was standing by the door. "No, not you! Get away! All of you, get away! Leave me alone!" she screamed.

Gwyn grabbed her firmly by her wrists and held her. Huw ripped the curtains from the window and tore them into strips. With these they bound Alison.

"Good work, boy," he said to Gwyn. "I'll take her to the car now."

"I'll do that," said Clive, suddenly recovering from his shock.

Clive turned the ignition on. The starter motor whirred and the engine roared into life. He backed the car down to the gate, got out, opened it, and backed onto the road. Gwyn stood and watched as the car slowly disappeared down the road in the early hours of the morning. He heard a swishing, and looked up. A giant owl was perched in a tree above him, looking out down the valley.

Shaun Wakeford

Although there are obvious weaknesses here—Roger's death for instance, is rather perfunctorily handled, and the dialogue is some-times wooden—they do not detract from what is genuinely impressive about this piece. One of the most striking things about it is the use it makes of repeated images, such as the owls and the slowly growing puddle of water on the kitchen floor.

The owls, of course, come straight from Garner's novel and, as symbols of the destructive forces that have Alison in their grip, they are no doubt being fairly consciously deployed. Nevertheless, Shaun doesn't simply use them as a "given." The moment in his chapter when the night air is filled with owls is itself filled with a genuine sense of terror:

Gwyn watched the two points of light getting closer to the house. Suddenly something passed within inches of his face. He turned around, but could see nothing.

Swish.

He felt a cold jet of air rush past the back of his head.

Swish, again.

Swish, swish.

Gwyn shielded his face as the night air was suddenly filled with owls. Hundreds of them, silently travelling through the cold night air.

He didn't know how long it lasted, but it seemed for eternity. When he finally did uncover his face, the night air was calm, ex-cept for the steady beat of the rain and the occasional howling of the wind.

The clipped economy of the writing—almost telegraphic in places—and the restraint with which the terror and menace of the moment are evoked, these could be Garner himself. Like Garner, too, is the way in which the writing conveys the feeling of some process having come to completion: "When he did finally uncover his face, the night air was calm, except for the steady beat of the rain and the occasional howling of the wind." All this is so convincing that it has an odd and almost certainly unintended effect. Gwyn's petty and childishly nursed sense of grievance ("All he wanted was revenge") is implicitly "placed" by being set against the malice of larger and more impersonal forces.

But, however calculated Shaun's use of the owls may have been, the symbolism that develops around the image of the growing puddle of water on the kitchen floor seems much less premeditated. Unlike the owls, one doubts whether Shaun could explain the use to which he puts the image, although there is no doubt that he is consciously using it.

At first, the puddle seems to represent the intrusion into the human world of those inhuman forces—symbolized in the rain and the wind—that are now massed against it:

A flying piece of wood smashed one of the panels in the kitchen window, sending glass across the room. The rain trickled in through the gaping hole and dripped off the sill, forming a puddle on the cold stone of the kitchen floor. The wind howled and battered at the door. Water dripped through the hole in the window. The puddle slowly grew in size.

Yet, in contrast to the wild fury of the storm, there is a sense of calm steadiness about the growth of the puddle, as if suggesting that once such forces find their point of entry into the human world, the course they take is steady, directed and inexorable. Perhaps it is this that accounts for the subdued sense of menace that we feel in that final sentence.

In any case, when the image is repeated later, we are left in no doubt about the way in which the growth of the puddle functions as an "objective correlative" for the progress of Alison's "illness":

The puddle now almost covered the whole of the kitchen floor but, because of uneven wear, odd humps of dry stone stayed above the water level. Alison lay still on the wooden table, breathing small shallow breaths.

Through what is a largely instinctive use of symbolism, Shaun has brought Garner's novel to rest in a way that suggests that it is through the destructive human passions that are played out here—

rage, hatred, and jealousy—that elemental powers find their lodge-
ment in the human world, which they then proceed inexorably to
use for their own ends. It is a vision I can imagine Alan Garner
finding congenial.

Conclusion

In the beginning of this chapter, I spoke of "dependent authorship" as enabling a surprisingly wide range of students to write
about their reading with an unusual depth and power of response.
The depth and power of these students' writing is, I hope, evident
enough. What I have not established is the range of aptitudes and
abilities represented here. For convenience, let me quickly offer a
contrast between two of these students: Sam (who wrote the continuation of Z for Zachariah) and Darren (who wrote the epilogue
to Lord of the Flies).

Sam's considerable difficulties with reading and writing (and,
especially, spelling) had convinced him, in his own words, that he
was "stupid" and "hopeless," and he had, in the past, received
special remedial help. Difficulties there certainly were. When I first
taught him, in Year 9 at age thirteen, he complained that he was
unable to complete reading assignments for homework because he
was unable to make sense of what he read on his own. (In order to
get him through the class novel, Blue Fin, I had to resort to putting most of it on tape for him.) A year later, however, he was
able to read most of Lord of the Flies on his own, slowly and with
continued complaints about how hard it was. But his comments
about the novel in class showed that he'd understood what he'd
read even if he hadn't particularly relished the experience. Throughout that first year I taught him, he was so anxious about the failings he believed his written work revealed that, with the exception
of one poem written at the very end of the year, it all fell illegible
and stillborn from his pen. He was deeply lacking in confidence—
confidence in himself and in his ability to adequately complete
even the simplest task. In Year 10, at age fourteen, his continuation of Z for Zachariah was a kind of breakthrough, though not
one that prepared me for his epilogue to Lord of the Flies:

Jack

Jack sat in an old cane chair on the verandah of his beach
shack. He looked down towards the beach and moved his eyes
up to the horizon. The water was smooth and glassy and seemed
to be repeating itself all the way to the skyline. His two young

children ran up the steep winding path that led from the beach to the house. The youngest of them ran up to her father.

"Daddy, look what I found!"

She held a large shell in her outstretched hands.

"And Dad, if you hold it to your ear, you can hear the sea."

She handed him the shell. Jack put it to his ear. He listened to the familiar echoing sound of the air moving in and out of the shell—constant, soothing, peaceful—like water breaking on a distant reef, with the sound of the smaller waves lifting and dying on the sand.

Then, slowly and faintly, another sound appeared, just barely audible. The sound began to get louder, as if it was growing in the shell, starting from the middle and winding itself around the spiral cavity. After a few seconds he could recognize the sound: "Kill the beast! Cut his throat! Spill his blood!"

Jack began to shudder.

And out of the chant came the three most horrifying words Jack had heard on the island.

"I meant that!"

Jack began to cry.

Darren, on the other hand, was the kind of student for whom schools seem to have been designed. Not only was he used to success—academic and sporting—but it came effortlessly. However, though he wrote easily, his imaginative work was either fluently superficial or conventional and dull; he never seemed to have been engaged by it in any particularly searching or sustained way.

For both of these students, "dependent authorship" was the means by which they were able to explore concerns of some significance to them—that is obvious from the seriousness of their work—with an assurance, a depth of penetration and a technical resourcefulness that had not previously been theirs.

What is true for Darren and Sam is true for the rest of the students whose work appears here: for these students, these pieces of writing had a revelatory power, for in them they saw themselves operating (to borrow a phrase of Jerome Bruner's) "at the far reach of their capacities." Their writing was a revelation to them, of their capacity to discover and realize meaning *through poetic means of statement*   Though they could not, characteristically, articulate the significance of what they had written in the way I attempt to in my analyses of their work, they were in no doubt that significance was there. In fact, they felt little need to explain; they were content to let their work speak for itself. And there, perhaps, the most significant link between their own creative-exploratory activity and that represented by the text has been forged.

7

Reading/Writing in the Culture of the Classroom

CLEM YOUNG and ESMÉ ROBINSON

This book is concerned with the ways in which readers read literary texts, the nature of their responses to these texts, and ways in which these responses can be made both richer and more satisfying. The emphasis is understandably on the reader and the text, and on their interaction. The writer/author appears as the maker of the text, and the act of reading is generally regarded as a response activity. activity.

It is our purpose here to focus some attention on the act of composing itself, on text construction and work creation.

The starting point taken in earlier chapters of this book has been Rosenblatt's distinction between *text* and *poem*: the writer constructs the text on the page; the reader creates the poem within the parameters provided by the text. The validity of this position is established on the basis of introspection by experienced readers ("I feel this is what happens when I read"), on the testimonies of a number of child and adolescent readers, and on a number of research studies which have reported a high degree of personal involvement and projection by even highly experienced readers of literature. In addition, there is a growing body of literary criticism which argues that readers bring their selves, their whole beings, to the process of constituting a literary experience out of the verbal constructs provided by another person, a writer, and that the study of the role of the reader in the text is a valid critical activity.

This model, however, raises a number of questions, some readily answered, others not so. Amongst the latter, we would like to point to the distinction that is apparently made between writers (who tend to be regarded as competent adults) and readers (who seem to be portrayed as children or adolescents learning to formulate their responses to what grown-ups have written for them). By what processes do the (child) readers become the (adult) writers? Should teachers intervene directly in this process? If so, what kinds of interventions are most likely to be successful?

Readers and Writers

Conventional wisdom teaches that reading and writing are separate and distinct (even if related) processes. Writers write: in Rosenblatt's terms, they put marks on the paper. Readers read: they give meaning to the signs according to their understanding of the coding process that has been undertaken by the writer, their own personal predispositions and predilections, and the cultural understandings they bring to the task.

Although reader and writer are regarded as being engaged in a process that is essentially interactional in its nature, their roles remain relatively distinct. Writers write; readers read. If readers are to become writers, they need to be given direct instruction in the process of writing, which is usually interpreted as meaning that they need specific instruction in a range of writing skills.

A number of writers have recently challenged this conventional distinction between the roles of reader and writer, claiming indeed that reading and writing are best regarded as two sides of the one process, that reading is an act of composing, and indeed that we learn to write—we can only learn to write—by reading in the role of the writer. As we read, we must take on the role of the writer, not just in the sense of giving meaning to the coded information on the paper, but in the sense that the reader must imaginatively become the writer imagining the work. Literary works of art are encoded meanings in the process of being made, and in order to experience them the reader must participate imaginatively in their making.

Smith (1983), in exploring the process whereby we learn to write, concludes that writing demands an enormous fund of specialized knowledge which could never be covered adequately through formal courses of instruction. This specialized knowledge covers such areas as the grammatical rules by which the language operates, the conventions of capitalization, punctuation and presentation, the conventions of form, the subtleties of tone and register, and sensitivity to the needs of audience, all of which cannot be learnt through formal instruction because there is simply too much to learn, and the rules and conventions are far too complex, too subtle, too numerous, and too specific to particular writing situations. In addition, we do not yet know all the rules, and even if we did, it is unlikely that we could teach them directly in such a way as to make them able to be both understood and applied by children.

Perhaps, then, we might conclude that we learn to write by writing—by being given copious practice in a range of situations, writing for various purposes for a variety of audiences and in a range of appropriate forms. Smith concludes, however, that the evidence suggests that children do far too little writing to learn the rules, conventions, and subtleties of the task by writing.

How then do children learn to become writers? Smith contends that in order to learn to write we must learn to read, *but*, we must learn to read in a particular way: we must learn to read in the role of the writer. That is, during the act of reading, the processes of reading and writing must lose their separate identities and be fused in the mind of the reader into a single act: the reader must become the writer. In this way, as Tierney and Pearson (1983) conclude, the act of reading becomes a composing process.

Reading Like a Writer

It is self-evidently true that the reader cannot literally become the writer, nor is it necessarily to be inferred that the reader simply adopts the persona of the writer and reconstitutes the writer's experience of the work as represented by the parameters provided by the text. The process of reading is too multi-dimensional, too text- and reader-specific to be reduced to such an equation. Rather, the act of reading as composing would seem to require of the reader a range of responsibilities such as the following:

1. Reconstitution of the text by the reader

It has been referred to elsewhere that without a reader the text remains as so many black marks on white paper. The initial task of the reader is to recognize that the marks have meaning within the culture, and to reconstitute these meanings according to the reader's personal experience and understanding of the culture in which these marks have significance.

2. Collaboration between the reader and the writer in the reconstitution of the text

The reconstitution of even the simplest literary text involves a degree of collaboration between the reader and the writer. The reader, for instance, must willingly attend to the matter at hand, and must accept the conventions imposed on the text by the writer, lest there be no story at all, or at least one very different from that which has been constructed by the writer. Just as the writer needs the reader to reconstitute the text (or else there is no story), the reader is obliged to undertake this activity within the parameters set by the writer. This process will involve the

reader in giving over (or attempting to give over, or being prepared
to give over) his or her mind to the task of conjuring up the writer's
text, of suspending (or attempting to suspend) disbelief in the
events described, of eschewing (or attempting to eschew any
hostility towards the perspectives on people and actions offered
by the writer, of postponing (or attempting to postpone) criticisms
and judgements until the whole be revealed.

3. Interaction between the reader and the writer mediated by the text

The reading of a literary text involves, in part, a meeting between the minds of the reader and the writer, mediated by the
text. Through the text the reader comes to perceive, to construct,
the existence of an author ("Dickens" or "Shakespeare" or
"Keats") who is the kind of person who would say the kinds of
things written in the text. It has been argued that when a person
undertakes the reader-role there is an obligation to let "Dickens"
have his say (by mentally reconstituting the text) and to help him
have his say (by being prepared to attend to the text as written
and not to allow personal preference, predilection, or animosity
interrupt the story).

However, these twin responsibilities of reconstitution and collaboration do not adequately describe the process whereby real
readers read real texts. Evidence drawn from studies of readers
reading (Slatoff, 1970; Bleich, 1975; Holland, 1975) would seem
to suggest that tension or conflict between reader and writer is a
commonplace part of the literary experience.

Readers, as it were, do not normally give themselves utterly to
the experience (no matter how much writers might wish them to
or even claim that they ought to, or indeed must) but rather adopt
a role which both allows themselves to engage the text and at the
same time retain the right to interrupt the flow, to negotiate the
meaning of the text, to argue mentally with the writer on the
nature of things as represented in or implied by the text.

This interactive process would seem to involve the reader in
moving between two "selves": the real self, the person who has
taken the decision to read and whose cultural history will be necessary for the reconstitution of the text, and the self that the writer
would have him or her become, the "person" to whom the text is
addressed, what Booth (1961) calls the "implied reader" of the
text.

The implied reader is the "person" that the writer has in mind
as the reader as he or she is writing the text, the "person" to whom

the text is addressed, to whom the story is told, to whom the nature of things is revealed. There is, of course, no such "person": each reader is invited, requested, sometimes required to take on this role so that the writer, through the text, may work on the sensibilities of the reader. The implied reader is an imaginative construct, a role created for the reader by the writer through the text, and which must be recreated by the reader in the process of reading the text.

Just as there is a distinction to be made between the real reader of the text and its implied reader, so there is, according to Booth, a distinction between the real author (or authors) and the text's "implied author." Just as the implied reader represents the author's ideal interpreter of the text, and functions as the role of the reader in the text, so the implied author represents the presence of the author in the text, the someone who tells the story—what Booth refers to as the real author's "second self."

The process of interaction between reader and writer in the reading of literature can thus be seen to be a complex involvement of the reader in a number of roles, and the reader must be prepared to participate in all these roles. The very act of reading puts the reader in the role of the writer as the story is retold. More than this, the reader imaginatively reconstructs the roles of implied author and implied reader (and, perhaps, narrator and narratee) as the story is told, and for the purpose of telling the story. It is because of the simultaneity of this process that reading and writing may be regarded as two sides of the one process.

Text Structures and Structured Texts

Thus far we have argued that the reading/writing process is one in which the reader must act, as it were, in a responsible manner towards the text, and that it is by taking on the role of the implied reader that the most successful readings of texts are experienced.

Literary texts, however, are not always constructed in such a way that the implied reader-role is easily identified. Barthes (1975b) has claimed that it is possible to construct a "basic typology of texts" on the single criterion of the way in which they require their reader to participate in their reading. Barthes distinguishes between the "readerly" (le texte lisible), and the "writerly" text (le texte scriptible) on the grounds that readerly texts are "products (and not productions)," while the writerly text is "ourselves writing." He concludes that the writerly text is of value "because the goal of literary work (of literature as work) is to make the reader no longer a consumer but a product of the text" (Barthes, 1974, p. 4). Moreover, Barthes has argued elsewhere (Barthes, 1975a, 1977) that the entry of the reader into the text spells "the death of the author": the reader must be free to respond to the text's signifiers without being or feeling constrained by what the author intended (or the reader believes was intended). Meaning is made by the reader, and the pleasure of reading (jouissance) is taken by the reader through the exercise of freedom, even license, in relation to the text.

Barthes's claim would seem to be that the literary experience that is of value is that which is required by the writerly text, the text which is constructed as "a galaxy of signifiers, not a structure of signifieds," and that the task of the reader in reading such a text is to participate in its production through completing what Iser (1978) has called the blanks in its construction.

Children Reading, Children Writing

Thus far was have examined some of the implications of the reading/writing process by focusing on a description of this process in terms of readers reconstituting texts. Now let us turn to the process of writing and examine the ways in which children learn to become writers of literary texts.

Frank Smith's argument is that children become writers by reading in the ways we have described, that is by reading in the writer's role. This assertion gives rise to several as yet unanswered questions. If Smith's claim is correct, for instance, one would anticipate a relatively high degree of correspondence between children's reading and their writing: one would expect a powerful modelling influence, rather than, say, a developmental process, to be at work. At present there is insufficient evidence from case studies for such a conclusion to be reached.

Similarly, one might question the role of the teacher in the child's development as a writer of narrative. Is it simply to provide the texts and to encourage a "writerly" response, that is to encourage children to explore the pluralities of the text, to take pleasure from their personal experience of a number of different possible, plausible readings? Or may more direct intervention be desirable? And if so, what kinds of intervention are most likely to be helpful, and at what stage of the child's development?

The Modelling Process at Work

Ruth Park's novel, *Playing Beatie Bow*, was published in 1980, and was awarded the Australian Children's Book of the Year Award. The novel begins:

> In the first place, Abigail Kirk was not Abigail at all. She had been christened Lynette.
>
> Her mother apologized. "It must have been the anaesthetic. I felt as tight as a tick for days. And Daddy was so thrilled to have a daughter that he wouldn't have minded if I'd called you Ophelia."
>
> So for the first ten years of her life she was Lynnie Kirk, and happy as a lark. A hot-headed rag of a child, she vibrated with devotion for many things and people, including her parents. She loved her mother, but her father was a king.
>
> So when he said good-bye to her, before he went off with another lady, she was outraged to the point of speechlessness that he could like someone so much better than herself that he didn't want to live in the same house with her any more.
>
> "I'll come and see you often, Lynnie, I promise I shall," he had said. And she, who could not bear to see a puppy slapped or a cockroach trodden on, hit him hard on the nose. She had never forgotten his shocked eyes above the blood-stained handkerchief. Very blue eyes they were, for he was half Norwegian.
>
> Later she commanded her mother: "Don't ever call me Lynnie again. Or any of those other names either."
>
> *(Playing Beatie Bow, p. 1)*

The opening paragraphs of the novel are interesting for the ways that the implied author invites the reader into the text.

The first sentence poses the conundrum that Abigail Kirk is not Abigail Kirk. (How can this be so?) She had been christened Lynette. (Ah! So she is Lynette Kirk. How did she come to be called Abigail?)

In this way from the very first sentence, the implied author, the "third person" who is neither "I" nor "we" but "someone," gives the reader sufficient information for him or her to reconstitute the tale of Abigail Kirk who was not Abigail. The text provides the parameters, but within the space of the first dozen words the reader is engaged in the process of wondering, speculating, and hypothesizing, of interrogating the author through the medium of the text.

The text continues to confront the reader with a series of binary opposites: Abigail—who is not Abigail—whose mother apologizes—

who adores her father—but he leaves her matter-of-factly—who is so gentle and considerate of feelings of others—but who punches her father on the nose. Things are not always as they seem, and people are not always what they appear to be: the structure of the text becomes its meaning.

Lynette, the implied author tells us, chooses the name Abigail because her (despised) grandmother calls her "a little witch with those wild eyes and her hair all in a bush," and she accepts the witch's role. Abigail is a witch's name.

So Abigail and her mother, we are told, settle down to their new life in Mitchell, a tower block in The Rocks area of Sydney, that part of the city that was once old Sydney Town, and which still retains some of its former colonial charm, with its old convict-built stone buildings and maze of small alleyways.

Abigail befriends a neighbour, Justine, and bored, occasionally takes Vincent and Natalie, Justine's two children, to play in a crowded playground nearby.

> The noise was shattering. Most of the children came from Mitchell, but others probably lived in the cottages round about. Abigail observed that those racing dementedly back and forth performed their charges in a certain order. They were playing a group game.
>
> "Would you like to play it, too, Natty?"
>
> Natalie shook her head. Her big grey eyes were now full of tears. Abigail sighed. Justine was forever trailing Natalie off to a doctor who was supposed to be miraculous with highly strung children, but he hadn't brought off any miracles yet.
>
> "Now what's the matter, little dopey?"
>
> "They're playing Beatie Bow and it scares me. But I like to watch. Please let's watch," pleaded Natalie.
>
> "Never heard of it," said Abigail. She noticed Vincent rushing to join in and thought how weird it was that in the few years that has passed since she was six or seven the kids had begun to play such different games. She watched this one just in case Vincent murdered anyone. She could already hear him squealing like a mad rat.
>
> Natalie took hold of a fistful of her shawl, and Abigail held her close to keep her out of the wind. The child was shivering. Yet the game didn't look so exciting; just one more goofy kid's game.
>
> First of all the children formed a circle. They had become very quiet. In the middle was a girl who had been chosen by some counting-out rhyme.

"That's Mudda," explained Natalie.

"What's Mudda?"

"You know, a mummy like my mummy."

"Oh, Mother!"

"Yes, but she's called Mudda. That's in the game."

Someone hidden behind the concrete pipes made a scraping sound. The children chorused, "Oh, Mudda, what's that?"

"Nothing at all," chanted the girl in the centre. "The dog at the door, the dog at the door."

Now a bloodcurdling moan was heard from behind the pipes. Abigail felt Natalie press closer to her. She noticed that the dark was coming down fast; soon it would rain. She resolved she would take the children home as soon as she could gather up Vincent.

"Oh, Mudda, what's that, what can it be?"

"The wind in the chimney, that's all, that's all."

There was a clatter of stones being dropped. Some of the younger children squawked, and were hushed.

"Oh, Mudda, what's that, what's that, can you see?"

"It's the cow in the byre, the horse in the stall."

Natalie held on tightly and put her hands over her eyes.

"Don't look, Abigail, it's worse than awful things on TV!"

At this point Mudda pointed dramatically beyond the circle of children. A girl covered in a white sheet or tablecloth was creeping towards them, waving her arms and wailing.

"It's Beatie Bow," shrieked Mudda in a voice of horror, "risen from the dead!"

At this the circle broke and the children ran shrieking hysterically to fling themselves in a chaotic huddle of arms and legs in the sandpit at the other end.

"What on earth was all that about?" asked Abigail. She felt cold and grumpy and made gestures at Vince to rejoin them.

"The person who is Beatie Bow is a ghost, you see," explained Natalie, "and she rises from her grave, and everyone runs and pretends to be afraid. If she catches someone, that one has to be the next Beatie Bow. But mostly the children are frightened, because they play it and play it till it's dark. Vincent gets in a state and that's why he's so mean afterwards. But the little furry girl doesn't get scared," she added inconsequentially. "I think she'd like to join in, she smiles so much. Look, Abigail, see her watching over there?"

Before the older girl could look, Vincent panted up, scowling.

"We're going to play it again! I want to! I want to!"

"No way," said Abigail firmly. "It's getting dark and it's too cold for Natalie already."

The boy said bitterly, "I hate you!"

"Big deal," said Abigail.

Vincent pinched Natalie cruelly. Tears filled her eyes. "You see? Just like I told you," she said without rancour.

"What a creep you are, Vincent," said Abigail scornfully.

Vincent made a rude gesture and ran on before them into the lobby. As they waited for the lift, Abigail saw that his whole body was trembling. She made up her mind to have a word with Justine about the too-exciting game.

"I saw the little furry girl, Vince," said Natalie. "She was watching you all again."

(*Playing Beatie Bow*, pp. 9–11)

As the reader's viewpoint travels along inside the text, the reader apprehends the events and attempts to determine their significance. In this, the implied author appears to play three roles, all of which play their part in allowing, helping, even requiring the reader to imaginatively create a literary experience from the parameters of the text.

Firstly, the implied author acts in the role of observer, describing the events that occurred ("the children formed a circle"), what people said ("'never heard of it,' said Abigail"), and the environment in which these events occurred (the playground, with its concrete pipes).

Secondly, as well as witnessing and recording what any intelligent participant could perhaps observe, the author also appears to know what no real life observer could possibly know, namely what people thought ("she thought how weird it was that . . . kids had begun to play such different games"), and felt (Abigail "felt cold and grumpy").

In this omniscient observer role, the implied author identifies with Abigail's view of events, presenting what Moffett and McElheny (1966) call a "single character point of view." In fact, so strong is this identification that on occasions authorial intrusions are presented as Abigail's reflections on events ("The child was shivering. Yet the game didn't look so exciting; just one more goofy kid's game").

The story continues with the omniscient author telling us and showing us more about Abigail and the effects of her estrangement with her father on her, her mother, and their lives together.

One afternoon, bored, she takes Natalie to the playground again.

The child whispered excitedly, "When I was watching through the window I saw the little furry girl."

Abigail hugged her, "You and your little furry girl! And how could you see her all the way down there in the playground?"

"I don't know; I just did. I wonder where she comes from?"

"I expect she lives in one of the little terrace houses," said Abigail as they went down in the lift.

"I'd like to live in a little house," said Natalie, "with sunflowers higher than the roof and little hollows in the stairs. And a bedroom with a slopey roof. And a chimney."

The little girl, freed from the oppressive presence of her brother, skipped blithely along, looking at the children sliding down slippery-dips, hanging on the bars like rows of orangoutangs and climbing over the gaudily painted locomotive that stood near the sandpit. Abigail lifted Natalie up to the driver's seat, but she was frightened at the height; and, besides, most of the children had begun their obssessive game of Beatie Bow, and she wanted to watch.

"Why do you want to watch when the silly game scares you so, Natty?"

"I just want to look at the little furry girl watching, because I like her, you see."

"You're a funny little sausage." Abigail sat on a cement mushroom and watched curiously while the children formed themselves into their hushed circle, and "Mudda" took her place in the middle. Natalie pulled at her shawl.

"There she is, Abigail. Do look."

Abigail looked. At the edge of the playground, absorbed in the children's activities, yet seemingly too shy to emerge from the half-shadow of the wall, was a diminutive figure in a dark dress and lighter pinafore. Her face was pale, and her hair had been clipped so close it did indeed look like a cat's fur. Eagerly she watched the children, smiling sometimes, or looking suspenseful, as the game went on, and then jumping up and down excitedly as Beatie Bow emerged from her grave and frightened everyone to death.

"I wonder why she doesn't play. Perhaps she's crippled or something," said Abigail. "Let's go and talk to her."

They were close to the child before she noticed them, so engrossed was she. She was about eleven, Abigail thought, but stunted, with a monkey face and wide-apart eyes that added to to the monkey look. She wore a long, wash-out print dress, a pinafore of brown cotton, and over both of them a shawl crossed over her chest and tied behind. Her feet were bare, and Abigail was surprised to see that the skin was peeling from them in big flakes.

"Hullo, little girl!" said Natty shyly.

The child whipped around in what seemed consternation. She looked an ugly, lively little creature, but scared to death. With a stifled squawk she fled along the wall and dived up one of the steep stone alleys that still linked the many irregular levels of The Rocks.

"Well, she didn"t like *us*," said Abigail. "Or perhaps she comes from another country and didn't understand we wanted to be friends."

Natalie nodded, her eyes full of tears once more.

"Oh, Natty, do stop crying. You're like a leaky jug or something. What's the matter now?"

"I don't know." But when Abigail had delivered her back at the unit, she gave the elder girl a hug and whispered, "I cried because the little furry girl has been unhappy."

"How do you know?" Abigail asked, but the child just shook her head.

(Playing Beatie Bow, pp. 24–25)

As the reader imaginatively reconstitutes the places and events described and the conversations recorded in the text, certain doubts or questions begin to arise in the reader's mind. Who is the "little furry girl"? Why is she afraid of them? Why is she dressed so strangely? Why is Natalie so interested in her? How could Natalie "see" her from the apartment? How did she know the little girl had been unhappy?

Why does this narrator who apparently knows so much (even what people are thinking) not tell us the answers to these questions? The answer lies partly in the nature of narrative itself, that events are lived in time-space sequences, and that the narrative in revealing its truths through a process of gradual unfolding represents what Barbara Hardy (1975) has called "a primary act of mind." Narratives are written that way because that's the way we perceive events.

This view seems to be borne out as we read the text, and the reader, having been taken into the text and found a role within it via an identification with an attractive character (Abigail), can now comfortably wait for the significance of these events to be revealed. Such a reading, however, is only partial, and avoids to an extent the more demanding task of reading in the role of the writer.

As well as providing the reader with necessary inside information on certain events, and describing others in such a way as to excite the reader's curiosity as to their significance and consequences, the author describes other events, and apparently fails to note the significance of some others, which are crucial to a complete reading of the story. (For instance, the shawls that both Abigail and the "little furry girl" are wearing, and Natalie's desire to live in "a little house . . . with sunflowers higher than the roof and little hollows in the stairs. And a bedroom with a slopey roof. And a chimney.") It is through the real author's creation of an apparently defective, omniscient implied author that the blanks in the text are constructed. It is in identifying and completing these blanks that the reader becomes essential to the full realization of the text.

It is interesting with these ideas in mind to turn to an example of children's narrative writing and see if the modelling effects of reading can be identified. Karen is 12 years, 8 months old. She considers *Playing Beatie Bow* to be "the second best book ever written—after *Tom Sawyer*." She reads with enjoyment and writes with enthusiasm. Here is the first chapter of her uncompleted story on a family of otters.

The Otter Family

Mr Otter slowly swam back to the holt, which is the name for an otter's burrow.

He had a large, and very fierce looking pike in his mouth. It was still twitching.

This pike had been bothering him for a long time, and for many reasons:

a. It was very large and vicious and therefore hard to catch.
b. It had a ravenous appetite, so it ate all the good fish Mr Otter and his family would have liked.
c. The pike was quite old, and so had been bothering them for a very long time.

Mr Otter had finally caught it by hiding behind a rock and surprising it.

As he swam back to his home he thought about how pleased his family would be.

There were four otters in the family—Mr Joseph Otter, Mrs Helen Otter, Thomas Otter, and Jayne Otter.

Mr Otter was a fisherman.

He worked in the river, where they lived.

Mrs Otter was normally in the holt.

She liked to keep it very clean.

Thomas Otter was a quiet animal he liked to stay inside the holt and read, and he had spectacles.

Jayne Otter, on the other paw, was completely different. She could be very difficult at times.

Mr Otter paddled up to the entrance to the holt.

It had a green door, with a doorknocker shaped like a fish on it. It was just above the surface of the water.

He opened the door, and stepped in.

"Hello!" he called.

He hung his coat up and took off his boots.

He held the pike in his paws.

"Hello darling," said his wife, "Oh, what a beautiful fish! You are clever, Joseph!"

"Oooh dad! How did you catch it?" asked Thomas, who had just come in.

"We'll talk about that later, son," said Mr Otter, "Right now, I would like to talk to your mother in peace."

Thomas went out and read his book.

Jayne was in her room brushing her fur. She had a date to-night with a beaver called Mike.

Mrs Otter stopped cleaning two salmon he had caught yester-day. "Is something wrong, Joseph?" she asked worriedly.

Mr Otter sat down in a chair.

"I'm afraid there is," he said seriously. "Before I came home I checked the stick, you know, the one I use to test the water level with, and it it two inches higher than yesterday.

Also, I swam down to "that place" yesterday, and found out what the humans are doing.

They're going to dam the river. I don't know why. At the rate it's rising we'll all be flooded out in three weeks!"

Mrs Otter began to cry.

"What'll we do?" she sobbed.

Mr Otter put a paw on her shoulder.

"Don't worry love, I'll think of something," he said.

He tried to sound comforting, but it was hard enough to stop himself from breaking down.

What could they do?

Karen, 12 years, 8 months

Karen, too, adopts the single character point of view, so that the reader perceives events from Mr. Joseph Otter's perspective. Her omniscient author knows a great deal about the family and its members, but indicates her apparently defective vision in the final, rhetorical question "What could they do?"

This text, too, recognizes the reader's presence, and relies on the active participation of the implied reader in its recreation. The reader's presence is directly recognized through the final rhetorical question, which is evidently inserted to invite the reader to speculate on the possible consequences of the family's dilemma. The reader's existence is also recognized in the two parentheses: "the holt, which is the name for an otter's burrow" and "the stick, you know, the one I use to test the water level with." The former provides information for the reader (and lets the reader create an image of the implied author as being someone who knows about animals) in a way which the well-informed reader will not find offensive. The latter cleverly uses dialogue between characters to provide information which the reader (but not Mrs. Otter, to whom it is addressed) needs to know.

In talking about her story, Karen showed some concern for the reader's response to the indirectness of the first paragraphs. She called her character "Mr. Otter," she said (rather than "the otter," or the more personal "Joseph Otter") because she wanted the reader to imagine him as a particular kind of character: adult, reliable, fatherly, a bit formal. The text, too, reflects the kind of character he is as the author (identifying with Mr. Otter's view of things) somewhat systematically, even scientifically, sets down his reasons for being bothered by the pike. Mr. Otter, to the reader who fills in the blanks, is just the kind of character who would use a measuring stick to record water levels in the river.

Karen's writing shows considerable development from the self-projective narrative of much young children's writing, though there is still a strong bond between the real and implied authors of the text. (It comes as no surprise to learn from Karen that she loves animals, thinks her mother is very concerned about tidiness in the home, sees her father as reliable but a bit stodgy, likes reading, had recently been required to wear spectacles, and sees herself as being very difficult at times.)

Karen's accomplishments as a writer of narrative have been developed through her reading. She writes extensively on a range of subjects, but has almost certainly never had any direct instruction in the principles of authorship which are evident in her writing. She writes with the reader in mind because she reads in the role of the writer. Reading and writing, to her, have become interchangeable roles in the composing process.

For teachers, the question must arise as to when students can benefit from being made more self-consciously aware of these techniques. We want to turn now to a brief description of three reading/writing projects which aimed to sensitize students to the problems authors face in creating writerly texts.

Hard Yakka

Hard Yakka is a group story, composed by class 10K, a group of fifteen-year-olds in an economically deprived area of Brisbane, during the last month of their compulsory schooling. School, for many of them, had been neither a happy nor a successful experience, and they look back on it with a sense of failure, and forward with a sense of futility at the prospects of unemployment and the dole.

During these final lessons, their English teacher talked with them about the documents they would receive from school (reports, references) and from this discussion emerged the notion of the documents that govern our lives. They decided to tell the story of their lives, as they saw them, through a collection of such pieces of paper, and to do this created the character of "Terry Wright" who was to be their archetype.

The teacher began by discussing with the class the types of documentation that might tell Terry's story: school report, reference, Board of Secondary School Studies Certificate, job advertisements, letters of application, employers' rejection letters, application for unemployment benefit, and so on. Each day the class, working in groups, produced samples of the documents, and an editorial committee worked on shaping them into a structured narrative so that a reader could piece together Terry's story.

As the story grew, Terry Wright, the alter ego of 10K, seemed to take on a life of his own. He had been so named as a combination of the names of two local politicians, both, in the eyes of the class, fighting a losing battle against a system which was stacked against them—Terry Wright couldn't win. Someone put a coat on a chair in the class, and this became "Terry's place." Someone else gave him an exercise book, and they took turns in doing his homework for him. "Ask Terry, Miss!" became a response to difficult questions.

The story itself is interesting for what it reveals about a class of children not noted for their achievement or their good behaviour. Terry is presented as being good at school, and "popular with both kids and teachers." But Terry finds it very hard to get a job, with rejection after rejection, gets into trouble with the police, and has a disagreement with his girlfriend. All of this is revealed through the series of documents that make up the text. The class was faced with a dilemma over the ending—should Terry be revealed as successful in his quest for employment? Should perseverance, hard work, reliability, good academic results, and good references be seen to be enough to overcome the statistics of youth unemployment? Or should Terry be presented as a failure, one of the growing numbers of the young on the dole? The class was equally divided on the question. The teacher (still uncertain of the correctness of her decision) opted for optimism, and Terry got a job.

In constructing their narrative, Class 10K were using what might be termed document narration, a variation on the use of letters or diary entries employed by such established writers as Henry James, Fyodor Dostoevsky, Ambrose Bierce. In Frank Smith's terms, Class 10K had joined the club of writers: they were trying to solve a communication problem by finding the narrative form whose shape would tell their tale.

As they created their literary construct, it was evident from the questions they asked they were aware of the demands their text would place on the reader. They were beginning to use compositional techniques which would place quite heavy demands on their readers' reconstitutive abilities. For instance, a job advertisement read:

Required

Two people to paint the
insides of vacuum cleaners.
Five days a week, an eight
hour day. Good wages.
No experience required.

Would their readers see the futility, the boredom, in the kinds of jobs available to Terry Wright? Had they constructed their textual blanks with sufficient skill and care that their ideal implied reader could adequately fill them?

Two pages later, the reader finds an envelope neatly addressed to

Master Terrence Wright,
23 Banksia Street,
Brisbane

Would their readers interpret this in the way that they as writers intended, namely that adults patronize adolescents at the point in their lives when they most need to be communicated with through adult forms?

As they wrote and rewrote their story, Class 10K explored their experience of their schooling through the life of their collective alter-ego, Terry Wright. They also learnt a good deal about the ways in which literary meaning is made. They learnt that they must, like Santiago, the old man of Hemingway's novel, lay down their lines carefully if they are to make their catch; and that, as composers of the writerly text, they must write in the role of the reader, that the roles of reader and writer are not merely inter-changeable but interdependent.

The Shoe Box

Dylan Thomas's short story, "Patricia, Edith and Arnold," is told from the point of view of an anonymous small boy who, while apparently engrossed in his play, "was listening carefully all the time . . . to Patricia and the next-door servant, who belonged to Mrs. Lewis, talking when they should have been working, calling his mother Mrs. T., being rude about Mrs. L."

Class 12A, a group of seventeen-year-olds, were looking at ways of "imaginatively recreating" the story, when one of the class suggested retelling it through a collection of artifacts. The result was not so much a recreation of the original as a new story, told through a shoe box and its contents, and based on Dylan Thomas's original notion of the child as observer and recorder.

In "reading" 12A's shoe box the reader is invited to interpret the significance (or otherwise) of the box and the items it contains. Apparently, the reader (in the role of historian/detective) concludes, there is something that binds these objects together; they relate in some way to each other. In the words of one class member, "They tell a story that the reader has to tell."

12A's observer is an undiscriminating collector—he takes up what others discard as useless, just as Dylan Thomas's observer regards and mentally notes those actions and events which others might see as peripheral, even trivial. His shoe box contains such items as old envelopes, discarded letters, wrapping paper, used theatre tickets, a bath cube, some ribbon, even a page torn from the agony column of a teenager's magazine. Many of the items relate to the story of Patricia, his babysitter, her friend Edith, and Arnold, the delivery boy from the nearby grocery store. Others are irrelevant, deliberately introduced to waylay the unwary reader, the reader who does not constantly think in the writer's role as the story is created from the constructs of the text.

The class had some difficulty in providing sufficient structure in the collection of objects for the reader to piece together a narrative (and in their discussion of this problem learnt something of the nature of narrative itself). Their solution was to provide several pages from Patricia's diary, torn out and discarded and presumably retrieved by the observer from a waste paper basket. This device allowed them to develop a time sequence for critical events and greatly enhanced their capacity to lay false clues for the reader.

In constructing their shoe box story, 12A too learnt much about the nature of storying, the mutually interdependent roles of reader and writer, and the way in which, in literature, the what and the how of telling are inextricably linked.

Thomas

12A was a class of students who knew each other well, many of them having spent their entire school life in the same group. As a class they felt safe to share personal throughts and feelings in discussion, in drama activities, and through their writing. Writing, in fact, had become a valued medium for these students, all of whom kept personal journals, which they called free expression books or resource books, and which were initially kept for their own private use, but which, as a result of the sense of trust built up in the class, came to be shared quite freely amongst class members.

The class had been working on an integrated unit based on an examination of the roles of young people in society. The material used was drawn from a wide range of sources: prose, poetry, fiction, non-fiction, drama, film, documentaries, newspapers, magazines, TV programs, art, music, and was read, viewed, discussed, criticized, and dramatized, as the class explored the theme.

The fiction from which students made their selection included protagonists with whom they could identify (*The Catcher in the Rye; The Chosen; 1984; Hard Times; A Candle for St. Antony; Cry, the Beloved Country; I Heard the Owl Call My Name*), and students were encouraged to link their responses to the texts to the full range of their reading and viewing. In Barthes's terms, they were encouraged to take their pleasure of the text.

The class was also used to presenting written responses in ways which reflected their personal explorations of the texts. Rather than producing literary critical essays, students were encouraged to find a form (or forms) which would adequately meet their communicative purposes. Responses to the texts included students' own poetry or songs, often with personal annotations, drama scripts, reviews, art work, juxtaposed with selections from printed published material. In this way, the form of the students' responses became a part of its content. Assignment submission days became exciting opportunities to share personal responses with a sympathetic audience, and students responded enthusiastically to each other's assignments as new texts.

This procedure had the effect of encouraging students to find new ways of expressing their responses. On this particular occasion, one student, Jamie, created a fictional character whom he named Thomas Albury and who purported to be the author of the assignment. Thomas in effect became the narrator, and Jamie remained in the background, acting as editor of Thomas's work, and annotating the text as appropriate.

Jamie's classmates found Thomas a fascinating character and were full of praise for his ingenuity in creating a persona through whom he could express and shape his own response. Thomas, in fact, was a part of each of them, and many of the class claimed they could see aspects of themselves in his attitudes and views on current events. He was also recognizably a part of some of the characters in the books they had read—he had Holden Caulfield's sense of idealism, for instance, combined with some of the metaphysical searchings of Mark Brian and the sense of helplessness of Winston Smith. Thomas Albury was recognizably a part of each of them, but also stood apart from them, like a character in a book.

Thomas's responses to the texts and to current events reveal him as a socially and politically aware young man, deeply concerned about the state of the world in which he lives. He is particularly distressed by issues of conservation, espeically of Queensland's historical heritage. This distress was brought to a head by the recent demolition of a magnificent old colonial building, the Bellevue Hotel, an issue about which many of the students in the class, including Jamie, had felt both anger and frustration at their powerlessness to intervene.

Thomas Albury's story is a moving account of a progression towards self-destruction The text concludes with his epitaph:

> Thomas John Albury
> late of Oppression Avenue,
> Nundah, Brisbane, in the
> State of Queensland, who
> died on or about the
> 23 day of August, 1979,
> at Nundah
>
> GOD REST HIS SOUL

The due date for the assignment had been 28 May.

The class felt the need to explore further the process whereby Thomas had been created, and the teacher suggested that this might be achieved by transforming the experience into dramatic form. The class canvassed their skills: Neil would transform some of the poems into songs, and a group would help write new lyrics as they were needed; others would work on the script, with Jamie as consultant; a dance sequence would be necessary to evoke the dreamlike qualities of some of Thomas's thoughts, but since there were no dancers in the class, they would have to obtain help from elsewhere—someone had a friend in Year 9 who would help.

And so *Thomas* was dramatized, with Sean in the title role, and other selected students playing themselves as class members. The setting, of course, was 12A's English classroom, and the class worked to recreate the experience of Jamie's response to the text through the creation of the frustrated idealist, Thomas Albury, who sees his classmates trapped by their innocence in a shallow optimism, while around them their world is being destroyed by the corruption and selfishness of the "tower people":

> If only they'd listen for a moment
> They could learn from a child . . .

But they do not listen, or if they do they fail to understand, and Thomas, the youthful idealist, he who thinks he can change the world "through an honest, hardworking approach," dies, himself transformed into a manifestation of self-destruction born of social and political impotence.

But Thomas Albury's death is not in vain, and his classmates, still struggling to understand who he was and what his life and death meant to them, sing:

> Now he's gone
> But who was he?
> With him went a part of you and me.
> Amidst the cries
> It's as if my eyes
> Were opened, and now I see.

Learning to Read Through Writing

Frank Smith's argument is that children learn to write by reading in the role of the writer. Our experience is that readers can also be helped to become writers—and become better readers in the process—by learning to write with the reader in mind. This means not simply being made self-consciously aware of the audience towards whom the text is addressed, and having classroom experience of writing for real audiences (though such experiences we believe form an invaluable part of the process of becoming a competent writer), but also being guided and encouraged to explore a range of literary forms which require a high degree of reader participation in their reconstruction.

This process requires a degree of sensitive intervention on the part of the teacher. The teacher needs to be able to draw on a range of text possibilities and help children realize the potential of these possibilities in their writing. In this way, readers become writers . . . become readers. . . .

8

Writing and Literature: Monitoring and Examining

LESLIE STRATTA and JOHN DIXON

Why examine English Literature? In most parts of the English-speaking world, the answer has been: to select entrants for university. And in our view the tradition that has developed in pre-university exams for 16–18 year-olds demonstrably distorts and perverts—as we shall show—both the teaching of Literature and the prevailing conception of literary studies. We shall begin, then, by analysing the critical limitations of that tradition.

Literature is one of the creative arts, yet it is an odd one out. In other creative arts, even within examination traditions, students are expected to submit a folio of paintings, for instance, or to perform pieces of music. Yet traditional Literature exams do not acknowledge that students may write poetry, prose, or drama themselves, and, though the study of plays is obligatory, their performance is ruled out. Students are limited to critical analysis and argument about texts. So because of university demands and their wash-back effect on teaching in schools, Literature courses have made a distorted and crippled contribution to the Arts in Education (Britton, 1963). Even though the majority of students have no intention of studying Literature at university, these restricted syllabuses and exams have been enforced for all.

We will point briefly, for the moment, to two consequences. First, because performance is ignored, many classrooms never experience literature as an enjoyable social occasion when all students contribute to a "concert" of recitals and acting. And, as a results, few students learn to discuss how best to render a line or to enact a speech. What this leads to is a tradition of Literature as silent reading, on the one hand, and, on the other, as interpretative commentary (or "notes") by the teacher—on the model of mass lectures at university. Second, students who are not encouraged to

174

write imaginatively, drawing on their own experience and visions of society, don't have first-hand knowledge of the struggle to make meaning of life that literature entails. As a result, they are less likely to have fellow-feeling with the writer's struggle and achievements.

Equally crippling in its limitations is the fact that traditional examination syllabuses follow a 19th century university model, and entirely exclude the modern art forms of radio, film, and television—the "literature" of most students' lives (and perhaps of most of their teachers!). Given the fact that many students spend more time watching television than they do going to class, it seems suicidal for schools to ignore the media (Central Statistical Office, U.K., 1985; Whitehead et al., 1975).

These omissions are serious enough; more damaging still is the conception of literary study enforced and encouraged by traditional examination syllabuses and papers. To begin with, texts to be studied are selected not by students or their teachers, but by an external examination board. The assumption is that the texts are in some sense authoritative and the student's role is to learn to "appreciate" them. What's more, their number is characteristically limited (currently in the U.K. to as few as four texts for 14–16 year-olds and seven for 16–18 year-olds—who are already "specialists" in Literature). The assumption is that for sections of the work, at least, study will take the form of line-by-line commentary. Certain authors or periods are required, whether they engage the students or not. So literature is a given body of material (a "heritage") out there, and the study of it is an induction into certain authorized forms of analysis and commentary. The ideological assumption is that there exists a group of people, an elite, who know what it is right and proper for everybody to study, and what should be excluded. In effect, the power lies with the university Literature departments; school teachers are cast in the role of maintaining this power structure.

The typical form of the exam itself takes this ideological stance one stage further. In effect, it authorizes certain kinds of writing, undertaken in highly constrained conditions. Texts are not allowed in the examination room; "questions" are unseen; and the characteristic time limit per question is 30–45 minutes. No sane person working seriously in the creative arts would behave like this. Ironically, it actually runs counter to the declared intentions of university teachers! The formative effect of these constraints is seen both in the questions that are asked and the teaching that results. There is a premium for teaching which trains the students to learn by heart a prepared group of quotations, to assemble material in readiness for the "five-paragraph" essay, to rehearse an authoritative set of generalizations, and to master—as we shall see—a highly esoteric form of "argument" aping traditional questions in university final exams (Dixon and Brown, 1984/5).

One further distressing element in the traditional exam paper is the "unseen" prose passage or poem. All students are expected to respond to a given text—on demand. There is no opportunity to read the text aloud and inadequate time to reflect upon its personal significance and take it to heart. Of course, an ultimate aim of literature courses is that students should become autonomous readers, able to realize complex possibilities in a text independently: the "unseen" questions is a caricature of that aim (Britton, 1951–2).

The Assumptions Behind Traditional Questions

Traditional questions follow a small set of formulae and these have three effects:

1. They carry presuppositions about the kind of knowledge to be derived from reading literature.
2. They require, and indicate in detail, the narrow forms of discourse which are authorized.
3. They express a limited ideological position about the kind of world to be found in most canonical literary texts.

Already by 16+ students in the U.K. have been instructed into major presuppositions about what *kind of knowledge* is derived from "reading literature" and what does not count as knowledge. As we have shown (Dixon and Stratta, 1985a & b), key words in typical questions assume that the knowledge of people, for instance, that we derive from literature is definitive and consensual. Thus, students are asked to describe "the" character, to outline "the" changes, to point to "the" differences. Then candidates are expected to take on an authoritative role and to assert the accepted position "we" have had "revealed." It is assumed that readers are passive and that the text makes "impressions" which "reveal" the truth to them. In answering such questions, students (and teachers) have to acquiesce in this travesty of reading theory. Thus, exams are transforming the reading of literature into a form of knowledge which is consensual, determinate, and unproblematic.

By 17 or 18+ in the U.K. the majority of questions demand a specific *kind of discourse*: generalized argument with a fantasy opponent over a single proposition. "'Donne is a scholar, not a poet.'

Discuss" (from an Oxford Delegacy literature paper). The pur-ported aim is to refute, or to argue "to what extent," or to give grounds for agreeing that X is the case. Thus, a peculiar form of pseudo-argument—a last vestige, perhaps, of medieval dialectic?— becomes *the* authorized form for articulating responses to litera-ture. All other forms are discounted—including, characteristically, the chief forms found in literature itself, narrative and dialogue. The hidden assumption is that the high peak of response is a gen-eralized proposition.

The *ideological position* taken for granted in exam questions at all levels is peculiarly lop-sided. There is a tacit assumption that the social interests of literary studies are limited to "the indi-vidual" (or "Man"), personal relationships, "the values they live by," and the "moral vision" of the artist in producing a "picture of the human race" (from recent Advanced level literature papers). In general, it is assumed that the economic and political world in which artists work is irrelevant to their "vision." The idea that a given artist's understanding of society will inevitably be limited, flawed. and, in addition, structured by the social milieu in which s/he lives, is never raised as a topic for consideration. Traditionally, the work is treated as an encapsulated object—timelessly floating through space—with no reference to the student's life and how s/he perceives society now. The questions our society is deeply involved in—about sex roles, racial oppression, or class conflict—are hardly, if ever, touched on in exams.

Outcomes of This Tradition

There has been a long-standing criticism of this tradition in many countries (in the case of the U.K. starting as far back as 1921) (Great Britain, 1921). But so far as we know, the actual outcomes— a representative sample of students' exam scripts—have not been available for rigorous and public scrutiny till this decade. Such a sample was drawn in 1977 and submitted for detailed commen-tary to a panel of thirty very experienced teachers of literature, from schools and universities throughout the U.K. (Dixon and Brown, 1984/5). It was clear from the comments on the whole sample that the panel were deeply disturbed about most of the essays they were scrutinizing.

To illustrate what they felt was going wrong with the majority of these essays, produced by 17–18 year-old students specializing in examined courses in Literature for the previous four years, we will begin with a typical essay from a student in the higher grades (the top 5–10% of the age group, according to the examination). As the examination board was guaranteed anonymity, it is not possible to quote the question verbatim. However, in general terms, the student was given the assertion that "Gulliver's Travels" has appealed to all kinds of readers since its publication and then instructed to give reasons why s/he should agree with this!

In terms of the question and its assumptions, we note the following:

1. The assertion (supported by a canonical critic) that the book from its publication has appealed to people of all kinds is taken to be authoritative and unproblematic.
2. Thus, if the student's response to the text is at all at odds with the assertion—if any part did not appeal—that response is discounted.
3. Even if the student does respond positively to the book's "appeal," it is not her own response that is to be discussed, but the appeal to people in general.
4. The student is required to account for the appeal to readers past as well as present!

In our view, it would not be surprising if directions and assumptions such as these defeated all but the exceptional candidate at 18+. However, the student was awarded a good mark, in keeping with a high overall grade. Here, then, is the student's answer: we give the opening and conclusion, omitting three short paragraphs in the middle.

Gulliver's Travels has been read by many people since its first publication. It has always, and still is read by many children, as a tale of adventure and even adults of a low educational calibre, enjoy it as an intriguing fairy story, about a man who travels to strange lands and meets very small, then large people who talk and act like any other human being. On the other hand, people of a higher education standard and more philosophical attitude may also enjoy the bitter satire and irony, underlying the pleasant story. Swift has masterfully accomplished a "happy medium," whereby all people, old and young, academically aware or not, may enjoy the humour and satire of Gulliver's Travels.

In book one Swift tells an amusing tale of a man caught by little people and who proceeds to live with them, in a land where every thing is one twelfth the accustomed size of ordinary life, and its objects. However after learning their language and helping them in their fight against an enemy, they turn hostile and after a threat of death or losing his eyes, Gulliver escapes. This story of the Lilliputians may be read as an amusing story or analysed as a bitter satire, against politicians and religious and political wars of the late 17th early 18th century. In this book Swift gives Gulliver the part of a camera, who sees and experiences many strange things, but is too naive and gullible to analyse them. Swift draws the observant reader's notice to the fact that the Lilliputians, in their pretentious, pompous way, are representing the politicians of Swift's time. When Gulliver is put in a large temple-like building, one can see that it might possibly represent Westminster Hall, where Charles I was beheaded. A similar crime committed within its walls prevents the Lilliputians from using it as an everyday building.

When Gulliver is given his freedom he is searched. The inventory of the contents of his pocket is amusing when see from the Lilliputians' point of view. Familiar objects take on strange forms and ideas. This event may be compared to the evidence drawn up against Harley and Bolingbroke, when their letters and papers were twisted to appear treasonable, thus making them look guilty. . . .

He therefore leaves the pretentious doll-like people and seeks sanctuary with the enemy who might represent the French Catholics and who are enemies due to the dispute over which end an egg should be broken. He then leaves.

Shortly afterwards on another journey he finds himself in a land of giants, Brobdingnag. Unlike the precotious Lilliputians these people are moral and live by simple laws and customs. Here Swift tells another intriguing tale, but at the same time is satirizing travel books. In such books of the time, details were grossly exaggerated and distorted. In this story we see how everything is enlarged so as to seem hideous to the small Gulliver.

Yet in the same way as the Lilliputians small people appear pretentious. It is no wonder that the queen's dwarf is the most vicious member of the household. The king of Brobdingnag, after hearing with disgust Gulliver's arrogant, proud descriptions of England and above all the use of gunpowder, concludes

"The bulk of your race to be, the most pernicious race of little odious vermin, that nature ever suffered to crawl on the surface of the earth."

We may see therefore that in Swift's amusing fairy tales are hidden many bitterly satirical comments. His main point being to give enjoyment to the less intelligent people who may enjoy the book purely for its story content and to the academic people

who can see the distinctions made between the vicious preten-
tions of the Lilliputians and the morality of the giants. Both
books together might form a Utopia, yet Swift points out the
same faults and failings in these states as in the media and government of the time, which cause him so much annoyance.

Let's now turn to the comments made independently by two
members of the research panel. As it happens both had considerable experience as chief examiners and had also undertaken original
research on response to literature. They were deliberately not told
the student's grade; thus, without their knowing this, their comments form an effective criticism of the grounds for awarding it.

On this evidence, "the reading that has gone on has been dutiful
rather than committed." "Whether he has enjoyed it on the more
simple level (what he calls the fairy-tale level) remains . . . an open
question." So much for the reading. How about the teaching?
"The writer has clearly been exposed to explanations of the satirical intent underlying some of the details in the first two books of
"Gulliver" and his inability to retail these rationally and coherently
provides negative evidence of his ability to respond to Swift's intentions on this political/satirical level." "His narrative does provide the material for his explication, (but) one suspects that the
latter is pretty derivative, probably from his teacher, because the
backslidings in his expression, such as . . . 'the gaining of favour by
certain acts, of politicians to the monarchy' . . . led me to disbe-
lieve that such responses as the following flow from the closeness
of reading: 'In this book Swift gives Gulliver the part of a camera,
who sees and experiences many strange things, but is too naive and
gullible to analyse them. . . .'"

Looking at the discourse, "This student begins weakly with an
opening paragraph which says little to us but that he knows the
text is satirical. Its language is . . . struggling to be literary: . . . 'has
masterfully accomplished a happy medium.'" "What is one to
make of 'pretentious doll-like people' as a description of the
Lilliputians? Is it a first-hand reaction, crudely and coarsely articulated? A misremembering of someone else's language? The answer
as a whole has so little *character* that it is difficult to know how to
'read it. . . .'" "What we have is mostly a list, a parade, of duly
learned and memorized details."

In our view, these judgements are fair—and completely unsur-
prising. On the evidence offered by this essay, the student seems
never to have applied the fable to political life as s/he perceives it
today. Thus s/he has no basis for talking about its "appeal" to her—
let alone anyone else. However, the traditional examiner appears

not to be disturbed. The candidate has, after all, reproduced received opinions about the social-satirical-political references in the book and translated the surface level of the fable. So s/he has joined the company of "people of a higher educational standard" apparently. The feedback from the examination board to the student and teacher is that this is the kind of knowledge of literature that is required.

This student is not untypical of roughly half those students who coped best with the examination constraints. These were not average students; they were awarded grades which pretty well ensured them a university place on a degree course in English Literature (in the elitist British system).

Moreover, the research panel's misgivings—although they commented independently—were consistently similar to those expressed above. The repeated demand for generalized answers had had its effects on the kind of knowledge displayed. "Very vague and general . . . the play has removed itself to a distance." "A routine manipulation of poorly understood abstract ideas." "Concern to . . . categorize the poems has inhibited him from displaying his own feelings." "May be a reasonably sensitive student but the account is mechanical . . . mechanistic, diagrammatic." "An unusually tidy performance . . . but it is quite external." "An exercise in emasculation . . . the writer's cool, prosaic, fluent account . . . written at such a distance from the experience of the play." In other words the examiners are rewarding a knowledge of literature that is external, prosaic, tidy, uninspired, routine, stock, and mechanical.

There were complex reasons, we believe, why the students should write in this way. These also were commented on by the panel. "Her mind is on notes rather than the book itself." "The ritualized method that many young people are taught to use in dealing with contexts." "Goes through the processes which will inevitably have been drilled into him." "Never risks getting so close to the play that an individual reaction is called for as opposed to a safe general comment." "More concerned with . . . the question than exploring anything about the character." "Attempts to grapple with a very poor (and difficult) essay title—one which rather than drawing him into the world of the book, forces him to see it as an object for analysis." "Determination to answer the question set . . . like a model answer" (Dixon and Brown, 1984/5).

The evidence we have quoted concerns up to half of those who "succeed" best, as judged by the prestige examination in the U.K. Readers will be able to imagine the crushing effects these conditions also have on the majority of students. Of course, under

different conditions, many of these students might be able to produce better evidence. As we have said, they are suffering in the
first place from the timed exam, the kind of discourse demanded,
and the kind of knowledge thought to be appropriate. But the
type of work rewarded in the exam feeds back into teaching, so
that students are trained to meet the exam demands at the expense
of learning how to develop their responses to literature of all kinds.
And there is more to it than this, we would argue: the dominant
ideological position handed down from the universities—and accepted by many teachers as well as examination boards—tends to
lock "the work" in the classroom, an object on the desk rather
than an active part of the students' lives. Until that is rethought,
changes in exam procedures, in the types of questions set, and in
the marking criteria will have a limited effect.

To sum up: the school of thinking represented by the traditional
examining consensus is without a theory of reading, without a
theory of written discourse, and without a theory of ideology. It is
clear, then, what the prerequisites are for any penetrating advance
beyond this position.

The Foundations for an Alternative Tradition

Currently, the traditional exams dominate the Literature curriculum in many countries of the English-speaking world. So the
first step is to reverse that. In England this could shortly become
a real possibility when schools are allowed to replace the external
exam paper at 16+ by a folder of written course work. But changes
will not be fundamental unless there is an active and coordinated
movement by English departments, the national associations for
the teaching of English, and the examination boards. This needs to
have at least three components. First, departments have to learn to
monitor for themselves the outcomes of their policies for literature
of all kinds. Thus, for example, do they find that students, as they
mature, are reading fiction, going to plays, and viewing television
documentary or drama both more widely and more selectively?
Are their students taking part in (and enjoying) poetry recitals,
play readings and presentations—in other words in active "readings"? Do the students' own imaginary stories frequently show the
quality of their encounters with "literature"? And, in general, is
this contact with literature in all its forms raising questions and
insights into themselves and their society?

Some of this monitoring is relatively straightforward. It is easy,
for instance, to make a crude survey of students' voluntary reading

and play-viewing over a week or month; to monitor the effects of literature in the broad sense on their imaginary stories; and to discover—as Yarlott & Harpin did in their research (1972–3)—whether leavers intend to go on reading literature. These are the crude findings that reveal some of the basic effects of teaching. In fact, the overall effects of the traditional examined courses in the U.K. stand condemned by the results of such surveys.

When the department asks whether that reading, viewing, acting out, and so on is not only more abundant, but is also being "enriched" by their teaching, the question is more complex. This leads us to our second component. What would constitute evidence of such "enrichment"? Is it restricted to the reading, viewing, and play-going—taking account, for instance, of the fact that we are in the middle of a second golden age of "children's fiction"? Does it allow for different ways of exploring literature, in its varying forms? What precisely constitute "development, maturing insight and understanding, deeper responses . . ."?

About such things the exam tradition has nothing to say. Indeed, it has said little beyond vague generalities about "standards" in exams. And in the century or so of its existence it has failed to provide any adequate collection of exemplars of the significant changes in students' achievements that a grading system, presumably, is designed to reward. So it is crucial for departments, acting regionally and nationally (together with the examination boards), to collect and analyse a wide range of exemplars and case studies of individual students as readers, in the broadest sense. This would lay the essential foundation not only for departmental monitoring, but for any system of external assessment.

Of course, even to collect an adequate set of exemplars demands an adequate theory of reading, writing, and ideology. And the analytic commentaries that are needed to accompany exemplars and case studies would incorporate and develop such theories.

The third component is to undertake a systematic review of the piecemeal advances that have already been made in opposition to traditional exams. New ways of exploring literature, new forms of questioning, new ways of writing—new evidence of what has been gained from reading, viewing, acting, and discussing: these have been emerging, unevenly and often without a clear sense of their potential. A synthesis is needed, the value of which will be seen more clearly in our final section.

We believe that until departments, working collectively, have established a tradition of monitoring their own work, they have no basis for saying what they want—or transforming the existing views of assessment. This is just one of the reasons why, for some considerable time, external assessment will persist. So during this period we see the coursework option as a valuable opportunity for departments:

1. to build up their own systems of monitoring, and the necessary understanding this requires;
2. by taking part in consortia, to open the way to experiment and jointly to develop the positive criteria needed to assess any student's work, whether internally or externally.

It would be dangerous to underestimate the effort that will be needed to transform a tradition that has shaped, after all, most of the existing teachers. Of course, there have been challenges to that tradition, but in the nature of things these have been piecemeal. To be true to learning theory, we have to recognize that departments, too, will have to set themselves short-term targets, to design their own enquiries stage by stage (and enlist the help of students), acknowledging that new theory and understanding can only be built up gradually. In this final section, then, we want to sketch some of the lines of enquiry that have already emerged and can be extended more systematically. For convenience, we'll take them under three main headings: kinds of writing, kinds of questions, and kinds of context.

Emerging Alternatives in Writing

Because the tradition has no theory of writing, any alternative has to begin by considering such concepts as the writer's role, purposes, and relations to reader(s). Moreover, there will not be simply one type of neatly packaged essay; to be fully valuable, writing will have to help the process of responding (and articulating response) from a relatively unformed stage to stages that are more consciously worked on and shaped. Thus, rather than assume that a fossilized "argumentative" structure is either inevitable or desirable, it has to be recognized that there exist a whole complex range of structures—which will be explored in journals, recreative narratives, ideological discussions and arguments with the writer, dialogues, and many other forms.

To illustrate what we have in mind, let us start with journals, basing our comments on existing work by David Jackson, Mike Torbe, and others (Jackson, 1982; Torbe, 1974). Or course, journals can have more than one view of their potential readers: some are quite private, only to be read by readers the student chooses; others are specifically written for sharing with wider groups in the class, even inviting response and comment on what is emerging.

Journals open the way for questions, notes, and jottings which are relatively unshaped, as well as more developed ruminative thinking, or stretches of narrative.

Let's look closely at two examples where David Jackson's 16–17 year-olds had been reading Heaney's "Blackberry-Picking." First, one that is quite short (Jackson, 1982).

> I've read it once and have nothing to say. So I'll try again. This time I understand it a bit—I think.
>
> This poem explains vividly blackberry picking as I know it. I feel that Seamus is not wholly thinking of the content of the poem as he writes. He seems to be mingling his thoughts with some murderous film or play he has seen.

What is this telling the teacher and how might s/he respond to it? We see the first admission as valuable: as David Jackson says, "Starting to see yourself as a person capable of independently making sense of what you read often takes more time than teachers suspect." Adrian's first sentence is a useful context for what he says after the second reading—"I understand it a bit." He has clearly been able to make a connection between the poem and his own experience, but he is still left tentative about the possibility ("seems") of another layer of meaning. So we'd be inclined to give him a chance to read the poem again (or hear someone else's reading) and to share impressions with others in the class, so that he can reconsider that Bluebeard reference among other things. (This is precisely what was done.)

The second example comes from a student who has already had time in her journal to "react to the poem's feeling centre and Heaney's sensuous extravagance with a matching up of her own language and experience," as her teacher says. Some time later—and after group discussion in class—she returns to the poem and finds time to ponder over a significant moment:

> It ruins the mystery to utter such realistic phrases as "You should have known they wouldn't keep—of course they'd turn bad." A child would not think of being sensible and freeze them. He just goes out expectantly to pick berries and then hoards them always believing that one year they would not go bad. I discovered that thread of hope when I was a child, simply reading through a fairy-tale. I put dolls' furniture at the bottom of the garden with liquorice cakes on the table and hoped that the fairies would come. An awful uncle informed me with harsh, shattering, down to earth finality that fairies did not exist—all that was left for me was shattered dreams and furniture warped by the rain.

In resisting someone's comment here, Fiona rediscovers in Heaney's poem and in her own experience "the tension between knowledge and a child's sense of wonder (or willed self-delusion)," as David Jackson observes. "All that was left for me was shattered dreams and furniture warped by the rain." So, from her own experience, she decides the poet is right—this is her positive evaluation of his truthfulness to childhood. Clearly, her insight is something to share with others in the class.

Journals, then, leave room for responses that are immediate, tentative, interim, fragmentary, but not yet deliberately shaped. When teachers and fellow students are trusted, such entries form part of a dialogue which give validity to student response and helps to develop it.

When students want to move on, to shape and work on their written responses (sometimes with a wider readership in mind), there are a range or purposes they may wish to follow through— each with a range of appropriate forms of writing. Thus, Fiona, as it happened, wanted to move into her own experience, giving it independent shape and significance. (In fact that part of her journal—quoted in David Jackson's chapter—is already enjoyable for a wide range of readers.) The decision to move from a poem to a (parallel) experience of your own is not necessarily egocentric; it may well be a kind of tribute to the contact the poem is making with your real life. And in some cases the student may be strongly aware of the way the very pattern offered by the poem fits experience as s/he knows it. This is exactly what happened to Michelle, a student in Betty Ratzin's class, when she heard another Heaney poem, "The Early Purges." In response, she wrote:

The Early Purges

I was only young when I first heard my parents argue
My step-father struck her, "the stupid old cow"
With harsh words; his voice booming.

His face hot and red, but the din
Was soon lost. I ran upstairs
Into my room, and I cried.

"Shut up you stupid fool," Ian said.
Like a shaking leaf she sobbed, till the anger was gone,
And silence settled, over the whole house.

Suddenly frightened, for hours I sat,
Brooding in my room, until calmness came,
And I forgot it.

But the sorrow returned
When I heard voices raised more than usual
Or cutting words used to hurt.

Still, living displaces false sentiments,
And now when I hear rows
I just shrug "Bloody fools."

It makes sense:
"Heated arguments" cause unrest in society
But in well-run families, feelings must be let out.

Although she was quite free to choose how to respond, Michelle
had no doubt what she wanted to do, to write about "when I was
very young." "I could relate to what he was talking about," she
said. "If I'd just had to write a poem on my own, I wouldn't have
done it that well, because I wouldn't have done it in three lines
like that. . . . The first line and the last line were the same as his
and I just moulded it around that." By a strange coincidence, she
had found a template in the poem to fit something in her own experience, and the way to deal with that was to write her own
poem, looking back at her own vulnerability—and a shade sardoni-
cally at her present self-protective shell.

This poem is a form of evidence for response, albeit indirect and
tacit. We find it impossible to believe that Michelle was not deeply
moved by Heaney's poem: the way she construes her experience
and the form she chooses are eloquent testimony. At the same
time, there will be many pieces of personal writing that move
much further away from the original than this but which still testify to the impact and quality of the literature the student has
been reading and watching.

Of course, artists have traditionally taken poems and stories
from the past and retold them in their own way, transforming
them in terms of their own culture and audiences: it is part of a
wider human propensity that affects all the stories of our everyday
lives. It seems a pretty natural step, then, for teachers to invite students to select and retell parts of a story they have enjoyed, adopting a new perspective—and producing a parallel text, as it were. We
have called this kind of response "imaginative recreation" (Stratta
et al., 1973). Let us illustrate briefly, from the work of Linda
Jones, what a fourteen-year-old student in a mixed ability class
might stand to gain.[1] One of the war poems they had been exploring was "Dulce et Decorum Est."

---

[1] We are grateful to Mark Boland and to Linda Jones, his English teacher, at Streetly
School, Walsall, for permission to quote this piece.

The Retreat

We were retreating—the wounded, the shell-shocked, the drop-
outs. Deafened by the constant thump, thump of shells, blinded
by the flash of flares: we were beaten.

A dull thud behind us make me look round. I saw another
crater in the Flanders mud, spewing out an evil green mist—gas.
Gas, . . . GAS! Then it hit me. A shouted warning, a flurry of
movement to fit gas masks . . . just in time. Then I heard someone yelling, screaming. I saw a man without a mask, choking.

I can still see him now, coughing up blood and vomit every-
time he moved—dying.

Why did it have to happen? Why? Old men tell children how
great war is. There is no glory, only Hell.

There is no attempt here to analyse the poem in a literary-criti-
cal way, but we believe the evidence of response it offers is equally
valuable—and probably complementary. The student's focus is on
the experience offered by the poem, and he is deeply immersed in
imagining this from the point of view of a different participant.
Teachers we have worked with have been in no doubt about the
quality of his imaginative involvement. But what also struck them,
as the piece was read aloud, was the freshness and originality of his
own language. In line after line, they realized how Mark was stretch-
ing the potential of narrative, learning new ways of using language
in his effort to express the quality of the imaginary experience and
its significance for him. "We were retreating—the wounded, the
shell-shocked . . . Deafened . . . blinded . . . : we were beaten." Although the focus is not on the language of the text, there is detailed
evidence of his tacit learning about its power.

Such narratives, in which students unconsciously emulate the
way poets use words, have been traditionally ruled out—if they
have ever been considered in the first place. But, if a crucial effect
of literature that we are searching for is to carry us into new experiences and, in so doing, to change the way we use language, what
more do we want from any fourteen-year-old!

Lyric poems and prose fiction especially invite this form of response. Drama and dialogue, when they are acted out, remind us
of a further role for the student writer, not as a participant within
the action but as a director, engaged and responding—but more
creatively conscious of what is to be represented. This leads to an
analytic awareness that is quite distinct from the kind demanded
by the tradition.

There are various forms in which this kind of analytical awareness can be expressed; several of these are illustrated in "Responses

to Literature" (Dixon and Brown, 1984/85). For instance, there is a director's narrative commentary on a scene from "The Winter's Tale": in this case the directions to the actors form a narrative, with interpretations of their actions interpolated within the structure (Dixon and Stratta, 1985a & b). The example we have chosen here takes a different form: notes rearranged in two columns, the left hand giving movements on the stage, while the right hand gives "the reasons" for these directions, together with interpretations of individual lines. The following excerpt (on *Richard II, IV i*) comes from the later pages of the notes (Dixon and Brown, 1984/5).

Richard looks stage left rear at soldier and orders crown to be brought. Line 181

Soldier looks at Boling. who
65 in turn nods his head without even looking at soldier.

Soldier only brings the crown when he has Boling.'s permission.

Soldier then walks to centre of stage between Boling. on stage left and K. Richard on stage
70 right but stands slightly at rear of the two holding crown.

Illustrates Richard's lack of authority and consequently illustrates the power Boling. has already established over many of Richard's subjects.
Also the fact that Boling. knows that the soldier wanted his permission without actually looking at him highlights the confidence he has in his own rule.

King Richard. Line 181
75

Boling. does not take the crown which is in the out-stretched arms of the soldier.
At this stage King Rich. is not touching the crown, leaving it in the arms of a soldier.
The soldier symbolizes the common people and reminds us of the time he left the coun-
80 try for the Irish wars leaving the throne floating for anyone to exploit.

On 'Here cousin'
Boling. puts his left hand on the crown.
85 As Boling. does so, Richard quickly puts his right hand on it and immediately says line 183

The crown is taken by Boling. without any violence.
From "The Cease of Majesty" by REESE: 'It has often been noted that the play lacks a central climax, that the actual transference
90 of power from Richard to his enemy is bloodless and perfunctory'

On line 188 Richard drops his hand from the crown.

Richard finally surrenders the crown physically, but still he feels responsible for the role of king.

Bol. takes crown and holds it.
95   Exeunt soldiers.

Line 191 King Richard walks to stage right facing that direction Again turns sharply on line 193 and directs speech at North/ York/Henry Percy.	Richard is quiet and thoughtful to think he's lost the crown. Then he is confronted with a feeling of anger and grief and points at his oppressors shouting line 193.

100

To begin with, we would like to quote the comments of one of the research panel: "The writer is obviously totally involved here. The device used has, in the first place, forced him to see it as part of the play not simply a text to be studied. Throughout he is thinking of the characters in relation to each other, and his stage directions are forcing him to look more clearly at the relationships between the characters. The writing gives the impression throughout that he is genuinely *thinking* about the scene, not merely echoing someone else's opinions (col. 2, 64 on) . . . just one example at random, and this gives him, I feel, the necessary confidence to pit his own opinion against established critics (col. 2, 16). It also gives him the confidence to express his feelings about the play in a telling manner. . . . whether one agrees with the comment or not, one has to accept that it is the considered view of a competent critic; it has force because it has the weight of the previous comments behind it."

Such writing, then, can offer evidence that the student is projecting a scene on the stage as s/he reads the text; is involved in the imaginative experience; is thinking of characters in relation to each other and looking more clearly at those relationships; and can even take issue with an established critic's interpretation. Again, we ask, isn't this kind of evidence preferable to what the tradition demands?

There is a double value in such writing, too: the most obvious response to it is to try it out, in acting the scene and discussing the insights this leads to. So when writing in the role of director, a student can have this purpose in mind, as well as that of personal exploration. Such writing, then, is not a product written for the teacher-as-examiner, though it offers one important kind of evidence that exams ought to be calling for.

Emerging Alternatives in Questions

Why do teachers set the same question (or a narrow choice) to the whole class? We believe that they are merely imitating the exam tradition. Even in coursework folders, such questions frequently seem to carry the message that the teacher, as authority, wants to discover whether or not the students have learnt what is required—just as in the exam. And, in general, this kind of restriction carries the presupposition that there has been no preceding work where the students have been given any responsibility, no invitation for them to make any preliminary exploration of response for themselves (as in journals), and thus no questions and investigations that have arisen from the dialectical relation of teacher and students.

However, it is precisely the traditional questions, as we have argued, that have engrained in the minds of generations of teachers the assumption that, in fact, students have nothing of importance to offer. The hidden message is to "be a passive recipient of the text: 'it' will 'create your impressions,' 'reveal the character' and 'show' what X is like, without their active participation. Thus, they can only offer consensual—not personal—knowledge, 'pointing out what is revealed,' 'our feelings toward X,' and what 'we (all) learn' about 'the effect on the reader'" (Dixon and Stratta, 1985a & b). These are typical wordings taken from actual papers. There is no admission that students must actively construct an imaginary experience from the text. Once that is denied, traditional questioning appears to be not merely inevitable, but right and proper.

So two stages are called for in changing this tradition as a whole: first, we have to learn to analyse and challenge the assumptions carried by the wording of questions we have all been brought up with, and second we have both to change the ways that questions are raised and to discover new forms. In doing so, we will be challenging the orthodox view of knowledge, discourse, and ideology current in literary studies.

Because this is a two-stage problem, we can get some help from a few liberal exam boards which have made the space for teachers to change the questions and the context for them. Although these are still restricted by exam conventions (and ideologically, too), there are possibilities that can be translated into classroom enquiries of a kind we have still not touched on in this article—a more analytical approach deriving from the human face of "literary criticism."

What kinds of joint enquiry do these revised questions encourage, then? They encourage students to look closely at a poem or a scene that seems important to them. They suggest that the teacher is interested in "your reactions as you read through," in "any lines that particularly interest or puzzle you," in anything you "find unexpected in (characters') behaviour, attitude and language—

recognizing that "your feelings may vary" as the poem or scene unfolds. They are interested in "your own interpretation" and "your understanding of the problems that confront" characters.[2] These are a selection of wordings from a minority syllabus, in which the Cambridge board allows students to take Plain Texts into the exam room.

Such questions allow the student to write as an "I"—to offer their personal constructions, their own interpretations of what's going on, and their own reflections on the significance of a scene for the ideological meanings they are constructing. Of course, there is not reason to assume that this "I" is necessarily an individual responding in isolation; joint enquiry allows for personal responses to be exchanged and developed within the group. Equally, these exchanges can offer a surer foundation for further personal exploration, continued in the act of writing—which itself produces a further exchange when the writing is read and discussed in the class.

We want to indicate briefly here the kind of discourse that can emerge and the changed view of what counts as knowledge. Let's look, then, at a group of 15–16 year-olds from Jean Blunt's class who had chosen a scene from "Billy Liar" to discuss and respond to in this personal way.[3] (It is the moment when Billy with his friend Arthur goes into the record shop and meets Liz again—a revealing moment in the group's view.)

Dawn's comments at times indicate that she is discovering more in Billy than she had expected: here are two extracts.

> When Billy first enters the shop his behaviour is almost boisterous and rowdy. He is full of his own self-importance, and appears to want to "prove" himself to Arthur. "Let's go take the piss out of Maurie."
>
> However, once inside the shop Billy begins to change. He is no longer so confident, in fact he feels "old-fashioned," and in and attempt to boost this he "puts on an intellectual act." But looking round the shop he is surprised to find that he doesn't know anyone, indeed I am surprised to find that he doesn't know anyone. . . .
>
> When it come times for Billy to leave the shop he's not anything like when he first came in. He wants to have a go at Maurie

---

[2] These are quotations from recent Ordinary level papers of the Cambridge English Literature (Plain Text) examinations.

[3] We are grateful to Jean Blunt and her fifth year pupils at Summerhill School, Kingswinford, Dudley for these examples.

but without Arthur to back him up," he was "loth to approach" him but "decided to do so for Stamp's benefit." Just when I think that Billy has lost all his self-confidence he once again surprises me by leaving the shop whistling, a sure sign that he is back to his "cocky" self once again. . . .

Dawn is telling us about shifts in her expectations as a reader. Michael as he sums up Billy's behaviour after a similar detailed commentary, acknowledges that he is making a personal interpretation:

> The main reason, I feel, for Billy's initial bravado, is to impress Arthur. In his presence he feels confident, knowing that he has an ally to back him up. But as soon as Arthur leaves him he is alone, out of place and insecure. I feel that this is why Billy is so outgoing and imaginative—to cover his basic insecurity. That is why he prepares himself before meeting Liz—he is unsure what her reaction will be. As soon as she gives an encouraging reaction he is able to be himself more and rely less on his extravertness as a prop.

Such evidence indicates a major shift, marginally recognized for the moment by the boards. It extends what is permissible in forms of knowledge and discourse, but even the board concerned wants to have it both ways; thus its mainstream examinations are still in the traditional mould. What is more, there is little, if any evidence that ideological issues have been considered at all—certainly we have not found examples as yet.

Of course, "ideology" is an ambiguous and slippery word; its meaning is inevitably contested again and again by different schools of thought, political, social, and cultural. The best we can do for the moment is briefly to indicate kinds of thinking that can actually go on among students, as they discuss literature, and the need to make room for such thinking whenever literature is assessed. Here, for example, is an extract from a group of seventeen-year-old Australian students' discussion of "Ozymandias" (Dixon and Gill, 1977):

G. What it could mean is that even though the king might have been mighty in his day, and that, been pretty strong and ruled a lot of people, that after a while everything that he's gonna done is gonna just fade away and there's only gonna be one thing he'll ever be remembered by and that's the statue.
W. Which is all spoiled.
H. They could say that about everyone, not just the king.
G. Just the king is what I mean.
   (Indecipherable)

G. It might end up just being a . . .

W. . . . stone statue

G. . . . a shattered wreck somewhere, and nobody will ever remember it.

W. He might have been great in his time—even though he's great then, he's not now, he's forgotten.

H. But we're not just talking about one king we're talking about everyone. Yes.

G. Anything else. We all know he's not implying just to the statue, but to . . . to . . .

W. Something in it, it was . . .

C. Like in the future, like whoever's prime minister now, when he, about a hundred years time will be nothing.

H. But they're not talking about prime ministers, they're talking about everyone.

C. Yes, those who think they're leaders.

H. Yes, those who think they're leaders . . . ole Gough Whitlam.

C. Like all the statues up in, you've seen in Ballarat gardens, all the prime ministers.

H. Yes, but I reckon a statue's got to represent something, it's not just supposed to be a statue. . . .

Shelley has a clear ideological purpose and these "non-academic" students not only recognize it, but apply it significantly to their own life and times. And they go on to explore the nature of the "respect" you get if you are like Ozymandias, and why you will be forgotten:

H. If you try to dominate everybody else, they'll remember all the worst points . . . they won't remember you as a person, they'll just remember you as a, a being.

G. A thing.

W. Yes, as a thing, to be respected.

H. But they'll lose the respect for you when you die.

G. When they don't have to fear you anymore. It'll just be like a statue.

Just as Fiona in her journal found parallels from her personal experience and thus validated "Blackberry-Picking," so these students in conversation are finding parallels in their social and political experience that validate Shelley. So a significant value of the poem is the way it helps them to reflect on contemporary experience and construe it, perhaps, in new ways. We have found little or no evidence that such reflective thinking is being encouraged by traditional examinations.

Emerging Alternatives in the Context

We are working here in a print mode; thus there is an inevitable bias towards response as writing and literature as texts. So we have to return now to our own introductory position, to place literary work in a dynamic relationship to modern art forms, especially radio, film, and television. By and large, these are excluded in Literature exams: if they are recognized, it is in specialized studies of Communication, Film, or the Media. For a generation, some teachers have questioned this. But the domination of the university demands, their unrevised models of Literature, and their ignorance or total lack of concern for the pressing needs of students 14–18 has stifled progress.

There is eloquent testimony to the teacher's struggle to change the whole context for Literature in a recent article by Roy Goddard, describing his department's dilemma in teaching an "alternative" course for 16–18 year-olds wishing to specialize in Literature:

> We wanted to see how far we could push an alternative A level beyond a narrow, closeted literary heritage model into contact with the discourses and cultural concerns of the real world, so that we would be drawing upon, and in some cases explicitly investigating, a range of material—film, TV, community theatre, news media, and writing outside any established canon, as well as mainstream literary texts. To that end we identified course units . . . [aiming] to have at the centre of the unit a particular discursive practice or area of social and cultural experience rather than the text itself. . . .
>
> Such was our attempt and although the effort did our teaching good, I can't pretend that we were successful and I'd like to say why we failed and why our failure points not merely to inadequacies in the teachers who undertook the enterprise but, more vitally, to limiting, constraining, inhibiting factors built into [the] alternative A level course, which many teachers, including myself, would see as the best of the new A levels (Goddard, 1985).

On the face of it, then, we still seem to confront an unchallengeable university elite, their self-interest and their power. But, before giving up hope, let's consider whether that position is so impregnable after all. First, we know that many university teachers already have grave misgivings about what is done in their name in pre-university teaching and assessing of Literature. Many more would have, if they saw representative samples of the writing that

results. Second, higher education itself is divided over the definition of Literature, the forms of study to be expected, and the
theory that is needed. Third, in England and Wales, possibilities
are about to open up for courses that integrate literature and media
work within English studies. If literary studies in the broadest
sense are going to have much meaning for the majority of students
in [high] school, this is where change must begin. Will such courses
help to win acceptance for a broader view of Literature? The answer depends on a commitment and united efforts within our
national associations, shared and promulgated through the International Federation for the Teaching of English.

9

Responding to Poetry:
Create, Comprehend, Criticize

MOLLY TRAVERS

I don't like these poems. No excitement, can't associate with
it, like the poems we are told are good by teachers.

(Tony, age 15)

I don't know, I can't really find any hidden meaning in it, the
sort of meaning that readers are supposed to pick out from
poems.

(James, age 16)

Very easy to understand. This helps with a poem. I don't like
poems with lots of symbolism that are difficult to understand.

(David, age 15)

These were good students with a particular bent toward the sciences, and they were amongst the most competent readers of
poetry, as measured on a published poetry reading test which included Dickinson's poems and Shakespeare's sonnets. Behind these
words lie a number of assumptions: that the poetry we are told is
good by teachers is not the verse which nearly everyone, from
infancy to adulthood, enjoys at some time, whether nursery
rhymes, playground chants, pop song lyrics, greeting card doggerel,
or the In Memoriam lines which mark our passing; that school
poems cannot be read for simple enjoyment but are there to test
the student with traps of hidden meaning; and that a poem can be
enjoyed only if it says what it means at the first reading. As we
will see, these views are representative of the majority of secondary
school students.

I want, in this chapter, to look not only at suitable poems and
suitable methods of teaching them, but also at what adolescent
poetry readers actually do when they approach poetry. Perhaps
when we know what they do, we can build on that. The adolescents quoted above came from a sample of several hundred twelve-

to sixteen-year-old students from a cross section of schools, and the examples quoted in the remainder of the chapter are from that group which scored above the norm in a poetry reading test; they were not necessarily poetry lovers.

What Is a Response to Poetry?

Before we go further, we should look at what has been said about the effect of articulating our responses to a poem. Remember Rupert Brooke's spiteful verse about the girl friend who "quacked" beside him when he was aesthetically absorbed in the scenery. Many of us experience responses to art which seem to be in some way fragile. One teacher said, "Poems dear to me are usually destroyed by an indifferent class," and another, "It's almost heart-breaking to read something you love to the sound of 'This is sick!'" Pupils complain that dissection of poems ruins them and resist attempts to have them reassess a first ecstatic reading. A study by Wilson (1956) concluded that the requirement to articulate a response in the form of critical analysis partially destroyed an initial emotionally involved response. David Bleich (1978) explains that when we talk about our responses, we are trying to objectify the "affective-perceptual experience" rather than the work of literature itself; in all events we are not recording the response, but a verbal symbolization of it. There is, of course, no better way to communicate our response, and the poet has been similarly restricted by language.

Louise Rosenblatt (1978) acknowledges the same problem by distinguishing between the reader's initial unarticulated responses, "the web of feelings, sensations, images, ideas, that he weaves between himself and the text," and what she calls the "second stream of response" which "includes setting up hypothetical frameworks, entertaining expectations, selecting from alternative responses, revising what has been read in relation to what follows—a kind of self-criticism." For this second stream of response, "in most instances the reader or critic resorts to words as the medium of interpretation," an activity which involves introspection and recollection, so that the reader looks back to restructure the poem: "The evocation of even the simplest work is tremendously subtle and complex, with its blending and balancing of overtones, attitudes, feelings, and ideas." Thus, "reflection on the literary experience becomes a reexperiencing, a reenacting, of the work-as-evoked, and an ordering and elaborating of our responses to it" (pp. 134–137). This process is what

Rosenblatt defines as interpretation, and is what readers engage in when asked to write about a poem.

As the verbal response, restricted, as it were, by the words of the language, is not the whole response, nor is it the first response to a poem. Nevertheless, there is agreement on the value of a reflective, ordered, verbal, and even written response in deepening and providing insights into the process of response. We as teachers want to know how our pupils are responding and we need some form of evaluation. If the means we use deepens response, then the process has some learning value, too.

I have taken it for granted that reading aloud, group reading, and solitary reading, as well as talk—by the teacher, in class discussion, in groups, in pairs, and even alone on to an audiotape—will precede much of the writing; and that the writing, whether it is creative writing, comprehension, or critical evaluation, will be discussed and shared with others—the teacher, in pairs, in groups, and in displays and publications.

I have classified the types of written response which we look for when we ask pupils to write about poetry as creative responses, comprehension or interpretation, and critical evaluation—creation, comprehension, and criticism.

Creation

Even if children enjoy reading poetry, they do not like having to write about it. In most secondary classrooms, discussion and reading are more popular. However, writing in response to poetry can also mean writing poetry itself—perhaps the most natural response. Small children imitate actions and speech which impress them. The writing of verse after reading the work of an admired poet could be considered the ultimate expression of appreciation—imitation the highest form of flattery. Many of the successful poets in Nemerov's (1966) *Poets on Poetry* went through a period in adolescence when they created pastiches of the works of their favourite poet. Judith Wright (1975), herself a poet, suggests poetry writing in schools as a solution to the problem of declining interest in poetry: the child should be encouraged "to play with words, their textures, their sounds and rhythms. He may never become a poet himself, he may never even become a reader of poetry, but he will feel more kindly disposed to it" (p. 23). T. S. Eliot (1960) was saddened by "would-be poets who write regular verse with, at least, dull metronomic accuracy," and at the same time deplored others who "write 'free verse' with an ear untrained by the practice of regular verse"; he also looked for readers of poetry, and later said, "it is probably better that they should like the second-rate, the unoriginal, than that they should not like any poetry at all." His objections to the efforts of the young lay in their ignorance of the craft of poetry rather than to their writing mediocre verses. Notice that it is the crafting of language to which these poets refer, not the unburdening of the would-be poet's soul—which many educationists see as the greatest value.

The Value of Poetry Writing

Teachers like Marjorie Hourd (1949) in *The Education of the Poetic Spirit* wanted children to express their thoughts and feelings sincerely. In her examples, she relates theories of conflict in meaning defended by form to the actual poems several adolescents wrote, in order to draw Freudian conclusions about the expression of their inhibitions and sublimations through metaphor and symbol; self-expression through poetry writing could thus be a solution to behaviour problems. David Holbrook (1964) in *English for the Rejected* had similar aims, though his working class adolescents' violent writing was far from the sublimated flower metaphors of Hourd's middle class girls. He believed that their writing could help them—in expressing the Oedipus theme, for instance—to order their experiences and fantasies, to cope with their personalities and their search for identity, and he even suggests that a course in psychoanalysis would help teachers (p. 17). Poetry therapy and recent studies of the personality problems which illiterates have suggest that Holbrook was on the right track.

Another suggestion was that since free verse was easier to write than prose, less able adolescents could get some rewards from such writing. Bantock (1963) put it this way:

> An imagistic, symbolic type of poetry writing meets their capabilities much more easily than does prose writing, with its more rigid structure and its greater technical demands of grammar and punctuation. . . . What provides the structure is an emotional reaction, a series of disparate raids on the inarticulate rather than a coherently linked configuration. Indeed, in poetry, logical discontinuity is not necessarily a fault: the ordering principle is emotional, evocative, imagistic, rather than logical, connected and rational (p. 214).

Even if this meant writing the kind of verse to which T. S. Eliot objected, teachers have found that adolescents can find some satisfaction in creating a piece which looks like a real poem.

Developing this approach further, John Dixon (1969) in *Growth Through English* advocated that the child use his own language to shape his experiences, writing his own poems from his own beliefs and sharing them with the class. He develops confidence in himself and learns to control his experiences through control of language. Language in control, not language out of control as Bantock's idea suggests. The suggestion is that a child moves from being a participant in human experience when he actually takes part, to the role of spectator when he draws back, orders the experience in his mind as he talks and writes about it, thus coming to terms with it, "resolving inner tensions," and thereby controlling it. The whole value of poetry in the classroom is associated with the development of language to order and control emotional experiences, sharing them with others. Thus the personal growth. The poetry they read will add some experience, but it is what they write that is valuable:

> When pupils' stories and poems, though necessarily private activities, reemerge as experience to be shared and talked over with teachers and classmates, they become the literature of the classroom (Dixon, 1969, p. 55).

Such an idea will be familiar to those who have read Don Graves' accounts of children's "ownership" of the writing which they "publish" for the other members of the class to share and read, as they read any other published books.

Nevertheless, there are problems. "There is," Britton (1970) said in *Language and Learning*, "a kind of sad stagnation about the poetry written by an adolescent who fills whole exercise books with his (her) lines but rarely if ever reads the work of another poet," and he suggests that "trying other people's voices may for the adolescent be a natural and necessary part of the process of finding one's own" (pp. 260–262). Which is what T. S. Eliot and the poets in Nemerov's collection have said.

In the last decade, we have been in a period of review and readjustment accompanied by disillusioned attempts to return to earlier practices, considered—mistakenly I think—to have been more successful. The arrival of "process writing" (Graves, 1983) has led to an increased concentration on the pupils' own writing, mainly to develop positive attitudes which will help in learning to write and to read. The focus is on prose, and poetry is seldom mentioned. Any suggestions like Bantock's about poetry being easier because it does not have to be so clear and accurate would horrify teachers of process writing, where careful group proof reading and attention to language is part of making meaning clear to the reader.

In addition, although process writing places importance on looking at the writing of published authors for information on conventions, and for ideas on content and style, the development of the writer's own writing, and not the appreciation of the author's, is the focus. Nevertheless, discrimination in poetry does result almost without the pupil realizing it, perhaps the only way it will. Adolescent writers learn to accept that if they are to become writers, they must know the conventions, the structures, the schema, which a culture has available and which readers in that culture expect.

We now have five interrelated approaches to the writing of poetry in schools:

1. Writing expressive, free verse as a way of releasing one's emotions and increasing mental health.
2. Writing experiential verse as a method of developing one's own personal language and increasing self-esteem.
3. Writing free verse because it is easier for less articulate pupils who have difficulty connecting ideas and using the language conventions expected in prose.
4. Developing an understanding of the structures of poetry in order to increase one's command of a variety of appropriate ways of writing to meet audience expectations.
5. Learning to appreciate the form, style, and techniques of poetry through writing from great poetry as a model, including pastiche.

Teachers need to know why they are doing whatever it is they decide to do. So if verse is the written response you are asking of your class, think about your objectives and where they fit into the five classifications above. As a response to other poetry, the last two approaches concentrate on the work being read as much as on the pupil's own composition. But whatever the purpose, writers still can make use of all the available structures or styles. The more we learn about the use of our language, the more we are able to say what we want to say, and the greater our power over our lives.

To read successfully, adolescents need to be able to respond with feeling, even with passion—which may be sorrow or even rage as often as it will be pleasure. They also need to be able to understand the plain sense; otherwise their anger may be directed at poetry and poets, who seem to set out wilfully to confuse and frustrate, as we shall see.

Comprehension

Poems are difficult to read. To find out whether pupils have understood the plain sense, we ask a series of questions on content, for which written answers are required, sometimes a single word, sometimes a paragraph. Multiple choice questions make marking easier. The plain sense means more than simple facts; for instance, meaning may be misinterpreted if the tone of the poem is misunderstood. Attempts to order levels of comprehension hierarchically from fact through to inference are not helpful. We may well sense the irony of a poem in a first, quite unclear reading; and an awareness of symbolic implications may precede a comprehension of an apparently more obvious sequence of factual events. Only after all that might we explore a poem's syntactic and semantic complexities, and its narrative content. Under the heading of *comprehension* I include everything from an understanding of vocabulary to the most complex interpretations of meaning.

Although I have rejected a hierarchy of interpretations or comprehension for the order in which a reader understands a poem, teachers commonly accept a particular order of difficulty when they decide what questions to ask their pupils in class. Usually, less able or younger children are asked for facts about the narrative: "How many . . . ?" and "What happened . . . ?", and more complex questions are asked of older or brighter pupils: "How do you know . . . ?" and "What is suggested by . . . ?". Only later do questions about tone, poetic technique, and other questions on form follow; and after that, imagery and symbolism and finally that "hidden" meaning which I take to go beyond comprehension of the poem's meaning to questions which relate to the reader's particular associations and attitudes.

We will look at the problem of the "hidden" meaning in the section on *criticism*. Here I want to look at some attempts by twelve- to sixteen-year-old readers to comprehend the plain sense of poems. Most were, once given the freedom to respond as they liked, involved in outlining the meaning, unless they found the poem too difficult and unusual, in which case many resorted to an attack on the poet. Some of the most interesting responses were to Jon Silkin's "Worm," which thirteen-year-olds found very difficult, and I have written about that elsewhere (Travers, 1982). We will look at attempts to interpret "Lone Dog," by Irene McLeod:

I'm a lean dog, a keen dog, a wild dog, and lone;
I'm a rough dog, a tough dog, hunting on my own;
I'm a bad dog, a mad dog, teasing silly sheep;
I love to sit and bay the moon, to keep fat souls from sleep.

I'll never be a lap dog, licking dirty feet,
A sleek dog, a meek dog, cringing for my meat;
Not for me the fireside, the well-filled plate,
But shut door, and sharp stone, and cuff, and kick, and hate.

Not for me the other dogs, running by my side,
Some have run a short while, but none of them would bide;
O mine is still the lone trail, the hard trail, the best,
Wide wind, and wild stars, and the hunger of the quest.

Those thirteen- and fourteen-year-olds who wrote about this poem set about interpreting it with anything from the most basic paraphrase:

> The dog is a dog which doesn't care what he does. He's been mistreated. This dog has talked to other dogs but he doesn't like the way they have an easy life. The dog seems to hate everything. He likes stirring sheep and people from their sleep. The dog doesn't seem to be able to find his quest.
>
> (Daren)

to a quite sophisticated account:

> The life on the trail seems to me wonderful and beautiful, to bring out a streak of primitive wildness that urges him to leave what he's doing and follow this call to the wild. Although it is hard, it is the best life; in a way the dog is trying to repulse society and yet at the same time call them to follow. In the first verse, he says he's wild, untouchable, teasing. In the second, he is openly disapproving of those who are weak, revelling in his strength and way of life. In the third, he tells of those who tried to join him but didn't succeed. Then he says his trail is hard but the best, even nature and creation seem wild and big and wonderful.
>
> (Brigit)

These young readers needed to sort out the simple meaning and to express it in their own words before or while recording their aesthetic or moral responses.

Retellings seem to be a necessary part of formulating more sophisticated critical responses. The retelling also lets teachers know what has *not* been understood, and it allows pupils to show how they feel about a poem (Brigit has a quite different attitude to the dog from Daren, which shows up clearly in what they select to tell as well as in their language, even given that Brigit is a more skilful writer). Teachers do not need to ask comprehension questions if they have this information from a retelling, though they do need to discuss with the pupil what it is that has been missed or misinterpreted.

Apart from retelling, these adolescents concentrated on several aspects in their attempts to clarify meaning. They nearly always discussed rhyme and rhythm, and occasionally repetition. Again on "Lone Dog," Merry wrote:

The rhythm is good and seems to flow along, but it's a kind of a jerky flow. It is very definite. The last line of each verse kind of is a different rhythm but it still fits, but it seems a bit awkward and clumsy to me. It's not so bad in the second verse. The other thing that draws my attention, but not a much as the rhythm, is the rhyme, not just the ones at the end of the line (Are they called internal rhymes?). I think now you know that I like the poem, and the rhythm and the rhyme strike me most, in that order.

(Merry)

Colin noticed the repetition:

I like this poem quite a lot, one of the main reasons being the way it flows smoothly and easily without pronounced stops during the poem as many others tend to do. I think this effect is brought about by the repetitiveness of rhythm in some of the lines, eg. "I'm a rough dog, a tough dog," and "I'm a bad dog, a mad dog."

(Colin)

Others noted if rhythm failed to meet their demands for obvious beat, or if rhyme was missing. Comments on a modern poem in free verse were:

The poem doesn't seem to keep a steady beat and that is why I think it is boring.

(Darren)

When you're reading it, it doesn't have the slightest bit of rhyme or rhythm.

(Mary)

I find this poem hard to say in any rhythmic way. It just doesn't fit.

(Kate)

Mark wanted rhyme:

Each line doesn't appear to have any rhyming, or even close to rhyming things, just the end words—self, blind, cutting, ringed—see, they don't even have any rhythm or rhyming,

but later he made a generous attempt to appreciate the poet's intention:

When I said before that it doesn't rhyme, I'm sure he hasn't meant it to rhyme. Maybe he thought he could be different by not rhyming. There are a lot of poems that don't rhyme, I'm sure. That might've added more to the poem without it rhyming anyway. Maybe it's a good thing it doesn't rhyme.

(Mark)

Although the next two adolescents did not comment on other sound devices like alliteration or assonance either by name or description, they did quote words or phrases with approval. The first examines a word from Jon Silkin's "Worm"; the second refers to a line from Cesare Pavese's poem "Ulysses" reprinted below.

I like the use of the word "unvenomous"—"it is graspable and writhes in your hot hand: a small snake, unvenomous." I think that's quite good.

(Mark, on Jon Silkin's "Worm")

Ulysses

The old man's fed up, his son was born
too late. Sometimes they look each other in the face
but once is enough for a slap. (The old man goes out,
comes back with his son who pulls a face
and won't raise his eyes any more.) Now the old man sits
until night-time in front of a big window,
but no one comes and the street's deserted.

This morning the boy ran off, and came back
at night. He sits there sobbing. He won't tell
anyone if he's eaten at noon. He'll even
be heavy-eyed and he'll go to bed in silence:
his shoes are muddy. This morning was fine
after a month of rain.

                    Through the cool window
comes a bitter smell of leaves. But the old man
doesn't move from the darkness, hasn't slept all night,
and would like to sleep and forget the whole thing
as though he'd returned from a long walk.
To keep himself warm he yelled once and struck out.

The boy soon came back, his father didn't hit him any more.
The boy's a young man now and every day
discovers something and doesn't talk to anyone.

There's nothing in the street he couldn't discover
by standing at the window. But the boy walks
the streets all day. He doesn't go after women yet
and no longer plays outside. He always comes home.
The boy has his own way of leaving the house
and it's plain there's nothing more to be done.

Cesare Pavese

The line at the end of the second stanza is interesting, I think: "This morning was fine after a month of rain." It's sort of abrupt, but it leads on to the description of "the cool window" and the "bitter smell of leaves," I think. I don't know why he did it, but I like it, though.

(Caroline, on Cesare Pavese's "Ulysses")

Both Mark and Caroline had been taught in class how to identify various poetic techniques by name, such as image and metaphor. It is important to recall that in this study, they were asked to say what they "wanted to say" and given two sessions of practice, so it seems that the naming did not form part of a comfortable response. I am inclined to agree with Barnett (1977) who found that his college students, once they had identified imagery as such, felt it became isolated and unrelated to the content of the poem.

When a Poem Breaks the Rules

In attempting to understand a poem, readers have in their minds an idea of what a poem should be, which includes the form it should take (rhymes, for instance), the language it should use, the topic it should be about, and what it should say. When these adolescents saw what they thought of as the rules or conventions defied, they attacked the poet:

This bloke must be pretty thick to write about such a thing in such a manner.

(Dan, on Silkin's "Worm")

The author is pretty hopeless because if he can't think of any interesting things to write about other than worms, he must be gone gone in the head.

(Ben)

I think the writer was a bit twisted or he had a very good imagination.

(Jamie)

Experienced critics are not above doing the same, and I see such attacks as signifying an involvement which at least gives teachers a way in. These rejecting comments always came at the end of an attempt to understand the poem and what the poet was getting at, and appeared to be an angry reaction to a failure to understand. I think we need to think very carefully about why adolescents reject poetry: failure to understand what the poet is doing and why he is doing it is clearly one reason, and disapproval when you do understand is another. All result from strong involvement in poetry.

Tedious comprehension questions requiring a detached, efferent reading, and the laborious writing out of answers, can destroy this

involvement. David Bleich (1975) in *Readings and Feelings* encourages students to write subjective reactions which are then discussed in groups. This discussion of strong reactions, where teachers
respect the strength of each reader's response, is more likely to
modify and develop feelings about poems than are requirements to
be detached. For teachers who want to know if the plain sense has
been understood, retellings appear to be more comfortable and
spontaneous responses from adolescent readers. D. W. Harding
(1968) in an essay called "Practice at Liking" puts the whole problem thus:

> Understanding and liking are not independent. . . . Feeling
> baffled by what is offered . . . sets up dissatisfaction. . . . Grad-
> ual mastery . . . itself brings satisfaction. Some degree of liking
> or disliking is therefore bound up with the degree of under-
> standing, regardless of the meaning of what is understood. But
> there will also be liking or disliking of the meaning. . . . Two
> pieces of verse may be equally comprehensible but one will be
> liked and the other disliked according to the interest and ac-
> ceptability of what they say, in terms of the reader's individual
> structure of values—his interests and attitudes (Harding, 1968.
> p.4).

Which brings us to the question of criticism, as opposed to simple
comprehension or more complex interpretation.

Criticism

A poet and teacher, A. D. Hope, has complained that adolescents will ask him what a poem of his really means. There is, he
says, a difference between what the poet meant to say when he
wrote the poem and other possible meanings for various readers.
Many explanations which readers give "go beyond the poem; they
are not the meaning of the poem itself, but the way the poem
takes on extra meaning when it attaches itself" to the reader's experiences and ideas. And so Hope cannot tell readers what extra
meaning his own poem will take on for them. The poem may evoke
ideas and associations which the poet may or may not have intended, but whether they were intended or not, if readers find
them, for these readers they are there. Judith Wright says of one
of her poems which adolescents wrote to her about:

> There wasn't anything difficult about the words, indeed they
> couldn't have been simpler. But apparently it was too simple. A
> trap was suspected. After all, it was set for examination; more

must be behind it than could be seen by the careless eye. . . . It must have a Meaning, however cunningly disguised, and it must have been designed, and set for schools, as a kind of test of the candidate's, and the teacher's, ability to find this Meaning (Wright, 1975, p. 16).

She goes on to say that the pupil readers had learned not to accept simple enjoyment at their own level, and no longer trusted their own responses. She concludes:

I don't want to give the impression that poems do not, in fact, imply a great deal more than appears on their surface. Any good poem is a never-failing mine of suggestion, allusion and illumination. It makes us feel, and the feeling makes us think, in many directions. What I object to is the notion that poems can be pinned down once and for all, paraphrased, translated into some statement which is What the Poem Means, and that this statement is then all you need to understand and appreciate the poem (Wright, 1975, p. 17).

Having seen what poets have to say about their own poems, now let's look at how adolescent readers state the problem; for we have in the classroom pupils as readers, the poem which the poet wrote, and ourselves as teachers. The confusion adolescents feel about the meaning of a poem is clear in James's essay, written in Grade 10 about Cesare Pavese's "Ulysses":

There has to be a significance in this poem. It can't just be about a man and his son. Maybe the irrelevances might be just there to confuse you. Why not? Poets seem to enjoy it. It has to mean something else. Generally you have to know the Encyclo-paedia Britannica backwards to find a meaning. Why don't they make it obvious? Poetry's economical on words but it drains the brain trying to work out what it means.

(James)

Despite this plaintive cry, others rather enjoyed the search. As Julie says:

This is a pretty surface poem in that it doesn't have any hidden meaning, which is good in a way, but in other ways it isn't, because sometimes I (it depends on what mood I'm in) I like searching for a meaning and sometimes I don't.

(Julie)

Adolescent readers do spontaneously look for associations in poems and these can give them the pleasure of recognition or an illuminating discovery. These thirteen- and fourteen-year-olds

produced an assortment of associations when reading "Lone Dog";
they were not asked to and did not when reading "Worm." Chris,
for instance, made a simple comparison with her own dog:

> My dog loves her comfort, and begs to be allowed inside in
> winter. This dog seems almost afraid of softening, and being the
> undesirable lap dog, spoilt and fat. My dog isn't that bad, and
> she loves wind and running.
>
> (Chris)

Several saw themselves in the poem:

> I like the idea of the independent spirit and not bending to
> anyone and not seeking people's approval, because I think I'm a
> bit like that.
>
> (Sara)

Or more detached:

> Perhaps the reason for the appeal is that the dog is somewhat
> like we would like to picture ourselves, "the loner," someone to
> whom danger and excitement are commonplace.
>
> (Colin)

The majority went further still, so that the poem was no longer
about a dog at all:

> It doesn't just symbolize a dog, it could be a dreamy loner,
> spurred on by unexplainable energy.
>
> (James)

> The image created in my mind is of a tall, rugged bushman,
> roaming around the outback of Australia by himself on a horse.
> I think, very subtly, perhaps that might be what the poetess is
> trying to put across.
>
> (Christine)

> It could be about people. A person who wouldn't like to
> bother people, trouble people, and doesn't like to mix. It could
> be about a poor person who will never ask for help from the
> rich. A tramp might fit.
>
> (George)

We have moved from desirable independence to an anxious outcast,
and others went even further:

> A leader, rather like a leader of skins or sharps, who is feared
> by the other members of the gang, but all the same respected.
>
> (Mike)

> A lone punk disturbing the peace, stealing, wrecking, on the
> dole, not liked by anyone, performing crimes by himself, not
> wanting to settle down, always on the run.
>
> (Dan)

These responses appear to be provoked by the poem itself, and perhaps Colin's observation is even more perceptive than it first seemed to be: "the dog is somewhat like we would like to picture ourselves" or possibly as we "do picture ourselves" in our deepest desires and anxieties. N. N. Holland in (1973) *Poems in Persons* explores such fascinating possibilities, using a Freudian framework for interpreting responses.

However, one of the most original responses was intellectual rather than personal, and in her response, Sara explains her discovery:

> The line "shut door, and sharp stone, and cuff and kick and hate," I don't quite see why he'd want that, it's the opposite to "sadistic," it's a person who likes to be hurt. He's very independent, but no-one really would want to be cuffed and kicked and hated. I don't know whether he wanted to prove what a bad place the world is, that he himself was the only one that's right. He almost seems as if he's trying to make a martyr of himself, one of those religious martyrs like in the 16th century when Bloody Mary was having them all burnt at the stake, and they were yelling out curses. He seems to be a bit like that when I read it again. I doubt that Irene McLeod would have written it like a religious fanatic, though I was saying that. But as I read it, it just seems more and more like that.
>
> (Sara)

She added later that "Irene McLeod probably just wrote that as an innocent sort of poem, but I have got this strange idea out of it"; in saying that, Sara makes the distinction which Judith Wright insists on. Sara had discovered a poem, one which was different from the poem McLeod intended, but that did not disturb her. The process is interesting: an inconsistency was worrying; she sought an explanation in the dog's character, and a parallel came to mind which coincided with historical figures from a period she was studying. Matching the comparison throughout the poem had the satisfaction of a game or a discovery. One has to admire her ingenuity.

Two interesting points arise from these responses. One is the question of how far a response can move from the original "simple" poem and still be legitimate. The second is the extent to which personal identification and associations lead to liking or a dislike of the poem. Both are important to teachers.

It may not be true that there are as many versions of a poem as there are readers. Sara recognized the possibility that the poem remained while her theory developed. Her driven martyr was not

Chris's laughing, teasing wag, nor Dan's "lone punk," nor Mark's leader of "skins and sharps," nor George's humble tramp. Each had created a version of the poem to satisfy individual perceptions of the work, directed by something in their own experiences and personalities. Usually, certain sections of the poem were ignored to complete the interpretation satisfactorily; "teasing," ignored by Sara as inappropriate to her martyr theory, was central to Chris's carefree and cheerful wanderer, while for Dan the word acquired sinister overtones. Is the teacher to insist on a more accurate reading, and perhaps to reduce some of the enthusiasm which went into these responses? The answer is to exchange and discuss the separate responses, to allow these adolescents to explain and explore further their own and other's responses, an activity which will inevitably point them again to the poem.

The second point on liking and dislike may help us to answer the last question. Although many were content to enjoy the dog as dog, perhaps one of the strengths of "Lone Dog" (one of my favourites as a child) is its openness to interpretations within the experience of fourteen-year-old adolescents, whether this experience is actual (as in Alice's case, where she made a comparison with her family who had been rebuffed in their attempts to help an Asian immigrant family), romantic, or historical. If the image was favourable, the poem was approved; if unfavourable, the poem was condemned. Dan, for instance, wrote after his description of the lone punk, "dogs can be an interesting subject to write about, but this poem stinks." He was unusual, but he does give some clue to why those who disliked the poem did so: their image of the rejected, unloved, hostile dog was too uncomfortable, possibly even too close to how they felt about themselves. Those who saw the dog as enjoying his independence, or at least confidently defiant, found the poem very satisfying. I do not think it is going too far to say that when we ask pupils to make an aesthetic response, we are asking them to talk about themselves and to expose something of their own hopes, anxieties and fears. Perhaps that is why teachers often move hastily to what Rosenblatt calls the efferent response—taking the factual information from the poem in a series of comprehension questions. In that way, when we mark an answer "wrong," we avoid hitting below the belt—or below the conscious to the vulnerable subconscious, which, if we accept Holland's (1973) view, determines how we will respond to poetry.

Comprehension or Criticism?

I have been making a distinction between comprehension and criticism. Something of the difference is explained by the poets

A. D. Hope and Judith Wright when they distinguish between the simple meaning and the extra meaning, or between what appears on the surface and the "mine of suggestion, allusion and illumination" which is evident only when the poem attaches itself to the reader's experience and ideas. Something of the difference is also explained by Rosenblatt's distinction between aesthetic reading and efferent reading.

Literary criticism involves something beyond the interpretation of the plain sense of the meaning of the work. W. Ray (1984) in his discussion of recent literary theories in *Literary Meaning: From Phenomenology to Deconstruction* outlines Hirsch's distinction between interpretation and criticism: "interpretation differs from criticism in that the former busies itself with simple meaning, while the latter is concerned with significance. . . . Significance is the relating of an author's meaning to something outside of it. Interpretation involves an attempt to understand the work, whereas criticism involves judgement—comparing the meaning of the literary work with some value criteria (an established literary standard for instance, or moral standard) or with anything else one likes to compare it with" (p. 95). If you look at Chris's or Sara's comments, you will see that that is what they are doing. Terry Eagleton (1983) in *Literary Theory: An Introduction* summarizes Husserl's interpretation: "significances vary throughout history, whereas meanings remain constant; authors put in meanings, whereas readers assign significances" (p. 67). Each different historical or cultural group assigns new significances to a literary work which may never have been anticipated either by its author or its contemporary readers. Sara recognized this in her dog-martyr theory, and was quite rightly not worried by it.

Discrimination and Moral Values

Two other areas of criticism which concern us in the secondary school relate to values: the value of a particular poem in comparison with poems of established quality (is it a good work of literature?); and the moral values which the poet and reader hold (does the reader agree with the values expressed in the poem?).

All evidence suggests that most adolescents (nor the general population, for that matter) do not learn to discriminate between what literary experts consider good and poor poetry. Research studies in schools report their failures, some with irritation: Abbott and Trabue (1921) long ago commented that a "marked preference . . . for this silly gush over real poetry reveals a weakness in human nature, or in English teaching" (p. 125) when their secondary and college students failed to discriminate, and subsequent studies concluded that the majority of adolescents have limited powers of discrimination, and actually rate poor poetry as better than good poetry. They base their judgements on the topic of the poem, the feeling the subject arouses, the obviousness of language and theme, and though they respond to good poetry if it meets their criteria, they are still unable to distinguish between the good and poor poems they like. A small group of adolescents, however, already have the ability to discriminate, and some make judgements based on formal qualities such as poetic technique and language, which the majority do not.

In the study discussed in this chapter, the majority of students aged twelve to sixteen chose the least sophisticated poems. This pattern was particularly marked by the older students, where two of the favourite poems were those included in the research as examples of poor quality in form and content. However, at fifteen and sixteen, some good adolescent readers did change their opinion after writing about one of the inferior poems, but not all.

As to the moral values expressed in a poem, we have been through a period where readers have been asked to detach themselves from "the emotional appeal of the subject matter," which Williams, Winter, and Woods (1938) dismissed as an "irrelevant factor"; and through a subsequent phase where we explored "themes" so that only subject matter—and sometimes only part of the subject matter of a poem—was seen to be important. However that may be, adolescents do judge poems and even poets by their subject matter; in fact, they often judge the deeds described in the poem and virtually abandon the poem itself, as we can see with Matthew.

In his writing, Matthew adopted similar strategies for approaching two poems. His first paragraph outlined the theme, and there followed an account of each verse which included judgements about the behaviour of the characters and some guesses about their future behaviour. The first poem was about an aging father unable to make contact with a young son. Matthew stated that the father and son "should get on with each other"; the son "really needs parental advice," is "maladjusted in society," "probably left school and is unemployed and is a Juvenile delinquent because there's nothing to do and his father (his mother probably died when he was very young) didn't teach him how to be a useful member of society," and "will probably end up committing suicide or being a criminal. . . . There is very little chance that the boy will become normal"—none of which was in the poem, but all of which was likely, given the atmosphere and the account of events.

His second essay was as follows:

This poem is by the girl who had a love affair with a boy who had since deserted her in preference for someone else. Because of their impulsiveness, low moral standards and "love" for each other, the girl is pregnant and the poem is set as being written on the night she is having her baby. To add disaster to tragedy, the girl is going to die. She has had to pay dearly for her rash love affair.

The poem does not suggest that her love was not genuine, and does not condemn their moral standards, nor indicate that she is paying dearly (we are invited to enjoy her tragic death and applaud her devotion to her baby's father); these judgements are added by Matthew.

He continued:

This poem shows up some of the disastrous effects that result from individuals behaving in a way dictated by today's low moral standards; effects that are not mentioned very often in today's popular films and books. If the seemingly less enjoyable, but safer code of morality had been followed, the girl would not be pregnant and if they had had a child, it would have been brought up in a stable family environment, not branded for life with illegitimacy.

Matthew's concern was with moral behaviour; he wrote about the poems as if they were accounts of actual relationships, his only concession to their existence as fictions being his comment on rhyme—"It is because this is such a negative and depressing poem, about people's failure to cope with life, that I don't like it. Also it doesn't rhyme. I like poems that rhyme."

The majority of adolescents also made moral judgements about the behaviour of characters in the poems, and in some cases the poet. "They ought not to—behave that way—write poems like that" was a common response from both thirteen- and fifteen-year-olds, so that Matthew's view was not so unusual. Readers do make such judgements as they read, and in fact literature which does not provoke such reactions is likely to be unstimulating.

The Adolescent Poetry Reader

These secondary pupils were aware of certain technical aspects, rhyme and rhythm particularly, and the majority sought poems where both were marked. These were good readers, and all but three came from classes where poetry was studied, so that a failure to accept modern literary forms was not through lack of familiarity. They noticed and quoted extensively any lines or images they liked or rejected, but few were able to make any comment on their reasons for selecting certain lines. However, subject matter and characterization absorbed them most. Topics and points of view were discussed in detail, often with misinterpretations resulting from a determination to support a particular view rather than from an inability to cope with vocabulary or syntax. Many rejected anything ambiguous or complex and refused to explore meaning. Poems were praised for being simple, straightforward, and having no "hidden" meaning. Pupils liked poems they could respond to personally. Favourite poems were often compared with their own feelings and experiences. At the same time, they sought positive or sentimental reactions, rejecting those which called for uncomfortable reappraisals of their established views.

In all, pupils looked for poems which were not only easy to read but also easy to feel. The good feelings arose from the topic, from stereotyped sentimental emotions, and from an easy, recognizable rhythm and rhyme. Jolts in ideas, emotions, or structure led to a rejection of the poem.

Several pupils had quite different preferences, enjoying all those qualities which the majority rejected and rejecting those which the majority enjoyed. Others who enjoyed the easier poems were able to write about their reasons with perception and conviction, or at least to talk about them. If poetry is to have any impact on pupils like these, then opinions, based on feelings which are part of an individual's personality and experience, must be taken into account, not only in the discussion of poems, but also in the selection of poems for classroom reading.

The Poetry Teacher

I have argued that if we are to make poetry important for secondary pupils, we must accept the way they can and will respond, and build from there. One teacher who took part in this study taught a class in which every child enjoyed poetry, and it may be of interest to take a closer look at him. He taught a class of over thirty pupils, packed into a crowded classroom with solid wooden desks. His first degree had been in science, and he had spent a year working on the railways, another on a farm. He had a passion for poetry and read a good deal himself. He believed utterly in its value, and that it could be made accessible to everyone. He found the hostility pupils often bring to poetry an "exciting challenge" and he would use anything to create interest, though he always emphasized the difference between light poetry and that which deals with the vital things of life. He worked furiously to counter the modern tendency to neglect poetry in the curriculum, but felt that often he was "piddling in the Pacific." He made coloured sheets of all kinds of poetry for his class, read aloud with vigor, and allowed pupils to contribute their own anecdotes and comments; but at the same time poetry was taken very seriously. He was highly organized, dominating but not a showman, and very accepting of the pupils' contributions. The secret appeared to be a deep personal conviction, a profound belief in the pupils, a wide knowledge of poems which appealed at all levels, an ability to read poetry aloud and talk about it at the pupils' level—but seriously, a wide variety of classroom activities, and an inspiring classroom manner. He was not a paragon; he seemed simply to like poetry, like his pupils, and like teaching, and he expected his pupils to enjoy learning. Research suggests, as I have explored elsewhere (Travers, 1984), that the teacher does make a difference, and plays more part in influencing whether adolescents will come to like poetry than the poems chosen or the methods used, and can influence most pupils, whatever their personalities.

10

The Hidden Life
of a Drama Text

ROSLYN ARNOLD

Once upon a time we thought that reading and relating to a written text involved chasing topical allusions through contemporary dictionaries in an attempt to unlock the secrets of the writer's mind. Sometimes erudite commentaries told us the significance of a phrase as it related to what the writer was doing on the day of its composition. It was part of the sub-text of that particular method that readers brought nothing of significance to their reading of the text. Now we know that the reading process is infinitely more complex than the allusion-chasing method recognized, requiring at least the need to unlock the secrets of the reader's mind as s/he encounters that text. Formidable as this might sound, in fact the process is illuminating and exciting once we see how much creativity goes into making meaning from print. The long term process of moving from an initial spontaneous reading of a drama text to an evaluative, discriminating rereading involves the reader, in part, in an engagement between her own assumptions and guesses at meaning and the structures, patterns, and language of the text. In that engagement there is a tension between what the reader wants to believe and what the text wants her to believe. It is in resolving that tension that personal meaning matches with public meaning (the text), and the reader gains a sense of belonging with the text. None of that engagement, conflict, and resolution can happen unless the reader sustains belief in her own ability to create meaning while preserving her own integrity and that of the text.

In the olden days we thought the text was a very stable entity, rather like a Gothic cathedral—beautiful on the outside and infinitely more magnificent inside—if only you were strong enough to open up the massive front door. Now we know that while the cathedral still stands, there is more than one door and some doors lead on to the altar of high wisdom while others lead into the crypt of confusion. Sometimes it takes a long time to find the best door, but you can go back and forth as often as you like. The cathedral will still stand there. All the doors have some purpose in contributing to a perception of artistic totality, and the skilful doorkeeper in the classroom knows that the traditional "lit. crit." approach is a very narrow, creaky little door indeed.

To take a different metaphor—though possibly still in the medieval vein—we have to acknowledge the tale borne by the reader encountering the text as well as the tale contained within the text. To know what belongs to the reader and what belongs to the text—keeping in mind that teachers too have their own personal histories as readers—takes highly developed analytic and empathetic skills. When you stop to think about it, there may be a cast of hundreds involved in the apparently simple dynamic of a reader, a text, and a teacher. If you think that is overdramatizing the process, consider experimenting with the method outlined below. I think it illuminates some of the complexities of the hidden life of a drama text, and the hidden life of readers. But it also helps readers to develop independence and informed judgement as they engage in making a text their own.

Background

In the early seventies in Sydney, the Nimrod Street theatre, a venue for the most innovative theatre productions in Sydney at that time, ran several teachers' drama workshops which I attended. One afternoon session with the actor/director John Bell was particularly memorable because he demonstrated to our group of about twenty teachers the methods of sub-texting he used with actors encountering a drama text for the first time. The fact that I remember the text he used, the method he demonstrated, and the heat and pressing lassitude of that hot January day has much to do with the powerful effect that session had upon me. It made explicit something I had secretly believed through all my university English courses, in the heyday of the Leavisite approach, that what the reader brought to the text did matter—not so much because it stood in opposition to another's interpretation, or even stood beside it, but because it was there as a factor to be taken into account, and to ignore it was to undervalue the dynamism of the reading process. How could literature make an impact upon one's life and search for meaning if there was no engagement between the self as reader and the words on the page? How could one be involved unless there was some risk-taking, some reevaluation of personal constructs, some shaping of tentative, early responses into more firmly held discriminative ones. Living out the text places it within the self. Readers love the texts they feel they can commit themselves to. To be told you cannot understand a text until you have read what the critics say about it is like trying to love a child through a thick glass wall—you can see her but you cannot touch or hear her—a recipe for the kind of literary autism which has beset many readers in the past.

The fact that John Bell could use the method successfully with actors who barely knew the texts they were using was very encouraging. Crucial to the success of the method is the teacher/director's willingness to accept that whatever the reader presents as the subtext is valuable material to work on: even silence can signal something important about the reader encountering the text.

The Method of Sub-Texting

Essentially, the method of reading the sub-text of a drama text is one of articulating and bringing to the surface all the ideas and associations the reader has in response to the text. Readers are asked to express as clearly as possible what is going on as they make sense of the lines on the page. It is similar to paraphrasing, but it may at first be much more liberal and liberating than a paraphrase. Obviously, in bringing to the surface one's personal responses to the text, there may be many responses which are largely irrelevant to other readers and some which even the reader may not want to retain into a second reading. What is important is the way in which the reader attempts to articulate what happens when a text is shaped by the individual reader so that the intricate process of forging meaning from the text is recognized for all its complexities. Done properly the process is difficult because so many readers have learned to repress what they feel and think about a text for fear of being found wrong or wanting. However, if the webs of personal responses are not brought to the surface and evaluated for their significance, their richness or their banality, they have a habit of interfering with the reader's refinement of response. In other words, the more we scrutinize our responses, the more we invest in the text; the more we understand who owns what response and idea, the reader or the text writer, the more we recognize those texts which stand up to the rigours of close scrutiny and those which fall apart when the stitches are unpicked and the fabric examined.

How to Sub-Text in a Group

It is helpful if the work of sub-texting is done in a group (ten is a good number because it allows sufficient turn-taking, variety and a range of responses). Each group member has a copy of the text or piece of the play under examination. The readers are asked to read a couple of the original lines just as they appear on the page, then, *in the first person,* as if they were the character in the play, they read the lines again giving as free a translation as possible of the lines in question. Readers are asked to read the text and give their sub-text in turn—working on enough lines to make a sense sequence (for young readers it may help if the teacher works out the readers' segments in advance). Ask the readers not to comment at this point on another's sub-text. Encourage guesswork if the text is difficult.

A number of interesting things happen when this method is used. For a start, many readers are very nervous of revealing their own interpretations. Speaking in the first person is very threatening because it assumes some ownership of the language, but insist upon the use of the first person. It is important that the teacher/ director establishes the validity of *every* response no matter how trivial, tentative, silly, or confused that interpretation might be. It can take a lot of skill on the teacher/director's part to liberate the readers sufficiently for the method to work. You have to believe that the secret life of the text is important or the students will escape confrontation with the text and resort to second-hand reactions. Hence the need to emphasize the collaboration of the whole group in bringing to life the language on the page and the shared meanings of that particular reading group. No two groups ever share exactly the same readings of the text, which makes the process particularly exciting. With shy groups it can help to hear a tape-recording of another group's efforts, providing that does not unduly influence their own work. Different passages to those being worked on can be chosen as models, and the basic idea can be introduced on the tape. It is easier, of course, if the teacher demonstrates the method, perhaps with a passage the students nominate so that the teacher's own hesitations and back-tracking are revealed as part of the authenticity of an initial reading of a difficult text.

When sub-texting is done in a group, it becomes obvious that different readers give different emphases to different aspects of a speech. Some readers give interpretations surprisingly different to those we might have been mentally rehearsing. One can be startled out of complacency by hearing another give an apparently aberrant sub-text to a well-known line. What needs to be kept in mind is that sub-texting is not only a matter of finding out what the text means but of finding out what the text means when it is enacted by readers: finding out the intricacies of motivations, symbols, thoughts, and feelings evoked by language as it is written on the page and language as it is read and spoken by readers. But for all the differences one might find among the interpretations made by readers, there will often be a thread of commonality among the responses. With an acute and perceptive ear one can become attuned to strong threads of agreed meanings beneath the surface of the sub-texts too. Finding a sub-text is not the end of the story; there are sub-texts within sub-texts too. Hence the need to rework passages to strengthen those commonly shared understandings.

When the text has been sub-texted once, it is worth reworking the same passage without too much comment or justification from individuals for their interpretations. What is often discovered is that on a reworking, aberrant interpretations are dropped in favour of more acceptable ones. This can happen almost unconsciously as the readers in the group intuitively recognize the differences between the claims of the very idiosyncratic response and the claims of the written text itself. That is why I think it is important to let early interpretations stand without comment from the director or the readers. If there is tacit acceptance for a reading, then it will withstand a reworking. It it is not accepted, it will bend under a reworking. I am arguing for letting the process of sub-texting do its own job without recourse to argument or justification, pervasive as such rhetoric is. Keep insisting that the readers continue speaking in the first person and emphasize that acceptable interpretations will be shaped by increasing knowledge about the characters and events as reading of the text progresses. In drama rehearsals the final point of the sub-texting process is to enable actors to utter spontaneously the original lines of the text with as much conviction and understanding as if they had created them themselves. Ideally, in the classroom situation the end point might be a reading aloud of the original text and an acting out of scenes. You'll find that while it may take time and effort in the beginning to establish the ground rules for sub-texting, once readers have had a couple of sessions working with the method, they find it relatively easy and unthreatening. The beginning is the hardest part, but once the dramatist's language is demystified, it actually becomes easier for it to be incorporated into readers' repertoires of language forms.

I have chosen for analysis here passages from Shakespeare and a passage from Harold Pinter's one act play, *The Black and White* (in *Theatre Today*, ed.: D. Thompson, Longmans, 1965). The contrast is deliberate because the different linguistic styles of each dramatist demonstrate the flexibility of the sub-texting method. With Shakespeare there is usually a paring down of the original language at first. With Pinter there is a building up and a fleshing out of the text. If anything, readers usually value the process of sub-texting more when they encounter Pinter because it can be difficult to interpret "iceberg" language. They come to appreciate the significance of the defensively brief exchanges between Pinter's characters and the role of pauses and gestures which counterpoint the brevity of dialogue.

To illustrate how sub-texting might work, here is an example from *King Lear*, I i 37–42:

TEXT	SUB-TEXT
LEAR: Meanwhile we shall express our darker purpose.	Meanwhile let me get on with something more difficult.
Give me the map there. Know that we have divided In three our kingdom; and 'tis our fast intent To shake all cares and business from our age, Conferring them on younger strengths, while we Unburden'd crawl toward death.	Give me the map. You know I have already divided the kingdom into three and I'm determined to give up all responsibilities so the young can take them on. I'm going to free myself of burdens as I face death.

A more liberal sub-text which is defensible in light of knowledge of the whole play might be:

	Look, you lot will inherit everything when I die, so you can make things easier for me now.

Consider then the exchange between Lear and Cordelia shortly after this speech (I i 87–95):

TEXT	SUB-TEXT
LEAR: What can you say to draw A third more opulent than your sisters? Speak.	This is what I've been waiting for. What can you say, Cordelia, to gain a third which is richer than your sisters (or: what can you say which is richer to gain a richer third). (The ambiguity is significant.)
CORD: Nothing, my lord.	I'm not going along with this. I hate my father's need for public displays of love. It demeans him and me.
LEAR: Nothing!	Did I hear right? You can't mean that.

TEXT	SUB-TEXT
CORD: Nothing.	I do mean it. I will not compromise.
LEAR: Nothing will come of nothing: speak again.	Look, I've set this up so words equal property. If you say nothing you get nothing. Have another go.
CORD: Unhappy that I am, I cannot heave My heart into my mouth: I love your Majesty According to my bond; nor more nor less.	I hate letting you down, but I can't say what I feel about you in this public confrontation. I love you as a daughter should love her father and you'll have to decide what that is worth.

Obviously not everyone would agree with the sub-text I have given to Lear's and Cordelia's words. For example, the sub-text "it demeans him and me" is a very free translation of her response and relies on further information about Cordelia than most readers would have on a first reading of the play. However, if an actor/reader were trying to say the original lines with as much conviction as possible, then it would help to understand the layers of feeling motivating Cordelia. Arguably, a feeling that her father was demeaning himself by this request for public acknowledgement may be one such feeling. If so, the "no" of the text may be said with some element of appeal to her father to read the situation more accurately, rather than as a straight defiance of him, as some readers interpret these lines. With all sub-texting, the interpretations are left open and subject to reworking as more information about the characters is revealed.

It is easy to move past that exchange in the text without recognizing how tremendously powerful it is. Because the lines are so brief, pointed, and unadorned, they are often skipped over. Yet they mark a pivotal point in the play and through the process of sub-texting one becomes aware of the drama of that moment. It marks the beginning of Lear's rejection of Cordelia and the beginning of his self-confrontation. This self-confrontation is essential because Lear had relied upon Cordelia to mirror his reactions and to confirm himself in her image of him. By her refusal to endorse his behaviour, he was confronted with his own ego blindness. To save face he had to reject her at that point. By saying "no" Cordelia was saying "I will not reflect back to you a false self." One might also argue that she recognized intuitively, too, his need to look inwards now as well as outwards for those reflections of self which help us all to maintain our integrity. It is interesting how often in Shakespeare's plays the most powerful psychological points in the plays are not always those couched in the most elaborate language; they are sometimes those which sound the most commonplace and are ignored. After all, we all know what "no" means, don't we?

It takes time to sub-text well, and it is worth selecting carefully those parts of the play worth working on in detail. I favour choosing contrasting elaborate and commonplace speeches (or parts of speeches) to make the point that reading is a matter of interpreting, predicting, hypothesizing, reshaping and guessing, bringing to bear our own life experiences and expectations, no matter how simple or complex the text is. Once students are tuned into the process it does not have to be overstressed. After all, what you are encouraging readers to do is to make explicit what happens naturally anyway.

Should you choose to sub-text Goneril's and Regan's responses to Lear's request (I ii 59–62, 71–77), which precede Cordelia's, you will find how skilfully Shakespeare has matched their language to their motivations. The students who try to sub-text those speeches have great difficulty in finding substitutes for the original words. They begin to repeat themselves and falter, precisely because the language of persuasive rhetoric employed by Goneril and Regan is hollow and deceptive. It breaks down under the scrutiny of sub-texting. The words are highly abstract and even contradictory ("Speech which makes breath poor and speech unable"), but as their primary function is to sound impressive publicly while concealing true motivations (greed, hostility, sycophancy), it becomes very difficult in sub-texting to do other than fall back upon the original lines. Another way to sub-text the lines could be to ignore their lexical context altogether and say simply "I'm going to get what I can by saying whatever the silly old man wants me to say." Experienced readers might take up that option, but with those new to the process of sub-texting you may need to offer help with Goneril's and Regan's speeches here. It can be a relief for readers to find that the apparently complex language is largely meaningless though rhetorically functional in context.

To demonstrate another aspect of the sub-texting process, it is worth considering two speeches of Romeo's in Act I of *Romeo and Juliet*. By careful sub-texting it is possible to see changes in Romeo's attitude to love within the same act. The first speech for consideration is Romeo's first entrance in the play. He is heavily involved in the rhetoric of love and self-dramatization, so when one tries to sub-text these lines, the humour, repetitiveness, rhetorical extravagance, and ambiguity of Romeo's words become all too apparent. When one considers what physical actions Romeo might be involved in here, attention-seeking movements like breast-beating and foot-shuffling come to mind. In other words (which is what sub-texting is about) Romeo wants the attention of all onlookers (audience included), and the subject of his "love" is none other than himself. As with the Goneril and Regan speeches mentioned above, the rhetoric of the speeches breaks down under the analysis of sub-texting. The real function of the words, to draw attention to the speaker's self-interest, is revealed. This is not to suggest that the words are not significant: rather to suggest that their significance is very different to that overtly stated by the speaker. It becomes a case of the audience/reader knowing more about the character than he knows about himself. Consider Romeo's first speech:

TEXT	SUB-TEXT
I i 165–188	

Enter Romeo

TEXT	SUB-TEXT
BEN.: Good morrow, cousin.	Morning, mate.
ROM.: Is the day so young?	What a bore . . . is it still morning?
BEN.: But new struck nine.	It's only just nine o'clock . . . what's up with you?
ROM.: Ay me! sad hours seem long. Was that my father that went hence so fast?	I'm depressed . . . time drags. Was that dad racing away?
BEN.: It was. What sadness lengthens Romeo's hours?	Sure was. Why are you depressed?
ROM.: Not having that which having makes them short.	I can't get what I want.
BEN.: In love?	I know . . . you're in love.
ROM.: Out—	Getting nowhere.
BEN.: Of love?	Oh, I'm wrong, you're not pining.
ROM.: Out of her favour, where I am in love.	She won't come across.
BEN.: Alas! that love, so gentle in his view, Should be so tyrannous and rough in proof!	Poor you . . . you're really tied in knots and love (or is it sex?) is meant to be terrific.
ROM.: Alas! that love, whose view is muffled still, Should, without eyes, see pathways to his will. Where shall we dine? O me! What fray was here? Yet tell me not, for I have heard it all. Here's much to do with hate, but more with love. Why, then, O brawling love! O loving hate! O anything, of nothing first created! O heavy lightness! serious vanity! Mis-shapen chaos of well-seeming forms!	I don't even know what love is . . . something's driving me crazy. Talk about eating? Not me? What's been going on here? No, I don't want to know. I've heard it all before. This is what happens when love and hate get mixed up. You can't tell the difference between one thing and another. Rhetoric tells it all . . . the world is full of confusing contrasts and I'm a victim of its paradoxes. I can't sleep, I can't think of anyone else I'm so centered on my own frustration. I hate this love/sex/romance business. You're not laughing at me in my serious misery?

Feather of lead, bright smoke, cold
                    fire, sick health!
Still-waking sleep, that is not what it
                    is!
This love feel I, that feel no love in
                    this.
Dost thou not laugh?

Now consider this speech when he first sees Juliet:

TEXT	SUB-TEXT
I v 45–57	
ROM.: What lady's that which doth enrich the hand Of yonder knight?	Who's that woman dancing with that lucky knight?
SERV.: I know not, sir	I don't know, sir.
ROM.: O! she doth teach the torches to burn bright. It seems she hangs upon the cheek of night Like a rich jewel in an Ethiop's ear;	She certainly turns me on. She's stunning. I'm dazzled.
Beauty too rich for use, for earth too dear! So shows a snowy dove trooping with crows.	She's too beautiful to use . . . too good for this earth. I'm suddenly shy. She stands out among the rest.
As yonder lady o'er her fellows shows. The measure done, I'll watch her place of stand, And, touching hers, make blessed my rude hand.	I know what she's like and I must take action . . . make contact with her.
Did my heart love till now? Forswear it, sight! For I ne'er saw true beauty till this night.	Did I talk like this before? No . . . forget all that. I can see now what I have to do. This is the woman who excites me to action. The past is forgotten. I'm a man of purpose now. Words are not enough.

The sub-texts I offer here are often very liberal and other readers would make their own interpretations and guesses at the character's motivations. Obviously, as you come to know a character better, the sub-texts become more accurate because you bring to bear fuller knowledge of the play and its dynamics. Interestingly, where the poetry is most aptly metaphoric, you feel a resistance to sub-texting it at all. For instance, in the final line of Romeo's speech above, "For I ne'er saw true beauty till this night," the poetic force of that line is lost when one sub-texts it. You become aware of the creativity of Romeo's language and the force of his feelings. In the earlier speech with all its rhetorical flourishes and exaggerated metaphors, you feel it doesn't matter whether lines are transposed or left out all together. In this speech, each line leads inexorably to a fitting conclusion.

When reading the lines aloud, you become aware of the place of rhythm in speech—it anticipates the closure of the final line and reflects the purposefulness of Romeo's state of mind. I would urge all readers in your working group to say these lines of the text aloud. There are special effects created by the poetry, rhythm, rhyme, imagery, and sounds of these lines which add special dimensions to their meaning. As one reads the speech, there is a sense of urgency impelling one to the final line "I ne'er saw true beauty till this night." This natural movement in the lines adds conviction to Romeo's words. In the earlier opening speeches the lines lacked a sense of natural movement and one felt lines could be transposed or skipped without loss of meaning. Here there is a tautness and internal logic which influences meaning and creates a sense of Romeo's integrity. The clarity of the imagery, its sensuousness, the vitality of the "t's" and "b's" in the first lines, the fact that his own words and the sight of Juliet impell Romeo to action are evidence of the genuine physicality and energy of his feelings for Juliet. There is a focus and clarity in Romeo's words now, and quite rightly he makes a decision "to touch" Juliet and transform desire into action.

I am not claiming that this is evidence of "true love," whatever that is, but it is evidence of a different Romeo to the man we met at the beginning. We see now the young virile man inflamed by the sight of Juliet, "Oh, she doth teach the torches to burn bright," and burning for physical action. A dramatic change from the self-dramatizing Romeo of the first speeches! He has become outward-looking and self-aware ("Did my heart love till now?"). I defy any-one to sub-text this with a lively group of adolescents without some marvellously funny moments when they realize what Shakespeare is really talking about through Romeo. You might even consider all the current and outmoded expressions for sexual desire and compare them with Romeo's phrases. Is explicitness better than subtlety? Is coherence in thought and desire reflected in language?

To consider part of a drama text where the sub-text is some-what more elusive than in those already discussed, here are two extracts from Harold Pinter's one act play, *The Black and White*. The scene is a milk bar table where two old women, unnamed, are holding an apparently desultory conversation. If students are asked to read the text for the first time, they are generally unimpressed with the dialogue and they have difficulty engaging with the two old women at all. After some work on the sub-text, they begin to gain insight into the force of the apparently facile conversations between the women and slowly recognize the skill of Pinter's creativity. The transformation in attitude towards the text can be very exciting. Here is the text at the play's opening:

TEXT	SUB-TEXT
(The first OLD WOMAN is sitting at a milk bar table. Small. A SECOND OLD WOMAN approaches. Tall. She is carrying two bowls of soup, which are covered by two plates, on each of which is a slice of bread. She puts the bowls down on the table carefully.)	
SECOND: You see that one come up to me at the counter? (She takes the bread plates off the bowls, takes two spoons from her pocket, and places the bowls, plates and spoons.)	Did you notice how men are still attracted to me?
FIRST: You got the bread, then?	I'm not interested in your flirtations. . . . I'm threatened by them. . . . I'll ignore that question. . . . keep to the basics.
SECOND: I didn't know how I was going to carry it. In the end I put the plates on the top of the soup.	O.K. I'll go along with you. We'll talk about safe topics.
FIRST: I like a bit of bread with my soup.	We get on well, when we keep the talk about food.
(They begin the soup. Pause.)	
SECOND: Did you see that one come up and speak to me at the counter?	No, I'm not going to let the matter drop. . . . I want you to talk about my my experience.
FIRST: Who?	I didn't notice anyone.
SECOND: Comes up to me, he says, hullo, he says, what's the time by your clock? Bloody liberty. I was just standing there getting your soup.	Good. . . . I can retell the story now . . . reenact it. I was that annoyed . . . flattered really . . . and I wasn't even inviting attention . . . just standing there playing maid for you.
FIRST: It's tomato soup.	I'm going to put you down. . . . ignore your story . . . you're having yourself on.
SECOND: What's the time by your clock? he says.	I'm still going on about it. Instant replay . . . here's how he tried to pick me up. Listen again to what he said.
FIRST: I bet you answered him back.	Knowing you, you wouldn't miss a chance.
SECOND: I told him all right. Go on,	Too right, I told him to piss off or I'd

I said, why don't you get back into your scraghole, I said, clear off out of it before I call a copper.

(Pause)

FIRST: I not long got here.

SECOND: Did you get the all-night bus?

call the cops . . . won't find me being an easy mark.

Let's keep to safe topics. . . . our relationship's too fragile for these threatening exchanges. . . . You could be just fantasizing anyway. . . . let's play safe.

Sure . . . we'll keep to the routine. . . . I don't want any confrontations either.

One could argue that the sub-texts offered here seem to have very little to do with the lexical content of the text. How can the phrase "It's tomato soup" possibly mean "I'm going to put you down . . . ignore you," etc.?—because language takes its meaning largely from context and when one knows the whole text of this play, it becomes obvious that the strained conversation between the two women is an attempt to hold together a very fragile, mutually dependent relationship where the characters know intuitively the boundaries of their everyday talk and their need to maintain a status quo at all costs. Once you "crack the code" of their conversation, the pathos of their plight is acutely felt. A comic and poignant exchange occurs just before the end of the play where the second woman boasts that the cops took her in, once:

TEXT	SUB-TEXT
SECOND: They took me away in the wagon once.	Anyway, the cops wanted me. . . . they took me in.
FIRST: They didn't keep you though.	Don't think you can impress me. . . . didn't want to keep you did they?
SECOND: They didn't keep me, but that was only because they took a fancy to me. They took a fancy to me when they got me in the wagon.	You're not going to take away my little victory. . . . I was just far too attractive for them. . . . quite excited them, I did. . . . especially up close.
FIRST: Do you think they'd take a fancy to me?	Maybe it was a pretty good thing. . . . I'll stick my neck out. . . . do you think they'd find me attractive too?
SECOND: I wouldn't back on it.	Ha, fell for it . . . now I can pay you back.

Immediately after that exchange, and the second woman's Pyrrhic victory, the defeated first old woman looks out the window to gaze at the world outside. She decides the outside world is pretty threatening too:

TEXT	SUB-TEXT
(Pause)	
FIRST: They'll be closing down soon to give it a scrub-round.	We'll have to go out soon.
SECOND: There's a wind out.	It'll be cold outside. . . . I'm a bit sorry I was nasty to you.
(Pause)	
FIRST: I wouldn't mind staying.	I'd rather stay here . . . even though we can be hard on each other at times.
SECOND: They won't let you.	It's not "us" who's the problem. . . . it's "them."
FIRST: I know. (Pause). Still, they only close hour and half, don't they? (Pause) It's not long. (Pause) You can go along, then come back.	Yes, but we can always come back and be together again.
SECOND: I'm going. I'm not coming back.	I don't like all this dependency. . . . I'm going alone. . . . maybe.
FIRST: When it's light I come back. Have my tea.	I'll always be here.
SECOND: I'm going. I'm going up to the Garden.	I'm stretching out . . . moving on.
FIRST: I'm not going down there. (Pause) I'm going up to Waterloo Bridge.	I'm not following you. . . . I'm going in another direction.
SECOND: You'll just about see the last two-nine-six come up over the river.	You can watch the bus . . . buses govern our movements.
FIRST: I'll just catch a look of it. Time I get up there. (Pause) It don't look like an all-night bus in daylight, do it?	Yes I can observe things which move people about . . . things look different in daylight don't they? . . . I still want to talk to you . . . exchange observations . . . share experiences . . . where does this leave our relationship?

I have worked on this play about thirty times now and I still find the experience of sub-texting it very moving and impressive. As much as anything because of the experience of watching how readers new to it develop a growing sense of excitement and discovery as the subtleties of the language unfold. Because the play is so brief (about eighty lines) it is possible to work and rework it several times over a couple of hours. Involved readers then find it easy to work in pairs on presenting a book-in-hand reading. Again it is fascinating to see how differently the pairs present their reading. Matters such as body language, proxemics, voice quality, expressions, movement, and the use of pausing arise as matters for discussion quite spontaneously. More importantly, the structure of the play (and Pinter's *Last to Go,* also in the same volume, *Theatre Today*) offers students a chance to read, sub-text, perform, and discuss a play, albeit a very short one, over, say four class periods.

One of the special advantages of working actively with the interpretation and enactment of a drama script is the possibility it offers for engagement with artistic language which gains meaning through contexts which can include physical movement, lighting, costuming, and design. That is, students can work towards the point where a throw away line like "It's tomato soup" can be said convincingly and pointedly with all the richness of connotation and motivation it bears in the Pinter play. A context where a line is part of an intricate network of meaning. Not only does such an enlightening experience enhance one's idea of what can happen when we read imaginatively and with insight; it can also carry over into renewed perception of the role and function of language in everyday life. Part of becoming a good reader is the ability to de-centre and consider other points of view—those of the characters in the text and those of other readers. Sub-texting involves a dual process of centring and decentring—moving from one's initial reading and interpretation to consideration of other possibilities in the light of others' readings and the disclosures of later parts of the text.

Sometimes readers express anxiety that "tampering" with the text by temporarily substituting one's own language is not authentic reading. I reiterate the purpose of sub-texting as one of coming to terms with the author's language through a dynamic process of making it one's own. When the process has been experienced effectively, the author's language lives for the reader, in its own right, and as part of the reader's range of experienced language options. Sometimes students working in drama workshops express reservations about the possibility of this method working in schools. I can only repeat that the process is one which occurs anyway when readers encounter language—not only poetic and literary language but everyday language. If in doubt, play a guessing game with students. Ask them to pose questions to you to which you can answer only "Yes" or "No." Ask the questioners to write down what you really meant when you said "Yes" or "No." (As the actor, you have to enter into the game by answering "Yes/No" as expressively as possible.) Most times the questioners can give you very accurate sub-texts for your replies because we do it every day, every time we listen to another speak. And the more the other's language concerns us, the more we invest in getting the sub-text right. How many marriage proposals and other life-changing situations have been realized through the participants' accurate "reading" of the sub-text? Knowing how to mean, in a large part, means knowing how to sub-text.

One of the very reassuring things about contemporary recognition of the complexity of the reading process is that while theory becomes more abstract and complex its practice has become more natural. By removing the adult-built structures which kept young readers from experiencing whole texts and by recognizing the intuitive power of what readers do naturally, we have allowed ourselves as teachers to become partners with readers in a mutually enlightening experience. Dialogue has become triadic (reader-teacher-text) or "trialogue," with webs of meaning interlacing all participants and all the language functioning in the reading experience, which includes the language used by the participants in establishing the context for the reading experience. From what we know of language exchanges in all kinds of contexts, we can be reassured that in most situations, most of the time, participants know what language means because they know how to weigh up the function of context in the exchange. So the closer our methods are to that impressively complex process by which even very young readers, writers, speakers, and listeners make sense of language, the more we are enriching the life of the reader and the life of the text. After all, inspiration does mean "breathing life into." Sub-texting is an inspiring experience.

11

Post Reader-Response: The Deconstructive Critique

PAM GILBERT

Reader-Response Theories

The assimilation of new critical theory into literature classrooms will certainly be a long time coming, but the assimilation of many of the tenets of "reader-response" theories may arrive more quickly. This volume is proof of that. Its introduction claims a commitment to "reader-response" aesthetics, arguing, as does one of the writers, that the reader-response theorists "describe, more accurately than anyone else I have read on the subject, what I feel I do when I read." (Evans, Chapter 2, p. 27)

Reader-Response Theories and Literary Criticism

Reader-response theories tell many "stories of reading" (Culler, 1983) and are not tied to any single philosophical starting point. What they do have in common is a focus on the reader's contribution to the meaning of a text, and in that way they are seen to represent an assault of a sort on the traditional notion of literature as "expressive realism"—the notion that literature is a reflection of the "real" world, that literary texts have single determinate meanings, and that the authority for their meanings lies with the author, who "put" the meaning in the text in the first place. Expressive realism assumes a communication model, with the text acting as a thread connecting two consciousnesses—that of the author and that of the reader. The author has something to communicate with the reader, and the text acts as a transparent medium through which the author's intentions are actualized. To understand the text, then, is to explain it in terms of the author: the author's ideas, psychological state, social background, and so on.

This delving into the author's past was brought seriously into question with the publication of Wimsatt's "The Intentional Fallacy" in 1946, in which he argued that the author's intentions had nothing to do with literary criticism. Wimsatt and the "new" critics insisted that the words on the page were all that mattered, and searches for things anterior to the text became less important. However, once the "author-ity" of the text had disappeared, "meaning" had to find a new warrant. If meaning could not now be traced to an author's intention, if it resided timelessly in the words on the page, then the only way in which meaning could assume some authority was if words were seen to stand for things or for experiences which inhered permanently in the world and in human nature. Words were thus regarded as labels for things that already existed independently of language.

Two of the strongest objections to the New Critics and the "words on the page" focus came from different directions: from theorists like Frye, who sought a systematic framework within which to order knowledge about the whole domain of literature and criticism, and from linguists, notably Saussure. Frye's (1957) *Anatomy of Criticism* attempted to provide answers to questions about the nature of a literary text and a literary reading of texts, whilst Saussurean linguistics challenged the relationship between language and the world, by undoing the link between word and thing, insisting on the arbitrary nature of language, and offering a "synchronic" approach to the study of language. Meaning could no longer be seen to reside timelessly in the words on the page and attention was focussed on what information about texts and the reading of literature readers brought to a reading.

This shift of focus from the words on the page to the interaction between text and reader inevitably led to a much closer scrutiny of reading practices and of readers and to the popularity of reader-response theorists, who sought to clarify the nature of this interaction. The account by Young in Chapter 1 provides a discussion of several of the chief protagonists in the field. The writers have different stories to tell about the nature of the relationship between the reader and a text, but they tend to agree that individual readers make personal meaning from texts.

The difficulty for reader-oriented theories lies in deciding the balance between text and reader. How much freedom is there for the reader? Are there as many readings for a text as there are readers? Either experience is totally personal and therefore totally plural, or experience is somehow controlled by the text so that meanings made through reading are substantially similar. Is a text's meaning infinitely plural (as experience is infinitely personal), or is there a model reader, a "good reading" which lines up with the intention of the author.

Chaos needs to be avoided, and various strategies are suggested to fend off total plurality of response. Fish (1980) describes "interpretative strategies"—a form of literary competence which seems to be natural and intuitive; Holland (1975) guides his readers' responses by asking "questions," ostensibly to elicit "free associations to the stories"; Bleich (1978) trains his readers in what to include and what to leave out in their "response statements." Iser (1978) tries to bring together the potential creativity and plurality of many of the "reader-power" stories with the need he sees of the text for a particular type of response. Iser wants "co-partnership in the literary enterprise" (Eagleton, 1983, p. 85) and posits a dualistic theory in which the claim is made that something is provided by the text and something else provided by the reader. Iser develops the concept of the "implied reader" to account for this.

> If . . . we are to try and understand the effects caused and the responses elicited by literary works, we must allow for the reader's presence without in any way predetermining his character or his historical situation. We may call him, for want of a better term, the implied reader. He embodies all those predispositions necessary for a literary work to exercise its effect— predispositions laid down, not by an empirical outside reality, but by the text itself" (Iser, 1978, p. 34).

Such a concept tries to avoid the pitfalls of the concept of the single, authoritative, "ideal" reader and of the omnipotent author-creator; and in their places supplants the concepts of the "implied" reader and the "implied" author. The "implied" reader is predisposed to the ideal reading because of the effects in the text implied by a shadowy author figure—the "implied" author. Presumably an experienced reader knows how to produce this reading from the text: how to act as the implied reader so that the implied author's intentions can be reproduced. The authority for the meaning of a text is now this model reader. The one "authoritative" meaning for the text is still sought, but it is sought from a different perspective.

This shift away from the author and away from the literary critic has been attractive to English education as Young (Chapter 1) has explained. The concept of textual meaning lying in the reader's hands—of the student reader as co-creator of a text—matches similar moves in language education in the seventies and eighties: sociolinguistic moves towards linguistic pluralism (Trudgill, 1975; Rosen and Burgess, 1980) and similar psycholinguistic moves which focus on the personal interrelationship of language and learning (Britton, 1970; Emig, 1983). The person has returned to the centre of the discourse, and school language texts assert the primacy of individual responses and of personal meaning. It is not surprising then to find a willingness to adopt reader-oriented aesthetics in the English classroom.

Within the English Classroom

The experienced English teacher, geared to reading and studying a wide variety of literary style texts in traditional ways, would probably adequately fill the role of Iser's implied reader, and like Evans (Chapter 2) could identify with such a description of what competent readers of literarure do. As well, reader-response theories offer concepts which are attractive for English classrooms.

1. A Plurality of Meaning. Theories which seem to be claiming the death of the single authoritative reading of a piece of literature—formerly the domain of literary criticism and associated in many English teachers' eyes with the worst aspects of elitist literary study—offer relief to teachers who have long struggled with the traditional "decoding," or "unravelling the mystery" aspects of literary study in schools. At last student meanings—in all their naivety, tentativeness, insufficiency, and outright "misinterpretation"—can be taken aboard as "legitimate" because they represent personal engagements with texts. No longer will teachers have to tell students they are "wrong," and fear the stunting of any further attempts to respond to texts. If readers create meanings individually and personally, then—the argument goes—all students have equal rights to create their own meanings.

In this volume, Evans (Chapter 2) sees the individuality of the reader being as important in the reading experience as the common availability of the text, claiming that works of art are never fully "made" when they leave the pen of their original maker until they are remade by each individual reader. Similarly, Young and Robinson (Chapter 7) refer to Rosenblatt's distinction between "the text" and "the poem." The text belongs to the writer—but the poem is what the reader creates from the text. Brown (Chapter 5) describes strategies for classrooms that demonstrate to students that readers do indeed recreate texts personally, using their own lives and reading experiences to make sense of texts, and Arnold (Chapter 10) claims that the reading process becomes "illuminating and exciting once we see how much creativity goes into making meaning from print."

All of the chapters in this volume acknowledge the importance of having students believe that their personal responses to pieces of literature are valuable and valid, and although some indicate an awareness of problems associated with this approach in classrooms, all are willing to espouse it.

2. A Plurality of Response Forms. The notion of personal "meaning-making" from texts offers a host of possibilities for classroom language activities and partly solves the problem of legitimizing the use of personal language (in preference to what was seen as the "impersonal" language of traditional literary criticism).

Protherough's chapter is appropriately called "The Stories That Readers Tell" (Chapter 4), and in it he offers case studies of written responses to texts. Similarly Adams (Chapter 6) gives us examples of "stories" his students wrote as responses to texts, offering at the same time the concept "dependent authorship" to describe "writing from reading." The use of the text as a springboard for a host of related language activities is also referred to in Corcoran's chapter (Chapter 3) in which he offers teachers advice for "interventions" (which will focus attention on the reading process) as well as for activities that "tamper" with the text. Corcoran suggests "the interrupted reading," literary cloze procedures, sequencing strategies, and the development of new story structures. As well, Young and Robinson (Chapter 7) describe classwork which encourages the use of less common narration methods—through documents, artifacts, or assumed personae.

3. A Focus on the Reading Process. Reader-response theories and their focus on the reader and on reading sit much more comfortably in English classroom pedagogy than does a focus on the study of authors—"the life and times of . . ." approach which had been difficult to make relevant or interesting to adolescents, and, once the thematic approach to literature study had become entrenched, difficult to research and justify. Perhaps also the teaching of reading is seen as a more acceptable and relevant role for classroom language and literature teachers, given the debate about the nature and role of classroom literature and literary studies over the past thirty years. The elitism of the Great Tradition is in disrepute; the egalitarianism of the reading process seems a much more worthwhile endeavour.

Brown's statement that "It's hard to make the move from seeing ourselves as teachers of literary texts to teachers helping students become better readers" (Chapter 5, p. 97) presents this shift nicely, and reiterates claims made earlier in many of the other chapters that teachers of literature need also to be teachers of reading. Protherough talks about "learning to behave as a reader and becoming conscious of being a reader" (Chapter 4, p. 79), Corcoran's text is entitled "Teachers Creating Readers" (Chapter 3), Evans's title is "Readers Recreating Texts" (Chapter 2), and Young and Robinson (Chapter 7) argue that:

> . . . reading and writing are best regarded as two sides of the one process . . . reading is an act of composing . . . indeed . . . we learn to write . . . by reading in the role of the writer (p. 154).

Reading is regarded as an active role for students—one that places them at the centre of pedagogy and the curriculum—and the value of the reading of literature is not questioned. Evans begins his chapter with the statement that

> This book is concerned with all readers of imaginative literature. Its authors also believe that that should really mean everybody (p. 22).

He then claims that it is an important need for all students that they be "able" and "happy" to read for "satisfaction" and "enjoyment," and in Chapter 5 Brown agrees with him, claiming that "rendering imaginative literature accessible to *all* young readers is at "the heart of this book" (p. 94).

The Literature Classroom: Responses and Readings

The foregoing chapters in this volume claim to offer many examples of the ways in which aspects of reader-response theories can generate not only a more student-centred literature curriculum, but also a more enlightened approach to the study of the relationships between reading and writing. Readers' personal responses are to be valued: writers are to be free to recreate literary texts in personally satisfying ways; reading processes become of key concern to teachers. However, within this reader-oriented discourse are a number of unresolved problematic issues. The assumptions that have been made about writing, about reading, and about texts do not sit easily in classrooms (as several of the writers in this volume testify). What checks are provided against chaos? How open is "plurality of meaning" and "plurality of form"? And how are readers' responses to be read by teachers?

The nature of the school text as well as the literary text needs reappraisal. What constitutes an "original" and "genuine" piece of writing in response to literature, and how are teachers to identify such a response? Is any reading of a literature text acceptable—or are some more acceptable than others?

Recognizing a Personal Response

The claim throughout this volume is that "what any reader does in reading an imaginative text is to 'recreate' it" (Evans, Chapter 2, p. 23). and the various chapters suggest and give examples of methods of this recreation in the form of written response. The nature and purpose of these recreations are treated somewhat differently throughout the book. What "shape" do such recreations take? What models are available?

Several of the chapters work with the conventions of literature texts (Corcoran, Adams, Young and Robinson, Travers, Arnold)—and yet there seems to be a reluctance to acknowledge and accept modelling of any sort. Stratta and Dixon (Chapter 8) describe it as a "strange coincidence" that a girl would choose to use a known poetic form when writing a personal response text, and Protherough (Chapter 4) wants to draw a distinction between "learned stories" and "personal responses."

Protherough's chapter offers examples from student responses written after initially confronting the novel *Catch 22,* and then later after studying it in class, and claims that in the latter, "students assure themselves and the teacher that they can now "understand," "see," "relate to" what Heller has "shown," "put across," "created" (p. 79). Protherough seems to be suggesting that this form of "storying" is unfortunate, in that it leads in the direction of "interpretation" and criticism common in unversity literature departments. His apparent preference for the initial responses, with their "personal" effects, compares with Corcoran's distaste in Chapter 3 (p. 50). for an "abstract, judgemental account" of a story, and with Adams's praise in Chapter 6 of a student writer's "inwardly felt" awareness and of another's move away from "the discursive statement of meaning" towards "poetic evocation through image and symbol" (p. 141).

Given the apparent preference for the "personal felt response" by writers in this volume, one of the questions that needs to be answered is whether or not such responses—the recreation of the text by individual students, apparently using their lives and reading experiences to make sense of it—are, too, a type of learned behaviour. Do students indeed "learn" how to make their stories sound personal? (Are not literary texts examples of how to do this?) Or do teachers only regard abstract and interpretative texts as "learned"?

Eagleton's claim that "Becoming certified by the state as proficient in literary studies is a matter of being able to talk and write in certain ways" (1983, p. 201) was not a reference specifically to secondary classrooms, nor to reader-oriented methods of literature teaching. However, it is relevant to this situation. Are there not still acceptable ways of talking and writing about literature—ways which privilege the personal over the impersonal, the subjective over the objective, the immediate over the reflective? Has not one system been exchanged for another?

Recognizing a "Good" Response

The new reader-oriented school story has several distinguishing features. One of the most obvious is that texts valued within this framework will be read in terms of the personal connections made between writer and text. Consequently, qualities of "genuine engagement," "emotional commitment," "serious intent" are prized, and chapters in this volume seek to reassure us that these qualities were present during the writing of student responses.

We find it impossible to believe that Michelle was not

deeply moved by Heaney's poem: the way she construes her experience and the form she chooses are eloquent testimony. . . .

(The student) is deeply immersed in imagining this. . . . Teachers we have worked with have been in no doubt about the quality of his imaginative involvement. . . .

The writer is obviously totally involved here . . . he is genuinely thinking about the scene, not merely echoing someone else's opinion (Stratta and Dixon, Chapter 8).

But the personal response is not all that the writers in this volume seek. Implicit in many of the chapters is the acknowledgement of the "real" or "hidden" meaning of literature texts—the public meaning.

Both Protherough and Travers discuss how to handle a student's "misinterpretation" of a text. If, in the literature classroom, every reader recreates texts from personal positions, if texts do mean different things to different people, how then do teachers deal with "chaos"—with responses which miss the poem's "hidden meaning"? How do teachers react to student recreations of stories which miss significances that the teacher-reader feels confident were author-intended (as in Protherough's case study of student recreations from *Woof*)? Travers (Chapter 9) suggests that the answer is "to exchange and discuss the separate responses" in the hope that the students will return again to the poem (does the text offer one true meaning if returned to and looked at carefully?).

However, Protherough (Chapter 4) shifts the focus. He regards difference in response as an indication of a student's stage of development as a reader, claiming that:

> The farther that development goes, the more likely it is that stories about response will become—in effect—statements about how a text ought to be read (p. 81).

Are different responses, then, indicative of various levels of literary competence? Is the fully developed reader one who arrives at a reading that was always intended? (Is the fully developed reader the "implied reader," the "model reader" of the text?)

And if there is one "true" or "correct" meaning, is this what should be looked for in examination and grading? How are students to be assessed in their responses to texts? Stratta and Dixon offer new modes of questions which claim to give primacy to students' personal reactions to texts, but how are these to be read and assessed? In terms of whether the students were "totally moved"and "deeply immersed"—or perhaps in terms of their "imaginative involvement"? Evans's partial solution is "to teach ourselves to judge the honesty and validity of different subjective attitudes, and record those judgements in our assessments" (Chapter 2, p. 27), but such a statement begs the question of what constitutes "honesty" and "validity," and, more importantly, what type of reading practice would produce such qualities. Will student responses that match with teachers' interpretations of literature texts be regarded as more "honest," more "valid"?

As Corcoran points out in Chapter 3, reader-response aesthetics is about more than eliciting "engagement responses from the very heart and soul of a student." By wresting the forms of literature teaching and resultant modes of classroom reading and writing away from the dominance of criticism, a tradition of "great books" and "great writers" has been brought into question. As Barthes (1977) has told us, the author has died, but the reader has been born. The significance for classrooms of this reader-orientation is important, as Chapter 1 has demonstrated. Students' meanings are accepted, students' needs are considered, and students' experiences are legitimized. As Corcoran (Chapter 3) can claim, "Those silent, reverent encounters at the high altar of literary religion" are made less often.

But in this heady discourse of student meaning, student need, and student experience lie paradoxes and contradictions about which meanings, which needs, which experiences. How much has changed for students? Has the literature text been opened out for a plurality of response, or is there just a different form of control over meaning?

In the last section of this chapter, the claim will be made that reader-oriented theories do not represent the radical shift necessary to shake free of the traditional epxressive realist model of literature and its critical practices to produce new approaches to reading and writing in the classroom. Alternative theories of writing, reading, and texts which acknowledge the culturally constructed discursive feature of "the author," the nature of learned reading practices, and the field of writing that the text represents suggest significantly new directions which make a dramatic break with the past.

Alternative Approaches

The Nature of the Literary Text

Within this volume, a number of different statements are made about the nature of literature. On the one hand, literary texts are claimed to be "original" and "unique"—the results of sensitive, perceptive human beings' perceptions of the world, translated into words so that others, too, can share in the special "uniqueness" of the authors' experiences.

However, there is a catch. "Good" literature is not easy to read. Only *some* individuals will know how to read the texts so that the authors' meanings will be revealed. Travers (Chapter 9) states bluntly that "poems are difficult to read," and Corcoran (Chapter 3) and Arnold (Chapter 10) offer ways of cracking this difficulty by focusing on the text's structures or by sub-texting the author's text. In fact, most of the texts in this volume are concerned in various ways with making authors' meanings more accessible to students, by providing teachers with strategies that will help connect students' minds, personalities, and experiences, with the minds, personalities, and experiences of "authors"—to jump through the density of the language, as it were, to make real connections with the human presence on the other side. In short, the potential of the literary text cannot be released unless it is read properly. Experienced adult readers know how to read literary texts properly, and they need to share this technique with less experienced students writers.

But there is a second type of literature referred to in this volume—the literature of the classroom. The co-editors claim that students write "literature" in schools, and Travers (Chapter 9) quotes Dixon's words in her chapter.

When pupils' stories and poems, though necessarily private activities, reemerge as experience to be shared and talked over with the teachers and classmates, they become the literature of the classroom (1969, p. 55).

Brown (Chapter 5) also speaks of the literature students write.

I'm coming to believe quite strongly that students' literary products—and of course they don't all have to be written—have to become the reference point we look to if there is to be any real sense of continuity in English courses.

This jells with Chapter 6, which is predominantly Adams's readings of student texts. In this chapter, Adams writes about his student writers and their texts (recreations from adult, published literature) in much the same vein as the sensitive expressive-realist critic.

So moving and so assured a piece of work almost defies commentary . . . (p. 126).

The hint . . . is taken up in the opening of Robert's piece and developed in such a way that one world, the objective world of the violently heaving cabin below decks, becomes a metaphor for another, the inner world of psychological dislocation and disorientation . . . (pp. 126–127).

The bare stating manner of the prose is not artless—it is the means by which powerful feelings are held in check. In the second paragraph, for instance, Anne's mounting dread as she begins to realize Mr. Loomis is never coming back is very powerfully conveyed by the pared-down terseness of the utterance (p. 134).

There seems to be an absence of any consciousness of self other than as an experiencing centre. What Sam has given us in Anne's diary represents what we might perhaps call the achievement of a difficult kind of sincerity, which, in its disinterestedness and its vulnerable openness to experience reminds me, at least, of some of Lawrence's last poems (p. 134).

Adams, too can see through the text to the author's real intentions. He compares the student texts with other texts he has read—"literary" texts—by reading these through the discourse of literary criticism. Although the questions of "uniqueness" and "originality" of perception bother him—these are, after all, only 'recreations'—he is convinced that these student authors have been "liberated" by writing texts such as these, and that such texts tap "deep springs of imaginative creativity." This willingness to attribute personal creativity to writing narratives or poems is perhaps why other writers in this volume (e.g., Brown and Travers) have also been prepared to call student texts "literary" texts, or to present them, as do Young and Robinson, as models of successful practice.

Adams, however, offers the most explicit description of the reading practice that will produce literary texts from school assignments, and his account may well be recognizable and intelligible to most literature-trained English teachers. We understand his "reading" of these texts. We, too, know about the "confidence" literary texts are supposed to have; we know about "wholeness of vision," about metaphor, about inner worlds of psychological disorientation; we know about "eloquent restraint"; and we know how important is the appearance of sincerity.

In short, we, too, know reading practices which allow us to read texts so that they become literary texts—but we also know how to read texts so that they become student texts. We know how to grade texts, how to rank order them, how to assess language competence. It is the reading practices adopted in the reading of a text which designate its function—not the text itself, and certainly not the writer of the text. Texts become what they become because of the way they function in discourse. As Barthes has claimed:

> . . . a text is not a line of words releasing a single "theological" meaning (the "message" of the Author-God) but a multidimensional space in which a variety of writings, none of them original, blend and clash. The text is a tissue of quotations drawn from the innumerable centres of culture (Barthes, 1977, p. 146).

And reading is not an innocent activity. Readers are situated in culturally determined discursive traditions, and the effects of these traditions determine the nature of the reading a text will be given and the meaning assigned to it. We recognize in the text what Derrida (1976) would call the "iterable" features—aspects which can be repeated and transferred from one specific situation to another. If features cannot be transferred, are not repeatable, the text cannot be a signifying sequence.

No language is original—texts are, as Barthes has claimed, "multidimensional spaces" in which "a variety of writings . . . blend and clash." Texts, including the literary text, are but tissues of quotations drawn from a range of other texts.

> All literary texts are woven out of other literary texts, not in the conventional sense that they bear the traces of "influence"

but in the more radical sense that every word, phrase or segment is a reworking of other writings which precede or surround the individual work. There is no such thing as literary "originality," no such thing as the "first" literary work: all literature is inter-textual (Eagleton, 1983, p. 138).

So where does that leave the author? What is the role of the author in literary discourse?

The Author

The Author-function has been one of the most cherished and significant aspects of literary discourse, and even in the texts in this volume—focussed presumably on the reading of literature—the author has remained a presence and power. Evans talks about "the author's written instructions" (Chapter 2), Corcoran mentions the writer's "deliberate patterning of words on a page" (Chapter 3), Adams says of one of his student texts that "writing like this . . . represents a point of meeting between two sensibilities, the author's and the student's" (Chapter 6), and so it goes on.

By drawing historically upon differing conceptions of authors and writers, both Foucault (1977) and Barthes (1977) have demonstrated that the concept of the author is a constructed one, a fairly recent and modern notion. In the Middle Ages literature was more likely to be seen as part of a collective enterprise, expressing no individual point of view, but in contemporary times the author is linked with concepts of "individuality" and "originality." The concept fulfils several important functions for the discourse called literature. Literary texts, unlike many others, are "authored":

> . . . in our culture, the name of an author is a variable that accompanies only certain texts to the exclusion of others. . . . In this sense, the function of an author is to characterize the existence, circulation, and operation of certain discourses within a society (Foucault, 1977, p. 124).

Consequently the "author" has come to represent the text's "truth," "honesty," "authenticity," and its ultimate unity and meaning.

> The image of literature to be found in ordinary culture is tyrannically centred on the author, his person, his life, his tastes, his passions. . . . The *explanation* of a work is always sought in the man or woman who produced it, as if it were always in the end, through the more or less transparent allegory of the fiction, the voice of a single person, the *author* "confiding" in us (Barthes, 1977, p. 143).

The bias that Derrida (1978) demonstrated in the Western metaphysical tradition toward presence, being, truth ("logocentrism"), and toward the living voice of the speaker ("phonocentrism") is obvious in this concept. The author has become the guarantee of "meaning" for a work: the presence behind the text, whose "voice" can be produced with a sensitive (literary?) reading. Consequently, literature can be marketed as a product, although the nature of the work or the production will be glossed over. The writing is bypassed in search of things anterior to the text.

The author's name on the cover, known, established, famous, is the guarantee of access to his or her imagination, just as the brand name of the product guaranteed the quality of the commodity. But the brand name on the product is the name of the employer or the company, not of the workers whose labour produced it. In a similar way, the author's name evokes given essences, qualities of insight and understanding, and not the labour of producing out of the available signifying systems of language and literature an intelligible fiction (Belsey, 1980, p. 127).

The author-function elevates the status of a particular discourse and circumscribes its boundaries, provides the appearance of a unity of meaning in a literary text, and acts as an illusory but necessary consumer guide to the quality of a product. If "the author" is removed from a text—if meaning is not sought in the author's "intentions"—then the literary work can no longer be regarded as a "veil" or "thread" between reader and writer. Without an author the work becomes the text: a network, a fabric, a texture to be ranged over rather than pierced. No one voice in the text is privileged. Reading thus becomes an active opening out of a text's possibilities, rather than a passive closing in to one reading, one position of intelligibility.

The Deconstructive Critique

Writing—as Derrida demonstrated in *Of Grammatology* (1976)—then becomes the field of study. Instead of focussing on constructions which are presumed to lie behind the writing, we need to accept Saussure's case that language is not a transparent "medium" allowing a reader to reach through to a tangible world on the other side. There are not "things" and then names for things; there are only named things.

If words stood for preexisting concepts, they would all have exact equivalents in meaning from one language to the next; but this is not true (Saussure, 1960, p. 116).

Saussure has amply demonstrated that different languages divide the world in different ways; language cannot be a system of naming existing things. Instead, language is a system of differentiation, and because of this system of differentiation, no concept can be completely free of "traces" (as Derrida calls them) or fragments of others.

But the system of differentiation is not entirely arbitrary. Language necessarily participates in the formation of ideological constraints. For instance, attacks by feminists on a language system seen by many to be "man-made" (Spender, 1980) have focussed attention on man-woman power relationships signified by language. Male terms (he, man, mankind) are used for concepts presumed to include men and women, with the result that women are seen to be a secondary sex, differentiated from the male norm. Similarly, feminists point to the supposedly equivalent terms for men and women—governor/governess, courtier/courtesan, master/mistress—to demonstrate other obvious phallocentricities in the language.

Far from being a transparent medium, language is ideologically constructed. Certain meanings are elevated by social ideologies to privileged positions, and their ideology is perpetuated by reading practices which seek to find unity of meaning and oneness of purpose in the text, instead of readings which seek out the "silences" in the text (Macherey, 1978), which refuse to accept the one offered "meaning" and instead look for evidence of other texts suppressed within the one pseudo-meaning.

Readings such as those suggested by Derrida, Barthes, Foucault have been termed deconstructive critiques. Such critiques seek to read in ways other than what seems natural, universal, and self-evident in order to show that what may seem given is but a cultural construct. They force a return to the "common sense," the "obvious," the "natural," in order that the reasons for such apparent common sense, obviousness, and naturalness may be made apparent. By focusing on the texts—and, as Derrida says, nothing can be said to be not a text ("Il n'y a pas de hors-texte": There is no "beyond the text")—we can confront the reading that the text apparently asks of us, and how and why it does this. But we can also confront the other readings (the other texts) and, as Belsey claims:

> . . . seek out the process of production of the text: the organization of the discourses which constitute it and the strategies by which it smooths over the incoherence and contradictions of the ideology inscribed in it. . . . Such a criticism finds in the literary work a new object of intelligibility: it produced the text (1980, p. 129).

And this is where deconstructive reading practices offer so much in the teasing out of the relationships between reading, writing, literature, and teaching. There is a discourse called "literature," because there are reading practices which can produce "literary" texts. There is a discourse which could be called "school writing," because there are reading practices which will produce student texts. And each of these discourses has its own conditions of possibility, although they are patently different, as even the simplest example of rule-breaking in syntax and spelling would show.

Whilst readings of the literary text regard rule-breaking as deliberate and intentional, readings of the school text regard such rule-breaking as faulty and inaccurate. To assume that texts have one meaning, recoverable through reading, is to underestimate the conditions of possibility of a text. A student text may well be read differently if printed in a literary magazine rather than submitted to the class teacher with a bundle of student assignments. Reading practices which produce the school text tell us about the constructed nature of such a text—just as reading practices which produce literary texts tell us of their constructed qualities. Nothing is to be assumed: all is open for analysis.

Readings which challenge the natural, the obvious, the common sensical, locate the ideological formation of our signifying systems. The women's movement has made that abundantly clear. By fostering in our students a genuinely critical stance towards language and its discursive formations, we foster "producers" not "consumers": active participants rather than passive recipients. Literature's "natural" features must be challenged. As Barthes has warned, literature need not be destroyed, but it can no longer be protected. And teachers are aware of this, as is evident from their willingness not only to broaden the field of literary discourse to include student texts, but also to "tamper" with the text.

> . . . anything that deflates the spurious authority of the text so that it becomes the object of engaging play is preferable to those silent, reverent encounters at the high altar of literary religion (Corcoran, p. 66).

But perhaps we need a more radical approach. Literature, as an ideologically constructed field of discourse, is a cultural construct, and the nature of this construct is what should engage students and teachers of literature. By asking students to respond to texts by linking personal experience to the experience made valid in the literary text, teachers have made prior assumptions which need to be reappraised. How are "personal experiences" culturally constructed? Which "personal" experiences do literary texts validate and why? Consider, for example, the paucity of female experiences, constructed by female writers, made available to adolescent girls in school literature classrooms (Gilbert, 1983). McCormick's discussion of the "focussed assignment" as compared to "the purely spontaneous response statement" (1985) points towards the classroom implication of literary theory beyond Bleich and Holland and Iser. Her paper addresses the cultural nature of the assumptions her students bring to the literature classroom, and her assignments are designed to focus their attention on those assumptions.

Post-structuralist, or deconstructive critiques offer approaches to writing and to texts which help to make intelligible the patterns of discourse that surround us all (teachers and students alike). Deconstructionist readings will not produce the one ideological construct—the literary text, the personal response. Instead, they demonstrate the process of production of that ideological construct and its conditions of possibility. That, I would claim, represents a radical—and powerful—expansion of our understanding of readers, texts, and teachers, and a direction in which we must move.

Bibliography

A. Works Referred to in the Text, and Further Reading

Abbott, A., & Trabue, M. R. (1921). A measure of ability to judge poetry. *Teachers College Record 22*(2), 101–126.

Abbs, P. (1983). Art-response in reading and writing. In B. T. Harrison (Ed.), *English studies 11–18: An arts-based approach* (29–41). London: Hodder and Stoughton.

Allen. F. K. (1977). Responses of young adults to literature, with special reference to student teachers. (MEd dissertation, University of Exeter. Unpublished.)

Applebee, A. (1978). *The child's concept of story: Ages two to seventeen.* Chicago: University of Chicago Press.

Arnold, M. (1869). *Culture and anarchy.* London: Smith, Elder & Co. Reprinted 1965, Ann Arbor: University of Michigan Press (page nos. given), 1932, Cambridge University Press.

Arnold, M. (1873). *Literature and dogma.* London: Elder & Co. Reprinted 1970, Ann Arbor: University of Michgan Press.

Arnold, M. (1888). *Essays in criticism: Second series.* New York: Porter, London: Macmillan.

Atkinson, J. (1985). How children read poems at different ages. *English in Education, 19*(1), 24–34.

Bakhtin, M. (1929). *Problems of Dostoevsky's poetics* (R. W. Rotsel, Trans. 1973). Ann Arbor: Ardis Publications.

Bantock, G. H. (1963). *Education in an industrial society.* London: Faber and Faber.

Barnes, D., Churley, P., & Thompson, C. (1971). Group talk and literary response. *English in Education 5*(3), 63–76.

Barthes, R. (1975). *The pleasure of the text.* New York: Hill and Wang, London: Jonathan Cape.

Barthes, R. (1975). *S/Z* (R. Miller, Trans.). New York: Hill and Wang, London: Jonathan Cape.

Barthes, R. (1977). *Image, music, text.* New York: Hill and Wang, London: Collins (Fontana).

Bates, B. (June 1984). Mick stability and gnome arks. *Contact* Newsletter 5. Education Department of South Australia.

Beer, N. (1983). Structuralism and the classroom. *Use of English 35*(1), 15–24.

Belsey, C. (1980). *Critical practice.* New York and London: Methuen.

Bennett, K. C. (1977). Practical criticism revisited. *College English,* *38*(6), 567–578.

Bennett, T. (1983). Text, readers, reading formations. *Literature and History, 9*(2), 214–227.

Benton, M. (1979). Children's responses to stories. *Children's Literature in Education, 10*(2), 68–85.

Benton, M., & Fox, G. (1985). *Teaching literature nine to fourteen.* London: Oxford University Press.

Blake, R. W., & Lumm, A. (1986). Responding to poetry: High school students read poetry. *English Journal 75*(2), 68–73.

Bleich, D. (1975). *Readings and feelings: An introduction to subjective criticism.* Urbana, IL: National Council of Teachers of English.

Bleich, D. (1978). *Subjective criticism.* Baltimore: The Johns Hopkins University Press.

Bleich, D. (1980). The identity of pedagogy and research in the study of response to literature. *College English 42*(4), 350–366.

Bloom, H. (Ed.) (1979). *Deconstruction and criticism.* New York: Seabury.

Blunt, J. (1977). Response to reading: How some young readers describe the process. *English in Education 11*(3), 32–41.

Booth, W. C. (1961). *The rhetoric of fiction.* Chicago: University of Chicago Press.

Britton, J. N. (1951–2). An enquiry into changes of opinion, on the part of adult readers, with regard to certain poems, and the reasons underlying those changes. (MA thesis, London Institute of Education. Unpublished.)

Britton, J. N. (1963). Literature. In *The arts and current tendencies in education.* London: Evans for the London Institute of Education.

Britton, J. N. (1968). Response to literature. In J. R. Squire (Ed.), *Response to literature* (3–10). Champaign, IL: National Council of Teachers of English.

Britton, J. N. (1970). *Language and learning.* Harmondsworth: Penguin Books.

Britton, J. N. (1977). Language and the nature of learning: An individual perspective. In J. R. Squire (Ed.), *The teaching of English: The seventy-sixth yearbook of the N.S.S.E.* (1–38). Chicago: University of Chicago Press.

Brown, L. (1982). Do we teach the way we read? *English in Australia 62,* 33–36.

Bruce, B. (1980). Analysis of interacting plans as a guide to the understanding of story structure. *Poetics 9,* 295–311.

Bruner, J. (1974). *The relevance of education.* Harmondsworth: Penguin Books.

Cahill, R. (1979). Confession: I read aloud to 'em. *English Teachers' Association of New South Wales Newletter*, 19–21.

Cain, W. E. (1984). *The crisis in criticism: Theory, literature and reform in English studies.* Baltimore: The John Hopkins University Press.

Carey, R. F. (1982). Making connections. *Language Arts 59*(4), 323–327.

Central Statistical Office (U.K.). (1985). *Social Trends 15.* London: Her Majesty's Stationery Office.

Chambers, A. (1983). The child's changing story. *Signal 40*, 36–52.

Chambers, A. (1985). *Booktalk.* New York: Harper & Row, London: The Bodley Head.

Chatman, S. (1978). *Story and discourse.* Ithaca: Cornell University Press.

Clark, M. M. (1976). *Young fluent readers.* London: Heinemann Educational.

Clifford, J. (1979). Transactional teaching and the literary experience. *English Journal 68*(8), 36–39.

Coleridge, S. T. (1817) (1949). *Biographia Litteraria.* Everyman's Library Edition. Totowa, NJ: Biblio Distribution, London: Dent.

Cooper, C. (Ed.) (1984). *Researching response and the teaching of literature.* Norwood, NJ: Ablex.

Crago, H. (1979). Cultural categories and the criticism of children's literature. *Signal 30*, 140–150.

Crago, H. (1982). The reader in the reader: An experiment in personal responses and literary criticism. *Signal 39* (See also Walsh, 1983).

Culler, J. (1975). *Literary competence.* Reprinted in Tompkins (1980) below.

Culler, J. (1983). *On deconstruction: Theory and criticism after structuralism.* Ithaca, NY: Cornell University Press, London: Routledge and Kegan Paul.

Davies, F., & Greene, T. (1984). *Reading for learning in the sciences.* London: Oliver and Boyd.

Derrida, J. (1976). *Of grammatology.* Baltimore: The Johns Hopkins University Press.

Derrida, J. (1978). *Writing and difference.* Chicago: University of Chicago Press, London: Routledge and Kegan Paul.

Dilworth, C. B. (1983). Structuralism, stories, and English teaching. *English Journal 72*(1), 81–83.

Dixon, J. (1969). *Growth through English* (2nd ed.). London: Oxford University Press.

Dixon, J. (1979). *Education 16–19: The role of English and communication.* London: Macmillan Education.

Dixon, J. (1984). Taking too much for granted? 'A' level literature and its assessment. *The English Magazine 12*, 21–24, 29–30.

Dixon, J. (1985). What counts as response? In K. Whale & T. Gamble (Eds.), *From seed to harvest.* Richmond Hill, Ontario: Canadian Council of Teachers of English.

Dixon, J., & Brown, J. (1984 & 1985). *Responses to literature— what is being assessed? Parts I, II, and III.* London: Schools Council Publications.

Dixon, J., & Gill, M. (1977). New directions in senior English. In K. Watson & R. Eagleson (Eds.), *English in secondary schools: Today and tomorrow* (109–129). Sydney: English Teachers' Association of New South Wales.

Dixon, J., & Stratta, L. (1985). *Character studies—changing the question.* Southampton: Southern Regional Examining Board.

Dixon, J., & Stratta, L. (1985). Unlocking mind-forg'd manacles? *English in Education 19*(2), 1–11.

Donaldson, M. (1978). *Children's minds.* New York: W. W. Norton, London: Collins (Fontana Books).

Durkin, D. (1981). What is the value of the new interest in reading comprehension? *Language Arts 58*(1), 23–42.

Eagleton, T. (1982). The end of criticism. *English in Education 16* (2), 48–55.

Eagleton, T. (1983). *Literary theory: An introduction.* Morris, MN: University of Minnesota Press, Oxford: Basil Blackwell.

Early, M. J. (1960). Stages of growth in literary appreciation. *English Journal 49*, 161–167.

Eco, U. (1979). *The role of the reader: Explorations in the semiotics of texts.* Bloomington: Indiana University Press, London: Hutchinson.

Eliot, T. S. (1960). On teaching the appreciation of poetry. *Teacher's College Record 62*(3), 215–221.

Emig, J. (1983). *The web of meaning.* Upper Montclair, NJ: Boynton/Cook.

Evans, R. (1982). The question about literature. *English Journal 71*(2), 56–60.

Exton, R. (1982). The post-structuralist always reads twice. *English Magazine 10*, 13–20.

Fillion, B. (1981). Reading as inquiry: An approach to literature learning. *English Journal 70*(1), 39–45.

Fish, S. (1980). *Is there a text in this class?* Cambridge, MA: Harvard University Press.

Foucault, M. (1977). *Language, counter-memory, practice: Selected essays and interviews.* Ithaca, NY: Cornell University Press, Oxford: Basil Blackwell.

Frith, G. (1979). Reading and response: Some questions and no answers. *English in Education 13*(1), 30–31.

Fry, D. (1985). *Children talk about books: Seeing themselves as readers.* Milton Keynes: Open University Press.

Frye, N. (1957). *Anatomy of criticism.* Princeton, NJ: Princeton University Press.

Genette, G. (1980). *Narrative discourse.* Oxford: Basil Blackwell.

Gilbert, P. (1983). Down among the women. *English in Australia 64*, 26–29.

Goddard, R. (1985). Beyond the literary heritage: Meeting the needs of English at 16–19. *English in Education 19*(2), 12–22.

Graves, D. (1983). *Writing: Teachers and children at work.* Exeter, NH, and London: Heinemann.

Graves, M., et al. (1983). Effects of previewing difficult short stories on low ability junior high school students' comprehension, recall and attitudes. *Reading Research Quarterly 18*(3), 262–276.

Great Britain: Board of Education (1921). *The teaching of English in England (The Newbolt Report).* London: His Majesty's Stationery Office.

Harding, D. W. (1937). The role of the onlooker. *Scrutiny 6*, 246–258. Reprinted in *Language in education: A source book*, prepared by the Language and Learning Centre Team at The Open University. Boston and London: Routledge and Kegan Paul.

Harding, D. W. (1963). *Experience into words.* New York and London: Cambridge University Press.

Harding, D. W. (1968). Practice at liking: A study in experimental aesthetics. *British Psychological Society Bulletin 21*, 3–10.

Hardy, B. (1975). *Tellers and listeners: The narrative imagination.* Dover, NH: Longwood, London: The Athlone Press.

Hayhoe, M., & Parker, S. (1984). *Working with fiction.* London: Edward Arnold.

Hillocks, G., Jr. (1980). Towards a hierarchy of skills in the comprehension of literature. *English Journal 69*(3), 54–59.

Hirsch, E. D., Jr. (1976). *The aims of interpretation.* Chicago: University of Chicago Press.

Holbrook, D. (1964). *English for the rejected: Training for literacy in the lower streams of the secondary school.* New York and London: Cambridge University Press.

Holland, N. N. (1973). *Poems in persons.* New York: W. W. Norton.

Holland, N. N. (1975). *Five readers reading.* New Haven: Yale University Press.

Holt, S. L., & Vacca, J. L. (1983). Reading with a sense of writer: Writing with a sense of reader. *Language Arts 58*(8), 937–941.

Hope, A. D. (1967). How it looks to a cow. *Idiom 7*, 3–8.

Horner, W. B. (Ed.). (1983). *Composition and literature: Bridging the gap.* Chicago: University of Chicago Press.

Hourd, M. (1949). *The education of the poetic spirit.* London: Heinemann.

Hunt, R. A. (1982). Toward a process-intervention model in literature teaching. *College English 44*(4), 345–357.

Inglis, F. (1971). Reading children's novels: Notes on the politics of literature. *Children's Literature in Education 5,* 60–75.

Iser, W. (1974). *The implied reader: Patterns of communication in prose fiction from Bunyan to Beckett.* Baltimore: The Johns Hopkins University Press, London: Routledge and Kegan Paul.

Iser, W. (1978). *The act of reading: A theory of aesthetic response.* Baltimore: The Johns Hopkins University Press, London: Routledge and Kegan Paul.

Jackson, D. (1978). Using *The midnight fox* with a group of secondary school first formers. *English in Education 12*(1), 1–8.

Jackson, D. (1980). First encounters: The importance of initial responses to literature. *Children's Literature in Education 11*(4), 149–160.

Jackson, D. (1982). *Continuity in secondary English.* London: Methuen.

Jackson, D. (1983). Learning to become an active reader. *Use of English 34*(2), 59–67.

Jackson, D. (1983). *Encounters with books: Teaching fiction 11–16.* New York and London: Methuen.

Jackson, D. (1983). Dignifying anecdote. *English in Education 17* (1), 6–21.

Jauss, H. R. (1982). Towards an aesthetic of reception. Minneapolis: University of Minnesota Press, Brighton: Harvester Press.

Jefferson, A., & Robey, D. (1982). *Modern literary theory: A comparative introduction.* London: Batsford.

Kahn, E. A., Walter, C. C., & Johannesson, L. R. (1984). *Writing about literature.* Urbana, IL: NCTE.

Kearney, A. (1984). Politics and English studies. *Use of English 35* (2), 11–20.

Langer, S. K. (1953). *Feeling and form.* New York: Macmillan, London: Routledge and Kegan Paul.

Lewis, R. (1975). Fiction and the imagination. *Children's Literature in Education 19,* 172–177.

Lunzer, E., & Gardner, K. (1979). *The effective use of reading.* New York and London: Heinemann Educational.

Lunzer, E., et al. (1984). *Learning from the written word.* London: Oliver and Boyd.

McCormick, K. (1985). Theory in the reader: Bleich, Holland and beyond. *College English 47*(8), 836–850.

Macherey, P. (1978). *A theory of literary production.* Boston and London: Routledge and Kegan Paul.

Mallick, D. (1978). Reading and writing short stories. *English in Education 12*(3), 58–60.

Martin, N. (1983). What happened to the stories? In R. Protherough (Ed.), *The development of readers* (38–54). Hull: The University of Hull.

Martin, T. (1985). Horizons, themes and protensions: How Sally solved the mystery of "Tom's midnight garden." *Reading 19*(1), 13–19.

May, S. (1984). Story in its writeful place. In J. Miller (Ed.), *Eccentric propositions: Essays on literature and the curriculum.* London: Routledge and Kegan Paul.

Meek, M. (1982). Children's literature: Mainstream text or optional extra? In R. D. Eagleson (Ed.), *English in the eighties* (114–127). Sydney: Australian Association for the Teaching of English.

Meek, M. (1982). Response—begin again. In D. Mallick, P. Moss, & I. Hansen (Eds.), *New essays in the teaching of literature* (85–96). Norwood, South Australia: Australian Association for the Teaching of English.

Meek, M. (1982). What counts as evidence in theories of children's literature? *Theory into Practice 21*(4), 284–292.

Meek, M. (1982). *Learning to read.* Salem, NH: Merrimack, London: The Bodley Head.

Meek, M. (1984). Speaking of shifters. *Signal 45*, 152–167.

Meek, M., et al. (1983). *Achieving literacy: Longitudinal studies of adolescents learning to read.* New York and London: Routledge and Kegan Paul.

Meek, M. (1984). Speaking of shifters. *Signal 45*, 152–167.

Moffett, J. (1968). *Teaching the universe of discourse.* Boston: Houghton Mifflin.

Moffett, J., & McElheny, K. (1966). *Points of view.* New York: New American Library.

Moy, B., & Raleigh, M. (1984). Comprehension: Bringing it back alive. In J. Miller (Ed.), *Eccentric propositions: Essays on literature and the curriculum* (148–192). London: Routledge and Kegan Paul.

Nemerov, H. (1966). *Poets on poetry.* New York: Basic Books.

Norris, C. (1982). *Deconstruction: Theory and practice.* London: Methuen.

Pearson, P. D., & Tierney, R. J. (1984). On becoming a thoughtful reader. In A. C. Purves & O. Niles (Eds.), *Becoming readers in a complex society* (144–173). Chicago: University of Chicago Press.

Petersen, B. T. (1982). Writing about responses: A unified model of reading, interpretation, and composition. *College English 44* (5), 459–468.

Petrosky, A. R. (1982). From story to essay: Reading and writing. *College Composition and Communication 33*(1), 19–36.

Phillips, T. (1971). Poetry in the junior school. *English in Education 5*(3), 51–62.

Prince, G. (1973). Introduction to the study of narratee. Reprinted in Tompkins (1980) below.

Probst, R. E. (1984). *Adolescent literature: Response and analysis.* Columbus, OH: Charles E. Merrill.

Probst, R. E. (1981). Response-based teaching of literature. *English Journal 70*(7), 43–47.

Probst, R. E. (1986). Three relationships in the teaching of literature. *English Journal 75*(1), 60–68.

Protherough, R. (1979). Children's sense of story-line. *English in Education 13*(1), 36–41.

Protherough, R. (1983). How children describe their reading of stories. *The development of readers* (55–70). Hull: The University of Hull.

Protherough, R. (1983). *Developing response to fiction.* Milton Keynes: Open University Press.

Protherough, R. (1986). *Teaching literature for examinations.* Milton Keynes: Open University Press.

Purves, A. C. (1969). Structure and sequence in literary study. *The Journal of Aesthetic Education 3*, 103–117.

Purves, A. C. (Ed.) (1972). *How porcupines make love: Notes on a response-centered curriculum.* Toronto: Xerox College Publishing.

Purves, A. C. (1980). Putting readers in their places: Some alternatives to cloning Stanley Fish. *College English 42*(3), 228–236.

Purves, A. C. , Foshay, A. W., & Hansson, G. (1973). *Literature education in ten countries.* New York and London: John Wiley. and Sons.

Raleigh, M. (1982). Independent reading. *The English Magazine 10*, 21–29.

Ray, W. (1984). *Literary meaning: From phenomenology to deconstruction.* New York and Oxford: Basil Blackwell.

Reid, I. (1984). *The making of literature: Texts, contexts and classroom practices.* Norwood, South Australia: Australian Association for the Teaching of English.

Richards, I. A. (1929). *Practical criticism.* New York: Harcourt, Brace and World, London: Routledge and Kegan Paul.

Robinson, A., & Schatzberg, K. (1984). The development of effective teaching. In A. C. Purves & O. Niles (Eds.), *Becoming readers in a complex society* (233–270). Chicago: University of Chicago Press.

Rosen, H., & Burgess, T. (1980). *Language and dialects of London school children.* London: Ward Lock Educational.

Rosen, H. (1983). *Stories and meanings*. Sheffield: National Association for the Teaching of English.

Rosenblatt, L. (1976). *Literature as exploration* (3rd ed.). New York: Modern Language Association, London: Routledge and Kegan Paul.

Rosenblatt, L. (1978). *The reader, the text, the poem: The transactional theory of the literary work*. Carbondale: Southern Illinois University Press.

Rosenblatt, L. (1985). Transaction versus interacation—a terminological rescue operation. *Research in the teaching of English 19*(1), 96–107.

Salvatori, M. (1983). Reading and writing a text: Correlations between reading and writing patterns. *College English 45*(7), 657–666.

Sampson, G. P., & Carlman, N. (1982). A hierarchy of student responses to literature. *English Journal 71*(1), 54–57.

Saussure, F. de (1960). *Course in general linguistics*. New York: McGraw-Hill, London: Owen.

Scholes, R. (1982). *Semiotics and interpretation*. New Haven: Yale University Press.

Scholes, R. (1985). *Textual power: Literary theory and the teaching of English*. New Haven: Yale University Press.

Selden, R. (1985). *A reader's guide to contemporary literary theory*. London: The Harvester Press.

Slatoff, W. J. (1970). *With respect to readers: Dimensions of literary response*. Ithaca, NY: Cornell University Press.

Smith, F. (1971). *Understanding reading*. New York and London: Holt, Rinehart and Winston. Sec. Ed. 1978.

Smith, F. (1978). *Reading*. Cambridge: Cambridge University Press.

Smith, F. (1983). Reading like a writer. *Language Arts 60*(5), 558–567.

Squire, J. R. (1964). *The responses of adolescents while reading four short stories*. Champaign, IL: National Council of Teachers of English.

South Australia, Education Department of (1983). *A single impulse: Developing responses to literature*. Adelaide: Education Department of South Australia.

Spender, D. (1980). *Man made language*. New York and London: Routledge and Kegan Paul.

Stanton, M. (1980). Art exists to . . . make the stone stoney . . .: A report from work-in-progress on the AEB 'A' level literature alternative syllabus. *English in Education 14*(3), 42–55.

Stratta, L., Dixon, J., & Wilkinson, A. (1973). *Patterns of language*. London: Heinemann Educational.

Suleiman, S. R., & Crossman, I. (1980). *The reader in the text.* Princeton: Princeton University Press.

Tabbert, R. (1979). The impact of children's books: Cases and concepts (Parts 1 and 2). *Children's Literature in Education 10* (2), 92–102 and (3) 144–149.

Tallack, D., et al. (1986). New ways of reading old texts. *English in Education 20*(2), 21–31.

Thomson, J. (1978). School writing: Product and process. *English in Education 12*(1), 22–29.

Thomson, J. (1979). Response to reading: The process as described by one fourteen-year-old. *English in Education 13*(3), 1–10.

Thomson, J. (1984). Wolfgang Iser's *The act of reading* and the teaching of literature. *English in Australia 70*, 18–30.

Thomson, J. (1986). Applying reader-response critical theory to a rereading of *Heart of Darkness. English in Education 20*(2), 1–12.

Thomson, J. (1986). *Understanding teenagers reading: Reading processes and the teaching of literature.* Australia: Croom Helm.

Tierney, R. J., & Pearson, P. D. (1983). Towards a composing model of reading. *Language Arts 60*(5), 568–580.

Tolkien, J. R. R. (1964). On fairy stories. In *Tree and Leaf.* Boston: Houghton Mifflin, London: George Allen and Unwin.

Tompkins, J. P. (Ed.). (1980). *Reader-response criticism.* Baltimore and London: The Johns Hopkins University Press.

Torbe, M. (1974). Modes of response. *English in Education 8*(2), 21–32.

Travers, D. M. M. (1982). Problems in writing about poetry and some solutions. *English in Education 16*(3), 55–65.

Travers, D. M. M. (1984). The poetry teacher: Behaviour and attitudes. *Research in the Teaching of English 18*(4), 367–384.

Trudgill, P. (1975). *Accent, dialect and the school.* London: Edward Arnold.

Tucker, N. (1972). How children respond to fiction. *Children's Literature in Education 9*, 48–56.

Walsh, J. P. (1983). The writers in the writer: A reply to Hugh Crago. *Signal 40*, 3–11.

Webb, A. J. (1982). Transactions with literary texts: Conversations in classrooms. *English Journal 71*(3), 56–60.

Whiffey, J. F. (1970). *Golding: Lord of the flies.* London: Edward Arnold.

Whitehead, F., Capey, A. C., & Maddren, W. (1975). *Children's reading interests: Schools council working paper 52.* London: Evans/Methuen Educational.

Whitehead, F., Capey, A. C., Maddren, W., & Wellings, A. (1979). *Children and their books.* London: Macmillan Education.

Widdowson, P. (Ed.) (1982). *Re-reading English.* London: Methuen.
Williams, E. D., Winter, L., & Woods, J. M. (1938). Tests of literary appreciation. *British Journal of Educational Psychology 8,* 265–284.
Wilson, R. N. (1956). Literary experience and personality. *Journal of Aesthetics and Literary Criticism 15,* 47–57.
Witkin, R. W. (1974). *The intelligence of feeling.* New York and London: Heinemann Educational.
Woolf, V. (1932). *The common reader. Second series.* New York: Harcourt, Brace, London: L. and V. Woolf.
Worsdale, M. (1982). Literature in the fourth and fifth year of secondary school. *English in Education 16*(1), 30–36.
Wright, J. (1975). *Because I was invited.* Melbourne: Oxford University Press.
Yarlott, G., & Harpin, W. (1972–3). 1,000 responses to English literature. *Educational Research 31*(1), 3–11 and *13*(2), 87–97.
Young, R. (Ed.). (1981). *Untying the text: A post-structuralist reader.* London: Routledge and Kegan Paul.

B. Children's Books and Short Stories Referred to in the Text

Adams, R. (1972). *Watership Down.* New York: Avon Books, London: Rex Adams, Harmondsworth: Puffin Books 1973.
Adams, R. (1976). *Shardik.* New York: Avon Books, Harmondsworth: Penguin Books.
Adams, R. (1978). *The plague dogs.* New York: Alfred A. Knopf, Harmondsworth: Penguin Books.
Aitken, J. (1962). *The wolves of Willoughby Chase.* New York: Doubleday, London: Jonathan Cape, Harmondsworth: Puffin Books 1968.
Bosley, G. (1976). The killing. *New stories 1.* London: Arts Council of Great Britain.
Branfield, J. (1972). *Nancekuke.* (In USA: *The poison factory.* Harper & Row and Ace Books.) London: Gollancz (O/P).
Briggs, R. (1977). *Fungus, the bogeyman.* London: Hamish Hamilton.
Briggs, R. (1978). *The snowman.* New York: Random House, London: Hamish Hamilton, Harmondsworth: Picture Puffins 1980.
Chambers, A. (1982). *Dance on my grave.* New York: Harper & Row, London: The Bodley Head.
Cormier, R. (1977). *I am the cheese.* New York: The Pantheon Press, London: Armada Books.
Dahl, R. (1959). *Kiss kiss.* New York: Alfred A. Knopf, London: Michael Joseph.

Dean J. (1982). Woof. In *School's ok*. London: Evans (Reprinted in *Mischiefmakers*. London: Collins 1983).

Dickinson, P. (1969). *Heartsease*. London: Victor Gollancz, Harmondsworth: Puffin Books 1971.

Garner, A. (1973). *Red shift*. New York: Ballantine, London: William Collins Sons, London: Fontana Lions 1975.

Lessing, D. (1957). Flight. In *A habit of loving*. London: Macgibbon & Kee. (Also in *Story 3*. Harmondsworth: Penguin Books 1973).

Lewis, C. S. (1950–1956). The "Narnia" books (*The lion, the witch and the wardrobe* to *The last battle*). New York: Macmillan, London: Armada Books.

Lingard, J. (1972). *Across the barricades*. New York: Lodestar Books, Harmondsworth: Penguin Books.

Pearce, P. (1958). *Tom's midnight garden*. New York: Dell, London: Oxford University Press, Harmondsworth: Puffin Books 1976.

Roueché, B. (1965). Phone call. *The New Yorker*. 1965. (Also in *The loaded dice*. Nelson (Australia) 1982).

Sendak, M. (1967). *Where the wild things are*. New York: Harper & Row, London: The Bodley Head, Harmondsworth: Picture Puffins 1970.

Tolkien, J. R. R. (1937). *The hobbit*. Boston: Houghton Mifflin, London: George Allen and Unwin.

Westall, R. (1981). *The scarecrows*. New York: Greenwillow Books, London: Chatto & Windus, Harmondsworth: Puffin Books 1983.

Wilder, L. I. (1935). *The little house on the prairie*. New York: Harper & Row, Harmondsworth: Penguin Books.

Notes on Contributors

PETER ADAMS is Head of English at Banksia Park High School in South Australia. He was a major contributor to *A Single Impulse: Developing Responses to Literature*, published by the South Australian Department of Education, and is currently co-authoring a monograph on the same topic for the Australian Association for the Teaching of English.

ROSLYN ARNOLD lectures in English Method and Drama in the Department of Education at the University of Sydney. She was director of the Third International Conference on the Teaching of English held in Sydney in 1980 and subsequently edited *Timely Voices: English Teaching in the Eighties*, a collection of some of the major papers presented at the conference.

LOLA BROWN has taught English in Secondary schools in England and Australia for over twenty-five years. She is now English Adviser for the Central Northern Region of South Australia and is the major author of a series of highly successful secondary texts, *I Mean to Say, I Dare to Say,* and *Shaping Up.*

BILL CORCORAN is Senior Lecturer in English Education at James Cook University of North Queensland, Townsville, Australia. He was a seminar leader in the Literature Commission of the Third International Conference. His special interests are in literary theory and its application to the classroom, and the dimensions of children's voluntary reading.

JOHN DIXON, formerly Senior Lecturer, Bretton Hall College of Advanced Education is a distinguished scholar and author in the field of English Education. He directed the *English 16–19* project in the U.K. and has recently co-authored *Response to Literature: What Is Being Assessed?* for the Schools Council.

EMRYS EVANS lectures in English Education at the University of Birmingham. He had a major involvement in the Schools Council English 16–19 project, and has particular interests in literary theory and the teaching of children's literature.

PAM GILBERT is a Lecturer in Language and Literature at James Cook University of North Queensland, Townsville, Australia. Her interests include the teaching of writing, the classroom teacher as reader of student texts, the place of "literature" in the classroom, and sexism and education.

ROBERT PROTHEROUGH lectures in English Education at the University of Hull. He is the editor of *English in Education* and the author of *Developing Response to Fiction and Encouraging Writing*. His most recent book is titled *Teaching Literature for Examinations*.

ESMÉ ROBINSON is a Senior Education officer in the Queensland Department of Education. She maintains particular interests in the teaching of literature and is active in the in-service education of English teachers.

LESLIE STRATTA, formerly Senior Lecturer in English in Education, University of Birmingham, is an internationally recognized scholar and teacher. He was principal author of *Patterns of Language* and is currently co-authoring, with John Dixon, a series of booklets on *Achievement in Writing*.

MOLLY TRAVERS is Senior Lecturer in English Studies, La Trobe University, Melbourne. Her particular interests are in the teaching of poetry and children's literature. She is completing a comparative study of writing about literature by groups of Australian, English, and Canadian students.

CLEM YOUNG is Principal Lecturer in Language and Literature at the Brisbane College of Advanced Education. Within the general framework of the teaching of literature he is particularly interested in the relationship between writing and reading development.